THE CRANES OF BLACKWELL

BY J.D. KELLNER

KYANITE
Publishing

THE CRANES OF BLACKWELL

Copyright © 2020 by Kyanite Publishing LLC

For permission requests, please contact the publisher, Kyanite Publishing LLC, via e-mail, with subject "Attention: Permissions Coordinator," at the e-mail address below:

info@kyanitepublishing.com

ISBN
Hardcover: 978-1-952152-39-9
Paperback: 978-1-952152-38-2
eBook: 978-1-952152-37-5

Cover & Interior design by B.K. Bass
Editing by Jabe Stafford

www.kyanitepublishing.com

Dedicated to my beautiful wife, our two wonderful boys, and my loving family and friends. All of you made this dream come true.

ACKNOWLEDGEMENTS

A special thank you to my patient wife and the wonderful team at Kyanite Publishing. Without their belief in me this book would not have been possible.

THE CRANES OF BLACKWELL

"Never to suffer would never have been blessed."

– Edgar Allen Poe

CHAPTER ONE

Bergden Crane tried to focus on his book as he heard them taking the neighbors away. Their cries muffled, their arms and legs bound as they struggled against their abductors. He knew them only as acquaintances. A family of four, the husband, the wife, and two sons all whisked away in the dead of night under the moonlit sky. Under the rule of the Regime in the city of Blackwell, such moments had become commonplace and a facet of daily living for its people. There hung in the air an ever-present aura of fear and the terror of being taken at any moment. Without warning. Without cause.

Bergden had grown accustomed to drowning out the pleadings for mercy, the somber cries, and the gasps and groans of physical pain that accompanied the usual beatings. Bergden Crane was habituated to the authoritarian symphony of anguish not because of the daily warrant-less arrests of his neighbors in his apartment complex or the horrific shrills of children being stripped away from their families, but because he was on the other end of the terror. He was a Regime Enforcement Officer or as they were known to the people across the Regime, black jacks.

After the silence once again settled in hopefully for the rest of what was turning into a very long night, he lay awake unable to shake the unnerving thoughts about the coming day. He had to work in the morning like all men and needed rest. He feared losing his job, worst of all. Unemployment meant an entirely different thing in the city of Blackwell under the Regime.

It meant you were dead.

Perhaps worst of all, it meant that your family would be cast out into the streets, forced to live as pariahs. Most moved into the dangerous slums known as the Skids to struggle to carve out a meager existence fighting for scraps.

Not even the march of time gave any respite from the daily grind. If you were an eighty-year old woman blinded by cataracts, the Regime had a use for you, a purpose in its eyes. Bergden could still picture his grandmother in the waning days of the war handing out propaganda leaflets on the corner by his grandfather's general market. It paid next to nothing, but she persisted, her shaky hands passing out the thin paper cards touting the grand victories of the Regime. Time would catch up to her before the end of the war. A sad twist for a kind woman who worked to the bone with unwavering patriotism and who never saw what became of the victor. There were times Bergden found himself jealous that she never had seen what the Regime had become.

As the sun crept through the white cotton blinds and into Bergden's room, his alarm sounded off its usual disruptive tune. The triumphant Regime jubilee rang loudly each morning at 5 am on the dot. Not a second earlier, not a second late. For the past three years, he had worked the same shift, but in his line of work the shift never indeed ended. He ate the same breakfast and drank the same state-issued coffee. A bland mixture that afforded him just enough caffeine to perk up and get himself out the door. Nothing about his mornings were special. He had learned to thrive on routine, on the mundane, and to him and his family, he was better off for it.

The Regime believed that hygiene was paramount for success, and Bergden agreed, but perhaps not with the state methodology. A brisk morning shower with a state limited amount of cold water and despite ten years of cold showers, he still longed for the refreshing feeling of hot water on a chilly autumn morning such as the one he experienced today. The Regime believed hot showers sowed the seeds of laziness and caused the blood to boil with thoughts of insurrection, but for him, it was a luxury long missed. If he knew the result of victory would never allow him to take a hot shower again, he might have rethought who he held a gun for during the war.

Bergden stood stared at himself in the bathroom mirror. He pulled open the medicine cabinet and took a bottle from the second shelf. Expired medication. Inside were not capsules, but a photograph. One of the few of his days in the army that remained. He smiled as he looked at his younger self. The same chestnut hair cut close to the scalp, his narrow nose and the chest of a man forced to do more push-ups than he could count. Now, greys crept into his hairline, his smile lowered, and his eyes no longer harbored dreams of a life of purpose. He was a man of thirty, but what he saw was an older face suffering from years of internal torment. A soul aged by artificial means. Not by the actions of his heart. He sighed as he walked back into the bedroom, a gray, thin towel slung carelessly over his shoulder. He made his way over to his closet and pulled apart the twin doors.

His black jack uniform complemented his athletic build he carried over from his military days. He cut his brown hair close to the scalp despite age, pushing back his hairline and sported a clean-shaved look. Only once could he recall having something of a beard before they were banned. In years past, his unorganized stubble was a result of spending weeks on tour and away from a sharp razor.

Vivid nightmares plagued him, stealing away what little sleep he could manage. Memories of the war and its atrocities sent him in a depressive spiral from which he struggled to emerge. He went to great lengths to hide his past from his family. To him, they had no use for knowing the things he suffered through.

The things he had done.

He made the twin bed that sat juxtaposed to the window. As were most of the bedrooms in the complex, his was a simple bedroom with few adornments save for a few trinkets and heirlooms. A few pictures of loved ones were permitted, but no room would be complete without an oil print portrait of the benevolent chancellor himself, Albrecht Kroft.

The framed painting was a gift for his service in the war. It depicted a much younger Kroft. Gone was the jet-black hair, the slicked back look a fashion of the time. Now, Kroft's crown held only wispy gray and white hairs, the thin strands greased back above his brow.

Kroft's eyes were now surrounded by crow's feet. In a typical man, it meant years of smiling, but Bergden doubted Kroft had ever truly embraced humor in any manner. The chancellor's uniform was the same as it always had been and much to Bergden's surprise it still seemed to fit. The jacket's high collar rose just beneath his chin. The gunmetal wool blend jacket was weighed down with more medals than a man could feasibly earn in a lifetime. A bevy of fabricated achievements meant to pump the ego and validate his position rather than represent real accomplishment.

Bergden put on the same uniform he had worn for the past

seven years. Black leather boots with a polished buckle at the calf, black wool pants with a faint blue stripe on the leg, a gray-blue shirt and steel colored, wool hat adorned with the Regime wolf on the facade. He did have the option of wearing a black wool hat or a more formal number should the occasion call for it. Considering his position, he often went for a more formal cap to show his authority in the station. The formal cap high peaked with a glossy charcoal, leather brim. A steel braided cord for show and, of course, the Regime symbol of the wolf planted right in the middle.

The wolf seemed appropriate, considering how cruel the Regime had become.

After a few final adjustments, Bergden made his way into the kitchen. He was greeted with the aroma of a homecooked meal. A hint of fresh-ground pepper filled his nostrils as he took his seat at the kitchen table and the best part of the morning approached. The kitchen was his favorite room in the apartment. In a sense, it had become his sanctuary. White walls, white windowsills, and steel appliances were a welcomed change from drab brown and dull gray painted interior of the apartment.

The best sight was not the warm meal on its way to him, but the beautiful and vivacious brunette smiling as she approached and placed his plate on the tabletop. His wife, Alyssa. She returned to the stove with her cream-colored apron slung round her slender waist. The apron blemished by coffee spilled long ago. The stains a mark of services to her family. Her hair was pulled back over her head, a silver pin keeping it in place. Bergden remembered when she initially showed him the broach on their first date. He pictured her hair as it fell to her shoulders and the glow on her face as she held out the pin. She said it was a gift from grandmother in her youth.

"I hope you enjoy your breakfast, my love," she said in her lyrical voice.

Bergden had met her shortly after the war ended just as he arrived home from the front. As a young woman, she moved from the formerly prosperous village of Oyster Bay to the centerpiece of the Regime, the city of Blackwell. In the waning hours of the war, Oyster Bay crumbled to nothing more than ash and dust under the fury of one, final bombing raid. Homeless, Alyssa had no choice but to abandon her home. The drastic change of scenery surely would have been dramatic had it not been for Bergden. Oyster Bay, a hinterland wonder with a glorious ocean view from the city and the wealth of the oceans to fill the pockets of its people, was in stark contrast to Blackwell, an industrial powerhouse where only the strong prospered, and the weak disappeared into the concrete labyrinth.

Bergden felt that life was what you carried with you no matter where your feet were, no matter where you landed, or who you were with. Materials and items were not what life meant, but the memories you carried, even those that burdened the soul. Alyssa had felt the same when she took the train south, ending her journey at a station in Blackwell. She wandered the city for two years taking jobs to get by and working towards reclaiming her life as a teacher. On the day the Coalition surrendered, she began her work as a school mistress in the local district elementary re-education center. The job paid the bills and kept her fed, but the joy of teaching was gone.

That's where Bergden came into the picture.

Broke and awaiting back pay that he would never see, Bergden opened an ad for a roommate at his apartment just to be able to afford housing. The mass migration to Blackwell made finding a home too difficult to relinquish his own home. To make matters worse, in post war paranoia, the Regime implemented new rules of law that made finding a place to live all the more challenging. The idea that non-blood related or unmarried persons shared domiciles seemed like an affront to common decency to men like Kroft. Kroft believed such living arrangements harbored anxiety, and anger eventually led to outright rebellion. That was something he would not tolerate and thus such arrangements were strongly discouraged.

When Bergden first laid eyes on Alyssa, he knew right then that there was something special about her. He saw Alyssa at an outdoor café a few blocks from his apartment. He, a war-torn man with a damaged past, and her, a spirited brunette with aspirations and curves that caught any man's eyes, were, in his eyes, a perfect match.

Little about Alyssa changed since they met those ten, long years ago. Her skin, long kissed by the coastal sun, still glowed even after being away for so long. Her brunette hair always bounced as she walked, and her perfect smile reeled him in every time he looked at her. He began to get lost in his memories.

As Bergden took a sip from his hot, yet watered down, coffee a high-pitched squeal of excitement from down the hall interrupted him.

A young boy barreled into the kitchen and into his father's arms. Bergden gripped him in a loving embrace. He could feel the joy in his son's youthful vigor, James. With a partially toothless grin, the short brown hair, and the forest green eyes, James represented what Bergden hoped for in the world. The hope for change in a desolate wasteland of tyranny. The irony of being a Regime baby was not lost on Bergden. James would likely never experience the world like Bergden did. The lack of fear that accompanied daily life was gone. The ability to get up and go wherever you chose no longer an option. It saddened him to think of the youthful days lost, not playing in the fields or gripping a baseball bat in his hands. Those were things for the idle mind. On the day of his sixteenth birthday, James would be assigned a job if his grades didn't improve. Forced to clean the streets, tending the Regime's higher classes, or worst of all, a grave digger for the dead tossed from Cherry Hill.

"James. Have you given your mother a log of your studies? I don't want your headmaster to call me again at work. The last time the call went through the Station Chief Aberdeen, and I can't say he was too pleased to be taken away from his work. I would prefer it if that never happened again."

James looked back at his dad sheepishly, then over at his mother trying to avoid eye contact, clearly hiding the fact that he had not provided his mother a log of his studies.

The Regime required that all children log their studies during the evening hours in lieu of entertainment. Playtime was saved for the weekends, and mastering the subjects of mathematics and Regime history was to fill the rest of those hours. James was a pleasant child despite the rigorous coursework always keeping his childlike demeanor at the forefront. Other children did not embrace life the way that James did. It is what gave Bergden his purpose to subsist in the Regime. It is what kept him going to work each and every day despite it all.

"Father, I have logged my studies, and I promise to give them to mother before school. Is it okay to play now? After we hear from the chancellor? I can't wait to hear what he has to say to us today," James said with a boyish grin, doing his best to charm his father.

Bergden nodded and watched as James scrambled to the living room to retrieve his toys. Figures of the "heroes" of the Regime were the appropriate toys for both boys and girls, according to Kroft. The great men and women who led the Regime to victory made fine examples and apparently acceptable playthings. The forced infatuation disgusted Bergden. He knew the horrors those so-called "heroes" had orchestrated. The men and women they sent to the slaughterhouse. Considering those were James's only toys, he couldn't take them away. He could only grin and bear it and watch as his son took pleasure in pretending to be what those whose faces were on the figures were not: human.

God damn Kroft.

While James played on the floor, Alyssa and Bergden read through the previous evening's post before the morning radio report would begin. The Regime mandated that all citizens listen in as Kroft gave a daily briefing of the world around them as he saw it. Knowing it was likely lies, Bergden still listened sifting through the message to get a feel for how the Regime truly was holding up.

The radio cracked and buzzed just as Bergden finished his cup of coffee. James threw down his toys and sat close to the speaker drinking in every word of the anthem.

"All rise and salute Chancellor Albrecht Kroft!"

Bergden listened as the anthem played loudly.

In Kroft's eternal light,
We stand united against the foreign might
To keep the peace, we sacrifice
We work till dusk
And shun all immoral vice."

Bergden walked out onto the balcony and listened. The smattering of voices echoed through the complex. Each and every room in each and every building listened in unison as the Regime's anthem blared, and should you not be in a room, then the street speakers were there to help you couldn't escape no matter what you did. Down on the street, pedestrians and shopkeepers alike stopped and sang, eyeing the black jacks that stood with a watchful eye making sure everyone praised the Regime.

Beyond the propaganda, there was a more important reason to listen to the announcements: Propaganda Inquiry Officers or inquisitors as they were called, walked the streets asking anyone about the details of the announcement. Should you fail to answer appropriately, you might spend the day or perhaps even longer in a reeducation center. Those who were forced into these places of "learning" were brutalized and fed propaganda until they broke.

Bergden was immune because of his chosen profession as a black jack, but he feared for Alyssa and James. The reeducation centers were not a thing to be taken lightly. No one ever was the same person when they walked out those barracks doors, and they weren't any safer than your average citizen.

The rest of the anthem slowly drowned out as Bergden focused on the newspaper until the radio announcement continued upon the conclusion of the anthem.

"On behalf of Chancellor Kroft, Commander Liam Grimm will be giving the day's announcements."

There were no gasps save for the sighs of a disappointed James. Bergden recalled seeing a relatively healthy Kroft meander to the podium to announce the great victory, but he still had aged terribly in the past ten years. No amount of makeup and posturing could hide that liver-spot-infested mug. For the first few years after the war, he'd give a live daily announcement about the Regime and update its citizens on the progress of the creation of a more perfect nation. Over time fewer and fewer improvements were needed as the Regime's iron grip crushed its inhabitants. Kroft spent more days than not away from the microphone leaving much of the speech giving to his second in command, Commander Liam Grimm. Grimm was a man that somehow frightened Bergden more so than Kroft. The man seemed to be even colder and if was possible, more ruthless.

Bergden took his place on the couch across from the radio, and it cracked once again as the commander began his speech. Grimm lacked the political, charismatic showmanship of the chancellor, but the chill that his voice sent down the collective spines of the Regime's citizens more than made up for it. Grimm had always remained in the background like a ghostly specter hanging ominously over Kroft whispering commands in his ear. Bergden often wondered who truly led the Regime.

Grimm's speech droned on about the great victories and arrests of dangerous saboteurs, but Bergden drifted in and out of sleep, his coffee clearly not having the effect he desired. It was the same report of the Regime's victories over subterfuge and the Coalition remnants. A false impression was given to the people that they were somehow better off than before because of the Regime's perceived generous offerings and illusion of prosperity with hard work. Their enemies smote with Kroft's own two hands.

The radio clicked off, and Bergden snapped back to reality realizing he would be late for work if he didn't get moving. Alyssa was gathering her items for work and preparing James to go to school. It was nice she was able to walk with him to work, the school being but a few blocks away. It kept the boy out of trouble. He on the other hand caught the train to Pemply Station where he would begin the workday. It was a crowded, noisy commute but it was the best way to get to work on time.

"I love you and James, Alyssa. Please be careful on the way to school. Avoid the inquisitors if you can. Those reeducation centers give me the creeps. I love the woman you are, not the one they'd make you."

Alyssa laughed and kissed him goodbye with a gentle smile. "We'll be fine, Bergden. Besides, I have my big strong black jack to protect me. You'd better get going."

Bergden enjoyed the train. The ride provided a moment to reflect before the workday began. It was 6:30am, and he was right on schedule. Blackwell came alive as citizens headed out to start their days. The others aboard the train sat motionless on the train, mumbling amongst themselves, reviewing the morning's radio announcement and what to do if an inquisitor crossed their path.

After the twenty-minute ride, the train reached Pemply Station. Pemply Station was one of the largest Regime Enforcement Stations in Blackwell, and he was the lieutenant of Pemply Station. Second in command only to the station chief. A veteran of the war and stalwart man named Dahlen Aberdeen. Station Chief Aberdeen earned through years of service and success. Long nights and long days filled with one interrogation after another was the recipe for his reward and when lieutenant Aberdeen became Station Chief Aberdeen at the age of thirty-five it was quite an accomplishment. Not all his colleagues gave him praise, however. Many of the other black jacks were jealous of his meteoric rise, but if they knew the hardship, the sacrifice it took to get there, perhaps the situation would be different. Even so, Bergden kept an eye over his shoulder.

"Good morning Bergden. I trust you slept well and enjoyed a hearty breakfast? I know Alyssa takes great pride in getting your day started just right."

It was Sergeant Carl Sonderberg. A bright-eyed sergeant, if there ever was such a thing, and Carl was his partner at the station and his closest friend. Well, as much of a friend as the Regime permitted. After-work drinks and laughs were enough to define friendship even if the revelry ceased by the time curfew arrived. The black jacks had a bit more leeway considering the stresses and the nature of their employment, but Bergden dare not abuse it. The Regime had a habit of not keeping its promises unwritten or otherwise.

"Marvelous as usual, Carl. Alyssa never ceases to amaze me when it comes to my morning routine. Indeed, she is a very astute cook. A sous chef, I might say."

Carl laughed and shook Bergden on the shoulder. "That is good, indeed. Mary is also quite the cook and my daughter is learning quickly. She will make a man happy one day. I'm just hoping that day is a way off."

Bergden smiled. He had never met Carl's family and her, his, but he was glad to hear that his friend led a happy life. "Let's hope not too soon," he joked.

He considered Carl a friend, for whatever that was worth in the Regime. He trusted him, and beyond his wife, faith in anyone was tough to find. Black jacks maintained an unspoken code, but that hardly called them friends.

Carl was different.

"How is James? Is his schooling coming?" Carl hinted. "I trust we won't get another call when we are on our route?"

Bergden frowned. He had hoped that the weekend would allow the matter to pass under the bridge, but sadly Carl, the first person he saw, was not quick to forget when he had an issue. He wasn't trying to press the matter, but it wasn't much of a secret that James's schooling had long been problematic. He just hoped to separate work from his personal life once he stepped into Pemply Station.

"Alyssa assures me his studies are complete. I've warned him in the past that he cannot become a black jack, even if I wouldn't want him to follow in my footsteps if he continues to neglect his Regime duties and stay focused in the classroom. Not that I wish for him to follow my footsteps, but he seems persistent on the matter," Bergden opined.

The station was bustling with more activity than usual. Usually, the night shift squads would come back with their fair share of perpetrators. Tired from the long night and trudging for the train station. Joining them were a mixed bag of thieves, dissidents, prostitutes, and the mentally disturbed often lined the holding cells, all of which would be subject to Bergden's review, but today was different.

Disturbingly different.

He saw the station secretary Dinah standing outside of his office.

"Are you headed to the auditorium, Lieutenant? The chief has an announcement for the station staff," he said.

Bergden had nearly forgotten about the quarterly address. He gave a hasty thank you before rushing into the auditorium to join the rest of the station, where the speech was already underway.

"Settle down, settle down. We don't have much time today. Today's address will include a special guest. I know that makes the rest of you sad that I won't be giving my normal quarterly exercise in how long you can stay awake, but I promise you that won't be an issue this day. Now, please put your hands together for chancellor Kroft."

After a brief hesitation and whispers among the station, they burst into applause as the chancellor climbed the staircase and walked unabated to the podium.

"I want to thank each and every one of you for your bravery and unwavering patriotism."

Bergden watched as cameras rolled into place, and microphones popped up from among the crowd. Whatever Kroft had in store for the station, it must be significant. He wanted his words heard and the people of Blackwell to get the message.

"These are dark days indeed, and I must admit I have grave concerns about the security of our greatest city, Blackwell. These concerns, however, are not for me, but for you, the people. The foundation of our nation..."

"Wonder what he's referring to?" Carl asked.

"Isn't it obvious?" a man offered from a few seats over. "They are afraid of the weak links and loose ends that fill the ranks of our station. That's why he's here. Kroft is gearing up to purge the ranks. Get rid of the traitors and bring order to Pemply." Bergden glared down the aisle and saw Rocco Draven. A private at the station, Draven had made his name as a ruthless pursuant of his version of the law. Two weeks ago, Station Chief Aberdeen confronted Bergden about alleged internal misconduct that had been reported by Draven. Bergden managed to convince his superior that the allegations were unfounded, but Bergden knew that with each report, no matter how true, the Regime's watchful eye soon followed.

Bergden diametrically opposed Draven's approach to enforcement, and thus the two had become bitter rivals. On more than one occasion, Bergden had to drag Draven off a suspect. The young black jack took pleasure in delivering his brand of justice.

The chancellor's mention of Liam Grimm brought Bergden back to the chancellor's speech.

"Commander Grimm has brought to my attention the alarming uptick in the number of internal investigations. These types of cases undermine the very people you serve and damage the reputation of the Regime. The people count on us to provide them with peace through security. When that security undermines itself, then we cannot provide peace. I trust that our dear commander will help us resolve this minor crisis," Kroft urged as he gestured for Commander Grimm to join him on stage.

Kroft continued, "It is with great resolve I announce a new initiative to banish these traitors from our ranks. Commander Grimm will provide further detail as I must attend to other Regime matters. Every day is a new challenge. Never forget why we came to power in the first place. We are the people's champions."

Chancellor Kroft exited the stage after the brief appearance to momentous cheers and chants of his name. Then Bergden saw something that he didn't expect. As Kroft and Grimm passed one another, there was a peculiar exchange of glances. It was subtle, but Bergden saw the frustration, even for just a moment, cross Grimm's face.

"Pardon me, but I will be skipping the formalities," Grimm orated, waving away the cameras and microphones. "I appreciate the introduction from our dear chancellor, but we do have serious accusations to attend to. Lest to say I am not pleased to be here this morning."

The Regime leadership rarely showed its weaknesses to the public, preferring to keep a close eye on the information that got out. Grimm would likely ensure the camera film was destroyed.

Grimm continued. "We have received numerous inquiries surrounding the alleged activities of our officers that are not in line with the Regime's code of laws. "Citations, in particular in Blackwell, indicate a hotbed of insider criminal activity, and I must admit, it is alarming to say the least."

Bergden could feel Draven's eyes gravitate towards him. Keeping his eyes fixated on stage, Bergden didn't move as the commander continued.

Grimm held up a form and spoke. "We are giving the officers the ability to submit accusations to my office that will be investigated by my personal staff. We are doing this in the name of fairness and for the sake of our integrity. That said, I am asking you to use discretion when submitting an accusation. This is not a time to cull the herd or throw your petty rivalries to the forefront. Anyone submitting a false claim will be punished. That I can promise, and my staff won't go easy on you. Is that understood?"

A collective "Yes, Commander" answered Grimm, followed by a quick salute. Grimm returned a halfhearted salute before departing the stage.

As the black jacks began to disperse, Draven approached, pushing aside his colleagues to get to Bergden.

"I hope you'll give me a few days before turning me in to Commander Grimm," he said coldly. "I'd give you the same courtesy."

Bergden doubted that if given a chance Draven would wait to turn Bergden into Grimm's custody, but he would have to violate the law first.

"Draven, you have given me no reason to do so unless, of course, there is something you're trying to allude to." Bergden sighed and put his hand on Draven's shoulder. "I may not agree with your tactics, but you do what is best for the Regime in your mind. I just ask you to use discretion when doing so and put the Regime above your own ambitions."

Draven smirked. "Right. Discretion."

"You don't think I know it was you that filed that internal affairs report to Station Chief Aberdeen?" Bergden revealed.

Draven waved him away and headed towards the exit.

Bergden knew that Draven didn't believe him, but his concerns needed to wait as he was already behind with a mountain of paperwork awaiting him in the office and a fresh crop of prisoners in the holding cells from the previous night's arrests. Draven's petty attempts at escalating their rivalry would have to wait for the moment.

Exiting the auditorium and continuing through the main lobby, Bergden passed a young redheaded woman sobbing. Most days, he would not give it much notice. Dozens, if not hundreds of people were shuttled through Pemply Station each week for one reason or another. They were questioned, returned to their domiciles, incarcerated, or worse. It was common practice for a black jack to arrest on suspicion if it meant putting someone back in line with the Regime. Often, interrogations were short and unproductive. He rarely delighted in utilizing advanced interrogation and deportation like many of his power-hungry coworkers. His time in the War prevented him from further indulging in the near fetish-like state of authority that many others enjoyed.

Still, as he passed her in the hall, the woman's sobbing was all he could hear. It was a feeling that he simply couldn't push away. He studied her and sensed a level of familiarity. Was it her hair?

Her clothing?

She looked up at Bergden. Judging by the deep dark, red rings that hung beneath her piercing blue eyes, she had been crying for hours, perhaps the whole day. The worst part of all was that he realized exactly who he was looking at. He couldn't mistake her as she reminded him of Alyssa in many ways. He'd seen her on the train, at the market, but he'd also seen her in his home. Her name was Sia Karns and a friend of Alyssa's. Alyssa often had her and her husband Marcus over for coffee or casual conversation. She was a genial woman. He wondered what she could have done to be in the station. He would have to figure out what happened for Alyssa.

After he tackled his work, that is. The Regime came first in all facets of life. Per Regime regulations, his office was simple. Rows of filing cabinets stared back at him from the opposite wall, a portrait of Kroft set above them. On his desk sat a picture of Alyssa and James. The image was a few years old now, his son had become taller, and his wife's hair shorter, but their faces brought him happiness just the same. If he could ever find time to get back into the portrait studio, he would—and buy a new frame to boot.

After a few moments of reflection, remorse got the best of Bergden, and he walked back out into the hall looking for Sia. The wall where she had crouched was now vacant and he became concerned that she was taken for interrogation.

"Can I ask where the young woman went?" Bergden asked Dinah, who sat pecking away at her typewriter before glancing up at the lieutenant.

"She was discharged from our custody and returned to her domicile," she answered. "I can provide you the address if you'd like, lieutenant."

"No," Bergden lied, trying to mask his interest. "I was simply indulging a curiosity about the prisoner. Please return to your work." He liked Dinah, but she tended to gossip. Gossip could get a man killed in the Regime.

Returning to his office, he saw a few new candidates for his review. The job of black jack did not appeal to the faint of heart, but perhaps even worse, it appealed to those looking to live a life of a never-ending power trip. Stories of black jacks running their personal lives in the same manner was not uncommon. The way Bergden handled the power may be the minority in most respects. The position invited persons who felt marginalized by those around them to lash out when given a chance. The Regime made that an easy task, and what eventually came to his desk were the young men and women the screening process deemed "acceptable."

The intercom buzzed on his desk.

"Sir, Sergeant Sonderberg is here. Should I let him in?" Dinah asked.

Tossing aside the first dossier, he picked up, annoyed that his work was delayed once again. "Sure," Bergden replied,

Carl came in and took a seat without introduction. At this point, the formalities of the supervised and supervisor relationship had lines long worn from the chaotic nature of an interpersonal relationship in the Regime despite its attempts to simplify it.

"Night shift picked up a few vagrants," Carl said, gesturing towards the hallway. "Apparently, a handful of drunks were trying to drink it all away. Couldn't answer the basics about yesterday's speech, but they became quite belligerent in the process."

"Dare I ask how they managed to get their attention?" Bergden asked. "Doesn't take anything more than looking in the wrong direction these days. I fear our officers are getting too aggressive."

"The black jacks that brought them in say they have connections to the Coalition resistance, but then again they say that about everybody."

Detractors of the Regime were immediately branded Coalition

sympathizers or more frequently members of the faceless resistance known only as the Remnants. The initials CR showed up throughout the city and across the countryside shortly after the end of the war. The Regime required an expensive and wasteful use of resources to remove the graffiti. As a young black jack recruit, Bergden spent his fair share of time scrubbing the concrete. Once Kroft heard of possible resistance, he put his efforts into crushing a potential rebellion. Ten years later, the silent war raged on refusing to let the people of the Regime know of the existence of the Remnants.

Carl leaned against the door. "Best we go take a look."

Bergden followed Carl to the holding cells and into the interrogation room. A single brown envelope containing a brief dossier on each of the men sat on a stainless-steel table. Peering through the glass, he saw three haggard men. Two of whom appeared younger than twenty and the last no less than fifty. One of the men had long, matted blond hair that caught Bergden's attention. The blond had a tattoo of an arrow scrawled across his neck. The other younger man shaved his head into a hairstyle that puzzled Bergden. His head was shaved along the sides and kept long in the middle. It felt tribal and, as with his blond compatriot, violated the Regime's mandated men's haircut of short and clean. The oldest of the three, likely the father, carried himself in a more traditional manner. The eldest of the trio appeared to be a veteran of the war. A "CR" tattoo was visible on his forearm. A not so subtle reminder of where his loyalties lay.

"I'm guessing only the father has ties to the Coalition, or at least he did during the War," Bergden said pointing to the tattoo. "Probably nothing more than just a common street criminal now doing what he can to undermine the Regime. There might be a loose affiliation with the Remnants, but that'll be tough to prove unless he coughs up some information."

Carl took the folder from Bergden and flung it open, tossing it on the table. He scanned through his notes from the arrest. Bergden knew that at some point the information would be bent or a result of torture tactics. "Looks like they've named two women as co-conspirators," Carl said, sliding the notes across the desk. No names listed though as each was left custody this morning." Bergden sighed. "Take them to the archives and see what else you can find out about these vagrants. Have one of the new people create a dossier for my review. I'm guessing a trip to the reeducation center will be in order. Don't need to waste the cell space at Cherry Hill." Bergden stood up from the table and headed for the door. "For now, I'll go through some of the older dossiers first and try to make a few links between the groups. Perhaps even this new crop could be circled into the resistance we already go locked up. It's my job to take the small-time arrests and bring them into the greater picture."

Bergden stood in silence, taking in the mess of his office. A mile-high stack of papers swayed with each step he took. The mere thought of sitting for an entire day sifting through paperwork depressed him. He doubted the current crop of cases would bring any relief from the feeling of dissatisfaction he experienced. He remembered his early black jack days before he realized the brutality of it all. The review and revision of criminal dossiers bordered on exciting learning the ins and outs of the resistance, criminal organizations, and internal corruption. After spending years reviewing similar cases, the excitement dampened and was replaced with a sense of jaded indifference.

A commotion roared from the hall interrupting Bergden's thoughts. He slid the door open, peered out, and saw a young black jack pushing around a few recent arrestees including a young woman.

Rocco Draven stood over a man who weakly held his hands up

in defense.

"Just confess to your crimes you pile of shit and accept your punishment," Draven barked. "You'll get a cozy jail cell at Cherry Hill, but if you don't, then you'll be considered a member of the resistance giving me full rights to execute you right here. No one will miss a waste like you!"

When none of the suspects responded, Draven pulled out his pistol, slid the slide back and pressed the barrel against the now sobbing man's head pushing him to his knees.

Bergden had seen enough.

"Private Draven, tell me what is going on out here? Who is this man?" Bergden ordered, pointing at the prisoner who faced down a gun only a moment earlier, cowering in a pool of his own urine.

Draven pressed the gun harder into the man's head, pushing him closer to the floor. "None of your concern Bergden. He's just another piece of trash Coalition holdout we found down on the edge of the wharf selling illegal booze."

Draven had made it a habit of trying to undermine Bergden. Nothing angered Bergden more than Draven's affinity for authoritative evasiveness.

"Considering the interruption I am enduring for my work; I'm at least entitled to an explanation not to mention I am your commanding officer. Speaking of which, it is Lieutenant Crane to you, Private Draven," Bergden said, belittling the angry Draven in front of the other black jacks and undermining him in front of his prisoners.

Draven fumed as his eyes darted around the room, finally relenting when he realized with whom he spoke.

"Well?" Bergden urged. "Care to explain yourself?"

"He was selling banned booze and propaganda on the dock," Draven stuttered. "We have them here if you'd like to take a look, Lt. Crane." Draven tossed a few books at Bergden's feet.

"Interrogate him and get what you need. Take it easy on the physical part. He's still a person for God's sake. He's no use to the Regime as a cripple, and if I find out you sexually accosted that woman, I'll make sure you're gone by tomorrow morning, understood?"

Draven could only nod as he met Bergden's fiery gaze.

Bergden took the books back into his office and shut the door. It was the standard affair for banned books. Most were by Coalition authors. Science fiction tales, alternative history without the Regime, and of course unapproved romance novels. He tossed them in the evidence locker in his office and went back to his stack of dossiers. During his lunch breaks he would sneak a few pages in from the latest haul. Just because the Regime loathed intellectuals among the ordinary people did not mean he had to ignore their contributions to society.

Bergden leaned back in his chair and took the first dossier from the pile, rubbing his eyes. Opening the file, it didn't take him long to realize he was going to have his work cut out for him.

Looks like we have a few people we need to visit, Bergden thought. It is going to be a long day.

CHAPTER TWO

An early autumn thunderstorm arrived, and steady rain began. The thunder rolled through the city, eerily calming the otherwise busy streets below his window. Bergden had taken a few moments to just listen to nature before returning to his work.

The day's dossier reviews took much longer than expected. For Bergden, days like today reminded him that his work struggled with the mundane. He doubted many of the younger black jacks really took the time to review their cases before storming out into the streets to flex their power, arresting the innocent based on a hunch or a loose narrative—the arrest itself often accompanied by ruthless and brutal tactics.

Bergden's approach to his job would seem unorthodox to all but the most experienced black jacks. He preferred to supplant a sense of trust in those he apprehended and interrogated them banking on a payoff for his compassion. The simple act of showing just a touch of humanity went a long way compared to thoughtless beatings. In a world without remorse, any ray of hope was welcome.

The cruiser continued through the downtown thoroughfare. Carl plowed through the back end of the rainstorm. Bergden and Carl always rode together, but adapting to the erratic behavior Carl consistently displayed behind the wheel never came easy for Bergden. He gripped the bar above the door as the cruiser whipped around a sharp curve.

"You mind slowing down, Carl?" Bergden asked as he pressed his hand against his mouth. "I'd hate to throw up on my uniform right before going into a home. Removes that aura of authority we're supposed to carry."

"Sorry Bergden, I couldn't hear you," Carl laughed, whipping around another turn and down an unmarked side street. "Listen to that engine roar."

For a moment, Bergden swore that he felt the car slide off the deluged streets and onto the sidewalk. Pedestrians scrambled to get out of the way, and vendors pushed their carts onto the road as the wild ride continued past.

Bergden turned on the radio, attempting to calm his nerves and drown out the thoughts of horrendous car accidents involving his mangled, lifeless body on the wet pavement. The radio broadcast reminded him of the inquisitors as the Regime's morning propaganda shows played on a loop. He found himself thinking of Alyssa and James. By this time of the day, the two should be in school, but for the inquisitors neither time nor place mattered. He had heard rumors of school children being yanked from their desks to be questioned, or old men dying in their beds forced to answer trivial inquests their answers

"A Tribute to the Treaty of Blackwell," Carl chimed in, cutting off Bergden's thoughts about his family. "A symphony composed by Gerich Braun at the end of the War." The sounds of a string quartet and a brass trio came through the cruiser's speakers. A symphony to celebrate the victory of the Regime.

"It's one of my favorites," Carl continued. "Really captures the horrors of war and the burned-out corpses it took to place Kroft in charge, doesn't it?"

Ignoring Carl's jab at the chancellor, Bergden instead chose to pull out the dossier containing the first people that he and Carl were to visit. Flipping to the first page, Bergden was greeted by the image of a thin-lipped, disheveled man. His hair was raven black with a strong chin, rough skin, and emerald green eyes. The woman, a pretty redhead, who still held her looks despite a scar running the length of her neck. The pock marked man's name was a general store shopkeeper named Alvin Black, and the woman was his wife Mattie. A middle-aged couple that was allegedly spotted consorting with known Coalition agents near the wharf. He personally wouldn't have added the pair to the list of priority interrogations, but the station chief saw it otherwise.

"Looks like this is the place," Carl said as the car stopped in front of the prewar era brownstone. "First floor first door on the left." The brownstone townhome, a typical walk up like the one Bergden remembered from his youth, housed as many as ten families in some areas of Blackwell. When he was a boy, Bergden's townhome had five families. His childhood house was long ago destroyed during the war and rebuilt into a new complex, but it just wasn't the same as his family home. Still, for a fleeting moment, the townhome brought back memories of his youth.

Straightening his uniform, Bergden took a moment to gain his composure. He followed Carl up the concrete steps to the large, wooden door. The Regime flag hanging dutifully above the door the bottom frayed from exposure. He could bring the brownstone owner in for allowing the flag to fall into disrepair, but that was hardly something he concerned himself with at this point in his career. A younger, less experienced black jack on a power trip would be more interested in such trifle. For his position, the paperwork alone turned off Bergden to the idea. He preferred to give the people a little rope. He just prayed they wouldn't hang themselves for it.

Carl knocked, and after a few moments with no response, he pushed on the door and the two watched as it swung open with little effort. Much to their surprise, the two men noticed the door had already been forced open. Carl drew his pistol and crept into the house. Bergden followed behind unbuttoning his holster and removing his sidearm. He glanced down at his gun. *God, I hope I don't have to use this today,* he thought as he fingered the hammer. He hadn't killed a man since the War.

As the two men proceeded farther into the house, the sounds of struggle greeted them.

Bergden cursed under his breath as they tread carefully into the abode's family room. The floor was already steeped in blood, and it flowed into his boots. He feared the worst as he entered the room expecting to be greeted by a maimed corpse.

Instead, he saw Draven standing over what Bergden could only presume to be Alvin Black.

"What the hell is going on here?" Bergden demanded.

Rather than receiving a response, he saw stares from the blood-covered faces of black jacks. The man lay unconscious on the hardwood floor choking on his own blood. A sickly gurgle following each labored breath. The man's eyes were swelled shut, and a collection of teeth lay on the wood floor like jacks. Bergden bent down and felt for a pulse on the man's crooked neck.

Still breathing.

He sighed in relief

Another look at the broken man was all it took for him to know it would not be much longer till he'd have to call in the coroner. He could picture the scene before he arrived. Draven and his goons taking violent liberties with Mr. Black even as he lay gasping for air. Kicking and stomping his limp, broken body. With a crushed throat and his skull partially caved in on the right temple, the prognosis was grim. The disgusting sight was all he could bear as he moved his gaze to the kitchen door where Draven stood, gun drawn.

"Draven, take your men and search the upstairs for any evidence that might assist in this case," Bergden ordered. "I'm going to have a conversation with Mrs. Black. I'm afraid to see what you've done to that poor woman."

"We didn't touch the whore," Draven barked back. "She's only got what was coming to her. She wasn't on the dossier, and she still resisted. She'll spend a night or two in Cherry Hill when I'm done with her," he huffed.

Draven signaled the others to follow him further into the house. Bergden shook his head. Thankfully for Mattie Black, the young private hadn't read the entire dossier.

Walking into the kitchen, Bergden found the woman sobbing at the dinner table with an overturned cup of coffee, the contents dripping to the floor. He studied her appearance for any signs that Draven stepped over the line. The woman's eyes were red, but no visible bruises or cuts. He took a seat across from the traumatized woman. Her face now buried into her hands, only taking a moment to meet his gaze before slumping her head back at the table, her tears continuing to fall. "Carl, see what you can do for Mr. Black. Try and get the bleeding stopped at least." Bergden turned to the grieving wife. "Mrs. Black, I'd like to speak to you in private. I only ask a moment of your time."

She eyed Carl as he went to care for Mr. Black.

Blood from the prone Mr. Black He stepped towards her to help her from the table. Her shoes, an embroidered, brown leather pump that tied up at the heel, likely a gift from her husband, were now soaked with her husband's blood.

Mattie Black led Bergden away from the kitchen and into a nearby sitting room. There were two leather bound chairs the fabric kept in place with a series of copper nails, a near empty bookshelf, and a window that had a view of the brownstone across the alleyway. He glanced outside and saw the neighbors had gathered at the window to take in the scene.

Across the room, a piano sat gathering dust near the couch next to another half-empty bookshelf. The home itself was substantially more significant than his own.

"Mrs. Black, I know this is difficult, but I need your assistance. I can help you and your husband if you cooperate. Are you able to help me?"

Mrs. Black paused for a moment, turning her head away in shame as if awaiting another blow.

"Please, Mrs. Black. I'm sorry I gave you that impression, but I assure you I only seek answers," Bergden said.

The horror of the black jack reputation often preceded a raid, and if the subject was a woman this was often the result. He assumed that Draven threatened her with enhanced interrogation often amounting to nothing more than sexual assault or at its worst, rape, rather than an actual interrogation.

"I'm sor—I'm sorry. I tried to cooperate. He wouldn't listen when my husband tried to explain. He kept saying we were with the resistance. We—we don't know them at all. We are faithful to the Regime. I swear it."

"I beg you not to apologize. The Regime thanks you for your cooperation, and I'll make sure it isn't forgotten."

"My husband lay in a pool of his own blood. I think our cooperation has been long forgotten. My son died fighting for

Kroft. His body was never returned, we never received any condolence from anyone. Yet we endured as loyal citizens. For what? So my husband could be beaten to death in his own home?"

Bergden gestured her to the couch and sat down beside her. Before he could begin his line of questioning, a clamor from upstairs. Draven tore through the couple's belongings, launching a loose drawer down the wooden steps. The only respite for Mr. and Mrs. Black was the fact that owning anything of real value was damn near impossible under the Regime. After the War, all things of monetary value were taken to help rebuild the state under the promise of repayment. Ten years had passed without a single cent returned to the former owners, and the people of Blackwell turned to any means necessary to make ends meet.

Back in the living room, Carl struggled to stabilize Mr. Black's condition. Bergden knew that his condition persisted without hope, and Carl's intervention would do little to elevate his chances at survival. He was neither a doctor nor a nurse nor a medic. Wartime training was fundamental and easily distributed to new recruits but proved useless in all but the most fundamental of situations.

"My husband is going to die, isn't he?" Mattie asked through a veil of tears. "He is going to die, and your men killed him, but who can I call? Who should I report his murder to? If you are the authorities, who can I expect to help me?"

Bergden said nothing as Mattie's anguish escalated into a full-blown wail. He sighed and frowned.

Once Draven finished ransacking the upstairs, Ms. Black faced detainment, and if Bergden hoped to get anything of value, he'd better do it now because once she was arrested there were no guarantees. If she was sent to Cherry Hill, then whatever she knew would die in her cell. Years in a Regime cell was far worse than death for suspected traitors no matter the age or gender. If you managed to leave the cell without a broken bone, call a priest because it was a miracle.

"Mattie, I can help you, but I need you to calm down and focus," Bergden asked with his hand over hers. "I will make sure the men who did this to your husband are punished, but I cannot do so without getting some information from you. Do you understand?"

Mattie nodded, and Bergden removed his handkerchief from his jacket and handed it to the distraught woman. She eyed the offer for a moment before taking the tissue and wiping away the tears.

Bergden continued. "The Regime has reason to suspect you and your husband are sympathizers, and even possibly collaborators with a Coalition backed resistance movement known as the Remnants." Bergden leaned in closer to Mrs. Black. "I need you to be up front with me Ms. Black. Is this true?"

He could tell she wanted to deny it outright, shaking her head, but the life ending groans reverberating from the living room stopped her before she uttered another word. She rose from the chair and walked out and stared out into the family room. She put a hand over her mouth as she watched her husband take his final breaths. She stood speechless in the doorway. He could see the anguish in her eyes.

Bergden came up beside her and rested a hand on her shoulder. "I need an answer, Mattie. I can help you, but I need information and I need it now. "It upset him to be so forward with a woman in pain, but he was left with little choice as Draven could be heard wrapping up his search. Any moment now, Draven would march back to the kitchen, and unless she provided them a reason to believe she wasn't a collaborator, even Bergden couldn't prevent her arrest.

The grieving woman slammed her fists against her thighs again and again before crying out. "You cannot bring back my husband! That is what I truly want! Why should I tell you pieces of shit anything? No matter what I say, I'll end up dead just the same. Whether it is in a cell or in my own home it matters little to me."

Bergden sat in silence as Mattie continued her blank stare at the carnage in the living room before turning her attention back to him. A moment of clarity appeared on her face. The dawning of understanding that there was a reason to live.

"But for his sake, I will tell you what I know. I think I owe him that much to try and live on." She took a deep breath and shook her hands, wringing away her anguish. "Alvin spent time at the tavern on the corner, *The Rung*. You know the place?"

Bergden nodded. He was familiar with the bar in so much as he'd raided it once or twice when he first got started. *The Rung* maintained a sordid clientele that beckoned trouble. The first visit ended in a barfight between his squad and a few degenerates. Bergden never thought a broken bottle could do the damage it did, but he used it to dangerous effect.

"Alive went after his shifts at the mill and before our usual dinner time." Mattie paused and composed herself before continuing. "One night a few weeks ago, he told me of a group of people who had access to prohibited goods, books, and even non-government issued alcohol and coffee. Things we haven't seen in years. At first, I wrote them off as drunken braggarts, but after a few weeks they would give us black market goods at a discount in exchange for doing minor jobs."

"What kind of jobs?" Bergden interrupted.

Mattie looked down at her husband's lifeless body before finding the strength to answer. "Running messages, delivering goods to shop keepers, that sort of thing."

"Please continue Mattie," Bergden asked.

Mattie fingered the handkerchief in her hands, no longer meeting his eye. "Eventually encouraging us to assist their operations for a greater cut. The money coming in..." She paused.

"You must give me more information, Mattie," Bergden urged.

"The money coming went untaxed and helped us finally get ahead. A taste of the good life we used to have you know before the War. We weren't supporting the Coalition. Just trying to make our lives a bit more comfortable."

He could sympathize with her. He'd missed some of the luxuries from before the War and had he known how the world would change perhaps he wouldn't have jumped at the chance to join the military. No one could comprehend the consequences of a Regime victory on everyday life until it was too late.

He placed a gentle hand on hers, trying to console her. "Thank you, Mattie. We'll make use of that information I assure you and I'll put in the file that you were not taking part in any illicit activities. I know it comes at the cost of your husband's life for you to avoid persecution. I will make sure he is not forgotten."

Mattie could only nod her response, still fighting back tears.

He hoped that what she gave him would be enough to convince the squad that Mattie didn't need to be arrested.

As Bergden exchanged notes with Carl he could hear Draven and his goons thunder down the stairs laughing and cussing. Their hands were empty, but their pockets spilled over with the Blacks' personal possessions. He wanted nothing more than to take them to task right then and there but under the Regime they had done their duty. The homes of criminals were permitted to be looted for the good of the Regime and to pay the black jacks.

"Let's go. There's nothing more for us here." Bergden turned to Draven. "Draven, tell your cronies to get the hell out."

Draven eyed Bergden before relenting. "Yes, lieutenant." The group left, leaving only the grieving Mattie in the home.

Outside, the rain had finally stopped falling and a hint of sun peeked through the graying sky. The car cruised over the streets, sliding into potholes. Their depths disguised by the heavy rains.

Carl had given up avoiding them as they had become far too numerous in the forgotten areas of Blackwell. Bergden reached for the handle again as the cruiser sped through the concrete streets.

The next dossier took the pair from the middle class of society to the lowest in an area known as the Skids. A rumored hotbed for the Coalition resistance and black markets, the Skids was the last hold out against Kroft's grip. Since the end of the war, years of black jack raids and bagging suspects left very few people interested in trying to stand up to the Regime, especially if the end result was a long term stay at Cherry Hill, or worse, an appointment at Singer. Yet, the Skids continued to impose its brand of injustice. Looting, destruction of property and vandalism. All for the last of those, Bergden realized that the black jacks did that a fair bit themselves.

The radio in the car began to buzz. The sound of Draven's voice broke through the static. "Bergden? You there?"

"Go ahead, Draven," Bergden responded.

"An accident just occurred," Draven complained. "We made it past, but it'll be in your path. I suggest taking a different route as there won't be a crew out for probably awhile, I imagine. Do you want us to just go in?"

Not on your life, Bergden thought.

"Let me take a look at the mission parameters," Bergden retorted. as he studied the dossier. "Just hold tight when you arrive but be vigilant. We aren't exactly in the safest neighborhood in Blackwell. Do not proceed unless I say so, is that clear?"

"Yes sir," Draven lamented.

Bergden flipped through the dossier and saw the image of a man who had some hard years staring back at him. Salt and pepper hair and a well-trimmed beard, he also had a tattoo of a wolf on his neck. It was an all too familiar ink to Bergden, for he had seen it many times before: It was a tattoo from his time spent in the Regime military.

"Edgar Krupp," Carl said, taking the dossier from Bergden. "Former Regime loyalist turned resistance after he lost a brother to an overzealous inquisitor. It looks like he died while incarcerated at Cherry Hill after the interrogation went south. Krupp served two tours during the War and came back to find his house had been confiscated."

Carl shook his head in disbelief as he pointed to the dossier "His brother faced a much harder fate. Poor bastard suffered from schizophrenia and the guards beat him to death. I can't say that surprises me in that hellhole."

"I'd be pissed too if I was this guy," Bergden agreed. "Looks like plenty of tattoos on him too. "

"Plenty of notable markings for sure," Carl continued. "The visible tattoo on his neck, two on his arms and one on his right shoulder. Damn, got it down to the last detail, didn't they?"

Bergden looked at each of the tattoos. The photo was taken at Cherry Hill but held up just the same. A symbol of eagle wings on the neck, twin sabers, one on each arm, and a pin-up girl on the shoulder.

"Any changes to your body by you or by natural forces were to be reported immediately to your commanding officer," Bergden added. "Wasn't forbidden. Pretty typical stuff I guess, but also useful when they needed to identify your dead body on a corpse-laden battlefield."

"You know Bergden. I think I know more about these pricks' histories than your own past," Carl said. "We're supposed to be friends, and you rarely ever, hell, you never mention the wartime Bergden Crane. How about giving me just a little?"

Bergden shifted uncomfortably before answering. "I'd rather not Carl. It might be too much to handle for you. I know you fought in the war, but we make such a great partnership without you knowing about the intimate details of my life. Besides, I like the perception you have of me just the way it is."

"I know you were in on the front lines when the Coalition were hit along the border," Carl huffed. "Does it have to do with that? Hardcore group of Regime diehards right there standing up in the early days. Most only made it back in body bags. Save for an exceptional few."

Bergden's mind drifted away from the conversation with Carl, and back to the day he first stormed the Coalition lines. The goal was simple. Break through and in a pincer, movement cut the enemy lines into pieces. The armored cavalry would follow and that would be it. Yet that's not what happened. The initial attempts to break the line failed. Wave after wave of Regime soldiers were cut down, torn to ribbons by machine gun fire, but leadership persisted in the initial plan until finally there were a few hundred men standing. He remembered wading through the bodies and blood to get back to the supply lines. He sobbed that first night until the sun rose.

"Bergden? Bergden, you there?" Carl said as he snapped his fingers bringing Bergden back to the moment.

He stared at Carl and for whatever reason he decided to relent. No one knew of his past, not even Alyssa. "Fine, but this remains only between the two of us. Is that understood? God forbid Alyssa ever find out." Bergden hesitated. "She'd never look at me the same ever again."

Carl nodded. "Of course, Bergden. Your secrets are safe with me. Like I said before, we're friends."

Bergden took a deep breath but suddenly could not find the courage to speak.

Carl shook his head and shared his experiences. "When I was on the front, I was a married man. I had an affair with a Coalition woman in a barn for three days until my commander caught us. I have no idea if she became pregnant, but I knew we were in love.

We were forced apart. That wrecks me to this very day even though I have a family of my own. I despise myself for that forbidden love. Now, you tell me something about you," Carl offered.

Bergden saw genuine intrigue in Carl's expression.

"Alright Carl. I'll indulge you," Bergden said in a low voice as if they were being watched. "When we finally broke the Coalition lines, we were down to barely a handful of men and as luck would have it, I was out of ammunition. The Coalition forces scattered, and the stragglers were rounded up. We were tired and exhausted, but there was work to be done."

Carl held up a hand. "Who was your commander?"

"A familiar face," Bergden conceded. "Commander Liam Grimm."

Carl laughed and shook his head in disbelief.

Bergden pressed on. "All I wanted to do was go home and beg for forgiveness from anyone who would listen, but Grimm told us that we couldn't handle taking anymore prisoners. We didn't have enough food to feed ourselves let alone the prisoners."

Bergden took a moment to breathe and sighed. "We had to execute them one by one, but we didn't have any ammunition. Men were gutted, throats slit, or heads caved in with shovels. Whatever got the job done. I've never been more ashamed of my humanity than I was that day."

Carl's face froze in horror. "It was war, Bergden," he maintained. "Things happen during war that are out of your control."

Bergden ignored Carl's sympathetic words. "I hadn't seen what the human brain looked like until a shovel was buried into it. How does someone react to that? Live each day with that image in their psyche? They don't. I bury it away in the deepest recesses of my mind, but it's always there." Bergden fought back tears.

The two men sat in silence as Carl turned the cruiser down into a side street.

"God man, I knew you saw the worst of humanity, but I didn't realize," Carl sympathized. I'm sorry you have that burden to bear."

For the first time, Bergden felt the impulsive need to defend his actions aloud.

"I'm not that man anymore. God will judge me for the things I've done. I've quietly made it my goal to make life under the Regime better for anyone I can. Alyssa, James or anyone that needs it," Bergden sighed. "I'm not that man."

The cruiser came to a stop outside a rundown tower, a housing project that had seen more prosperous days.

"I know man, but now we need to take care of business," Carl said.

"We're outside. Not liking the look of this place," Draven interrupted.

Bergden and Carl got out of the car and approached the dilapidated housing project. Draven stood by the front door, his pistol at his side.

The Regime's reconstruction initiatives only stretched so far into the city limits. Clearly the home of Edgar Krupp did not receive the same treatment as Bergden's abode. The concrete seemed to crack and fall in the breeze. There were more windows made of a thin tile of plywood than glass which had been broken long ago. The complex itself, likely built prewar, was not up to the Regime's strict construction codes, not by a long shot. With the location on the outskirts, the regulation teams hadn't made out in quite some time.

The group entered the dimly lit building and fanned out pistols at the ready. The rainwater dripped through the ceiling and onto the rotten wooden floor causing each footstep to squish into wood muffling the sounds of their boots. The conditions were deplorable, and a portrait of Kroft hung above the entryway into the lobby, the face besmirched by vandals. That was enough to get a man killed.

"He's on the ninth floor according to the report. Do you trust the elevator? I doubt anyone's been on it in years," Carl asked Bergden, gesturing over to the decrepit life.

Bergden punched the call button, and after a few moments it did not arrive. He pried at the door, but years of rust and black mold nearly sealed them shut. The pungent stench of decay found its way through the door. Bergden suspected that the smell came from more than just poor upkeep and Draven came over with a pry bar. The squad was not greeted with a functioning elevator car, but the skeletal remains of a man who had hung himself. The rancid flesh hung from the poor man's face. His eyes had long been consumed by the fury of rats that raced through the Skids.

"Head for the stairs," Bergden relented, closing the door. He'd call it in when he got back to the station although he doubted a crew's arrival to the heart of the Skids.

The stairs strained under their weight each step. The wood creaked and groaned from years of neglect. He wondered if the building itself was actually abandoned and they'd been given false information.

"Case notes say he's up on the ninth floor. I can't believe there's anyone living in this hovel at all," Carl said.

Reaching the ninth floor without incident, Bergden, Carl and Draven split up and searched the floor. The lights managed to be darker than the lobby's and the stench somehow worse than the elevators. The odor permeated through the hallway as the trio went room to room many found to be unoccupied for a while, yet the former inhabitants had never left. Bergden heard Draven drumming on an apartment door. Bergden pushed past and further down the hall gun drawn and flashlight forward. He leaned against a partially rotten door listening for any sign of anyone home.

Gunfire thundered down the hall, jolting Bergden to action. Racing to the sound, he ducked behind a doorway taking aim at the direction of the shots.

"Bastards are armed!" Draven yelled down the hall. "Where the hell did, they get guns? They were all confiscated and destroyed!"

Bergden stifled a laugh. Draven was so used to facing no resistance that anyone that could fight back would be quite the surprise. The Regime put a stop to legal personal firearms years ago, but only those who were agreeable to the laws would this apply. A decades-long war made it easy for anyone to get a gun and some of them packed a serious punch.

Bergden and Carl followed the sound gunfire and entered the hallway on full alert, taking cover in a niche back away from the apartment before advancing on Draven's position.

"How many contacts?" Bergden asked Draven.

Before he could answer, a round crashed into a nearby wall. Glancing out into the hall, he watched two men duck behind a doorway taking aim. It was the first time since the war ended that Bergden saw the barrel of a gun pointed at him. He flashed back to the first time he lowered his rifle with the intention to take a man's life. He never blinked except when the kick of the gun banked hard against his shoulder. He never saw the man fall, but he knew in his heart he had killed him. Now, he faced down another over ten years later.

"Carl, give me cover. I'm going to head for that room over there and get a better angle. If he is ex-military, he might give me a go of it," Bergden said as he ducked low and worked his way to flank the men firing at them.

Carl fired off a few rounds and Bergden watched as the men ducked down avoiding the errant fire. He wormed his way to a doorway that provided just enough cover and gave him the advantage. The elders of the two men saw Bergden and popped off a few rounds before hustling back down the hall.

Bergden pulled the hammer back on his pistol and swung around the corner. Falling to one knee he fired taking the two men by surprise and striking one of them in the chest. The man stepped towards Bergden before slumping into the wall. Bergden watched the life drain from his eyes before realizing that he still had the other man to worry about.

He was struggling to find the apartment key when Bergden came up behind him.

"Step away from the door," Bergden demanded. "That's an order. Disobeying an order—"

Before he could finish a shot rang out. Draven stood in the hallway, his hands shaking. "Fucking bastard damn near clipped me. You shoot at a black jack this is what you deserve."

Bergden ignored Draven as he studied the two bodies. Two men lay dead up against a wall, the blood splattering on the wood panel behind them with four or five holes. Bergden looked down and saw that their man, Edgar Krupp, was not one of the dead.

"Pick up their guns and put them in for evidence. Maybe we can find the prints on them. Did you leave anyone alive to even question?" Carl barked at Draven, who was examining the exit wound from the back of the skull almost marveling at the destruction. "First time you've shot a man, Draven?" Carl asked.

Draven glanced up from the man's corpse. "Never saw it up close before. Never saw a man's head explode like a melon." Draven rubbed the back of his neck. "Not sure I feel right."

So, he does have a soul, Bergden joked to himself.

Walking into the apartment, Bergden looked down at two younger men that lay dead in a pool. Blood pooling around them. Their lives taken by their own hands choosing death over arrest. The crimson liquid still dripped from the fatal wounds and onto the rotted, wooden floor dripping down through the porous floorboards. As the three proceeded into the adjoining room towards a den with a collapsed bookshelf and a dust covered coffee table, there appeared another man. He sat propped up against the couch clutching his shoulder. One of the rounds managed to go right through him and hit the wall behind the bloodied man, the shot shredding his shoulder in the process.

"Let's just end the asshole's life already," Draven said as he placed his pistol against the wounded man's temple ruining Bergden's hope that he had a soul in the process. The man sat in silence defiantly facing his executioner grimacing as he fought off the pain.

"Give me a second to talk to him Draven before you go blowing his brains out." Bergden waved back towards the hallway. "Go search the place for any evidence. Any books resistance notes or other contraband. Most importantly make sure the place is clear," Bergden ordered.

Bergden wanted answers he could hand the station chief, but with the least amount of blood on their hands as possible.

"Are you Edgar Krupp?" he asked the man who clenched the mortal wound.

"I'm going to assume you are Edgar Krupp based on the picture in our files. Mr. Krupp, you need to listen to me. That man will kill you with no questions asked," Bergden said and pointed in the direction of Draven who was digging through the kitchen drawers. "I'm giving you the opportunity to help your situation and maybe save your life."

Still bleeding, the man cracked his neck in an abrupt upwards motion then spit at Bergden. The blood-filled mucus grazing his shoulder. Surrounded by squalor, the act didn't anger Bergden. Moldy bread and tainted water were all that a man like Edgar Krupp could survive on. Edgar Krupp knew the Regime did not look out for him and if he did turn to a resistance movement or the

Remnants, it wouldn't be for any other reason than survival. Bergden asked himself if this man even cared to live.

Yet, after several more attempts to get the wounded man to converse, Bergden felt defeated. Each time Bergden spoke, the more Mr. Krupp spat in his direction. He had a wife and child to take care of and getting a disease from this man, no matter how badly he wanted to help him, was not an option. Unfortunately, Mr. Krupp had left Bergden no choice as Draven came around the corner.

"Bastard not talking?" Draven asked he dug his pistol into the open wound on Mr. Krupp's should.er "Don't worry I'll get him to speak up!" Draven barked, pulling the hammer back on his pistol.

Bergden stepped between the two.

"Get the fuck out of my way, Bergden," Draven growled, shaking the pistol towards the wounded man. "You've had your crack at him, now it is my turn!"

Bergden stepped closer to Draven and glared down at the diminutive private. "We can't just kill him without getting some sort of intelligence from him. Get him to talk and let's get him out of here. Understood?"

Bergden hated leaving the short-tempered private to his own devices but coming back empty handed to the Station Chief looked bad for any black jack let alone a lieutenant. He felt for Mr. Krupp. Bergden winced as the truncheon struck Mr. Krupp with a dull thud. The advanced level of interrogation that Draven prided himself on was nothing more than a street beating. Batons, a chair leg or just his fists were enough to do the job.

Nearly an hour of beatings passed until Mr. Krupp caved. Not his resolve, but his skull his gurgled screams were not of pain or indignation, but rather insurgent in tone and message as his life slipped away.

"Resistance...Remnants...resistance..." Edgar Krupp struggled to say as Draven struck another blow against his back sending him to his knees. Each blow softened his voice, but the words of rebellion crawled out from his bloodied jaw.

"Res... Resis... Resistance. All resistance... Remnants are coming." A near-silent murmur followed as he collapsed to the floor. Bergden and Carl sat in silence waiting for Draven to confirm the obvious. That death found Mr. Krupp. Draven dragged the limp, lifeless body into the main room and propped him against the wall.

"He's alive, don't worry," Draven said, much to the surprise of the two senior officers. "Not much to say after all that, I guess. We'll have to leave it up to the boys at Cherry Hill to get him to spill what he knows. Let's go get some drink lads!" Draven cheered, gleefully celebrating the fact he beat the man to a pulp. Bergden reasoned briefly that alcohol was the young private's way of coping with the constant stream of violence, but watching him check the man's pockets for valuables reaffirmed his belief that Draven was nothing short of a common thug.

"I'm afraid I can't, Draven," Carl declined. "It's getting late and I don't get much time with Mary these days. I'll see you in the morning."

Draven looked at Bergden, whose face must have said it all. The furrowed brow of an angry man Draven waved his hand at Bergden in disgust before heading back downstairs.

Resistance is coming? Bergden thought. What did this man honestly know? He could only hope he survived until morning. Bergden hid his head in shame. He had let Draven do what he had been trying to avoid.

He'd have a rough time looking at Alyssa tonight when he told her about the day's events.

CHAPTER THREE

Silence marked the ride back to Pemply Station. For Bergden and Carl, death had become commonplace on the job. Only the most resolute-willed man could witness the brutal, fatal beating of a human being and walk away without a mental scar. The two men reflected in a quiet stillness as the cruiser made its way back to the station. More rain-leaden clouds crept along in the distance, but for the first time in the day, the rain had found another place to fall, and the fog slowly sank in behind the rolling clouds.

The car zipped through the empty streets. The workers had taken refuge back in their homes, their long workdays coming to an end. A few would go to the taverns, but intoxication, especially behind the wheel, was a one-way ticket to Cherry Hill.

Bergden thought about how to describe such a day to Alyssa. He had worked later than usual, but Alyssa accepted that as a side of effect of the nature of his job. What worried him was not the timing, but the look he wore walking through the front door. He never wanted to give his family cause for alarm, but days like today made it a monumental effort to be a stoic, never mind trying to feign happiness.

Edgar Krupp sat in the back of the cruiser in silence, bound and broken. A black bag draped over his gaunt, bruised, and bloodied face. For a moment, Bergden thought he'd find a dead man waiting for him when they got to the station.

"We're nearing Pemply Station," Carl said as the car began to slow. "I can let you out at the train station if you'd like. I can handle our friend back there and the initial paperwork. You've been working late too frequently, and Alyssa can't be happy with that. I know you are missing precious time with your boy too."

He was not one to turn away a chance to be home, especially after a day like today.

Bergden decided to take Carl up on his offer. "I appreciate it, Carl. I'll give your regards to Alyssa and James. I'm sure they will appreciate the gesture even more than I," Bergden said as the car came to a stop. Usually, he'd go back to the office to get started on the paperwork, but he just couldn't tonight.

The train car, nearly empty save for a few strays headed home, ground to a halt as it pulled into the station. A thick, low-lying fog shrouded the housing complex as he approached. He was tired, hungry, and ready to sleep. The twin high rises lined with shapeless windows disappearing into the formless clouds. At the peak of the high-rise apartment complex sat the Crane residence. It would be good to be back, giving them both a loving embrace.

On any given night, Alyssa would greet him at the door with a warm and James by her side. James looked forward to getting a chance to see his father just before bedtime and the later the night, the worse Bergden felt about those missed opportunities. It was one of those moments that only a father could cherish with his son—a moment to forget the day and return to what he considered normal in an abnormal world.

But as he approached, the immediate and alarming feeling that tonight that his typical late-night situation had somehow changed darted through his mind. The front door was slightly ajar, and the smiles of his family were removed from the scene. Instead, he was greeted by an apartment devoid of light save for the faint flicker of candlelight from down the hall. He felt an uneasy sense of fear as he crept into his home. Drawing his pistol, he leveled the barrel at the source of the light. Slipping in silence through the family room and farther into the darkened home.

Thinking the worst had happened to his family caused his hands to shake uncontrollably, unable to steady his aim as he stepped further into the darkened house. For but a fleeting moment, he sat still until the sounds of a muffled cry emerged from one of the bedrooms. He restrained his design from rushing as he approached Alyssa's room, the source of light growing broader and brighter. He peered through the crack in the door and saw a single candle illuminating the wall—the familiar portrait of Kroft staring hauntingly down upon Bergden as he proceeded into his wife's room.

He cracked the door and peered into the room; his pistol leveled—the muzzle facing the light. There sat a darkened figure facing street-side by the window. He studied the form as he realized they had not noticed his presence. He could tell it was a woman not by her form, but the robe around her blocked her face from view. "Alyssa?" Bergden asked the figure hesitantly.

He gripped the pistol in his hand until his knuckles were white. The figure turned, and he exhaled when he saw Alyssa. Tears dripped like candle wax from her eyes. She clutched her handkerchief tight before turning away from Bergden. Her somber whimpers muted. He shot a look back to the doorway wondering if something had happened to James. He left the room and raced down the hallway. He peered into the boy's room. Beneath the images of Regime heroes, model planes and a map of the world, the young boy lay quietly asleep. The moon emerged from the fog-laden night sky peeking into the young boy's room. Gently illuminating James's face. He exhaled in relief before returning to Alyssa's room.

"Bergden. They took him," Alyssa wailed through more tears. "They took him without any warning. The bastards took him!"

In the dim light, Bergden could see her reach for a wine glass. It had been a long time since Alyssa had a drink of something other than the usual coffee or water, but he watched as the red-tinted liquid spun around the crystal ware. The familiar aroma filled his nostrils. A hint of chocolate masked by oak-aged juices. The same wine from their wedding night. To be distraught to the point that she opened a bottle when the occasion did not call for it, was a bad sign. He had studied her proclivities throughout their marriage and unsolicited wine was hardly a moment of clarity for his beautiful wife.

He set aside the bottle from the nightstand and put it on the small oval table near the door table. It was half-empty which was plenty enough to get Alyssa to forget her faculties for a woman her size. Her face finally revealed in its entirety barely masked the pain.

"Who did they take Alyssa? James is in his bed. I checked on him only moments ago. Who must they have taken if not for our son?" Bergden asked, concerned.

"Sia's Marcus. Our neighbor and friend. Enforcement officers, your black jacks, came for him this evening, and I haven't seen either since. I could hear Sia scream as he resisted. She ran after their cruiser down the boulevard. Her anguished echoed off these very walls," Alyssa said rubbing the plasterwork. "I don't know what happened to her," Alyssa said before falling into Bergden's arms grasping for him and clutching hold of his back. His memory came rushing forth. He remembered seeing Sia's face at Pemply Station in the morning. She was the redheaded woman at the station; her makeup had smeared a black stream of eyeliner surrounding her bloodshot eyes. She must have been at the station all night long waiting for Marcus's release.

"Alyssa, I saw Sia at the station in a perilously fragile state, but she was still there unharmed. I did not recall it being her until this moment. My day was challenging to put it mildly, but I assure you she is alright. Unfortunately, I can't say what happened to Marcus. He was gone before I could press for his release."

Alyssa's body shook as she poured another glass, the wine splashed out onto the hardwood floor. The dark red liquid running to the soles of his boots. The wine resembled the bloodstained hardwood floors of Mr. Krupp's decaying apartment. Images of Draven's violence and the muzzle flashes from his sidearm rushed without pause forth from his imagination. He shook his head trying to reel in his emotions for his wife's sake.

"Tomorrow, I will find out what happened to Marcus. I will make sure Sia is home safe, and the two of you will be sharing coffee again in no time," Bergden offered, hoping to resolve the issue before retiring for the night. He could only hope his assurances would be enough although he feared for Marcus's wellbeing. He stopped short of promising anything to his concerned wife.

But before he could leave, Alyssa hastily poured another glass of the wine finishing off the bottle. It became clear that her fury kept building, barely in check.

"How could you not have known about any of this? You are the lieutenant, are you not? You tell me time and time again that all of the Regime's suspects in our district come across your desk. That you get the final say." She swigged from her glass, the wine spilling from the corners of her mouth as the final drop dripped into her blouse. The glass fell from her hands and shattered on the floor.

In a violent, jerking motion, Alyssa flung herself towards Bergden. "If Marcus tells them what they've done, Bergden, we'll all be in danger. The Regime will know what I've done! They'll take James away, Bergden! They'll take him away and it will all be my fault!"

Bergden was taken aback by this sudden change in the story. *What did she mean what she's done?* he wondered.

"What is it that you've done, Alyssa? Why would the Regime arrest Marcus? Why come after our family?" Bergden questioned. He knew that Alyssa used some contraband in her cooking in the past and the wine was not made of Regime grown grapes, but those were minor offenses easily overlooked when your husband was an REO lieutenant.

Alyssa turned donning a much sterner look on her face, the tears and sorrowful expression melting away.

"It's nothing Bergden," she whimpered, walking back her words. "I'm tired, and I fear I've had too much wine. I am going to wash up and go to bed. You've had a long day. We can talk about this in the morning. I just got carried away for a moment. Sia is my best friend and I just worry about her. "Alyssa stepped over and gave him a kiss, her breath heavy with the dull earthly tones of aged wine.

"I'm not sure what I'll find, but I'll look into Marcus's dossier in the morning," Bergden said to Alyssa as she stepped past him. "In the meantime, this conversation never happened, Alyssa. We don't need to rouse suspicion from the Regime for things we did not do."

Alyssa stopped her protests and forced a smile. "Of course, not dear. Good night."

Bergden walked back to his room. The grayed walls, the rasping hardwood and the portrait of Kroft above his bed were a depressing macramé—a reminder that the individual was gone and in its stead was cold authority. His room had become a prison when it once stood as a bastion of autonomy in a land where the mere idea was but a whisper in a darkened alley.

He felt a part of the machine more now than ever.

He stared up from his bed, trying in desperate vain to close his eyes forcing them to shut until sleep washed over him.

"The night sky hung high above him. The earth, cold beneath his feet as he walked from tent to tent. The near-silent groans were the only sounds to greet him as he pushed further into the camp. Tent by tent his foes fell at his feet. Their faces disappearing into the darkness leaving an emotionless husk, but to him it did not matter he chose not for whom he fought. He was a harbinger from the damned. No soul here was blackened but his, but not by his design. Doing as the earthly demigod has spoken was the path he took. He was a younger, brasher man beholden only to those who would lift him up in a mortal world.

He was a death dealer, a black angel, and scoundrel, but no one would know him. Tent to tent he made his way to the center. It was not a sense of pride that drove him to kill, nor was it his duty. Nothing could describe why he pushed forth until finally reaching the center. To greet him was a pyramid of heads from those he had butchered a testament, not a monument, to his revelry in the art of silent murder. Those who refused to accept it call it assassination, but he...he embraced it for the good of the Regime.

Soon he finds himself at the center and a table that has turned. He no longer wears the sign of the wolf, but the colors of another. He stands before a woman that is familiar but unknown to him. She wears the rose colors of a headmistress. She is to be his last target.

Approaching her like silk following in the breeze, he approaches her. A step before a step his blade slung low at his side. She was unaware until it was too late. The sharpened edge sliding across her throat. He could feel the warm blood spill into his hand, the liquid surprisingly thick.

He let her fall to the ground, the deed was done, and the mission complete. He rolled the body over to take a final look.

Bergden snapped awake in a cold sweat the nightmarish thoughts fading from his mind's eye. An iron grip across his chest with each breath more labored than the last. He ripped off his nightshirt and stood up pulling at his hair. His knees, weakened by the terror he felt, nearly gave out. When a man is part of many traumatic experiences it's not uncommon to reminisce with a degree of volatility but to see the face of the one you love, your wife hanging lifeless by your hand. It was an image he could not bear. He forced himself from his bed and opened the window breathing in the crisp night air.

His attention returned to his room as he heard the door into his room open. He turned, surprised to see Alyssa standing there in the only set of clothes that God gave her. "Southern Sea Distillery rum," she said bluntly as she slowly walked towards his bed.

One step at a time, her curves drawing him further and further away from his nightmare. Each little detail of her body echoed his desire and titillated his senses. Even if she wasn't trying, Bergden took the bait.

"Rum?" Bergden asked in a daze, her naked body seductively undulating closer to him, her curves hugging the night air, her feminine features slightly bouncing, inviting him with each step she took. He shook his head and refocused.

Did she say rum? he asked himself.

The Regime considered rum, as with most non-Regime originating spirits, contraband and thus very much illegal, but before he could process her words, Alyssa coyly slid into his bed, pulling the covers tightly to her bare chest. Her bosom heaved, inviting him to join her. A shiver of ecstasy rolled down his spine and into his toes. He could feel the hair stand at attention on his neck. She wagged her finger in a come-hither motion and, snapping himself out of his lust induced daydream, he crawled into the bed with her.

Without saying another word, the two lovers met lips in the starlit room. He could taste the freshly applied lipstick pressed against his own, her feather-soft lips enticing him further. The smell of rosehip rouse filling his nostrils, he caressed his hands through her silky, brunette hair pulling her closer to him. He could feel the heat from her naked bosom against his chest, her breathing increasingly became faster and faster in anticipation. He worked his way down the curve of her ever-beckoning neck and across her shapely breasts. She quivered in desire the further down he moved on her naked form until, without hesitation, she climbed to the edge of the bed and lay, welcoming him on all fours. He lunged towards her with primal instinct and pulled her to him. Her back arched as she moaned in passion and pleasure. In this precise moment, he was one with Alyssa in defiance of the Regime.

Alyssa and Bergden stared at the ceiling fan as it raced rhythmically round and round, the heat of their night's passions flowing out into the world. For the first time in years, Bergden lay without a care in the world, Alyssa clutched lovingly in his arms. The Regime forbade spending the night in the same room no matter the marital status. The only days permitted were anniversaries, birthdays, or Victory Day. The Regime used the two-room mandate as means of birth control, but for just this night he could not care about the Regime's authority. Men and women were supposed to love and lay with each other. That was the nature of things and the thrill of raw, sexual satisfaction right under Kroft's nose pleased him.

"That was amazing, my love. I wished it not to end!" Alyssa said as she pulled herself closer to him. "I don't know what had come over me, but my room felt lonely. I know it's the state mandate, but I needed your embrace more than ever."

Regime policy, based around the concept of isolation and dependency, stripped the intimacy from many families in the Regime. When the population boom occurred after the war ended, the Regime struggled. Feeding its newfound population became a full-time job for Chancellor Kroft. Within a few years, Chancellor Kroft ordered what became known as the Great Seclusion. "Building Character Through Personal Resolve" was the tagline of the policy when the public heard the announcement nine years ago, but the truth was far more sinister. Removing human emotion thus eliminating sexual desires among conventional society. Alyssa heard rumors that the upper class enjoyed more freedoms, but those were nothing more than salacious stories for housewives.

She knew they wanted her to feel empty, emotionless, but her dependency was not easily persuaded in the direction desirable of the Regime command. She yearned for more as she always had and thankfully for Bergden it was companionship this time. He felt the same pangs of lustful yearning more than she, but rarely acted out of fear. The Regime had nestled itself into his chilled psychological state long ago driving him into subservience to it rather than romantic endeavors. But no more. Alyssa reminded him of their love once again and he wouldn't take that for granted. He owed it to her, himself and their son, James. The boy needed passionate parents if he was going to succeed in a passionless world.

Alyssa turned and brushed her fingers against his naked back. "Bergden, I must confess something to you,"

Bergden turned and knelt beside the bed. "What is it? You know you can tell me anything Alyssa. You are my rock."

She sighed heavily.

A lump formed in Bergden's throat, waiting nervously for his wife's news to drop. He had forgotten about their conversation when he came home. The word "rum" crept back into his mind as the two sat in silence.

Finally, she broke the tension in the air around them.

"I had to lie to an inquisitor the other day. When I was taking James to school, I made a little detour to Whalers Wharf to buy a few provisions." She looked away in shame before continuing. "Things that the Regime markets rarely carry anymore—never carry."

Hiding it the best he could, Bergden could feel his lips purse in disappointment. He knew what she meant when it came to goods that the Regime "rarely carried anymore." The wharf was a hotbed of smugglers, rapists, and a rumored stronghold for the Remnants in Blackwell. Pemply Station recruited special squads to investigate all of the complaints. Unless you were a sailor, it was uncommon for any citizen to be spotted there and not face questioning.

"What did he ask? Why were you there?" Bergden hesitated before adding, "Was James with you?"

He studied Alyssa as she ran her hand through her silky hair, biding her time for a moment, trying to think of what to say. Years of being a black jack in Blackwell guided him when it came to the art of reading body language. Alyssa's subtle facial tells, and the gentle shutter of her shoulders told everything Bergden needed to know to deduce that something was amiss.

"I dropped James off first." She took a deep breath before continuing. "I met with Marcus at the wharf. Marcus sold me the rum in addition to some other supplies. Coffee, paprika, and a bottle of wine."

She held up the bottle showing Bergden it was empty.

"I've never been an over-indulgent person Bergden, but life...life has become difficult to bear at times. The constant sense of fear, the state-driven insanity. The rum takes the edge off in a way that the Regime's wine or beer cannot. Brings me back to my rebellious youth."

Alyssa got up from the bed and headed for the door. Her hands cupped over her eyes hiding her face in a desperate attempt to fight back the tears. He placed his hand on her back and gave the small of her back a firm but loving rub, trying to coax her to continue.

"I'm ashamed because I know that means little to you because you've seen the worst humanity has to offer." Alyssa began to cry. "You must think my troubles trite and pointless."

For him, each person who walked the world had their own problems. There are no levels of difficulty in the dilemmas one may experience in a lifetime. Each was separate and distinct from another and no two issues were precisely the same. Sure, her image of a rough life drastically differed from his, but that wasn't his place to judge.

Besides, she was his wife. Her problems meant the world to him.

"I wanted to instill that same feeling each day even with the Regime watching. I couldn't maintain my life without it. The freedoms that we had before the war and the freedoms were promised." Alyssa continued the revelation, stunning Bergden.

Wanting a happy home and a loving family was hardly a crime even under the Regime but masking the dreariness of the dystopia pit that surrounded them with alcohol would only work for so long. It had been the one escape from his reality he hadn't tried because he knew how it ended. A cold, lonely death surrounded by only the clang of empty bottles as they hit the floor.

"Many families around us, even in this very building, have items they shouldn't keep. I have my old ball glove in the back of my closet. Recreation is not considered working and thus contraband. I keep it hidden until the moment is right. When the day comes, I'll get to play catch with James."

Alyssa smiled.

"Yes, you do have a penchant for undermining the rules of the

Regime," Bergden admitted. "Ironic, I know. But more importantly, we are both naked in your bed beyond curfew hours, we made love on a day not sanctioned by the chancellor and we finished a bottle of wine on a work night. I'd say that is punishable by death, no?"

"But it wasn't just the rum, Bergden," she continued. "The inquisitor asked about Marcus in particular. He saw me and threatened me with a trip to Cherry Hill should I not be honest, but I was not honest. He asked about Marcus and Sia's affiliations. I told him I did not know, which is a lie."

Bergden had told her many times over to never veer from the truth when questioned, but now he was not so sure that was the best advice, and he was fortunate she had not listened.

"I know those people are part of the Remnant movement. I know they do everything to sabotage the Regime's efforts to control us and I applaud them for it. The shackles with which we live our lives are not a burden we should bear. Buying a few illicit goods is my way of helping out."

Bergden thought hard about Marcus. For their wives being close friends, he barely knew the man. Bergden had watched many visitors come and go from their apartment down the hall, but not once was it reported to Pemply Station. He thought little of it until this very moment. He only knew him as the husband of his wife's friend. Nothing more. He was in essence, a stranger.

"What part of that is a lie?" Bergden asked, pressing Alyssa for details. Bergden felt as though he was interrogating his wife, but needed all the information available if he was going to keep the family safe.

Alyssa closed her eyes, trying to contain her emotions before pressing on.

"Marcus and Sia run a club out of their apartment," Alyssa said as she pulled at a loose nail. "It is where he gets his alcohol from contact outside of Blackwell before I buy it at the wharf. People come and go from their apartment at all hours, but I do not know why. I know they are long past curfew and any assembly, peaceful or not, is illegal. You've seen it yourself, Bergden. You've arrested dozens for doing the same."

Alyssa spoke the truth and he knew it. There was no freedom of assembly under the Regime. None at all. Of all the laws put into place after the war, it was the one Kroft enforced the strictest. Considering the consequences of allowing the liberty to discuss the tyranny of the Regime, undermining his authority, it made sense even if it went against everything the world once stood for.

Alyssa sighed. Exhausted from the questioning. She struggled to maintain her composure "I don't know what goes on there, but I am certain he is in league with the Remnants. I just hope that he is alright—for Sia's sake."

If duty had bound Bergden in the way it did others, he'd be obligated to take not only Sia to the station but Alyssa too. Thankfully, he had long since pushed duty aside in the name of rationality.

Bergden embraced Alyssa. "I'm relieved Alyssa that you have not gone to their house for these gatherings. I am going to propose a trade and an apology if that is okay."

Alyssa nodded, pleased that her husband didn't take the news as a black jack, but as her husband. "Of course."

"Stay with me this night and the next night until our very last," he said smiling. "I cannot permit you to see Marcus at the wharf any longer and not because I think it is wrong, but for your own safety you mustn't go ever again. If you are arrested and taken to Cherry Hill, there won't be anything I can do, and I'll be damned if James is raised without his mother."

He paused, momentarily overcome with the gut-wrenching thought of Alyssa no longer in his life. Looking back at his life with James, one could argue James's fate was an orphanage.

"But worst of all," he continued, "I couldn't live without you. Can you promise to lay in my arms each and every night?"

Without anything else but a coy smile, she curled herself up next to him, her warmth still glowing from her sending a torrent of chills and goosebumps across his skin and down his arms lifting each and every hair into a frenzy of sensuality.

"This is all I've ever wanted in my life," Alyssa answered, holding his face in her hand. Bergden placed his hand over hers.

"I will review Marcus's dossier tomorrow and see what might be going on here," Bergden offered. "If I can secure his release, I will, but that I will not promise for fear of compromising our lives as well. James being forced into a reeducation center. The constant barrage of propaganda soldering his mind into a Regime puppet removing independent thought Not to mention a lifetime of suffering at the hands of Dr. Vossen for us if either of us gets sent to Singer. If true evil existed, it is found in Dr. Vossen. That woman is a monster."

Alyssa trembled at the thought. "I agree and be careful. I feel for Sia, but I would never be able to forgive myself if something terrible should happen to you or James. "

Again, they lay in silence. The hour was unknown to Bergden, but Bergden knew it was late and perhaps reaching into the early morning hours. The tall buildings surrounding their complex hid the sun from view longer than usual, so it was tough to say. Tomorrow would be a rough day indeed if only for the lack of sleep. He took a moment to reflect and abruptly he remembered why he awoke in the first place.

Looking over at Alyssa, he did not wish to wake her, but he felt that now was the best time to tell her of his nightmare, of the horrible thoughts that plagued him.

He shook her from slumber with a gasp. Her eyes fluttered until a smile cracked through the drowsy morning mental fog.

"What is it, Bergden? Is everything okay?" she asked, clearing her throat—his sigh matching the tone of her own from earlier.

"I have a confession I must make to you as well, Alyssa," Bergden said. "I had a horrible nightmare about you; about us."

"Your past is behind you Bergden," Alyssa said, rubbing her eyes. "What you did as a soldier during the war, those days are behind you. If you can bear it, I can bear it. I vow it."

The problem was he couldn't stomach the memories, the violent and terrible memories of the war. The images of the dead and the screams from dying, forcing him into a state of mental drudgery, he used to fight those powerful thoughts. The acute awareness of a living hell never let a man's mind be at peace.

"I had a dream or rather a nightmare that I cannot recall specifically as being something from my past. I was walking through a military camp with a butcher's blade in hand. The idol of the wolf on the handle slaughtering those who stood against the Regime. Many of the faces were a glimpse into my past. Others were new. Even in my nightmares I could not escape my actions... Like a machine I pressed through the camp taking life after life, drowning in their filth!"

Bergden had purposely kept details of the war away from Alyssa. In all the time they've known each other, he never uttered a single word about the things he saw—the things he did. Now, his memories spewed forth like an endless fountain of torment.

"The past is in the past," Alyssa reassured. "You are not the man the Regime tried to make you. You are a good man. Those were your enemies, and it was a time of war. I doubt any other soldier sleeps at night without facing those same demons over and over."

"Nightmares did have a tendency to exaggerate even the most innocuous details about one's life," Bergden reassured. "Still, I killed people, Alyssa and not always from a distance. War tends to get very personal without your consent. I can force the mental pictures from my mind."

Bergden sighed, "Their deaths weigh upon me as if a mountain sat atop my shoulders, but that is not the reason for this admission. There was a final target in my nightmare—a woman. I cut her down without question. Do you know who it was?"

Alyssa shook her head to the negative, but she could hazard a guess.

"It was you, but in my nightmare, I did not recognize you until I awoke, but I knew it was you all the same," Bergden wailed in anguish. "Dreams and nightmares often reflect some sort of spiritual truth, but I cannot wrap my head around why this time. I fear that my actions will be the death of you—of James."

Alyssa embraced him again; her bare chest pressed against his own. Bergden felt the hurried beat of her heart, their hearts beat in unison and calm coursed through his veins.

"There is nothing to forgive Bergden. It is just a dream. I am here. James is down the hall, and we are both alive and well. You are not going to be the death of me I promise. Now, come to bed. We have a long day tomorrow."

Bergden smiled and kissed her forehead.

"Of course. It was nothing more than a dream," he reasoned to himself. "I'm sorry to get you worried. I needed to say something. That's all."

But Bergden was worried. Was the nightmare symbolic of the days ahead?

What ramifications had they brought upon themselves by merely being acquaintances of Marcus and Sia? If Marcus was convicted by the Regime as a resistance collaborator, then Sia would be next, and then one by one all of their visitors would disappear. It would only be a matter of time until their entire network of associations would be bagged and locked away. He feared for Alyssa and James. He wanted to take them away from Blackwell and into the countryside, but was running implicating guilt for his family? As a black jack, when a suspect ran from an interrogation, then the Regime saw them as hiding the truth and pursued them to the ends of the earth.

He prayed that night for the first time in years.

CHAPTER FOUR

Alyssa awoke from a dream stretching her arms high into the autumn morning glancing back at her husband who still slept soundly by her side. With a smile, she slipped from the room and tiptoed nude into the hallway. It had been the first time in nearly three years they had slept in the same room let alone the same bed. The Regime had done its job of stifling sexual rights in Blackwell even among married couples. The War devastated the population and when the soldiers returned from the front a baby boom soon followed forcing the Regime to stifle procreation. Chancellor Kroft decided it was easier to manage citizenship when they weren't having babies all the time. Married couples weren't banned from procreating, but he did what he could to stifle the desire.

Years earlier, Alyssa left Oyster Bay after the War came to her doorstep, her family only a memory now, and her home a battered husk. Homeless and alone, she went to pursue the arts as an escape from her reality. The problem with art of course is that for most it is a profession mired in a land of feast or famine. She left her home in the hopes of finding a place not pockmarked by bombed-out buildings or farmland misshapen by sulfur-soaked craters.

"Bergden, I've made you some toast, an egg, and your usual coffee," Alyssa yelled back to the bedroom. A playful tone in her voice.

Bergden trotted out from the bedroom still naked from the night before and sat down and sipped on the steaming cup of coffee. "Last night was amazing, Alyssa. I didn't want it to end."

She grinned and pulled up a chair across from him, her expression a not so subtle reminder of their time together; a rare night filled with bliss in a listless world.

Bergden nodded and smiled his mouth full of toast and watered-down coffee. He was exceptionally pleasant this morning. Not surprisingly of course, considering the previous night's rendezvous. She had to admit that the torrid lovemaking had left her feeling particularly giddy on what would otherwise be another stressful morning.

"Mom, Dad, hurry, hurry, the radio is coming on! We get to hear the chancellor speak. I hope he tells of another mighty victory!" James hollered as he ran into the living room to listen to Kroft's morning announcement. Alyssa and Bergden traded a pair of sly glances before laughing. In his haste, James took little notice that his parents were both naked in the kitchen. Pressing her finger to her lips, the two sneaked back to their rooms to get ready for the day and save their son the mental scarring.

Alyssa returned to the living room to see James playing with the dial, trying to get the perfect clarity on the station. She had done an excellent job of ignoring the messages spewed by the propaganda machine for the past few years. She could sit in the den and stare at the radio fully intent on listening, but she heard nothing. The speeches did little else aside from providing inquisitors with any excuse to round up the Regime's undesirables.

The radio static blared momentarily until the anthem rolled. James stood at attention and waved his parents to join in. Alyssa had enjoyed the youthful vigor and inspiration she saw in James. As time moved along, she knew that robust, child-like aspiration would be replaced with dutiful ambition and narrow-minded sense of nationalistic pride. It was the poison that the Regime had laid out before the children in Blackwell. An assurance of sorts that the future of the Regime could persist in the hands of a new crop of brainwashed masses. "Please stand by for the daily Regime announcements," the announcer commanded. "Today's speaker is the altruistic Chancellor Kroft himself."

Alyssa glanced over at Bergden. Bergden nearly launched his coffee across the room in surprise. Kroft hadn't spoken in a morning message for at least a year. She decided that maybe this morning, it would be a good idea to listen as the inquisitors would be out in force today, looking for any excuse to question the masses. There was a good chance the reeducation centers would be filled to the brim come tomorrow more.

Prerecorded applause marked the opening of the announcements as Kroft's voice could be heard in the background, unaware that the mic captured every word. The beleaguered Kroft began muttering about how it was too early in the morning and how it hadn't seen what dawn looked like in years. Alyssa tried not to laugh but a giggle slipped through her lips. Bergden too could not contain himself as he began to laugh. James continued to sit legs crossed, patiently awaiting Kroft's words of wisdom undaunted by the chancellor's complaints.

"Good morning, at 6:45pm yesterday, we apprehended several known resistance collaborators that were organizing a plot to undermine the

utopia we have created for their own selfish ambitions. I say to you, the people, to rise up and squash these roaches before it's too late! You might think it is harmless to buy from a black market or take pleasures of the flesh with individuals other than your spouse, but rest assured these actions will collapse everything that you and I have taken so long to build! I applaud the efforts of our Enforcement Officers and the Political Inquisition, but they cannot do it alone. At every turn, Remnant partisans await to defile our right to exist! I call upon you, the people, to come forth and wrest these infidels out from the shadows! Make them known to all!"

The message was as prophetic as it was fiery. Chills raced up Alyssa's spine as the brief statement was in line with the recent events surrounding Sia and Marcus. The thoughts of what she knew about her friends raced into her mind. The pleasantries begotten from such a passionate night disappeared in an instant. For what she did not tell Bergden was that Marcus and Sia were not married but living against the Regime's law. Marcus was in fact a homosexual and Sia lived with him and played the role of his wife as a cover. In reality, Sia went about her day as a married woman, but at night she helped Marcus fund a black market that funneled resources to a group known to Alyssa only as the Remnants.

Bergden's description of her at the station was not at all surprising. Sia and Marcus certainly loved each other, just not in the way the world thought they knew.

"That was an arousing speech wasn't it, Dad?" James asked, interrupting her thoughts. The young boy was incensed by Kroft's ability to rouse his base. James hardly understood the world and knew nothing about how it truly worked before Kroft's rise.

"The word is rousing, son, and yes, Kroft always gives us a look into his thinking when he decides to talk," Bergden replied, trying to answer the question without actually answering the question. Alyssa could see her husband shifting uncomfortably. Not because his son suggested he was excited by Kroft's words. The meaning of the words caused Bergden's demeanor to change.

"Your father's right James. Kroft is quite..." She paused, searching for the right word. "Insightful to our plight, but you need to focus on your lessons," Alyssa ordered, hoping to divert his attention away from the chancellor.

James lowered his head.

"You're improving, but your teachers say you still are having issues reciting the names of the Regime leadership," Alyssa consoled. "I'm tired of hearing about your shortcomings because you aren't taking the time to study. You're too bright to be making these mistakes." She hated not being straightforward with James about the dangers of developing an unhealthy infatuation for a man like Kroft. She despised the fact that such a trite and meaningless lesson was perhaps the one that dictated his educational development the most. The ego-driven curriculum of the Regime defined children's education in Blackwell. The idea that a group of people ranked above math and language was insane. She could picture the figurines of Commander Liam Grimm, Headmistress Gretchen Longmire and Kroft perched above her son's bed. His toys were politicians and dictators. Whatever happened to a train set or truck? Even a tin soldier would be more agreeable to her.

The kitchen clock rang out the hour and Alyssa realized the time.

"James, you and I need to make haste if we are going to get there before the morning bell. You can't be late on my account!" Alyssa shouted as she gathered her things and headed to the door.

Alyssa ran over and kissed Bergden and brought him in close for a passionate embrace, before racing to the door.

"See you after work. I love you," she exclaimed as she ran into the hallway, dragging James close behind the young boy struggling to pull on his coat.

James and Alyssa took the elevator, and when it arrived on the lobby floor the two rushed out into the busy city streets. Their high-rise towered over the most active street market in Blackwell. It was a convenient place to pick up the essentials and her morning coffee. The coffee beans came from the same state grown trees, but something about the corner cafe's coffee enticed her to grab a cup every morning. The shopkeeper was an older gentleman who helped his granddaughter throughout the day. It was a way for him to stay busy in his advanced age and still prove useful to the Regime even in such a small way.

"I'll take a medium roast coffee," Alyssa asked pleasantly while trying to catch her breath. "If you have any cream and sugar that would be wonderful. Tough to get these days so I'll understand if you can't spare any."

The older merchant grinned and reached down into the bag of coffee grounds. "I do, and it is Regime-approved if you can believe that. After that statement from Kroft this morning I want my customers to know I'm only using approved foodstuffs. I'm too old to spend even a night in that dreadful Cherry Hill."

Alyssa smiled as the old man began to pour her coffee into a small paper cup. "Do people often question the origin of your coffee?" she asked, saddened by the idea that people would challenge such an elderly man and his granddaughter on the integrity of a mere cup of coffee.

He again smiled. The lines on his face told stories of his life and how it came to pass that he would spend his golden years helping the family.

"It's not the people, my dear, but can I say something? You look so much like my granddaughter. You see, her parents were killed in the war and a few years back she lost her grandmother. It's just been the two of us and it is kind people like yourself that keep this place going and food on the table. Can I get your name young lady?"

It warmed her heart to see that there were still friendly folks hidden in among the people.

Flattered by his kind words, Alyssa smiled and answered. "It's Alyssa. Alyssa Crane and it is always a pleasure to come into your cafe."

He handed her the coffee. "Come again won't you Mrs. Crane? You too, mister?"

"James, sir," the boy said.

"Mr. James, please come back, won't you?"

Alyssa smiled and nodded as she headed back out into the thoroughfare. The streets seemed fuller than usual today and were abuzz with Kroft's speech. Alyssa knew it was more than a simple message of pandering to the public for help. If he wanted to do that, he would've had one of his underlings do the dirty work. She did hear him mutter about having to wake up so there was something significant about today's message. She saw people conversing over Kroft as they once did. His charisma on display in a short yet message laden attempt to satiate his paranoiac lusts and rile up the masses.

"Mommy, look at that man over there," James said tugging on her dress. "Is that an inquisitor?" Alyssa looked up and saw the familiar uniform of an inquisitor, the design a deviation from that of a black jack.

The slate, blue jacket adorned with medals of various designs and the almost cartoon-like pauldrons perched atop that bounced with each step he took. Alyssa, hoping to avoid a confrontation, looked for a place of refuge, but the crowded streets prevented her from ducking into the store and the inquisitor was headed straight for her. It was as if he was on a mission to find her and her alone. After a few moments he finally made his way through the crowd to Alyssa. She turned and tried to walk away, but the crowd swept her back towards him.

She felt a finger tap her on the shoulder, and she cringed. "Ma'am if I could get a moment of your time?" the man asked, holding up his identification badge unnecessarily. Alyssa closed her eyes as she faced away and swore under her breath before turning towards him. The crowd around, suddenly realizing what was happening began to part around the two.

Her first reaction was to say that he could not and that her son would be late for school, but Bergden taught her that avoidance was paramount to lying to the Inquisitors. It would be a better tactic to simply lie to their face and believe in that lie than to run from an Inquisitor.

"Of course, sir. How can I assist the Regime today?" Alyssa asked. She did her best to not sound nervous. The inquisitors were quick to condemn a person just for being skittish.

The man smiled and bent down to look at James. James was aglow with the thought of meeting his first inquisitor. Considering who his heroes were made to be, it wasn't the least bit surprising to Alyssa.

He studied James with a grin. "Your son seems quite enthusiastic. Mind if I ask him a question about the Regime?"

Alyssa hesitated before giving a slight nod in agreement. She desperately hoped James was as attentive as he appeared to be during the announcements.

"What is our dear chancellor's birth city, young man?" the inquisitor questioned, peering into the boy's eyes while still keeping a steady grin.

Stumbling through his excitement, regaining his composure, James blurted out the correct answer much to her relief. "Blackwell!" James said, looking to the man for approval and then to his mother.

"Good answer, my young gentleman, and how about you madam? Can I ask you a few questions?" the man asked, satisfied that the lad was able to answer.

Alyssa fought the urge to turn and walk away once more. To get out of this situation could not come soon enough.

"Of course. I'd be happy to oblige," Alyssa answered. Her hands began to sweat profusely, changing her once delicate milk like palms into a sticky and pasty mess.

"First, tell me your name. Second, did you familiarize yourself with the chancellor's statement today?"

"My name is Alyssa Crane, and of course I listened to this morning's broadcast. I wouldn't miss any of Chancellor Kroft's inspiring proclamations," Alyssa lied.

"Excellent, Mrs. Crane." The inquisitor eyed Alyssa. "I'm sure Chancellor Kroft himself would love to know a woman of your beauty enjoys his broadcasts. Now, have you reported any suspicious activity recently?" he asked as he held his pen to the paper, waiting patiently to scribble down his notes that no doubt would be archived somewhere in the Regime's extensive bureaucracy.

Alyssa thought carefully about her answer. The simple answer was no, but in the Regime, there were no simple answers despite how much they wanted things to be simplified for the sake of control. No could have meant, never or not recently, or it could be a lie.

Thankfully, it wasn't up to her to decide what was a lie and what was not. The inquisitors were tasked with rooting out the differences with such things.

"No, I can't say that I've noticed anything suspicious recently," she lied again. "I am a schoolmistress. The children are my focus and my life's work. The Regime deserves children to be taught by those focused on the art of education."

He looked up from his paper and smirked.

"That's all Mrs. Crane. Have a nice day," he said, tipping his hat. She had no idea if she answered his questions to satisfaction and for the moment she could not care. She was now late as was James. Perhaps worst of all her coffee had gone cold.

Late, the pair hurried through the crowded streets towards the academy. As they approached, Alyssa noticed that a crowd had gathered in front. A line of people stood outside the gates waited patiently to enter. She was unsure what the holdup was, but it prevented her from being late for work if there was a silver lining to the situation. At the front of the lineup was Schoolmaster of the Pemply Station School Darcy Plante and the Headmistress of the all Regime's schools herself, Gretchen Longmire. Alyssa's mood went from an optimistic outlook on an unpleasant situation to dreadful consternation. Longmire rarely made an appearance at the academy unless it was something seriously wrong.

"Welcome students, educators, and parents. I apologize for the delay that this interruption is causing but I promise this will be brief. Your children's education is at the forefront of Regime priorities I assure you and what I am about to demonstrate will be a learning experience for us all," Longmire announced.

Longmire was a woman in her fifties. She carried the features of a woman who was a beauty in her formative years, yet she retained a level of elegance in her looks. Her hair was silver and her skin pale, but she was authoritative in her every move, her hawk-like gaze startling. Alyssa imagined Longmire still curried the favor of younger men looking for a place in society or who wanted to rise through the ranks, but her domineering attitude scared off the hardiest of upper society bachelors. Words like brutal and mean were an understatement.

"Schoolmaster Plante, would you mind coming to the stage? You should be present," Longmire commanded, gesturing the schoolmaster to the forefront. Plante had been in charge of the academy from the beginning of the Regime's rule over Blackwell.

She had molded many young minds throughout the years, including James.

Schoolmaster Plante was decidedly different from Longmire. She was shorter than Longmire, and her hair a hue of copper. Plante had a reputation as being a Regime diehard, but only to keep Longmire off her back. Alyssa and Plante met for lunch, talked about the students and how to improve the school. She was an excellent schoolmaster. Alyssa worried what Longmire planned for schoolmaster Plante.

Standing next to Plante, Longmire raised her hand and beckoned for a squad of black jacks to come forth, and from the back of the crowd emerged four heavily armed black jacks. Alyssa scanned their faces and saw that none were Bergden much to her relief.

"Schoolmaster Plante, I will make this brief so the children can get to class," Longmire said. Clearing her throat, she pulled out a piece of paper and held it aloft for the crowd to see. She wore a menacing grin. "You are charged with conspiracy to commit crimes against the Regime by virtue of association with convicted resistance members—criminals and vagrants, in particular—and a nefarious association with the terrorist organization known as the Remnants."

In a split second, the Schoolmaster Plante's face went from confusion to anguish.

Vehemently shaking her head denying the accusations. She scanned the crowd. Most were children, but the parents stood in silence as Plante pleaded her case.

"That is preposterous, Headmistress! I am nothing, but a loyal servant to the Regime and always have been. I love Blackwell. I love Chancellor Kroft! Why on earth would I ever, ever do such a thing as to backstab the land I love?!"

Longmire stood by stoically showing no emotion waiting for

Plante to calm down. Plante continued to plead her case.

"I am an innocent woman! You cannot treat me this way! I demand to speak to Commander Grimm at once!" she implored to Longmire before making a break to the back of the stage. "He will show I am innocent of these preposterous charges"

Plante raced to the end of the makeshift stage.

Longmire grimaced, annoyed that Plante was not taking the accusations in a dignified manner. She gestured for the black jacks to drag her back to the center of the stage.

"You will no longer be permitted to do a disservice to the children of the Regime through your distasteful propaganda! Your lies will no longer poison their fragile minds," Longmire cajoled as she ordered the black jacks to arrest her.

If the goal was to make an example or a spectacle of Plante, it was working. Alyssa stood horrified as a pair of black jacks pushed her to her knees as she threw a bag over her head. A third black jack came over and swung the baton down landing with a crack on her head sending her to the floor of the stage. The woman moaned in agony from beneath the burlap sack as she blindly wormed her way across the stage. Children screamed at the sight of blood as it started to seep from the bag and onto the ground below. One of the black jacks walked over to the struggling Plante and again struck her, this time across the spine with an audible crunch. Plante fell silent. The sounds of broken bones hushed the frantic crowd. The black jacks dragged the lifeless Plante away from the crowd, a trail of blood in their wake.

Alyssa looked at James in dismay. His mind had been subjected to the entire brutal spectacle.

I should yell out to them. Defend Darcy. She was a model citizen, not a traitor, Alyssa thought. Her sense of morality shaken to her very soul by the actions of her husband's colleagues. Throughout the years, she convinced herself that Bergden surely wasn't capable of such barbaric acts. Never did he once return home covered in the blood of others or the look of shame from his actions on his brow.

Or maybe she was just fooling herself. She lamented before regaining her composure as best she could.

The stage was cleaned up and the gates opened to the school. A somber march of silence and sniffling school children pushed through the gates flanked by the bloodied batons of the black jacks. None showed even the slightest expression of remorse on their face. Alyssa looked at Longmire as she passed, she prayed for an inkling of sorrow in his expression, but only saw the icy gaze of a woman indoctrinated by the sense of duty and self-righteousness. She refrained from showing her disgust for fear of meeting a similar fate as Darcy Plante in front of her son. Longmire had never shown fondness toward Alyssa. Alyssa felt like an outsider from Oyster Bay. Nothing more than a heathen. Had it not been for Bergden she would probably be up on that stage.

The somber mood carried long into the school day. Alyssa had a free period of the day to grade and prepare for the next day, but today she could not bring herself to do it. The endless charade that the Regime called education finally brought her to a breaking point with the events of the morning. Leaders, battles, places and disparaging falsehoods dictated how these children would behave. James was a model student, but unfortunately not as versed in practical knowledge. The kid could name off every Regime jackass that ever walked the wretched earth, but the inventor of the light bulb, civil rights or even mathematics? No, those were not a priority for Kroft. Zombies to fill the ranks, populate and propagate the ideology. Thought soldiers without the capacity to think for themselves beyond the orders they were given.

"I can't believe what they did to Plante," a fellow school mistress named Andrea said as she poured herself a cup of coffee in the lounge. The blackened sludge immediately turned Alyssa off to the idea of another cup. "Poor old woman didn't even know what happened."

"That makes two of us," Alyssa replied.

Andrea was a quiet woman. She has been a schoolmistress since the Regime took power. The students loved her. She tried her best to make learning fun under the wilting oppression. Not an easy task, and Alyssa admired her for it.

Typically, in the workplace she kept a very docile and introverted demeanor. The Regime frowned upon open mindedness in the first place. If a woman expressed her emotions, especially unprompted, to say it was frowned upon was an understatement. Another control mechanism that over time became a passive sense of authority unjustly and unwittingly accepted by society. Rarely did she find herself out of sorts or fervently charged about a particular idea. That sense of complacency is likely what kept the machine going in her eyes and made her a part of it.

Luckily for Alyssa, class started again without a mention of the happenings out in the yard. The accompanying sense of relief underlined the fact that the children likely were indoctrinated to the point that those types of actions were viewed with abject normalcy even after an initial display of rational fear. The daily quizzes she passed to their desks asked the same three questions: Who is the chancellor? Who won the War? And lastly, is your family loyal to Kroft? It was a not so subliminal way of asking if your family were members of an organization that sought to undermine the Regime or bring anarchy to the streets. For a second, her heart dropped. She wondered what James told his teachers each day. The young boy was enamored with his father's work so that gave her a measured level of assurance.

Bergden at least gave the family the appearance of being on the party line.

One by one the children handed in their quizzes until a little girl approached her. "Mrs. Crane, can you take a look at my quiz?" a young girl asked. Her name was Beth, and she just so happened to be Alyssa's favorite student in this cohort. She carried a kindness for a child that was alarmingly absent in the youth under the Regime. She wished that James could show that same level of innocence sometimes. She still worried tremendously about her. She rarely spoke of her family.

"Sure, my dear, let me take a look," Alyssa said knowing that it was a formality. The answers lay out before her: Kroft, the Regime and —

My God, Alyssa thought as she read the final answer.

"The uniformed men came and took Daddy last night and Mommy after her coffee this morning. That is the answer to the third question, right?" the girl asked. "I had to walk to school all by myself today. I hope they come back soon."

Alyssa nearly collapsed into her desk chair slack-jawed.

"I want you to come home with James and me. Beth, is that understood?" Alyssa asked.

Beth shrugged her shoulders unconvinced or perhaps unknowing of the situation. "OK. I'll just have to tell mommy when we get there I guess," she replied.

Alyssa nodded and ushered Beth from the room. She watched as the girl made her way to her next class, oblivious of the danger her parent faced.

The school day dragged on forever until the final bell rang. She sat stoically at her desk and looked out the window. The autumn sun was beginning to make its descent and she had no desire to move. That frenzied fear she had felt the night before crept back into her mind.

The fear for Beth only worsened the problem. Alyssa closed her eyes and breathed deep. A tear leaked out her eye and down her cheek before sliding onto her blouse. She wanted to let them flow but crying in her place of work would draw suspicion.

Mustering up what courage she had left she walked out into the hall to look for Beth. The children had all but left. James would be at the playground waiting for her to walk with him home. She always caught a glimpse from the second floor as he sat on the jungle gym, but as she looked out into the glaring sun panic set in. James was not at his usual spot.

Momentarily forgetting about Beth, she raced down the hall before nearly colliding with Headmistress Longmire.

"Slow down Mrs. Crane. This isn't a gymnasium. You can work out in your own spare time," Longmire joked.

"I'm so sorry Headmistress," Alyssa apologized. "I did not mean to rush."

"Where are you off to in such a hurry?" Longmire asked. A woman in her late fifties, Longmire's hair was white as snow and her eyes nearly all black. A small scar ran the length of her chin. A physical reminder of the part she played in the War of Wars. She was the perfect person if one looked for such a terrifying look to enforce authority. Longmire intimidated any who crossed her path. Alyssa wasn't even sure if she had ever smiled before in her life. None of the portraits even hinted at a single grin or inkling of anything that could remotely embody joy. A woman of her age should have smile lines, but the sides of her eyes were smooth to the touch.

"My son...." Alyssa stammered. "I'm supposed to pick him up from the playground."

From behind, Alyssa could hear the clacking of boots as they hit the hardwood step after step, and as the sound came closer and closer. Something told her to flee but could not. She remained frozen, unable to move out of fear. Running would do nothing but put her life and possibly James in jeopardy.

Alyssa managed to take a step backwards.

"It would be best if you remained in your place, Mrs. Crane," the Headmistress offered. "Resisting will only make the matter worse, and besides; it is your duty to comply with my orders."

Longmire signaled for the two black jacks to restrain Alyssa. She fought the urge to resist knowing that it never ended well. Bergden had told her on more than one occasion that resisting arrest resulted in a savage beating and was accepted as a level of culpability in a crime.

"What am I being placed under arrest for? I at least desire to know that. Where's James Where's my husband? Where's Bergden he will tell you that whatever the charges they are false!" Alyssa found herself twisting away from the black jacks. She managed to get within inches of the Headmistress.

Longmire stared back at her with an icy, penetrating gaze. "He too is finding his day could have gone better my dear. As we speak, he should be facing the same situation. Now, we could simply take you down to the station, you answer my questions and that will be the end of it. What do you say to that? Be honest and you might get to go home tonight."

Alyssa fought back tears. This couldn't be happening to her. *What was going to happen to James? Poor Beth?* she thought.

"Where is James?" Alyssa repeated as she struggled with her restraints, the metal cuffs digging into her delicate wrists. "What will become of him?" Alyssa asked, begging for an answer and continuing to fight back tears. The realization of her situation sank in at the thought of James. Would she ever get to see him again? What was going to happen to Bergden? What was going to happen to her?

"James is under the care of the Regime for now. Your future interactions with him will depend on your cooperation in the present." Longmire held out her arm to lead the group out of the school.

As the exited Longmire pulled Alyssa close.

"James will be better off being under the care of a true patriot. As for the little girl, her parents are finally getting what they deserve. One day she may even thank me," Longmire laughed before pushing Alyssa further ahead.

Once out of the school Alyssa's predicament did not improve. A crowd had gathered to watch. It would hardly be the spectacle they saw this morning, but nonetheless another teacher was being taken out in chains. Alyssa scanned the crowd, the young faces of her students sitting somberly as she was paraded past, the other instructors forced to watch as the venerable Mrs. Crane, a do-gooder and friendly person, was shackled and marched to a waiting Regime cruiser. As the group approached the car someone yelled out from the crowd as her head was pushed inside.

"Onwards, you Remnants!" a man cried out at the top of his lungs.

The black jacks immediately ran after the man giving chase into the emptied playground. The children began to laugh as a game of cat and mouse ensued. The man bobbed back and forth around the jungle gym. The black jacks raced from one end to the other, trying to apprehend him as he continued to crow "Coalition Forever!" The chase continued for a few more minutes until a shot rang out. The stunned crowd shocked into an eerie silence.

The black jack forced Alyssa's head downwards as she entered the back of the cruiser. She watched as she was secured into her seat as the remaining black jacks searched the man's body and pulled out his wallet. The money was pocketed without question. It was nothing more than the thievery of a dead man. The body was covered up and left next to the swing set. Alyssa sobbed as the children were forced to walk past the body as they exited the yard. She couldn't tell if it was an act of intimidation or just careless neglect of a child's fragile mind. This was what the Regime was propagating to its children? That fear was a tool designed to make the strong kneel and the cowardly blend in. For the souls that used it, only damnation awaited.

Suddenly, the passenger door swung open. A sharply dressed man sporting a minimalist, sharp fitting dark blue uniform emerged.

It was Commander Liam Grimm himself.

"Unfortunate turn of events out on the playground. I can't say I anticipated a revolutionary hiding amongst the children and their parents," he groaned before sitting next to Alyssa.

Alyssa looked at the commander. He was a man in his mid-forties. His skin was light, and his face gaunt with sharp almost hawkish features. His figure was hardly imposing until you stood before him. He was a tall, raven, haired authoritative man. His black boots taller than her legs and his hands twice the size of hers. It was easy to see why he could be intimidating.

"Where are you taking me?" Alyssa questioned, hesitating to ask for fear of his reaction, but much to her surprise, he acknowledged her.

He signaled for the driver to leave the school.

"Singer Psychiatric War. A doctor's visit if you will, but please do not fret. You'll understand what I mean when we get there."

Alyssa silently prayed to herself as the car sped down the busy street. She thought about Bergden and hoped that he hadn't been arrested, but she did not have much hope. James was gone, and in the hands of the very people she had begun to hate so long ago but waited in spiteful silence for years since her parents' house was destroyed during the war. For now, she needed to survive and get back to James. He would be lost without her.

All she could do was try and face down the good Dr. Vossen.

CHAPTER FIVE

Bergden walked the hall toward the kitchen. The morning sun peeked through the curtains, casting a shadow with each step he took. He closed his eyes, remembering the night and hoping to see Alyssa sitting at the table, the steam from her brewed coffee rising high into the air as it did every morning, and the smell of fresh cooked bacon titillating his senses. She had crept out of bed without waking him. He could picture her beautiful, womanly form tipping on the hardwood, trying not to wake him.

After the night they had, he had no intention of going back to his own room after the night they shared.

Alyssa served him breakfast, poured a cup of coffee, and the family sat down to listen to the morning announcements from the chancellor's office. A typical morning, save for the fact that the two were still naked from the night before. They exchanged silent, deviant smiles as he placed a kiss on her lips. For the first time in his career as a black jack, he seriously contemplated skipping work and damn the consequence.

The morning continued as usual, and with the sound of Kroft's voice on the announcements, he decided today wouldn't be the best day to be cavalier about his work. Citizens in Blackwell got three sick days that needed to be attested to by a physician and, of course, the state sanctioned holidays, Kroft's birthday and Victory Day. He had played hooky before, but that was before he had a family to worry about and more friends at the station.

Shortly after the speech ended, Bergden bid adieu to his wife and son. He kissed Alyssa goodbye and waved to James as the two made their way to the school. The past few days had been stressful, and receiving validation of his wife's love was always a breath of fresh air in his stale world. He never questioned her commitment to their marriage but living with the brutality of the Regime even the hardiest souls caved.

He had a few minutes before he needed to leave, so he decided to brew a fresh pot and relax on the couch, taking in the sounds of the morning in the city something he hadn't been able to do for quite some time. He sat down, opening yesterday's newspaper. The hot coffee warmed his chest, but rather than perking him up, he began to feel too relaxed and within moments fell back asleep with his cup of coffee still in hand.

He awoke to the sounds of sirens, spilling the now cold coffee onto his lap. Muttering obscenities in his half-awake state, he stumbled back into his room to get a new pair of uniform pants. As he rubbed his eyes, he searched for the time, realizing that he was terribly late for his shift. He'd have to drive today if he wanted to get to the station at a reasonable time to avoid arousing suspicion with the chief.

He was already late, but not just a little late, he was really late.

He had never been tardy a day in his life for anything. He would just as soon miss an appointment completely than be late. Personal pride in punctuality had prevented such an occurrence from ever happening before, but there was something about the night before that helped him to forget the stresses that drove such mannerisms. The night he spent with Alyssa was both a night of ecstasy and reflection. He hadn't had such a night in years, and clearly, it had a severe effect on his psyche that carried over into the morning routine.

Reflection on the pleasantries of the night could wait till later. Now he needed to get to the station and fast. Racing through the apartment, he grabbed his keys, his coat, and hat in record time and headed to the door. He heard the sirens once more, but this time they appeared to be closer to the echoes, almost as if they were right outside his doorstep. He backed away from the doorknob and peered out the window being careful not to be seen.

Something was amiss. Years of military training had never failed Bergden before. The black jacks surrounded the front of the complex, forcing people back into their homes and arrested anyone who resisted. Across the street, a group of black jacks stood outside of their cruisers, and the Regime special tactics teams began cordoning off the area. The complex was under his station's jurisdiction so maybe luck was on his side. He could casually join the operation with no one being the wiser, but as he turned the knob a knock rapped on the door.

"Bergden? Bergden, are you in here?" a man's voice called out from the other side. The tone in the man's voice was...panicked. "You there, Bergden? We need to move!"

"Carl?" Bergden asked.

"Yes! You gotta let me in, Bergden."

"What is going on out there? Looks like every black jack from Pemply is out there. Something going down in my complex?"

He could hear Carl groan in frustration, followed by louder and more urgent knocking.

The sounds of furious fists slamming on the door, demanding an answer.

Had it been anyone else from the station, his nerves may have very well jumped from his stomach and out onto the finished hardwood. Carl's presence signaled that the situation was not all that serious. Carl was his friend, after all.

"Carl, I know I am late," Bergden admitted as he tucked his sidearm into the holster on his belt. Alyssa and I had an emotional night and I fear I let it get the best of me. If you want to go wait in the cruiser, I'll be there in a moment. God forbid I should forget anything in addition to being late."

The sounds of sirens wailing through a nearby open window. The droning had become quite irksome to him, and he rushed to close it hoping to snuff out the sounds.

"What of those damnable sirens, Carl? The station making a mass arrest somewhere in the complex?" Bergden called out into the entry way from the den. "I think I would've heard about a raid."

"Bergden, you need to let me in right now!" Carl pounded on the door repeating the request again and again. "Open this goddamn door!"

Shaking his head, Bergden inched the door open just barely enough to see Carl's face. He looked like he ran the entire flight of stairs. A bead of sweat crept down his cheek from his forehead. He was breathing heavily and shaking profusely as if he had caught the flu.

Alarmed, Bergden swung the door open, and Carl rushed past him before slamming the door behind him. Without a word Carl pulled the blinds closed and checked the back rooms. To Bergden he appeared more anxious than usual and almost...frightened.

"Are you alone?" Carl demanded, grabbing Bergden by his

Regime jacket collar.

"Excuse me?" Bergden said as he pushed Carl away.

"Are you alone?" Carl pressed as he looked wildly about the apartment. "Of course, I'm alone. Who the hell else would be here at this hour?"

Carl exhaled and collapsed on the couch, but only for a moment before once again succumbing to urgency and rising to his feet.

"We need to get you out of here, Bergden. Where are Alyssa and James?"

"They left over an hour ago to head to the school. What's going on? Are they in danger?!"

"Just come with me, and I'll explain in the car. If we don't move now, we'll both be dead," Carl said as he pushed Bergden towards the door.

He hesitated for a moment, but Bergden followed Carl. The two men hustled down the apartment stairwell, opting to avoid the elevator. The thought of his wife and son slowly found its way into his mind as he kept pace with Carl. Part of Bergden wanted to turn around and go look for Alyssa and James, but the nagging sense of trouble pushed him away.

He followed Carl as they wound their way through the elaborate hallways darting in and out of areas of the building that even Bergden was unfamiliar with. Without warning, Carl stopped sharply and held a finger to his lips motioning for silence. He stooped down and peered out from behind the corner at the steps. Bergden followed suit and listened as the pounding of military boots hit the pavement.

He listened carefully and tried to count the footsteps as they pushed upwards toward them.

"One...two...one...two," he whispered under his breath, counting the steps and trying to gather how many black jacks were coming for him.

As the last boots fell, he realized that the whole station must be at the complex.

Something big was happening, and fear crept in. Fear not for his own person, but fear of the fates of his wife and son. If the Regime had come for him, then inevitably his family also faced the same trouble. His mind continued to race, but he couldn't pinpoint what exactly he might have done to get unwanted attention from the Regime.

Carl gestured for Bergden to follow him frantically, waving his hand as he ducked down to peer over the stairwell. The black jacks had pushed past the floor and were probably breaking down his apartment door as they spoke.

Carl wiped his brow and breathed deeply, taking a position out of sight from the central stairwell. "I parked the car out back. We need to get moving before they realize you're gone and expand to a city-wide search. They'll tear this whole brownstone complex apart."

Bergden wanted to turn himself in for his family's sake. For a moment, he thought the Regime would have mercy on him for his years of service. He shook the thought from his mind as Carl still had not told him what the black jacks wanted or where he was going.

Staying out of custody would be critical. He himself had been in the room when former Regime members were beaten and tortured based on nothing more than rumors. Treason and espionage suspects received the worst treatment, but once he watched an old commanding officer cave a man's skull for skipping out on the commander's Christmas party. Thinking about the consequences he could face pushed him back to the present situation.

"We need to find a way out onto the fire escape," Carl said, looking for Bergden's assistance.

"The building's single fire escape runs along the back of the building. Each can be accessed from the back bedroom of the apartment. That is, of course, if the layouts are the same in each. Regime design is typically uniform, as it was easier to build during the war by minimizing resource costs. Any vacant room should do, and we can just go out the back," Bergden replied.

Bergden and Carl looked for a room for a vacant sign. It didn't take long before they stumbled on an unlocked door. The door was unlocked for repairs, and thankfully no one usually was making repairs this early in the morning. Bergden looked out the window at the street below. A marked Regime car sat parked only a few yards away from the bottom of the fire escape and no sign of the black jacks yet. Carl held the window open as Bergden climbed out and onto the iron causeway. The metal clanged as the pair descended down to the streets below.

"The station chief thinks I'm guarding the fire escape in case you decided to bail. I'll explain it away later, but we've got to get you out of the city as fast as we can, Bergden."

The two men leapt into the car with Bergden taking a position in the backseat. There was a large canvas tarp on the floor. Large enough to cover a vehicle, let alone a single man.

"Just keep your head down and get under the canvas. I'll let you know when it is safe to get out," Carl demanded as he sped off down the alleyway behind Bergden's apartment complex.

Bergden could feel his stomach drop as Carl drove wildly through the streets with his heart racing with a mix of both fear and adrenaline. It wasn't the first time he'd been smuggled away. He recalled a close encounter with Coalition forces once during his days in special operations being tucked away in the back of a supply transport. The back of Carl's car, while vertigo inducing, was nothing compared to the slop he had to lay in to escape that mess.

Bergden heard Carl swear under his breath as the cruiser slowed. The sounds of muffled commands came from outside of the car.

"Fuck, fuck, and holy fuck. There's a checkpoint up ahead. Not black jacks either Bergden. They have the mark of soldiers. Keep your breathing as slow as possible."

Trying to stay as flat as possible, Bergden lay on the cruiser floor. He took a deep breath and concentrated on managing his breathing, keeping his chest shallow, and as inconspicuous as possible.

"Care to tell me where you're going flap jack?" a man unknown to Bergden mocked Carl. The military frowned upon the black jacks viewing the position more a neophyte enforcement agency than hardened gestapo. More a rabble of kids with guns than trained paramilitary in the eyes of soldiers. However, like most veteran black jacks, the man didn't realize both Bergden and Carl were ex-military. Bergden doubted that the man at the checkpoint even had half the experience of either, but he bit his bottom lip in silence.

"We're looking for a conspirator charged with crimes against the state. Wagering on him, taking the highway to the outskirts of Blackwell. Commander Grimm himself seeks his apprehension. You are slowing down my pursuit of bringing an enemy of the state to justice!" Carl replied, trying to retain a level of dignified composure.

Bergden fought the urge to peer out from the canvas covering. He still had no idea what was going on, but if he were to be caught, it would be awfully suspicious to be hiding in the back of a black jack cruiser and trying to avoid detection. He'd had experience talking himself out of jams but explaining this one to the station chief would be damn near impossible. Especially since it was him that they wanted.

Bergden held his breath to slow his breathing trying to appear as motionless as possible but then cringed as he heard the man ask the question he had hoped to avoid hearing. "What do you have in the back? Under that canvas?"

He waited for the door to swing open and to be arrested right on the spot. He'd have to sit in the tank and await the inevitable Draven beatings that would accompany. The delight that man would take for his turn at Bergden made him sick to his stomach, but much to his surprise, Carl provided a logical explanation for the crumpled mass of canvas in the back.

"The canvas provides cover to my vehicle when I need to keep it hidden. Can't just park it along the road out in the country. The anarchists look for cars like mine when I'm out patrolling. I think it would be pretty ignorant of me to park it out in the open without some sort of cover. The canvas keeps prying eyes from looking in the windows while it's parked. Don't you agree? "A moment of silent hesitation from the manmade Bergden's heart beat nearly out of his chest. He steeled his breath, trying to say calm. He could feel his eyes prying around in the back of the cruiser. The eerie silence continued as he awaited the man's verdict. The sounds of his uniform buttons gently caressing the vehicle's glass clearly peering into the back seat scanning for any signs of suspicious activity.

"I'm taking down the plates, but you're free to go," the nameless soldier snarled. "Do something for once, get out there and find that piece of trash. I'm sick of you black fats getting credit you don't deserve."

Bergden muffled a sigh.

The car ride began to get rougher as the cruiser left the well-maintained city roads of Blackwell and onto the barely paved streets of the surrounding counties. The Coalition had bombed the streets leading into Blackwell for many months during the war. After the treaty was signed, the Regime didn't feel it was a priority to repair infrastructure unless it was in a major production center like Blackwell. As they moved along, Bergden wondered aloud where they might be going.

"You'll see Bergden, but you should be okay to come up to the front seat now," Carl said

Bergden crawled to the front of the cruiser and surveyed his surroundings. Gone were the towering expanses of the Regime bannered skyscrapers. In their stead, the buckwheat fields and rolling hills of the countryside. He'd forgotten how serene life could be outside of the city. The War saw to prying away those memories. Yet, as he watched the crops sway when they drove past, he had a moment of calm, a sensation he rarely felt anymore.

"Alright, Carl, tell me what the hell is going on here? Where are James and Alyssa? I want to go back and get them. I need some answers before I continue any further," Bergden demanded.

Carl looked at Bergden in the passenger seat and grimaced.

"I don't know what happened to them, Bergden," Carl admitted. "I can't tell you if Alyssa is alive or what the Regime did with James. What I do know is I had to get you out of there or else there would be no chance of saving yourself or them."

That moment of calm and clarity burned up in Bergden's anger.

"What the fuck do you mean you don't know what happened to my family? What is going on?" he shouted.

Relenting, Carl took a deep breath and started giving his side of the story. Bergden listened intently as Carl told him about discovering a vile plot devised by Draven. Draven sought to have him arrested and imprisoned as a conspirator at Cherry Hill Penitentiary, eventually to be wrongfully convicted as a traitor and executed, with his family doomed to a similar fate. Draven devised a plan based on Alyssa's relationship with Sia and Marcus that Bergden, too was involved in Remnant activities. Carl had reasoned that Draven had manufactured stories of Bergden's involvement with passing vital Regime information to Remnant spies and being lenient during arrests and interrogation. Bergden admitted that he did try and give some of those they encountered a reprieve from the harsh reality of being in the custody of the Regime, but adamantly denied passing intelligence along.

"So, this is all that piece of shit Draven's doing?" Bergden asked, fighting back anger.

He knew the bastard felt a sense of hatred towards his commanding officer, but never on this level to have him killed. Suddenly a sense of disappointment flooded his emotions at the thought that the station chief, a man he had fought with in the war, would side with Draven's word against his.

"I was called back into work the other night after we raided that rat's nest of an apartment. Draven was in the archives pulling files. At the time, I thought he was reviewing case notes, but now I realize he was setting his plan into motion. They were expecting you at the morning meetings, Bergden. You were to be arrested then and when you were late. I saw a chance to help you escape so I offered to go ahead and see if you were home. They sent Draven and the rest shortly after."

The series of events that led him to his current predicament confounded Bergden. Being late, Carl suspecting foul works afoot and the canvas it all seemed too convenient for Bergden to believe. Carl likely knew more than he was allowing himself to admit, but right now, he was Bergden's only ally and he needed to play this out if he planned on getting back to Alyssa and James.

If they were even alive.

"So how exactly did Draven put this all together?" Bergden asked.

"Draven took the intelligence you gathered from the investigation and added details into the investigation against Sia and Marcus. The added details spun it in a way that implicated you and Alyssa. He added some false intelligence he extracted from

Marcus during interrogation to seal the deal. Information that was obviously false, but just enough to stoke the coals for Draven. No one at the Regime even questioned where he got the intel. That poor bastard Marcus suffered tremendously before finally succumbing to the pain."

Black jacks were trained in understanding manipulation and when a suspect was giving out falsehoods. Draven had the same training as the rest of them, and despite his bullish mentality he carried with him a high degree of intelligence. He took information that was merely said to placate the interrogator and wrote it down as fact. A simple thing to do, but no one would question him. Bergden would have, but he was none the wiser.

"How does Alyssa fit into this situation? She is innocent, and James is just a child. There is no way he knew about any sort of conspiracy. What did Draven concoct about them?" Bergden pressed.

"I hate to say it, but Alyssa was already on the chopping block for her association with Sia in the first place," Carl conceded. "The Regime decided to crackdown on ranking officers abusing privileges. If I had known Alyssa was buying rum from a targeted Remnant anarchist, I would have told you. The Regime had planned her arrest even before Draven's plan was hatched. The problem is, the arrest order added more probable cause to Draven's case."

For Bergden, the idea that a handful of black-market goods could lead to such a disaster perplexed him. He had arrested dozens of individuals suspected of smuggling goods not produced by the Regime, but never in his wildest imagination did he believe his own wife would get caught. It had been common practice that ranking members of the Black Jacks often had indiscretions swept under the rug even with the proposed Regime changes.

"I just don't see the connection made here. Marcus and Sia dealt in black market goods, and I read over the notes from the interrogation notes from our raid. I saw nothing there that would implicate my wife. Unless..." he trailed off, bringing his heartbroken gaze to Carl.

Carl finished Bergden's reasoning. "Draven altered the intelligence to implicate your wife in something substantially more severe than rum. Sure, she was going to get a trip to the reeducation center, but when Draven added to the story, it became alarming to Regime officials. Unfortunately for her, the reports on Marcus were damning for him and also, true. He ran a sex club out of his apartment, and Sia brought in the willing customers. The proceeds were sent to Coalition resistance networks most notably the Remnants. The black-market stuff was a side gig so to speak. Draven saw the list of clientele serviced in the club and added your wife to it with the stroke of a pen. She wasn't going to be arrested just for buying black market goods, but as a sexual deviant too. That would be the charge that would stick under Kroft's morality codes."

Bergden instantly regretted not performing the interrogations himself. Marcus and Sia would be alive and, at the very least corroborate Alyssa's innocence. He let Draven run the show and this was the price to be paid. He wanted to go back to Blackwell and confront his wife's accusers riding a wave of indignant feelings of social injustices that long defined the Regime's governance. He knew it was only a dream, an act one perpetuates in a moment of solitude, but it would only bring about doom to broach the subject in the face of such totalitarian platitude.

In the face of such a task, a normal man might cower away or rather a rational man might seek to wait out the matter, but Bergden found the breaking point of his own rationality. He had been fighting the indiscretions of the Regime passively for a decade.

"I want you to turn this fucker around and get me back to

Blackwell, Carl. I cannot leave my wife and son back in Blackwell to be killed by the Regime. I won't let that happen! Pull over!"

Carl pulled the car to the side of the road, slamming on the brakes. A cloud of dirt and dust shrouded the cruiser. Carl stared at Bergden, not with resentment, but patience. The look of panic had receded and in its stead was a steely vision of purpose.

"Listen, I can't promise you that Alyssa is still alive or that James is not in a reeducation center, but I will find out what I can. If either one of them is in Regime, then it is already too late to help them. The best thing you can do for them is to help yourself. You can't help them if you're dead. We need to regroup and strike. Don't let your emotions take over. Remember what the Regime taught you."

Knowing when someone has a point is especially tricky if it makes too much sense, and Bergden above all knew when to stop arguing with the truth.

"Now, you need to get out of that goose stepper's uniform and into something a little more inconspicuous. You'll stick out like a sore thumb where we're going."

Bergden sat in a fuming stillness as Carl opened the trunk of the cruiser and pulled out a duffel bag. He immediately recognized it as it was his from the station lockers. A black leather bag. Bergden kept an extra set of clothes at Pemply Station. If a day had been particularly exasperating, he took a hot shower at the station. Private residences may not have the luxury of a steam shower, but a government facility was afforded the comforts of the prewar era. Before he met Alyssa and long before the birth of his son, he had spent more time at the station merely lounging and taking in the day's news than at any bar.

"Sorry, I swiped it before I left the station. I saw that you had a set of clothes in there. I have a few more things in the trunk if you need them, but I'm not sure they'll fit," Carl admitted.

Both men were roughly the same height, but Bergden was considerably more muscular in stature. His years in the Regime military molded him, and his days a black jack kept it going. Carl was more or less of average build, but the clothes were about as plain and civilian as Bergden could hope for. A pair of slacks, a plain Henley-style button down, brown boots and a brown belt. Nothing in any article had the mark of the Regime. Thankfully, he had stowed away a small bundle of cash as well in case of an emergency. The clothes, he hoped, would fit for the time being.

Carl started the car again and headed back down the road. In the distance, Bergden could make out the silhouette of a small town beneath the midday sun. The pair had been on the road for a few hours, and it was good to see another city. During the war, he remembered fighting Coalition forces in the trenches outside of Blackwell before becoming an operative and before Kroft released the weapon that changed the war turning the tide in favor of the Regime.

The two men sat quietly for the rest of the drive until the cruiser came upon the small town. As they drove down the main drag, it became apparent its inhabitants had seen better days. The streets still bore the damage from the Coalition war efforts, the sidewalks nothing more than crumpled and pulverized brick. An old advertisement had been partially painted over on a nearby building. What remained looked to be an ad for a type of men's razor. Advertisements had been banned years ago by the Regime, and it was almost a shock to see one even partially intact.

"What is this place?" Bergden found himself asking as he took in his surroundings. The town felt like a step back in time. The war-torn streets were filled with crumbling concrete, broken glass and burned out vehicles. The people wore tattered clothes staring dead-eyed at the car as it wound through the rubble-strewn street. A small marketplace sat in the center of town selling meager trimmings and what was left from before the war.

"Welcome to Harvick. It's remained outside of the watchful eye of the Regime since the end of the war. Bastards thought it was abandoned due to the damage. Once ardent supporters of Kroft's promises of an economic utopia, the people replaced admiration with fear and loathing once the bombs started dropping," Carl said, turning the car down a side street in much worse shape than the main street. There was an empty lot at the corner filled with debris from a bombed-out building.

"This is where I must leave you Bergden. By now, the station will be on full alert in Blackwell looking for you. I don't suspect we were followed, but I can't take that chance. If I hang around too long the Regime will eventually catch word that I'm missing and send out a hit squad."

Bergden stopped Carl from taking off.

"I know we've been partners for a long time and you're basically my only friend so forgive me for asking this Carl, but how can I trust what you are telling me?" Bergden questioned.

Carl sighed. "I suppose you can't. I know that really isn't much of condolence, but it is the best I can do. I will not put you in harm's way. You have my word."

If a greater plan was in motion, he knew he wouldn't find out his involvement until the right moment.

"You drove me out here away from my family, and now you are just going to dump me off?" Bergden scolded. "With nothing but a few dollars, old clothes and my uniform?"

Carl reached across and snagged his uniform from Bergden's grip.

"Not the uniform. I'm going to report you as dead Bergden or they'll never give up looking for you. Station Chief Aberdeen will believe it coming from his partner and if they question, I'll give them the uniform. That should buy you enough time to fade into the background," Carl retorted. "Listen, I'll check in on Alyssa and James. If I find out, I'll try to get the word to you. You need to keep your head low for a while. Just stay in Harvick and try to fit in."

"Harvick? The ruined town the Regime bombed right before the end of the War?" Bergden asked.

"The same. It's still a bombed-out pile of rubble but that's what keeps the Regime from paying the people there a visit," Carl reasoned. "More importantly Bergden, I have a connection here that is going to seek you out and give you more instruction. I radioed ahead while you were sleeping."

Connection? How did Carl have all of this knowledge about Harvick? Bergden questioned. *He never mentioned the place before.*

Carl apparently was more involved in the Regime's underground affairs than Bergden could comprehend, but now Bergden was alone in a town he did not know. From what he could remember, Harvick was a town east of Blackwell that went mostly untouched by the Regime until the end of the War. It was a small, rural hamlet riddled with abandoned buildings, empty streets and burned out store fronts.

Now, he needed the town to buy him time to find his family.

"When will they find me?" Bergden questioned, asking about the contact.

Carl shook his head. "They'll appear when they think you are ready. Good luck Bergden."

With that Carl started the car and headed down the road back toward Blackwell.

Bergden didn't know if he would ever see Carl again, but he supposed he should thank him for saving him the indignity of getting arrested by the men he once commanded and most of all his life. He could not say if it relieved him of his current predicament and the fate of his family.

He stared around the street looking for his next steps duffel bag in hand. Across the street was an old tavern. He couldn't make out the name as the sign had rusted nearly clean off. If he knew anything about gathering intelligence in a strange place, it was that the best information came from the local inn keepers. Who knows? Maybe he'd find a room to spend the night or if he was fortunate, a job. He was settling in for the long haul. He just hoped that whoever this person was that Carl had trusted his fate would show up soon.

Then he could begin his journey to find his family.

CHAPTER SIX

Alyssa lay helpless, naked and shivering on the cold, stone floor. An empty bucket that once held ice water, used to great effect to lower her body temperature, lay adjacent to her, its contents splashed on her over and over. Her captor continued to scream and berate her, but Alyssa focused the pain inward and out of her mind. She had endured their profane laced tirades and physical abuse for what felt like days.

When she was first incarcerated at the Singer Psychiatric Ward, she was inclined to be agreeable to their questioning, hoping to use cooperation as a means to procure her freedom. Bergden had taught her that in the event she found herself on the wrong side of the table, to cooperate and answer what she could and not attempt deception. She had done just that, or so she had thought. She had responded to questions about her youth, her parents, her family, and most importantly—what she knew about Bergden. Not once did they address the obvious question as to why she had been brought here in the first place. Again, she would answer what she knew, and again, she'd face her captor's wrath.

She just wished for the pain to end.

"Get the fuck up!" one of her captors commanded, striking her across her back with a leather crop. Alyssa hardly winced at this point. The incessant barrage of ice water had numbed her to the point that the beatings were no longer effective, or rather she could not feel the blows. Alyssa's vision had become faded throughout her ordeal, but she could still make out the feminine features stowed beneath a Regime officer's uniform.

"If I have to ask again, I'll make sure you can't get up!" the woman commanded. With that she strode over and struck Alyssa three times. *Whap, whap, crack!* The third strike broke the skin, sending a torrent of blood to the floor, which pooled near a drain before quickly receding to the pipes below. The room had been designed for the ease of clean up from the torture results.

Alyssa stared up into the light. Her vision blurred, but could see the woman looming above her, crop held high. Alyssa weakly held her hand up in submission. She had mustered the strength to yield once again, but as with the attempts before her hands were slapped away and she again was struck. *Whap, whap, crack!* The skin again ceasing in its efforts to resist the damage from the crop. Blood seeped into the drain below. Alyssa could only watch as her life force disappeared beneath her feet.

Near the precipice of passing out, Alyssa was shocked back to reality when a bucket full of cold water was splashed across her naked body. The water felt surprisingly good on her fresh wounds but chilled her to the core after that a brief repose from pain. She braced once more for the lash of the crop, but instead heard the sounds of a speaker warming the static cracking to reveal the sound of a man.

"Please place Mrs. Crane in the chair, Dr. Vossen. I will be in momentarily," the man's voice ordered over the loudspeaker. Alyssa felt a haunting familiarity as the words poured out from the speaker. She couldn't place it.

Dr. Vossen groaned her disapproval and dragged Alyssa across the floor by her hair to a steel stool. As she forced Alyssa closer to the seat, she grabbed her by the throat, the tormentor's fingers squeezing tightly before releasing her grip and sending Alyssa to the floor.

Alyssa's tormentor leaned in close and whispered. "Don't think I won't kill you if you try anything. Now, get your ass on that stool before I break it over your back."

Alyssa's body was tremendously weak, but she feared that any relapse to the cold stone floor might very well be her last. She forced herself on the stool and nearly fell back in a heap before struggling to regain her strength. Breathing deep, she looked up at the woman who almost seemed disappointed she had not fallen back down.

"We'll meet again Mrs. Crane. The good doctor always accepts new patients," the woman said, winking at Alyssa before leaving her alone in the room.

A man clad in a steel gray uniform strode in past Dr. Vossen. Alyssa struggled to focus on his face, but could see he was wearing a simple uniform tightly kept with knee high riding boots and a high peaked cap very much like the one Bergden would wear to work except the embroidery along the brim was surprisingly plain by comparison. Due to her blurred vision she was unable to make out any other real distinctive features suffice to say his voice was still eerily familiar to her.

"Mrs. Crane. It is good to see you again. I must apologize for these conditions, but here at Singer Psychiatric Ward Dr. Vossen is in charge and this is how she chooses to spend her free time. For you see only those deemed a danger to the well-being of the Regime are placed here. The chancellor believes that Dr. Vossen can find a cure for anarchism, and unfortunately for individuals in your predicament, he waived any common medical decency."

He took out a handkerchief, the symbol of the Regime embroidered on it and wiped his brow. "I suppose it is an appropriate level of respect for those who wish to undermine the authority of the Regime. I doubt very much that Dr. Vossen can find any sort of cure for a social issue, but I'm not in a position to stop her from trying. The order of course coming down from Kroft himself."

Alyssa was stooped over the stool shivering, finally realizing the pain from the lashes as they throbbed down her spine. She slipped off the chair, shivering uncontrollably. That was likely the first stages of hypothermia as it made its way into her veins. Days upon days of laying naked, cold and wet without the will to carry save for the fact there was the slimmest of chances she may get to see James and Bergden once more. Hunched over and her vision returning, Alyssa noticed out of the corner of her eye the man signaling back to the iron door. It creaked open and her previous tormentor returned with a towel and a set of clothing they weren't hers from before, but anything was preferable to being cold and naked. She watched as the woman scowled as she tossed the clothes at Alyssa's feet before looking disapprovingly back at the man.

The man gestured Dr. Vossen to leave the room.

"You can have a fresh set of clothes provided you allow me to have a conversation with you. If it alleviates your concerns it will not be in this chamber. I prefer a more comfortable atmosphere for conversation. Dr. Vossen's methodologies probably served their purpose whether you consciously realize that or not. I dare say she is not as versed in the art of civil discourse as you or I might be, preferring a more savage approach despite her title. Do not doubt the chancellor's reliance on her though, for she is quite good."

Alyssa had no doubts that her tormentor was a savage. Her actions made that quite clear. Alyssa did not doubt the effectiveness of her interrogation. After all, she was a school mistress not a hardened criminal. Bergden taught her much about the Regime's tactics, but even he couldn't prepare her for the real thing. Yet, the longer and harsher the treatment, the more she grew numb to her tormentor's tactics. She had only spoken truths from the onset of the interrogation and in doing so avoided compromising her integrity. Now she was at the mercy of a man that put her in this position in the first place.

"Please Mrs. Crane, get dressed and I will have Dr. Vossen here escort you, sans violence, to my office," the man urged. It was then she recognized his face from beneath the shadow cast by the wide brim. It was Commander Liam Grimm. The man from the cruiser who shuttled her away from the schoolyard and away from her life.

Despite this fact she was strangely relieved, she took the towel and began to dry herself off. The towel was scratchy, but it felt warm against her ice-cold skin. The clothes too were made out of the same wool-like material, but she took nothing for granted for at any time she could be strewn out on a cell floor again. They were simple garments, but they covered her all the same.

Dr. Vossen returned to the cell and grabbed Alyssa by the arm, forcibly guiding her down the hall. As she was pushed farther down the hall, she peered into the other cells.

Unfortunate men and women, wretches in the greatest meaning of the word, hung from their wrists to the ceiling, chained to the floor or hiding from their tormentors in the darkness of the cells. Pock marks and gashes covered their pale, naked forms. Dr. Vossen stopped for a moment to spit on a prisoner as he reached out of the cell towards Alyssa. She gazed at the broken man's face. His teeth were beginning to rot and he had a long unkempt beard, but what implored her to stop were his eyes. So beaten were his orbital bones he could scarcely open them. He moaned in pain as Alyssa reached out to him and for but a moment, she gripped his hand. His fingers were broken and his skin nothing more than callous bumps. Her heart ached.

"Move it!" the doctor yelled as she shoved Alyssa away from the man, taking a moment to slap his hand with the crop. The man bit his lip in pain as the riding crop slapped his bony appendage, his hand retreating back into the cell. Alyssa could see the pain in his eyes grow as he slunk into the back corner. The conditions of the cell were horrid. Finally recognizing the smell caused Alyssa to stop and gag in revulsion.

Eventually, she was led to a small office at the far end of the hallway.

"Commander Grimm is waiting for you. Sit on the chair and do not move. Is that understood?" Dr. Vossen barked at Alyssa with a stern look on her face.

Alyssa took her place on the wooden chair across from a near barren desk. A single coffee mug stood alone on the metal table. She could see the steam from a fresh cup of coffee, but the smell eluded her as the pungent odor of the man's cell still hung in her nostrils. She was surprisingly calm considering her predicament. The commander had been much kinder than she imagined and although she had suffered a great deal, it was not from his hand directly. There remained a glimmer of hope in his custody. She feared if she remained in the hands of Dr. Vossen, she would not survive.

She sat alone for what felt like hours periodically looking over to the door to see if the doctor had peeked inside. Suddenly, her stomach growled as a reminder of her hunger. Since she arrived, she had not had a single meal. Throughout the torture and pain the pangs of starvation were a mute feeling, but as she sat waiting the groans reminded her that she needed to eat something. Her eyes fluttered as she fought sleep. Until the door swung open behind her and in walked the commander. He had changed into less formal attire. Simple, blue officer's shirt and slacks. His appearance had a calming effect that steadied her nerves. As he sat, he took a sip from the mug and frowned.

"The coffee isn't the way I like it. I'm sure you could care less considering your position, but I'm used to certain standards. Spend a few weeks in my position and you'll come to expect things that the average man or woman would not or could not. Even with something as trite as a cup of coffee. The bitterness of Regime-issued beans is disconcerting."

Commander Grimm reluctantly sipped on the drink before pulling a folder from the top desk drawer. He placed it on the table in front of Alyssa. She could see the initials *A.C.* in the upper right-hand corner of the folder. She made the reasonable and expected assumption that the information contained therein was regarding her arrest, but she was curious if there was more involved. Did the commander have an extensive file on her? On her family? Bergden rarely talked about the particulars involved with the Regime's vast intelligence network.

The folder sat on the desk in plain view, cutting the air between them. She doubted that the commander was overtly taunting her with his silence, but it felt that way just the same. Inside the manila envelope sat either her salvation or destruction. Her mind wondered. She thought about the information the Regime might have on her and her family. Buying forbidden goods on the black market had become so commonplace under the Regime's nose that she reassured herself that that alone would not cause her incarceration.

"I'm sure you are sitting there asking yourself what could possibly be contained in this little folder," Commander Grimm reasoned. "Believe me when I say I've seen far worse come through these doors, but that does not excuse what has been presented. It doesn't make you any less culpable for your actions."

As the pages turned, the commander's expressions did as well. Gone were the hopeful grins and in their stead was a grim reminder of the reality of the situation that Alyssa faced. He continued scanning through the documents stopping abruptly and peering up from the desk. She knew he was studying her face. Bergden often remarked on how, in the present moment of a situation, that body language and cues could determine an individual's guilt or innocence with or without their knowledge. The process seemed purely arbitrary to Alyssa, but Bergden assured her that the Regime discriminated in other ways so egregiously that it was more of a formality after the evidence had been collected. She thought about what the commander said in her face, but evidently it had not been much.

She watched his movements intently picking up on subtle cues and how each changed with every word. From one side of his mouth raising and narrowing of the eyes to the more overt signals of a smile and nod. Commander Grimm was a confusing array of emotions and his true feelings challenging to detect.

"I read what the black jacks at Pemply Station wrote here and I have my suspicions regarding the validity of the charges against you. Why do you think I feel that way?" the commander asked, clearly baiting Alyssa for a response.

Alyssa decided to remain quiet and shrugged her shoulders in cold response. He hadn't been vicious as his reputation had preceded him, but the truth of the matter was she hadn't a clue. Her days were as mundane as anyone's and her nights the same. The same in and out routine followed her from one place to the next. From home to work to bed, her life met with only a few select moments of diversion. The extent of her deviance began and ended with buying black market spices from Marcus and Sia to provide a small luxury to her family. Was that indeed a crime worth being locked up in such a place?

"I don't know and that's the honest truth," Alyssa admitted.

The commander closed the folder and tapped his fingers on the table in contempt.

"Glancing at the first few pages of your record is boring, but I'm assuming you knew that," he admitted. "Rum from a black-market merchant is about as lame a reason to get arrested these days as I can conceive. I know the Regime wants our citizenry to avoid anything that might inadvertently or directly support what little remains of the Coalition or its constituents; however, that is rarely cause for alarm for the wife of a black jack and school teacher."

She suspected as much from the report, but she became increasingly discouraged that there was more information that she could not even begin to speculate on. She decided to break her silence.

"If it was not the rum, then what falsehoods are contained in your report?" she questioned. I'll freely admit to buying small items with little value from Marcus, but that is the extent of my indiscretions I assure you, Commander. No doubt the ranking members of the Regime trade in worse things than illegal alcohol."

He smiled and shook his head.

"I'll give you a moment to think about your past injudiciousness and if you can recall any other events from your past that might warrant further investigation then I suggest you tell me," he warned. "However, if you cannot, then do not. Lying is counterproductive even if you think it is what I and by extension, the Regime, would like to hear."

Alyssa thought carefully about her response and dug deeper into the recesses of her mind. Deception on the part of the commander was to be expected. The Regime deliberately manipulated situations to gain the results they wanted. If the commander wished her to admit fault, she would not do so willingly but he would eventually elicit an admission.

Her conversations with Sia had, in the past, yielded much information about her private life, but Alyssa had not made the emotional investment to properly listen. She remembered stories of Marcus, her and strangers engaging in salacious deeds. Such discussions were often one sided as she and Bergden rarely took part in those activities. Bergden was hardly strait-laced but obeyed the Regime's morality laws. He considered it counter-intuitive not to examine his role in its enforcement.

"Perhaps you have me confused for another revolutionary commander?" she joked. "I have thought carefully about what you have insinuated and cannot recall any additional moments that did not fall under the Regime's watchful guidance."

Her hopes of feigning her knowledge of the situation were dashed with a wave of his hand.

"Enough Mrs. Crane. I'll ask you kindly again to tell me the truth. If it helps, I have irrefutable information in front of me that can only be refuted by yourself. Thus, if you do not tell me the truth, you are proving its merit," he demanded.

Alyssa shot back. "Tell me what happened to Bergden and James. Is my husband still alive? And James, is he still safe?"

The commander steadied himself in his chair and stared at Alyssa for a moment then pursed his lips again, tapping the folder impatiently.

"I told you that lying is counter-productive, and I suppose that means for both of us. Yet honesty is often painful. Mr. Crane, Bergden, I fear is likely deceased. He too was going to be brought him for questioning to Singer but elected to challenge the Regime when confronted and reported dead. I cannot say for certain though as the body has not been returned. Considering the overwhelming odds of him escaping, I would not hold out for hope. At best he's in a cell at Cherry Hill rotting from the inside out."

Alyssa feared the worst, but without a body, she would keep hope. She could not say for certain if the commander told her the truth yet had he wanted her to honestly believe, beyond a doubt, of Bergden's demise then why leave open a window of probability?

"And my son James? Where is he? Can I see him?" Alyssa tried in vain to stifle her exasperation with the vague approaches to her predicament by the commander. She continued to press about her son. "Let me see James just to know he is safe, and I will tell you anything. You have my word. "

Commander Grimm almost seemed disappointed that Alyssa tried to negotiate her way through the questioning. She had no leverage other than information that she did not know or was not true, but she continued to pose as though she could provide value. For Alyssa, that became a means to the end, whatever that may be. She would do anything, at any measure, to find out what happened to her husband and to see James safe.

"James is safe I can assure you of that," Commander Grimm promised. "He is in the loving hands of the Headmistress at the Kroft Academy and is getting his education steered to something more appropriate for his particular skill set. I dare say that he is on the right path, but we can address this later. For now, we have more to discuss and we need to determine your innocence or guilt."

A sense of relief that her son was safe stayed her nerves for the time being, but the thought of Bergden's death crept in. She fought back her grief by remembering that Bergden would not hide information from the Regime. It was hardly a secret to her or his closest friends that he had a penchant for going easy on people who did not nothing more than catch an Inquisitor on a bad day. He was a good man and perhaps that was what placed him under the Regime's microscope.

"There is nothing more to tell, Commander," Alyssa conceded. "I have admitted my guilt about buying black market goods from Marcus. I should have been aware of his other activities, but to be fair I was not and am still not inclined to take part in that lifestyle. I do not know where you got your information, but I can assure you that it is utterly and ultimately factually incorrect."

Commander Grimm turned his head and mulled over his next move before passing the folder over to Alyssa. "I'll let you see for yourself," he said grimly.

Alyssa read through the notes and became alarmed at what she read.

Instances of infidelity that she allegedly committed in the company of Marcus and Sia. She bore witness to sodomy, and herself took part in illicit behaviors long condemned by the Regime and supposedly assisted in the propagation of a business founded on such behaviors. She could not believe what she read. Endless lie with each page. Stories placing her in areas of Blackwell she had never even seen, providing sexual services to inquisitors in exchange for them turning away at her other illegal undertakings. The list went on and on and the more she read, the more anger built inside her. She suppressed her desire to lash out and slid the folder back across the table and onto the floor.

"That is a folder of nothing but falsities and slanderous tales," Alyssa implored. "I have never been so sure of anything in my life than to know that nothing that I have read contained in that folder was true. Whoever reported this should be punished and removed from whatever position they hold!" Alyssa's fury had boiled over causing Dr. Vossen to race into the room, a pistol leveled at Alyssa.

"Is everything okay?" Dr. Vossen questioned, staring down Alyssa. "I heard shouting. I can take her back to the cell. That'll teach her a lesson about how to treat superiors."

Commander Grimm dismissed Dr. Vossen's concerns.

"It is quite alright Ana, and while I know you would relish the opportunity to continue your work, but I don't think that will be required though," Commander Grimm replied. "Mrs. Crane and I have much to discuss still. I will call you in when we are completed."

Ana's gaze never left Alyssa as the doctor strode from the interrogation room. Alyssa did not know what she did to draw the ire of such a woman or if that was her very nature, but either way she wished to never confront her again.

"You needn't worry about Dr. Vossen," Commander Grimm insisted. "She's good at her job although perhaps a bit overzealous." Alyssa peered at the door and for a second, just a blink of an eye, questioned if she had the mental and physical fortitude to remove herself from her position, throw the door open and race to the prison exit. Her captivity, however brief, emboldened her as nothing had ever before. Was it the humiliation? The beatings? She dared not hazard a guess to the origins of her newfound flame, but instead chose to embrace it. Yet, rationality prevailed once more as she optioned to stay put.

Commander Grimm grinned and laid his hat upon the table and positioned himself across from Alyssa. "I am going to make you an offer, Alyssa, that you will find difficult to refuse. For, you see, refusal is the less desirable option of the two and hence the decision will be obvious to anyone who has not been diagnosed as a fool. I must ask then if it is even worth the effort to provide you with an option. You'd be the first in Singer to receive such an honor. Most here are resigned to their fates."

Again, the urge to flee bubbled inside her mind boiling her rationality nearly to breaking. She could feel herself gathering her courage without prompting. Would her body do what her mind was unwilling as it fought what was sensible? She needed to stifle these urges before they got out of hand.

James. She thought of her son and the ability to see him once more even if from a far. It was all she needed to tune out the instinctual flight mentality and reaffirm her faith in finding her family.

Alyssa closed her eyes and took herself back to a time of happiness. A time when her family was just a family and not subject to the Regime's subjective whims. She could picture Bergden sitting at the kitchen table drinking his coffee and waiting for her to join him. James would be in his room reading his lessons and preparing for the school day. She would fry eggs on the stove and listen for the toast to be finished, happily serving Bergden and calling James into the kitchen. The serenity of each morning came and went but it was what drove her happiness in such a desperate world.

"Commander, I dare not say what I believe my choices to be in this prison, but I am willing to listen. If it means someday my life can return to some semblance of normalcy with my husband and my son then I will do what you ask. In my heart I do not believe that Bergden is dead and I do not believe my son will succumb to the pressures placed upon him by the Headmistress. We are a strong, proud family, Commander. The Cranes of Blackwell do not break."

Commander Grimm remained unmoved by her speech instead of choosing to take the time to light a cigarette he pulled from his jacket taking an excessively long drag before sending a cloud of smoke from the corner of his lips taking care not to blow the smolder towards his prisoner's face. He gently dabbed the butt before squashing the flame dead.

"I can assure you that your life will never be the way it was Mrs. Crane," Commander Grimm quipped. "The Regime will see fit to destroying you no matter the outcome of this investigation. But I believe you and I can come to some sort of agreement. Do you know what I'm thinking?"

Alyssa shook her head and waited in silence.

"I think that this report is exaggerated. I think that the black jack that put together this investigation used largely unfounded information. Normally, that wouldn't matter as the Regime typically does not challenge the investigations put forth by its agents with any real effort. I see something different though. I see an opportunity that could benefit both of us," he offered. She worried where this was headed. It was not lost on her that senior leaders in the Regime often took advantage of prisoners for personal satisfaction. She was a young and attractive woman in a vulnerable state, desperately seeking an escape from this hell.

"As I discussed earlier, you have two options, Mrs. Crane," Commander Grimm reminded Alyssa. "Only one takes you away from this place. I am offering to take you into my home."

Her fears began to feel validated, but as the commander continued, she felt strangely optimistic and from that optimism emerged an offer she didn't expect.

"My wife Jocelyn and I will host you. I reviewed your record at the academy. You are a strong instructor," Commander Grimm raved. "Your students perform remarkably well and often exceed Regime standards. Because of this, I am going to place you in the Kroft Academy. We are in need of a new school mistress and I believe that you would serve him well."

"And if I refuse?" Alyssa challenged.

The commander motioned to the door. Dr. Vossen stood tapping the glass with the butt of the pistol, a devilish grin stretched from ear to ear.

"Then I call Dr. Vossen back in here and you never escape this hell," Commander Grimm warned. "I assure you that you will be treated well in my home. I may call upon you for duties that may seem unorthodox. I can promise you there is a purpose for such things and if you should refuse then you will return here. Is that clear?"

The door seemed farther away than ever. She doubted she'd survive another week in Singer, but she dreaded at what other duties the commander had in mind. Was he going to make her break her marriage vows in some way or would it be something worse? He was not lying to say that she really had no alternative. Alyssa thought of the man in the cell on the way to the room. How he wasted away, forgotten. A man that once had a family much like her and a family that likely missed him. She did not want to fall victim to the same forgotten memories. She took a deep, heavy breath.

"It is a clear decision for me, Commander. I will accept your offer. I only ask that I be allowed to see James and learn of what became of Bergden. It will pain me so if I cannot garnish some closure during my time with you and I fear that it will encumber my work."

The commander again was not moved by her pleas.

"You'll do well not to let that happen. You are not in a position to make demands, Mrs. Crane. You will do what I say, when I say it. This is an opportunity that many in here would kill for. I suggest you do not delay and try my patience any longer. Now, as a mistress in the Blackwell Academy you will gain access to some of the most important people in the Regime. You will do well not to forget that."

The commander rose from the table and pulled out his lighter. Holding the folder high he lit it aflame dumping the contents on the steel table.

"Consider it a new beginning Mrs. Crane. Ana? Please come in here and escort Mrs. Crane through the back and to my cruiser." He turned his attention back to Alyssa. "A driver will get you to my residence in the countryside. You will be given a day or two to rest and recuperate. I will not have a mistress at the school bruised and battered." He bowed politely. "I bid you adieu and long live the Regime." He raised his hand in a salute.

Shortly after the commander exited Dr. Vossen marched in. Her demeanor had changed little, and she grabbed Alyssa tightly and forced her towards the door.

"Just remember sweetheart, if you screw up once then you're right back here with me and if you think for even a second, I will take it easy then you have another thing coming," she warned.

Alyssa didn't bother to answer. Ana had blustered and boasted of her demise since she was first processed, but she was given a chance to free herself from these shackles. She could hear her go on and on about the pain she'd receive. Alyssa nodded her head before stopping cold. The man from before again reached out to her his hand clasping around an unknown object. She looked at him and past the pain, she saw a man with hope. Somehow, she knew that the man had discovered the commander's plan for her. He appeared to be mouthing something as she tried getting closer. Suddenly, he shot out grasping at her clothes. Alyssa struggled to get free, but as Ana hit the poor man over and over, he whispered to her.

"He is not what he seems to be. Listen and watch closely," she hinted.

Before he could speak another word, Ana struck him knocking him out cold. Alyssa looked in bewilderment. She wanted to know more. What did the haggard man mean? She wanted to know more, but for the moment she just needed to continue her mission. Her mission to survive and see her family together once again.

CHAPTER SEVEN

Nearly a month had passed since Alyssa was taken away from her family and forced to endure the grueling and grotesque conditions of the Regime's Singer Psychiatric Ward. She had not experienced a hell like that so-called hospital in her lifetime and hoped to never meet Dr. Vossen again. When at her lowest point at the hands of Dr. Vossen, in a whirlwind moment, she whisked away to the countryside home of the Regime Commander, Liam Grimm. She could tell he expected her to be more grateful, but for what reasons should she extend pleasantries? The false accusations that led to her torture. Being ripped from her family? The humiliation at the hands of that witch, Dr. Vossen? She decided to reserve her supplications for the moment she laid eyes on James and Bergden again. In spite of reservations she could complain about her accommodations. It was not as though her new abode would be uncomfortable or undesirable.

The moment the cruiser pulled into the governor's driveway, she realized that the commander lived in an opulent countryside mansion. Away from the city, far from the authoritarian politics and crime, where their only neighbors were the trees surrounding the property. The three-story villa was whitewashed brick with six bedrooms, a servant's quarters, a lounge and a dining room with a huge oak table able to sit twenty. Hung over each balcony was the Regime's banner, all of which were rolled up when the weather turned foul. There were stained glass windows inlaid into a great oaken front door, allowing the sunlight to peek into the immense home's entryway. The colors dancing on the granite floors that greeted the commander's guests. There were innumerable antechambers that Alyssa hadn't even started to see.

The commander and his wife Jocelyn shared the immense home with only a few servants. No children, no other family were to be found in the mansion. At first, the commander and his wife were keeping their distance from Alyssa even going so far to ignore her at every turn. She had been given access to the lower vestibules. Nor was she to exit the home at any point without permission from Commander Grimm. Not that she would have a place to go after walking out the door. Without knowing the whereabouts of her family, it would be a fruitless vent. She was afforded a single set of clothing, no real bed to speak of and if it wasn't for the observations of an older servant named Hari, she'd likely have starved. Hari was a quiet foreign man of few words, but of great compassion. He had taken it upon himself to watch over Alyssa and for that she was grateful.

"Miss Alyssa, I dare say that you've managed to lose even more weight. I can try and speak to the commander and the misses if you'd want. I could perhaps sway them to pay more than a never mind to your presence here," Hari asked as the two supped on a simple meal of bread and water near a courtyard window. Alyssa enjoyed his company and even though his repeated stories of his homeland bored her, she smiled when he told them.

Hari and Alyssa would spend their time conversing when he was not called upon by the commander. He regaled her with tales of his youth. He was a spirited youngster from the tales he told. A young man who preferred the wonderment of the wilds and exploration of the concrete edifices of a city. He told Alyssa about the day the Regime entered his town. He was much older than, but not too old and he, as he often tended to be, was walking through the forest and sketched the world around him. When he returned, the town had been emptied and anyone the Regime saw as a traitor or threat had been promptly executed. Most were simply gunned down, others hung, and the worst were burned alive. Alyssa tried to imagine such a horrible thing taking place and could not. Not even during the war had she been exposed to atrocities on that level.

"How did you come to be in the commander's employment?" Alyssa asked, trying to establish the relationship between this pleasant elder and one of the Regime's top figureheads.

Hari gave a surprising smile and promptly lit a cigarette.

"Much like you, the commander swept me up from the hellish oblivion in Singer Psychiatric Ward. I tell you this, the commander is not the man he appears to be in the public eye. He is a wiser man than you might expect and for your incarceration here on the lower floors there must be a purpose. It is a maddening process, but take my assurances, he does everything with a purpose," Hari said cryptically.

She found it hard to believe that there was purpose in her confinement, but Hari, despite having ample opportunities, chose not to speak ill of the commander. Instead, he told her of the good things he had done and the work he does behind the scenes that serve a higher purpose for the people living in the Regime. The commander was a man of integrity and promise in Hari's eyes, but for Alyssa these were terms all too commonly used when those who were blinded by their transgressions described Regime elites.

Despite Hari's assurances that things would change for her, Alyssa's days began to slow to an excruciating, tedious crawl. Alyssa resigned herself to the belief that she was to remain residentially incarcerated in the 1st floor vestibules and be in the company of Hari for the rest of her days. She could hardly say she didn't like Hari, but after a few days his stories no longer carried the momentum from dawn until dusk. In fact, he barely spoke at all if she didn't ask.

Another week passed until her stagnations were broken with a simple knock on the door.

"Hari? I think someone is at the door, Hari?" She called out, but silence was the only response. The commander ordered her not to open any doors. She wondered if that meant doors within the confines of the mansion itself.

Alyssa slowly crept over to the door and gently pushed it open and much to her surprise there stood a woman of some considerable clout. She wore fine jewelry, mostly diamonds, and her hair was raised above her head. Her dress was a black and form fitting with the shoulders removed exposing her caramel colored, flawless skin. It was more formal attire than Alyssa had seen in her life.

Was this Jocelyn? Alyssa asked herself.

"You must be Alyssa. Liam has spoken of you from time to time at the dinner table and before departing for work. Hari said you were experiencing a significant and prolonged state of ennui."

The woman gestured for Alyssa to approach.

"You are a pretty, little thing, aren't you? I suppose it is no wonder my husband brought you home with him." The woman eyed Alyssa from head to toe, her eyes following each curve of her body. The overt nature of her ogling made Alyssa feel uncomfortable. The woman ran her fingers through Alyssa's hair. "You should fit right in with our particular arrangements. Come, follow me and stay close please."

Alyssa struggled to remain at the woman's side. The uncomfortable exchange notwithstanding, she was in awe of the décor of the home. Much of what she gazed upon had been illegal under the Regime for years. For a time, it angered her that people were arrested and accosted for much, much less, but her morose demeanor faded as she took in her surroundings with intrigue.

"I suppose I should introduce myself to you Mrs. Crane. My name is Jocelyn and my husband has asked that I escort you to his study. For the purposes of what I cannot say, but I do believe you are going to be pleased with your stay with us. It has to be better accommodations than that dreadful penitentiary. Although I have not been there myself. I doubt it is too bold of me to say such things. Rumors of Dr. Vossen's accommodating nature are greatly exaggerated."

Part of Alyssa wanted to lash out and reproach Jocelyn for her incarceration but doubted that would help her situation any further. She remained quiet and studied her new custodial. The wife of the second most powerful man in the Regime was not to be trifled with and, while her lodging did differ in comforts, a prison was still a prison. She took notice of the immensity of the house as the two walked across a granite floor wonderfully adorned with a forest mosaic. It was a scene taken straight out of an ancient folktale.

Alyssa decided to break her silence once they exited to the lower floors in an attempt to build a report with her host's wife.

"You have a beautiful home, Jocelyn. I have never seen anything like it."

Jocelyn grinned and stopped Alyssa gently, placing her hand beneath her chin and craning her head sky-wards.

"Look up." She pointed.

Above the pair hung the most enormous and most lavishly adorned chandelier Alyssa had ever gazed upon. Opals, diamonds, and emeralds and many stones she did not recognize circled the wonderfully, white lights. A macramé of light danced from stone to stone and down to the floor below. She found herself awash in glorious, luminous splendor.

"Where did the commander, I mean, your husband, find such a beautiful piece? I am from modest means but took pride in having seen many magnificent things. I am nearly lost for words at its splendor," Alyssa said as she stared up in the light. Each stone reflected in her pupils.

Alyssa seldom awed in the material goods of others, in particular when it came to Regime leaders and what she saw in newspapers or overheard at the market. Bergden told her anecdotes of black jacks arresting a suspect tearing apart the abode to search for items beyond the purpose of evidence, valuables. It had been common practice, and these ill-begotten gains hardly warranted the attention of the hard-working classes that could simply abscond with other's properties.

Much to her surprise, however, the commander received his from different means.

"The house used to belong to Chancellor Kroft himself. A trophy from the War of Wars.

The original inhabitant was President Henry Gaines until Kroft's men stormed it at the beginning of the conflict.

Jocelyn pointed out into the courtyard.

"Right there is where they hung him," she noted coldly as she urged Alyssa forward. "After the war, Kroft took tribute funds and expanded the mansion to suit his needs." Alyssa's face must have been showing a state of disgust as Jocelyn continued. "I doubt it was much of a secret that Kroft broke his promises to the people to use the tribute to rebuild the country, but again, who would be able to stop him? He did win the war after all."

"Why build a house out in the country? Why not in the city?" Alyssa inquired.

Jocelyn continued, "It is something akin to a hunting lodge from my understanding. A bit too gaudy for my flavor, but most who visit remark upon its splendor. The chancellor took great pride in its construction. Even to this very day the chancellor writes to Liam lamenting his departure, but he knew he's pride and joy couldn't just sit empty. Hence giving it to Liam. Such a home should always have an occupant."

Alyssa, feeling emboldened by the conversational nature of their discussions asked the obvious question.

"Why did he leave if he is so sad? Why leave such regal surroundings behind if he laments it so?"

Jocelyn continued to walk, guiding Alyssa out of the great hall where the chandelier hung and into a library. The number of books seemed endless, and again, as before, there appeared to be an abundance of literature long banned by the Regime. At the end of the room was a large, closed steel door. She found it rather odd that such a door would be in such a place.

The two women again paused just outside the door. Jocelyn decided to proceed with her explanation of the chancellor's lamentation.

Jocelyn finally took a moment to answer.

"He wanted to be in the heart of Blackwell. He remarked in speeches to his staff that he feared getting out of touch with his country if he stayed out here. Personally, I believe he was and still is begetting an aura of paranoia allowed to be impressed upon the people by a personality cult at the peak positions within the Regime itself. I can tell you that Liam was more than happy to leave the city once he saw Kroft's idle pleasantries and passing rumors swiftly becoming policy and law."

Alyssa again pressed her position.

"Do you believe that to be the case? I have minimal experience diagnosing paranoia in another. Naturally, I have felt it from time to time, but it was more about my son's grades or my husband when he was out late for work."

Jocelyn appeared to think for a brief second before responding. Alyssa surmised that she carefully calculated a rapid yet thoughtful response. Or perhaps she saw an opportunity for her to back track on her previous works of indiscretion against the chancellor. Alyssa wondered momentarily if she crossed the line. It was remarkable considering her captivity that Jocelyn was so conversationally open to begin with, that Alyssa found herself scolding her boldness.

"In the coming months, I imagine you'll get exposed to his world in one way or another Alyssa. Kroft is a peculiar man and his idiosyncrasies can be alarming. If you get the pleasure of meeting him, you'll know exactly what I mean. That's all I will say for the moment, but now we shouldn't keep Liam waiting. Please come with me."

Jocelyn rapped on the steel door with her fist. The sound of the impacts each making a thud...thud...thud. Beyond the thick door, a near inaudible voice murmured, and the faintest echoes of footsteps could be heard. Alyssa tried to make out the words but caught herself leaning closer to the door. She snapped back away and looked over at Jocelyn who could only smile and shake her head at Alyssa's innocence.

The heavy door lurched upon with the force of the commander. The weight of the steel taxing the commander as he leaned on it in a heap visibly exhausted from the effort.

"Apologies, Mrs. Crane. This door is quite cumbersome. And

the weight. Don't get me started on the weight." The commander composed himself and pushed the door closed.

Alyssa glimpsed into the room. It was a strange room that did not seem to befit a mansion of this magnificence. A darkened room with a microphone perched atop a single desk. A lamp hung from the ceiling and spotlighted a pen and paper.

"I'm sure you are wondering what that room is for Alyssa. Well, there aren't a lot of things that aren't of your concern, but that is one of them. Now, I hope you will follow me." He turned his attention to his wife. "Thank you, Jocelyn. Have Hari prepare a meal for we have much to discuss."

Jocelyn smiled then eyed Alyssa, her once welcoming demeanor appeared to change in an instant. Alyssa instinctively stepped back to which the commander must have taken notice.

"Do not fear my dear wife, Alyssa. She does not like the idea of having a younger woman around and alone with me. She would much prefer to accompany us as I take you to the bedrooms. Please, do not mistake this as anything more than an excursion into the remaining areas of the house you have yet to grace."

Alyssa didn't respond and chose instead a path of silence as she walked a pace or two behind the commander. The staircase stood before her in magnificent splendor. Dueling sets of stairs led up to the second floor. The walls were adorned with paintings and pictures from all throughout history, most long banned by Kroft as being anti-government, perverse, or even pornographic. Every few steps hung another portrait, but strangely only a handful were of the chancellor. It was a drastic change from the ordinary citizen's home. The other figureheads of the Regime seemed to stand at attention. There was even a portrait of the commander himself. He appeared iron-like in his stoic pose. His serious tone was highlighted with a mouth that did not grin a single inch. He was dressed in his Regime best. Another slate gray number, but this time two massive pauldrons hung from his shoulders, a series of bombastic medals pinned to his breast and a black leather holster on his hip. She studied the portrait closer and realized he was a younger man when the painting was commissioned. It might have been a case of artistic privilege, but the picture lacked the wisdom that comes with age.

"The majority of the second floor is also not accessible to you. However, there is a study, a private bath that I assure you will be as I said, private. The library has old books and pieces of literature that have long disappeared from the general public. Kroft took careful measures to preserve history while denying those around him the ability to study it. You will have the opportunity to study them should you choose it."

Alyssa wandered into the library and pulled a book from the shelves, *A History of the World*. The title seemed harmless enough.

"Why deprive a good history lesson to the people?" she asked as she flipped through the pages. The title of each chapter reflected a time when the world was not under the Regime's heel.

"People are supposed to learn from history. God knows that isn't always the case, but Kroft is not a man ready to take chances after he seized control before the war. The process was really quite remarkable. The rounding up of intellectuals, artists, or anyone that could remotely provide a substantive argument against him. Anything that could de-legitimize his power was lightning fast. His supporters swept into the streets, people very much like your husband, and took them away." The commander sighed. "Not many are left alive after that initial sweep."

Hearing Bergden's name tossed among the thugs that crushed whatever hopes were left for a free world angered Alyssa. She knew her husband and knew that what he did was not because of any personal beliefs that Kroft instilled within him. As many did during those early years, it was out of necessity; otherwise, perhaps

130

he would have been one of the countless dead. There would be no James, no them. The mere notion he was a common thug pained her to think about the fact that it had become a reality in the blink of an eye.

She decided to get straight to the point with the commander with what her true feelings were.

"Can I see my son, Commander? It has been months and I have heard nothing. He is the last remaining light in my heart. If I can never see my husband alive once more than I must be able to see our offspring. Please, Commander, I will do anything and everything to see James."

The commander brushed past her to another door without acknowledging her request. He pushed it open, revealing yet another stunningly decorated room. The commander strode into the room flinging open the closet and pulling out each drawer revealing endless clothes. Many were exotic in nature or not befitting of the Regime's morality standards. Short dresses, low cut tops and even garters hung from hooks in the closet. Many were similar things that she remembered from her youth, but the Regime had snatched away when they marched into Oyster Bay.

"Mrs. Crane, my dear this is your room. It is yours to do as you please. My wife and I only ask that during lights out that you remain in your room and be quiet. Everything in this room is yours including the clothing. If they do not fit, then please let Hari know and he will tailor them to your needs. Don't worry about the style while you are in my house. Wear what you'd like knowing you will not face repercussions."

The commander went to the door and turned back to Alyssa, who stood silently by as if waiting for her next command.

"We are going to eat in an hour, and during dinner I'll speak to you about your son, James. Please, find something suitable in the wardrobe and like I said just summon Hari with the servant's phone should you need anything."

A sense of relief swept over her at the mention of James and inspired her to go through the fineries as the commander ordered. She started with the closet. The closet itself was the size of her room in their apartment in the city. A single wall rose from the floor to the ceiling with shoes of all types. Heels, pumps, and flats were laid out before her. She was glad to see that the shoes were mostly in her size and picked out a pair of heels then headed for the dresses.

The dresses were more numerous than the shoes and were of all types and shapes. Jet black, fiery reds, or even florals it did not matter. Anything and everything appeared before her as she shuffled through rack upon rack until pulling free a bold sapphire dress. She stood in front of the mirror and pulled it up. It was a form fitting number that showed every inch of her curves and for a moment she felt as though she was going back to the time when she first met Bergden. She had a very similar dress she wore on their first date. She fought back her tears and took a deep breath stepping out into the room and much to her surprise Hari stood in the doorway.

"You look ravishing, my dear." Hari stood dumbfounded until realizing he was staring. "I'm sorry I didn't mean to intrude. The commander wanted me to inform you that dinner is ready and to make sure everything was to your liking."

She was strangely happy to see Hari and smiled.

"What do you think?" she said as she spun the dress. "Think I can impress the commander and his wife enough to let me see James?"

Hari sat on the bed and asked Alyssa to join him, brushing his hand across the satin comforter. The comforter was intricately woven with a myriad of geometric designs and shapes. She marveled at the attention to detail and ran her hand across the embroidery. Her mind still focused on her son, James.

"The commander will get you to your son Alyssa. He has reasons for what he does, you'll see soon enough." He paused and grinned devilishly. "You are a beautiful piece if you don't mind me saying. Now, get downstairs. They are expecting you."

Alyssa followed Hari down the staircase and into the dining room area where the commander and Jocelyn were seated across from one another. A chair had been placed at the end of the table and in between the two. She hesitantly sat down between husband and wife as they casually placed dinner napkins upon their laps and ushering in more servants to pour the wine.

"I believe you picked out the perfect dress Mrs. Crane. I'm sure you've not seen such a fine dress in the entire city of Blackwell. You'll be glad to know that Jocelyn had a significant hand in picking out the wardrobe," the commander said, sipping on his wine. He wore a smile of satisfaction, almost proud of the fact that his wife's choice in aesthetics had been met so eagerly.

"Yes, it was quite the undertaking rifling through the former chancellor's mistress's belongings. She, thankfully for you, was of a similar build," Jocelyn said dismissively. Bergden often mentioned the rumors surrounding Kroft and his line of mistresses. Kroft himself was not a married man, but many of the women he chose to join him in his retreat were. She met the thought of such infidelities with disgust but was reassured by the commander's wife that the wardrobe in her chambers had never been worn.

The dinner continued on in silence for the better portion of the meal, which was of roast duck. It had been many years since she had poultry beyond that provided by the Regime and to taste duck was divine. The duck was tender and meaty, reflecting the taste of a perfectly cooked pork shoulder rather than the Regime-assigned meat that was purchased at the market. Sometimes she would buy a pheasant or two from Marcus, but only on rare occasions. Bergden feared the smell of cooked pheasant would attract unwanted attention from the neighbors who might have seen it fit to turn them into the black jacks or call upon an inquisitor. Yet, here she sat eating duck without a worry about being arrested.

"So, Alyssa, let us talk about James," the commander said, breaking the silence and instantaneously piquing her interest in the conversation.

"What about James? Where is my son at, and is he okay?" Alyssa asked, begging to know more about her family and their whereabouts.

The commander sighed with a sense of reluctant admission. "James is in a reeducation center in Blackwell and me as I said before he is quite fine. What I would like to discuss is not his wellbeing, but your opportunity to finally see the boy."

Alyssa barely contained her excitement, and it must have shown as the commander hold up his hand to steady her temperament.

"While I see you can barely contain your enthusiasm for your son, it does not come without a price."

She had expected there to be a catch. Nothing the Regime did came for free, and it was not tit for tat. The Regime took what it needed without question and often without cause. For the sake of power was more than enough reasoning for Kroft. In reality, she doubted that Kroft really had much input on the day to day seizures, but he profited just the same.

"Didn't I say that I will do anything? I'm not sure if you have children Commander, but the depths of my love for my son knows no bounds, and I think if you were in the same situation as I, then you would be more than willing to do what it took." Alyssa stepped off of her soapbox and waited with bated breath for his response. She glanced over at Jocelyn who met her gaze with daggers. The presumptuous approach to the lack of children appeared to strike a nerve in the chancellor's wife. The joys of childbirth did not befall

all women. She knew the anguish all too well. James was their miracle and his absence wore upon her like heavy rain.

"No, my wife and I do not have children. It is not for lack of wanting that much is certain, but that is not the point. The Regime requires new blood to be injected into our education system. Kroft himself has expressed concern that our current stock of instructors has become complacent, leading to the degradation of the Regime youth."

"So where do I come in, and how does this get me to James? To Bergden?" Alyssa asked.

The commander rose from his chair and walked, contemplating his response. Jocelyn maintained her icy gaze at Alyssa, raising the soft hairs on her neck. Eventually, she would need to address Jocelyn and apologize, but for now her fate rested in the hands of the chancellor.

"I am going to give you the position of school mistress at Blackwell Academy," he replied.

Blackwell Academy was the premier school in the Regime and the envy of the rest of the world. Kroft himself often made appearances, and the children delighted in his presence. Alyssa's personal evaluations were sent to the Headmistress for review and her curriculum reviewed to comply with the Regime's core evaluations. It was the pride of the Regime's education system and any schoolteacher worth their salt would jump at the opportunity to be a part of the Academy.

"How will this get me to see my son?"

The commander smiled. "You will teach on the same floor as his class. I have had a chance to review your past evaluations with the assistance of the headmistress whom I know you are familiar with. She was naturally reluctant, but I was able to convince her you were the right person for this position. I see grand things for you, Alyssa, and although it may not seem it, you are doing a great service to the Regime."

At the mention of James, a feeling of warmth spread from head to toe. News about her family could help her shake away from the depression that had begun to overwhelm her soul, and although the commander likely would not mention Bergden she still believed in her heart of hearts that somewhere out there he was alive. The opportunity to see James was all she had been asking for in thought and prayer.

"Of course, I will accept that role, Commander, and I want to thank you for allowing me the chance to see my son. Can I ask and forgive me if this is too forward, but can I ask for the whereabouts of Bergden?"

The commander looked at the floor avoiding eye contact with Alyssa before craning his neck and sighing.

"As I've said before, we believe your husband to be deceased. Reports indicate he was in a stand-off with the Pemply Station black jacks in your former apartment. I cannot say for certain where his body was interred. If it pleases you, I'll do some digging in the Pemply Station archives for what might have happened."

Holding out hope for Bergden was all Alyssa could do in her present situation. Doubt crept in at the prospect that the commander would perform a search of the archives, and if he actually did let alone find anything that would alleviate her fears or satisfy her urge for closure, should she accept his death as an inevitability.

"Anything you can do for me, Commander, would be greatly appreciated. If there is anything else, you need please let me know."

The commander finished his glass of wine and signaled for Hari to come and clean the table. While Hari hurriedly took away the dishes, he leaned in close to Alyssa parting her hair from her ear delicately.

"Do not dare ask again about Mr. Crane. If I should hear you mention your husband's name once more, then I may not be as kind. There are things in motion all around us that are beyond your control. Each mention of his name brings that which surrounds us closer to the forefront. If and when I find information regarding his fate, I will tell you, but until then just do what you're told and we will be just fine."

Hari came to help Alyssa up from her seat. Her time with the commander and his wife had come to an abrupt end. Tomorrow she would return to her profession of choice and the chance to see her son once more. Part of her felt a greater distrust towards the commander and questioned if he was a man of his word. Yet, the memory of Singer Psychiatric Ward was as fresh as ever, and if serving his purposes at the expense of her will kept her from that dreadful Ana and the torture she would play along.

Hari and Alyssa climbed the grand staircase and unlocked the massive ivory door into her bedroom. The clothes she had thrown about were once again packed away and her covers drawn away from the corner.

"I suppose it is lights out, Mrs. Crane. I've prepared your bed for you. Please let me know if you need anything else," Hari said before bowing out of the room.

The room no longer felt welcoming as it once did. The commander's home again felt like a prison keeping her caged and away from the outside world. Bergden might still be alive, but then again, he could be dead. Alyssa thought to herself. The only way to find the truth was to endure. Endure the pains put forth by the Regime and to take each opportunity given to her and the first step was to reestablish her family bonds with James. Who knows? Perhaps James knew something about his father. Only time would tell, and that time was fast approaching.

Tomorrow morning, she would awake once more, as she had done so many times before, as a teacher.

CHAPTER EIGHT

The smell of burning oil filled Bergden's nostrils and flowed further into his sinuses, each breathe burning in his chest. He coughed voraciously, spitting thick, blackened mucus onto the rig's grimy floor. The scent and even the taste were familiar to him and in spite of the burns, reminded him of his younger days in Blackwell before his current predicament placed him in Harvick. There were indeed moments in his past he wished to relive and the work itself notwithstanding, he longed for simpler times before he agreed to be a pawn in the Regime. His first stint as a pipe fitter on a rig marked a time when he first met his true love Alyssa. That love never died, but soon the violent grip of his black jack career smothered any hope of a lifestyle of normalcy. It had become demanding work and often took him from his betrothed and their son far into the long, cold night.

Suddenly, he longed for his family, and with each pound of the hammer another memory came rushing to the forefront.

Almost a year since Carl dropped him off on that corner in the center of Harvick, Bergden lucked his way into finding a job as a pipe fitter. He only had to survive a few days of living on the streets. He had spent countless hours in the pouring rain during the war, so a few days under a vacant shop overhang was almost a paradise. Within a few days he found a modest apartment three blocks from where Carl had dropped him off.

The town of Harvick suffered from a state of perpetual despair and gloom filled delirium brought upon it by the lack of access to the Regime, the lasting effects of the War of Wars, and any recognizable economic benefit to being an inhabitant in such a place. To say it was boring was perhaps a disservice to the term boring. Bergden spent the better part of his days either at that very bar or back in his apartment reading books long removed from any Regime library as being revolutionary propaganda. Writings marked as lewd or rapacious by Kroft's lackeys. He recognized quite a few titles that he picked during raids. He smuggled back as many as he could into his own personal library, but when he joined up with Pemply Station, he watched the literary funeral pyre tower into the night sky.

A giant hand clapped his back just in time for Bergden to regain his balance gripping the steel rung tightly.

"Catch you taken' a nap there, Bergden?" a gruff voiced joked. "Not taking a break on me are ya?"

It was the job site foreman and Bergden's boss, Roderick Trents. Bergden, by sheer happenstance, met Roderick at a bar called Deville's the very same evening Carl left him standing in Harvick, duffel bag in hand. He was a tough man to miss. Roderick could classify himself as a giant Bergden surmised. A hulking brute at first glance, Roderick had grown up in the mills surrounding

Blackwell before fleeing to Harvick when his father had been arrested as a Coalition sympathizer during the war. Roderick oft remarked on the size of his father and his bravery in the face of tyranny. Being able to even get him into a cruiser would have been an extraordinary feat if he took Roderick's word for it.

"Just end of the day exhaustion, I suppose Roderick. I appreciate the catch. Sure would've knocked some sense from me should I hit the floor," Bergden said, yawning from a long day's work and stretching his hand into the air, his hands meeting behind his head.

"Perhaps it would've knocked some sense into you." Roderick laughed. "You okay to go to Deville's? Some of the boys are going, just wanted to see if you were tagging along."

Exhaustion continued to seep into Bergden's bones, but he had barely come to know anyone in his new home. He feared it becoming known that he had once worked for the Regime. The people of Harvick weren't fans of the Regime. Quite the opposite, really. As he spoke with the townspeople, the more he learned about the Regime's influence outside of Blackwell and the hopes of acquiring the fate of his family increased. Bergden clung to the belief that James and Alyssa were still alive, and that the Regime likely fed them the same spoonful of lies that he had perished in a blaze of black jack bravado laced glory. He had the experience within a system designed to deceive and manipulate to know that the truth was never presented as a main dish. Carl likely didn't know what happened on that fateful day but took measures to prevent Bergden from racing back into Blackwell by instilling fear of a worst-case scenario into his emotions.

"I can probably stop in for a few. I'll meet you there and buy you a drink. I just need to stop back at the apartment really quick to grab a few things," Bergden said, slinging his duffel over his shoulder.

Roderick nodded and smiled, "Suit yourself but don't take too long. I'm buying the first round and I can't promise it'll be there for you when you arrive," Roderick joked. "You know how the boys get when the booze free."

Bergden sauntered back to his apartment the day's work weighing heavily on his mind. The sun had long disappeared beneath the nearby mountains, and the dimly lit alleyways in Harvick offered little to ease his mind. Harvick was hardly a dangerous town, but crime found its way after dark. He'd fought off more than one mugger after the day was done.

He trudged block after block until he reached the darkest stretch of street that led up to his front door. He stared blankly into the blacked-out alley. The specialized training he received as a Dealer served its purposes in one form or another, and in this particular instance, it proved a valuable ally in preserving his own well-being. Not that this sort of issue cropped up with any regularity. Unpreparedness was not an option for Bergden. Not now, not ever.

Bergden changed from his oil-soaked work clothes, rinsed off, and headed back down to the tavern. Spending his free time in a tavern wasn't ideal, but the men he worked with were innocent enough and provided camaraderie. The men would regale the bar regulars with stories about their time in the war, the women they'd been with or the times they indulged a bit too much in booze. The radio echoed in the background with music and the news from Blackwell. Kroft's speeches replayed from the morning and were greeted with a rousing set of taunts and expletives. Not a single portrait of Kroft or banner hung in any building signaling that the Regime long abandoned their presence in Harvick or rather, gave little notice to such an insignificant town.

"Those bastards destroyed our homes and pillaged our coffers, then marched right back to Blackwell, leaving us for dead with nothing but ruins in our hands!" Roderick's complaint brought out cheers from the patrons and the clink of glasses in a toast to his outcries. Bergden smiled and held his glass high masking the underlying truth that he at one time embodied the Regime in thought, word and deed. If it had not been for the love of Alyssa, he'd likely been utterly immersed in the political machine and an unnerving monster of a man. He suspected that no one in Deville's would be quite so endearing to him if they knew of his past.

The bartender, Darby, came over to refill Bergden's glass once more. The soot-colored beer oozed out into the empty pewter mug. He had almost grown accustomed to the texture and learned to tolerate the taste. It was hardly an appealing sight for Bergden, and when he first drank the local swill he gagged, nearly throwing it back up on the bar. The warm summer months did not permit anything more than a lukewarm respite from the day's heat. Ice was at a premium in the small towns around Blackwell and the freezer was often on the fritz. It was a rare moment when he was thankful for the winter months.

The night ended similar to how it began with a toast to the health of Harvick and the downfall of the Regime. Bergden stayed much longer than he had desired and felt the effects of the alcohol more than he had wanted. The streets seemed to spin as he stepped out into the snowy twilight. What few lamps remained illuminated and shone with a concentrated brilliance off each snowflake as they fell to earth, but nary lit the path for a man who had given way to consumption.

The alleyway approaching his apartment was once again dark, but not as blackened as when he departed for the moon had made an appearance. He stumbled through the darkness gripping the timeworn, red brick walls of the nearby building for balance. The words "laws of men have no meaning" had long ago been hastily etched into the brick. As he continued, he found himself increasingly lightheaded and in the presence of a small yet visible white light. Briefly, Bergden wondered if the alcohol had increased his blood pressure to a level high enough to bring him to faint resulting in the appearance of a white out environment, but as he regained his footing he soon realized that it was in fact not the detrimental results of beer. The apartment door had been opened and the light from which brightened an otherwise darkened alley.

Bergden, regaining what composure he could and trying to shake off the spinning sensation crept to the apartment door inching past the wooden frame and peering into the tiny one-bedroom abode. He fought against the lingering effects of the alcohol as he scanned the room, trying to focus. It appeared to be empty and nothing disturbed save for a single sheet of paper on the kitchen countertop.

Meet me at Sadie's Diner tomorrow morning at 9 am. I'll get you a cup of coffee. You look like you could use it after tonight. Information on Alyssa. Tell no one.

A.E.

Bergden looked around once more only to find his apartment as empty as before. He returned to the kitchen and read over the note again but could hardly focus. He decided it was best just to take his leave. He locked the door and propped a chair under the handle just in case his guest had stuck around. His bedroom welcomed his weary and half-drunk mind as he collapsed on the bed, asleep.

The morning sun pummeled through the blinds, focusing squarely on Bergden's eyes.

He struggled against the blinding light before realizing it was almost mid-morning. As he crawled out from the sheets, he remembered the note from the night before. Clamoring into the kitchen, he saw that it was 8 o'clock and sighed in relief that he had not missed his mysterious rendezvous. Forgiving himself would not be easy if he passed on a chance to learn more about Alyssa.

An icy shower and a fresh set of clothes set Bergden on his way to Sadie's Diner. He had seen the place on multiple occasions, but he never believed it to be operating. The windows were dirty, and the door ajar. Stray cats and dogs wandered in and out throughout all hours of the day. If there was indeed a business inside, they did a poor job of advertising food with the less than ideal conditions.

Much to his surprise, the diner was filled with people all chatting over coffee and enjoying a breakfast roll. The smell of freshly brewed coffee and bakery fresh bread reminded him of Alyssa, and the time she would take each morning to feed her beloved family. Happy memories drove him to find whoever had written the note.

As he scanned the crowded diner, and after no one approached, he took a seat at the end of the bar with a vacant chair next to him. The waitress brought him a cup of coffee and a newspaper. Anxious to meet this potential benefactor, he hurriedly glanced over the front page. The news hardly changed as the same headlines were plastered each morning. Arrests made here, Coalition Terrorists stopped, quashed and the chancellor's latest miracle for the economy. The Regime did a fantastic job spreading propaganda and sowing fear in its people. Blackwell was in his past, but he still looks over his shoulder for inquisitors. The effects of the Regime were everlasting.

Bergden became engrossed in his coffee and the aura of normalcy that the cafe seemed to afford him. Harvick's allure was hardly the businesses, the people, or even the distance away from the Regime, but rather the ability to keep to one's self sane. He had managed to do so for the large portion of his stay. On this particular day, that solitude within a public forum helped to nurse a hangover that was driven by the cheapest of beers. A headache perpetual. As he began to sink into himself once more there came a tap upon his shoulder.

"Mr. Crane, follow me to the back if you will," the stranger ordered. The man moved quickly and remained shrouded beneath a dark brown hood. None seemed to notice the two disappear into a backroom. A half-circular booth, the kind used by the crime families in the pictures, sat alone dimly lit beneath a stained-glass lamp. Instinctively, Bergden looked over the room for any signs of a trap. To his relief, the room was empty save for the booth. Bergden took a seat across from the man who was now revealed to him, and to his surprise, the man was black.

"My name is Andre Erasmus, Bergden. I'm glad you took my note seriously. Can I get you some more coffee?" the man said politely as a waitress appeared from the diner's front room and filled up the pair's mugs.

Bergden sipped his coffee in amazement, not at the taste, but with the appearance of his guest. It had been many years since a person of any ethnicity could be found in the Regime. The racist propaganda still echoed in his mind and the lines pounded into his psyche during boot camp roared back into memory.

"Andre, was it? Forgive my astonishment, but it has been some time since I've seen a person of any ethnic background in Regime territory. Kroft's thugs hardly acted kindly towards anyone but their own."

Andre smiled and poured sugar into his coffee. Sugar was a rare commodity in the Regime. It was heavily regulated and a likely catalyst to his entire situation if the reports were to be believed. Black market goods of any kind normally landed a man behind bars in Cherry Hill. Andre offered a spoonful, and Bergden graciously accepted.

"We'll get to that in a moment, Mr. Crane. Can I call you Bergden actually? The formalities will have to be dispensed with at some point. Now is as good as a time as any," he said, smiling as he sipped from his ceramic cup.

With a nod as he sipped the hot brew, Bergden insisted Andre continue. The urge to ask how Andre knew him rose into Bergden's throat, but he decided to let his new friend speak.

When gathering intelligence, you learn little if you only hear your own voice.

"I've been watching you for quite a long time, Bergden. Ever since Carl brought you here, I've had you under my watch. It's not every day a Regime party member such as yourself is dropped off in Harvick and not torn to shreds. I gather you've noticed by now that there aren't many Regime supporters roaming these streets," Andre said as he appeared to measure up Bergden.

"I've kept that part of my life a secret. No need to rile the masses. Although I do not consider myself part of the Regime any longer and haven't for probably longer than even, I realized," Bergden said as he finished his coffee.

"The remnants of the Coalition are based in Harvick, Bergden. The base of our operations is right here in this very diner. Each of those people out there, the men, the women, and the children are all looking for a way to restore the sanity that once prevailed over these lands. No matter their age and occupation they serve a greater purpose than our own. The restoration of freedom for all peoples."

Bergden peered past Andre and out into the main area of the diner. The customers each went about their business talking about the day and enjoying the fact it was a weekend, and work was still a few days away for most. The radio played only music, a rarity in the Regime, and much of it was banned for years. It was like looking back into a time warp and seeing what was and what might've been had Kroft failed in his attempts to control the world.

"The obvious question on my mind is, why follow me? What do I have to do with the resistance movement?" Bergden asked.

Andre got up from his seat and closed the backroom door

checking the window to make sure none could peer in.

"Your boy Carl told us a while back that you were different from the rest of the jackboot thugs that filled the ranks of the Regime, and admittedly I was skeptical. Tours of duty during the war, a brown cap, a dealer and finally, the coup de grace, a black jack? Tough credentials to make anyone believe you don't bleed Regime black and blue. If it were up to me, you'd have been shot on sight just for being a dealer."

Andre's perceptions of Bergden's past hardly surprised him. He had made a living on looking past initial perspectives to find a deeper and more substantive approach to understanding the mentality of another human being. On paper, it should be easy to dismiss him as nothing more than a Regime crony, but a person is not defined by anything more than who they are at any given moment. A historically loving father and devoted husband could in an instant become a cold, calculated murderer. The present is what defined a human in the eyes of another. The past is the past for a reason and men of intelligence know this.

"You can choose to believe me or disregard it as nothing more than pandering to your personal proclivities when I say that I am fully resolved to the dissolution of the Regime. That is your decision naturally as to whether or not you believe me, but I wonder if Carl would've bothered to save me had this not been true," Bergden countered with measured deviance.

Andre studied Bergden for a moment, clearly evaluating whether or not his words were trustworthy. For Bergden, it should've been a moment of truth. A chance at finding purpose in a purpose driven world, but instinctively he pushed aside the ability to care about what others think. He found it reassuring to know that he could still maintain individuality in the face of divisiveness and when his world was at its lowest point.

"Taking into account your history with the Regime, I guess it will be up to me, but you're going to need to prove to us that you are beyond a doubt a reformed soul before we let you join us," Andre offered.

Bergden began to contemplate what Andre and the other resistance members might be alluding to when they meant he needed to prove himself. What task could he do to ensure that he gained their trust? Besides, who gave this man the idea that Bergden had any interest in joining a resistance movement? A Regime exile in a town predominantly run by Remnants, Bergden doubted the feat would be anything less than dangerous to his very well- being.

"Listen, normally, I wouldn't be so eager to let you in on our mission plans, but if Carl thinks you're the guy for the job, then I'm just going to have to go with it," Andre admitted with apparent reluctance. He fingered his hair, stressed by the situation.

Andre had a series of tattoos on his neck, starting below the ear and ending at the shoulder. To Bergden they were nothing more than symbols with no apparent or specific meaning, but for Andre it was a mark meant to be seen.

"Can I ask about the tattoos?" Bergden said, breaking the awkward pause between the two men.

Grinning, Andre craned his neck and moved side to side, causing it to crack before rolling his shoulders and sighing. "I suppose it might be good for you to know why there's a black man in Harvick. You did a piss poor job hiding your expression of surprise when you first laid eyes on me." Andre stared at Bergden uncomfortably for a moment before laughing. "Happens all the time, Bergden, and I suppose it is only fair I tell you a little bit about me since I know so much about you."

Bergden finished a second cup of coffee as he waited for him to continue.

Andre said, "Four years into the war, about the same time you were doing secret operations missions on the western front, I was drafted into service," he said. "Ethnic troopers were rare, but I guess the Regime wasn't doing so hot at the time. I was the only eligible man in my family."

Andre tried to fight his grief, but he teared up as he continued to tell his tale.

"While I was out fighting for a cause I didn't believe in, Kroft decided to do away with what he deemed a drain on his great society. Chiefly, people like me. We helped him turn the tide in his favor, and he repaid us in blood, our own blood." He dabbed his tears with a handkerchief. "When my tour was up, I went home and saw what horrors could be sown by such a man. My mother, father, grandparents and my sister were hung in the street along with our neighbors. I suspected they were up there for a few days as the crows had gotten to them. Took me two days to bury them all."

Bergden could picture the gruesome scene. Not for a wanton pleasure in the obscene, but from the experiences he witnessed himself. The steady tide of Regime soldiers into Coalition towns marked the beginning of the terrible violence. The brutality of it all is what began to sway him ever so slightly. The rape, the murder, and the destruction were often too much for a single, conscience heavy, man to heap on his shoulders. The real pain came from turning away from the actions of his Regime comrades. It shamed him so and he lived each day with the guilt. He remembered writing up reports to the commanding officer only to be labeled an outcast.

"I'm sorry for your loss Andre. I wish I could empathize, but I hope my dearest sympathies will suffice," Bergden said, trying to avoid falsely relating to a situation that only harbored his actions on one side of the fence. He knew the pain, but not the moment.

"It hurts me every day, Bergden, but that's why I am doing

what I am doing and why I need to vet anyone who is going to be involved. I want that son of a bitch dead. You hear me?

That's the ultimate goal here. Kroft's unmitigated demise," Andre said, wiping away a final tear.

Bergden could feel the stress mount in his mind. Do or die moments rarely came to a man more than once in a lifetime, and here was yet another laid out before him.

"You mentioned having information pertaining to my wife in your note Andre. I should like to hear what you have to say," Bergden said, bargaining for information about his family before letting Andre continue.

Andre took a deep breath and exhaled audibly. Broaching the subject of Bergden's wife, a man who helps the resistance needed, must have been challenging. Strangely, it gave him hope as it was easier for a man to speak of death than of life. The hope of survival was masked by the conditions she likely survived if it all.

"Your wife Alyssa is purportedly and thankfully very much alive. Carl, your friend, alleged that after returning to Blackwell, he learned more details about her fate, but only so much as to say she survived her arrest and captivity," Andre offered.

The news of her survival at the hands of the Regime warmed Bergden but sent new fears into his mind. The prisons, which he himself had sent the Regime's enemies, were notorious for the conditions in which the prisoners were forced to live and the daily torture of anyone suspected of being even remotely affiliated with the Remnants. The ability to crush the will of the most ardent souls was the Regime's forte. Alyssa was a strong woman, but if she broke down Bergden could hardly blame her.

Even worse, she could land in Singer Psychiatric Ward and undergo horrific medical testing. Rumors of Dr. Vossen's cruelty were widespread and her efforts to "cure" radicalization often killed her so called 'patients.' "Has Carl reported anything about my son James?" Bergden questioned.

Andre shook his head.

"Carl hasn't heard a thing about James," Andre confessed. "I'm sorry, Bergden. I lost family and I do not wish it upon anyone. I hope we find your boy."

Reformation Center, Bergden thought. The Regime did not squander its youth. James was the perfect age to mold into what they wanted him to be and with his impressionable mind, that wouldn't take long. That was Bergden's fear, time. Time was against him. Time would determine how long Alyssa would survive if she was in prison. Time would tell how quickly James became nothing more than an indoctrinated Regime thrall, which was as good as dead.

"So, what do you need me to do?" Bergden asked, newly determined after hearing the news of his wife's survival.

Andre nodded and finally broke a smile pleased that Bergden appeared to be warming up to the idea.

"Once I tell you what we need from you there is no going back. Understand?" Andre hinted.

Bergden nodded in silence.

"Alright. We received intelligence from one of our contacts in Blackwell that Major Andrew Ridgway, the hero of the Coalition and a man many thought dead, is in fact alive. Kroft, for whatever reason, chose not to execute him. Our contact informed us that he is being imprisoned in one of the two Blackwell prisons either Cherry Hill or Singer Psychiatric Ward."

Bergden realized that this mission wasn't just a run of the mill resistance snatch and grab, it was turning into the roots of a revolution.

And he relished the thought.

"What do I need to do?" Bergden asked dutifully.

"You need to figure out which prison he is in and get him out.

Simple as that."

Yes, simple as that, Bergden thought as he rolled his eyes. Suddenly realizing that the mission was far more complicated than any he had undertaken even during his years as a Dealer.

"Why pick me if this task is so important? Why select a man you just met?"

Andre shrugged his shoulders. "Because Carl is vouching for you and he's done more for the resistance than most of us combined. He traverses the darkest corners of that city looking for opportunities to stick it to Kroft. You were his pet project. Watching and learning from everything you did. He believes you are the best man for the job. By now, the city should have forgotten you and with your knowledge of the Regime, we surmised you to be the greatest hope we had. Plus, you know how it operates and how to act to get what you need."

Bergden could have never suspected Carl of being anything more than a faithful Black Jack who worked long hours, but the more he thought about it the signs were there. He always spoke of a family, but Bergden never met them in fact, he had never even seen his home. Most of Carl's personal time was an enigma to Bergden. He would often take off without reporting in and yet still come to every meeting armed to the teeth with knowledge of the underground. Bergden took as nothing more than good police work, but in reality, it was so much more.

"I'll do it on the condition that if I find my wife in one of the prisons, I'm going to free her and Ridgway. If I don't, I want help tracking her down or I'll bail on the whole mission, understand?"

Andre nodded in agreement and shook Bergden's hand.

"Get some sleep tonight Bergden. Your journey to normalcy begins tomorrow. Roderick will pick you up at sunrise and you'll be on your way home."

Without another word, Bergden left the diner, went back to his apartment, and passed out, the stress of the day forcing him to sleep.

He awoke several hours later. The sun had gone down, and a steady, cold rain had moved in. The patter of each droplet as it hit the metal reverberated through the tiny apartment. He cracked a window and listened to the peaceful metallic tones. He felt surprisingly serene as he walked over to his closet. He began to pack his duffel for the mission until he stumbled across his old Regime Black Jack uniform. He tossed the uniform on the bed and stared at it. He had not looked at the black and blue suit since the day he arrived in Harvick. It was still neatly pressed, his medals hanging proudly.

Memories of his exploits as a Black Jack raced back into his mind. The times he tried to save those who were wrongly persecuted, pulling them away from the hungry maw of Kroft's propaganda machine.

He stared at the uniform even closer, studying each stitch and as he did thoughts of James and Alyssa crept into his mind. Memories from a time when everything wasn't as it should be, but they were happy. The mornings filled with banter about the day, the sounds of breakfast cooking and James studying for the day's lessons.

Bergden suddenly fell to his knees and wept. His tears flowed freely for the first time in years. Pent up emotions about the state of the world and the love of his family. He cried for hours before taking out a pen and paper to jot down his final will and testament.

Bergden had a predictably rough night's sleep and the sun came without warning as it peered between the blinds. A cold shower and a half-cooked breakfast later he stood waiting on the street for Roderick, duffel bag in hand. Within a few moments an old sedan clunked up to the corner.

"Get in you bastard. We're running late!" Roderick yelled as he leaned out the driver's window, slapping the side of the car.

Bergden climbed in the passenger side and closed his eyes.

"You ready for this, Bergden? This isn't exactly pipe fitting you know," Roderick laughed. "Bet you didn't think old Roderick could possibly be a Remnant, did ya?"

Bergden was ready to see his family again and ready to take the fight back to the Regime. If his actions brought peace and freedom to just a few people, then his life would be worth it. He needed this atonement, even if it was just to put his soul at rest.

The car ride seemed to take hours as the cityscape of Blackwell appeared on the horizon. The city was as he remembered it. The towering skyscrapers piercing through the late morning fog and the streetlights illuminating the road into the city. It was a stark contrast to the small-town streets of Harvick. It was an oddly heartwarming sight, like he was returning home. His wife and son were somewhere in the city and he needed to find them.

"So, where do I start?" Bergden questioned as he stared out at the street signs. Roderick gave a cunning smile.

"We're setting you up in an apartment on the south-central side of the city. You're to meet a contact there and she'll give you more information. She's been at the location for a week now scouting ahead and reporting in on Regime activity."

Bergden was getting deeper into the resistance movement every turn he took, but if it meant getting to see Alyssa and James again, he'd go to the ends of the earth.

"How far away from Pemply Station is the apartment?" Bergden asked, realizing that if anyone was going to recognize him it would be his old colleagues.

Roderick thought for a moment, puzzled.

"I'll be honest Bergden I really have no idea. I just drive to the rendezvous point and drop off our contacts. I'm a bit oafish to go wandering around the city. Inquisitors would be all over me. By the way, if they stop you, you're not connected to the town of Harvick in any way is that understood? If the Regime finds out we're operating so close, we'll be purged in no time flat. Hell, they may just send in bombers."

The rickety car came to a stop near a grocer.

"Get out here and make two rights. You're in room 310. If the first mark doesn't lead you to Ridgeway, then you'll rendezvous. Good luck."

Bergden got out of the car and stood, staring up at the massive buildings. He was back in the city that shaped him and now he was here to bring it crashing back down.

CHAPTER NINE

Can I still call this place home? Bergden questioned himself as he stood staring up at his old complex. The swirling snows masked the facade, hiding his window from view.

He started his own family here, but never did a place feel less like home as he clung to any semblance of a hopeful reunion with his former life. By contrast, Harvick, despite all of its peculiarities, felt closer to his heart. The small town had a sense of belonging. That feeling brought its people closer, a more intimate affair. The cold, damp alleys, the warm beer and even his dollhouse sized apartment appealed to him more than the busiest city in the world now that he was back.

The cruiser backfired as Roderick drove off causing the people to stop momentarily and stare at Bergden. Trying to keep a low profile, he set out on his own towards the safe house to meet his contact. The mid-morning sun cast a blinding glare on the snow filled streets. Markets and cafes all teeming with activity provided the right amount of cover as he strode in a hurried pace keeping his head low. If an inquisitor, or worse, a black jack, caught up with him then the game was over. Roderick dropped Bergden off on the south edge of Pemply Station's jurisdiction. Getting spotted by those familiar with him would end the mission particularly quick.

He mingled among the people as best he could, his tattered clothes doing little to isolate him from the rest. A large portion of the population toiled in the factories that powered the Regime's efforts. It was a hard life of oppression filled with a mountain of dirt and dust.

He froze as he felt a tap on his shoulder. For a moment, he thought about walking away and pretending he felt nothing, but if it was a Regime official that would only make it worse. He took a deep breath and slowly turned to face this mystery person.

He felt his heart fall into his stomach. It was an inquisitor.

Bergden stifled his panic as his eyes darted for a way to escape should the need arise. He stared back at the inquisitor. A man probably in his early forties, brown eyes and a well- trimmed goatee, his uniform pressed and neatly tucked into his trousers. A very average citizen in the Regime granted above average authority over his peers much like Bergden had. Thankfully, he didn't appear to recognize Bergden.

"Can I help you sir?" Bergden asked politely. He had dealt with dozens of inquisitors as a black jack. Most needed to fill a quota of citizens each day to question and on a frigid day like today any old person would do just to fill the books.

The inquisitor ignored Bergden and frowned as he checked out Bergden from head to toe. He slowly walked in a circle around Bergden poking and prodding at his jacket checking for a concealed weapon or anything that might be out of place.

"Haven't seen you around here before sir. What is your name?" the inquisitor asked, his breath clouding in the cold, midwinter air.

"James...James Kroft" fell from his mouth without thought.

"Can you tell me what the chancellor said today about yesterday's arrest of several resistance accomplices?" the inquisitor asked, still eying Bergden with suspicion.

Chancellor Kroft said nearly the same thing about each arrest each and every day almost too verbatim. The propaganda machine realized that after a while, no one really focused on the details choosing to just listen to the morning briefings as a part of their everyday routine. It hardly meant you were safe from questioning, but for most it was just a matter of replying in a manner vague enough to discard suspicion.

"The resistance members were captured, and a major criminal element was removed from the city of Blackwell. Preserving the sanctity of our population and upholding the law. Something along those lines. Forgive me if I cannot do it verbatim," Bergden answered confidently.

Bergden became impatient as the inquisitor wrote his answer down on his pad. Bergden glanced down hoping to catch a glimpse, but before he knew it the questions continued and to his chagrin it pertained to his current place of residence.

"What is your address?" the man questioned plainly.

It was a simple question, but one that Bergden could not supply an answer to. Andre and Roderick had provided a location, but only through landmarks, not a formal address. Nor would it provide a suitable response considering it was a Remnant safe house. His mind raced as he searched for a response but came up uncharacteristically blank. Standing there in the snow, Bergden met the question with silence prodding a negative reaction from his interrogator.

"I don't think I need to remind you that I am an inquisitor and if you refuse to answer my questions then we're going to have to take a trip to a reeducation center. Understood?" he threatened him, lifting a pair of cuffs from a hip pouch on his left side, his baton resting on the other.

Bergden hurriedly studied his surroundings as he gathered his thoughts. The square was busy, but no one seemed to pay heed to the interrogation. He glanced to his right and saw an alleyway. Choosing to flee was a dangerous prospect. He'd likely outrun the inquisitor and evade arrest for at least a while, but eventually Pemply Station would be on full alert blowing up the entire operation.

"Sorry, sir. I live on the corner of Market and Cornwall. I just moved into the city a few weeks ago so forgive me as I get my bearings. I meant no offense."

The inquisitor nodded as he wrote down his response. After a few tense moments, he turned his attention back to Bergden.

"That'll be all Mr. Kroft. I hope you'll be a little more attentive next time. I'll be seeing you around." He eyed Bergden as he stuffed his notepad back into the pocket on his chest.

With that the confrontation ended, Bergden could breathe a sigh of relief as he made his way to an alley to collect himself. He needed to keep a low profile and stick to the mission. He needed to be strong for himself, but more importantly it was imperative to stay on task for Alyssa and James. His hopes of seeing both again rested on the success of the mission.

The jarring sound of a child's scream abruptly pierced through the frigid air. A high-pitched squeal of terror instantly grabbed his attention. Leaning out from the alley, he saw the cause and groaned in frustration.

He saw the same inquisitor that approached Bergden, but now he was after a woman and her daughter. He had a grip on the daughter's hand as the woman struggled against him. Bergden could hear the inquisitor threaten the two as he pulled at the little girl's arm. Without thought, Bergden stormed out from the alley and towards the inquisitor.

"If you don't let go of this little girl, I'll make sure you rot in Cherry Hill you whore!" the inquisitor commanded, pulling violently on the little girl's woolen jacket while keeping the now hysterical mother at bay with his baton.

Bergden tapped him on the shoulder pressing down on his jacket.

The inquisitor spun around letting go of the girl's arm. She ran back and leapt into her mother's desperately waiting embrace.

"What the hell do you think you're doing?" the inquisitor barked.

The anger on the inquisitor's face was etched into Bergden's mind. The abuse of power to take this little girl away for her mother for no reason other than she couldn't remember the propaganda-laden speeches of an old tyrant frustrated Bergden. He could see the same arrogance on his face that Draven used to have. It made his blood boil.

So much for being calculated, Bergden thought, and without uttering another word, he forcibly jabbed the inquisitor in the throat sending the man to his knees gasping for a breath that was not there as he frantically clutched at his bruised neck. As the inquisitor attempted to get to his feet, Bergden's instincts again took over as he heels kicked the man's knee sending him to the ground grasping desperately at his leg in pain. The crack and pop of broken bone and torn cartilage echoed down the street. The inquisitor rolled and writhed in the icy slush cursing before Bergden delivered a knockout blow to the temple.

As Bergden hung over the broken man, a small crowd began to gather. He realized that he attracted the wrong type of attention with his stunt. He needed to get himself away from the situation and fast. He could feel the eyes of the entire square on him as he took off running down the street. The faint but closing sounds of cruiser sirens hurried his pace as he took off towards the hotel where the safe house awaited him.

Black jack cruisers screamed by without so much as a glancing eye as they sped towards the scene too busy to notice the man walking casually down the sidewalk. Keeping his head low, he eventually arrived at the entrance of the hotel. It was an older hotel in a part of the city once known for its tourism. The building's red bricks losing their original crimson hue, whitened by the vicious sun, the windows stained with years of neglect and the once great monolithic gargoyles crumbling to the street stone by stone.

"Can I help you?" the front desk clerk asked Bergden as he strode in, surprised that a guest would arrive at the height of the workday in a city where work was paramount.

"A friend of mine is staying here. Not sure of the room. Maybe you can help me?" Bergden asked. He had no idea what room the contact was staying in and whether or not they even expected his arrival, but to his surprise and relief, a note had been left behind with the clerk.

"She's left something here for you mister," the clerk said.

The clerk shuffled through her notes, then looked up at him in a moment of satisfaction. Her smile was yellowed from what Bergden imagined was years of tobacco use.

"Room 301, Mrs. Stein is expecting your arrival Mr. Lucas. I appreciate your patronage. Enjoy your stay." She handed him the extra key before going back to her work. He felt a sense of relief knowing he wasn't arriving entirely without notice.

The elevator was out and looked as though it had been for quite a while. Bergden entered the stairwell and climbed the steps to the third floor. The wooden steps creaked and groaned, amplifying the obvious age of the building itself. On the third floor, an empty maid cart sat idle in the hallway, a collection of dust gently rose as he brushed past. He continued towards the room glancing around for other guests and soon found the floor devoid of other people.

"*301,*" Bergden mumbled to himself as he approached the end of the hall. Just like the others, it was a door with a plain "301" plated to the wood, but unlike the others, the door was already open. He crept toward the opened door, peering back over his shoulder before retreating at the sudden greeting of a foul odor. Covering his nose with his sleeve, he gagged as he pushed further into the hotel suite. Bergden was all too familiar with that smell. The stench of death hung like a lowland fog as he slowly inched his way into the room.

It was a larger room, probably a suite at the height of the hotel's popularity. A couch, a radio and even a kitchenette made up the amenities. He scanned the room and upon first glance, he couldn't find the source of the pungent scent of the deceased. As he walked through the room it became clear that the smell came from the bathroom.

Thrusting open the door and flipping on the lights, half of which worked, was the terrible sight of a woman's decaying form. The corpse was hung from the shower rod and stripped. A dry pool of blood at her feet. It was a ghastly sight and made him cringe in disgust. The violent death had all the hallmarks of a Regime hit squad. Her eyes and mouth were sewn shut. The victim's hands and feet were bound in chains. The cuts running deep into the bone. Further investigation revealed the words, "A traitor died here," etched into her flesh.

Grisly and sadistic, it was meant to send a message to whoever came across her path. "She was a good person, Bergden. A vital member of the Remnant resistance in the city," a voice somberly cracked behind him.

Bergden spun around to meet this new voice. "Carl?" Bergden

asked as the man emerged from the living room.

Carl stooped and studied the body, shaking his head at the sight.

"Who was she?" Bergden asked somberly as he started to untie her. The rope had cut deep into the flesh and with each tug more meat pulled from the bone, causing him to dry heave. The stench of the fetid muscle tissue nearly overwhelmed him.

"Poor girl. No one should die like this," Bergden said, cringing as the last of the rope fell to the blood-stained tile floor.

Carl helped to get her down from the shower rod. The body slumped to the floor, falling apart from weeks of rot. Bergden covered his mouth and held his breath as the smell of her death seemed to magnify ten times as the cold, mangled corpse came to rest on the tile floor.

"Her name was Tori and she was our contact for Pemply Station. Your old friend Draven or should I say, Lt. Rocco Draven, was responsible for this slaughter. A few months back, after your disappearance, he created a hit squad with the sole purpose of sending these brutal messages into the hearts of those who would resist the Regime. He's been on a rampage since he took your position. Station Chief Aberdeen has completely lost control."

It wasn't hard for Bergden to believe that Draven, when left off the leash, would go to such extreme levels of violence.

"I'm going to call this in to the nearby sleeper cell and I'll take you to the second safe house." Carl sighed. "Plan B was always in our back pockets. We had worried her identity had been compromised but couldn't confirm it. Never easy to watch one of your comrades fall."

Bergden took a final look at the woman's body. Tears welled in his eyes at the thought of her agonizing last moments. A crippling fear had seeped into his mind that if he didn't act quickly, Alyssa could be next. The image of her mutilated corpse caused him to stop and physically shake the horrid psychological conception away.

"I'll have one of our boys pick her up. Give her a proper burial. The coal ovens don't deserve her," Carl said. referencing the massive crematories that still burned on the outskirts of the city. The smoke of burning flesh choking the sky. A stark reminder of the consequences of standing against the Regime.

Carl and Bergden took a cruiser to the next safe house just a few blocks away. The two began to reminisce about the days when Carl first joined the black jacks and how he blossomed under Bergden's tutelage. The glory days of the station were so far in the past because of Draven that most forgot what it once was. But Carl saved the most impactful revelation for the ride.

"How long have you been with the Remnants, Carl?" Bergden inquired.

Carl laughed and sighed looking down at his bloodied hands. "Since the beginning of the end. I was the first contact at Pemply Station. I was promoted to handler until they worried, I would be compromised. Then I was asked to take a more prominent role. A commander of sorts. We've been raiding Regime farms, factories and bases in the areas around Blackwell for years. They did their best to make sure that news never got to your ears. That's where the black market came in."

It was a stunning bit of information for Bergden. "When did I figure into this mess?" he asked.

"Because you were good at your job Bergden. They thought that you found me out, but I knew you would be a valuable asset to the Remnants and despite your history with the Regime, you were no longer in line with the party, no longer able to turn a blind eye from the oppression."

"When did you figure out, I would be the guy?" Bergden asked, curious about how long Carl studied him without him having the slightest of clues.

"From the moment I met you and spoke with you. You clearly did not fit the description of a typical Regime black jack thug. At first, I kept my distance thinking you were a member of Internal Investigations, but after a few arrests I realized you had something most of these jackboots don't have." Carl smirked.

"What might that be?" Bergden asked, looking into the rearview mirror. "Compassion."

The rest of the ride was quiet until the cruiser came to a stop at the corner. The streetlights flickered as they turned on illuminating the street with the sun fleeting in the distance.

"Now, we are nearly at the next safe house. Notice anything familiar?" Carl said, hinting.

Bergden peered out the window. It didn't take him long to remember the hallmarks of his old neighborhood. Only a year had passed, but much changed in his eyes but not so much he didn't know where he was. The corner cafe was boarded up, a market torn down and the park paved over, but the big oak tree still stood tall in the courtyard.

It was a sobering sight.

"What happened here?" he asked.

"After the Regime tried to capture you the neighborhood went into lockdown mode.

You were seen as a significant threat, so they turned most of what you see into a checkpoint. Bastards hung around right up until about three months ago. Harassing the locals, stealing what they could and even arresting a few people as supposed collaborators," Carl said.

Bergden stared out at the remains of an old machine gun nest sitting where the local newsstand once stood. The gun still perched, but long rusted out from exposure to the elements. "And now?"

"Station Chief Aberdeen convinced Commander Grimm himself that it was a waste of resources. The tightwad old son of bitch retreated as quickly as you could blink. Grimm does things with minimal financial backing at this point. No idea why. Rumor is he's holed up in a mansion outside of the city."

The cruiser came to a stop outside of the gate.

"Here we are. Your old brownstone complex. I hate to bring you here Bergden, but it turned into a safe house that gave us prime real estate in the Pemply District, but it will be exclusively yours. I promise the apartment is in as good of shape as you left it," Carl reassured.

It was the memories that worried him more than any changes in the apartment. Memories of his family, memories of his past and the fear that came with the future.

Carl and Bergden walked up to the brownstone complex. The sign had rusted, and the plants withered and died, but it was home. The stone stoop crumbled into disrepair, and as the pair approached the front door he sighed, choking back tears, and forced himself to turn the knob. The wind whipped wildly around him, setting the scene and sending a haunting chill into his heart. The memories he recalled were sorrowful. Alyssa and James being stripped away from his care and he, forced into hiding, flooded back into his mind. He tried to turn and run, but his body refused, and they proceeded inside and up the elevator.

"You'll shack up in your old place for the evening and meet with the first target at a diner called the *Corner Spot*. The target's name is Scarlet Marsh. She is a prison administrator at Cherry Hill. Pretty little brunette, short hair with hazel eyes. No more than thirty years old. She'll be wearing her uniform. She doesn't go straight home after work.

We've been watching her for months. I doubt her routine will change overnight."

Bergden only knew Cherry Hill from the rumors and horrible stories of the terrible sights and of the putrid conditions the other black jacks described. It was common knowledge even among the population that most who were unfortunate enough to be sentenced rarely saw the light of day again.

"I'm not going to delay this any longer Bergden. We're running out of time. The mission is to find out if Andrew Ridgeway, former general of the Coalition armies, is incarcerated there and you are to free him by any means necessary." Carl sighed and continued. "I wish I could give you a better plan on how to free him, but our contacts within Cherry Hill went silent weeks ago. I'm putting my faith in your military skills to get this done."

General Andrew Ridgeway was the hero of the Coalition until the Regime turned the tide two years into the war. Ridgeway won battle after battle much to the chagrin of Kroft until finally the Regime gained the upper hand through superior engineering. Technologically superior weaponry had turned the tide and pushed Ridgeway to the negotiation table. After the treaty was signed, a bold raid was conducted to capture Ridgeway for fear he would lead a resurgent Coalition army. If he was in Cherry Hill, Bergden doubted that the man was still alive, but Carl and the rest of the Remnants still held out hope no matter how fleeting the odds may be.

"Good luck Bergden. I'll check in with you after you speak with the target. Oh, and one more thing." Carl turned as he went to leave.

"What's that Carl?"

Carl put his hand on Bergden's shoulder.

"Do not go taking out inquisitors again. We were able to sweep this one under the rug at the expense of some dumb bastard, but I can't promise we'll be as lucky next time," Carl ordered. "Now, I've got to go. The station will be wondering where I'm at. I'm already late for my shift. I'll be in touch." And with that, Bergden was once again left alone by Carl. This time in his apartment.

The pain of the memories, both good and bad, surrounded him. He felt an aura of suffering overcome him. He collapsed to his knees and wept in the kitchen. He could smell Alyssa's perfume and he could hear the sounds of James reciting his lessons. He longed for his life to return to normal even under the yoke of tyranny. James and Alyssa could still be in his arms and they could be a family once again. He wanted to charge into the station, find Draven and gut him where he stood. Not since the war had he had such a desire to kill a man. He stormed to the door and nearly left until he saw it. A picture, a small picture, but a picture, nevertheless. It was illegal in the Regime to have a picture of anyone other than Kroft, but there it sat as he left it. A picture of James, Alyssa and himself at the beach. He picked it up and remembered why he returned to Blackwell.

For his family.

Bergden was able to find a set of his old clothes before departing. It felt good to be well dressed and out of the rags he wore in Harvick. Bergden left the apartment and headed towards the *Corner Spot*. The sun was beginning to set, and the bitter cold replaced with milder temps. A wintery moon had emerged beyond the buildings as he approached the *Corner Spot*. A half burned out marquee loomed over the entrance as he approached.

There were three big windows leading into the main dining area. There was a diner's bar in the front and more seating in the back and there sat the target. Carl had understated her beauty. She caught the eye of every man that wandered past the bar, but none tried their luck.

Until Bergden strode in and stood next to the brunette. "Mind if I take a seat?" Bergden asked confidently as he approached the bar. The woman seemed disinterested but nodded her approval. He smiled and pulled out the stool taking a menu from the rack. He casually looked over the menu all the while making passing glances at her. He watched as she reached for her drink. It was a beer, likely an ale judging from its amber color, she had worked her way through most of it as she had reached the foam at the base. It was the perfect window of opportunity.

"Can I buy the pretty lady a drink?" Bergden flirted. He could hear himself and immediately realized he sounded like any common drunkard hitting on a barmaid. Social refinement is what defined him from them and that was what swooned Alyssa.

He cleared his throat. "I'm sorry miss. That was a bit forward of me. Care if I buy you a drink?"

She eyed him intently and for a moment she hesitated before relenting.

"Of my choice?" she asked, holding the corner of her mouth in a smile. Her crimson lips, ever so enticing. Bergden swallowed hard trying to remember himself. He quietly nodded.

"Well, you are a fortunate fellow. I do appear to be out of drink." She waved the waitress over. "This gentleman, with no ulterior purpose I'm sure, would like to buy a lady a drink."

"Vodka and tonic. Pre-war vintage vodka. Oak aged tonic." She gave her order before passing a wink at Bergden.

Bergden could see Scarlet out of the corner of his eye as he fumbled through the menu listings. She went about her nightly ritual at the diner bar. A drink in hand, a voluminous Regime approved book and a smile. She was younger than Bergden and all seemed right in her world. As if none of the hardships of the Regime could touch her and that she towered over the challenges in her life. He envied her in a way.

He wondered if he envied her ignorance, a sense of delightful ambivalence of the world around her or perhaps that she overcame the morbid reality of total and abject repression. He wanted to feel the same way after all of this was said and done, but finding Andrew Ridgway was his only purpose at the moment. If he was going to be reunited with his family without the Regime constantly over their shoulder, then he needed to find out what Scarlet knew.

"I recommend the stew," she joked. "The stew is the only thing I think has any Regime-approved flavors."

Bergden smirked. He realized that he neglected nourishment since entering the city.

The overwhelming emotions of his clandestine return fueling him.

He nodded to the waitress who had overheard the conversation.

"I can't say I've ever seen you in here before," Scarlet said, turning her attention away from her book and to Bergden.

Bergden fibbed. "It's my first time in the city. Just looking for a way to create some familiar faces."

He studied her body language carefully. She moved aside her hair exposing the nape of her neck and as she did, he saw no wedding ring. A good sign of interest and a good sign that there wouldn't be any angry spouses to worry about as he turned on the charm.

"Well, you seem pleasant enough," she admitted. "Tell me, what brought you to Blackwell? I've heard a million different reasons, but not yours."

"I want to open a diner. Much like this one or perhaps this one." Bergden laughed trying to dodge the question. "What does anyone come here for? Work." The waitress brought the stew to the table. Bergden's stomach chimed in again.

"I got to say, my mother always told me that two parts of a man carried the whole thing and at least in your case, the stomach called the shots," Scarlet laughed, but the innuendo was not missed.

Bergden tried the stew in the most gentlemanly manner he could muster in spite of his ravenous hunger. The smell of peppers and sausage filled his nostrils. If he was going to get the information he needed, he was going to have to play the situation in the same he would as any single man. But first, he needed to knock off the rust.

"You're right about the stew. Can I ask your name?" Bergden asked, almost forgetting he needed to confirm the target.

"Scarlet Marsh. And who might you be?" He thought about his response.

"James Kroft. What do you do in Blackwell? That looks like a Regime uniform." Scarlet looked down at her outfit and frowned.

"I'm a prison administrator at Cherry Hill. I don't find the uniform very flattering, but a job a job."

Bergden begged to differ as he looked at her. It was a two-piece form fitting suit. A charcoal gray, two button wool military coat with the Regime wolf on the sleeve. The pants were plain black and hugged every curve. Her leather boots came up just below the knee. It was hardly an unflattering uniform on a woman like her.

"I think it projects authority while still allowing the feminine form to be its natural self," Bergden remarked.

Scarlet finished her drink. "Another?" she insisted, gesturing towards the empty glass.

Bergden nodded knowing that she was hooked. If he could put a few more drinks in Scarlet, then hopefully she would be more insightful about her position at the prison.

Scarlet continued to drink and whilst the two made small talk, Bergden plotted. He needed to know for certain that Ridgway was held in Cherry Hill Prison before he could push forward with any plans of a jail break.

"Tell me more about Cherry Hill Prison. What is a beautiful, young woman such as you doing in a place designed to house the most hardened criminals in the Regime?" Bergden asked, watching as she threw back another glass.

"Why do you want to hear about a prison?" she asked, slurring each word, the alcohol clearly having the desired effect.

"I find it fascinating that there are those out there that skirt the Regime's law and dare risk being put there. Call it a sick information fetish of mine," Bergden rebutted.

The waitress interrupted the two.

"We're closing in five," she muttered, sliding the bill over to Bergden.

Scarlet took Bergden's arm to get up from the diner counter and stumbled knocking a glass to the floor. The glass shattering at his feet, Bergden realized the woman was sloppy drunk. The nature of consumption changed from person to person. Other more adept drinkers, commonly known as alcoholics, would likely not be remitted to such a mental and physical state. She might be a Regime lackey, but he wouldn't take the moral free fall that others had before him just to obtain information. There were ways and means to do that without completely ruining this poor girl's life.

A cold, drizzle of rain floated to earth as Bergden guided Scarlet out into the night. He held his jacket over their heads to block out the weather as they made their way to Scarlet's blood colored cruiser. As they walked, her knees gave into her inebriated struggles nearly dragging him to the rain covered streets. Just when it seemed as though she was indeed worse for wear, Scarlet stopped cold in her tracks. Bergden took a step back anticipating the inebriated prison administer to vomit and without warning she lurched up, pulled him close and kissed Bergden. Instinctively, he pushed away.

"You don't...don't think I'm pretty?" Scarlet asked, stumbling through her words.

"I just have a thing about kissing in public. Call me a prude I suppose. Perhaps we should take this off the street?" Bergden said, thinking on his feet.

Scarlet took out a set of keys and scrapped the door of the

cruiser before handing them over to Bergden.

"Drive us to the prison. I'll let you see my office." She winked and smiled biting her lower lip.

Bergden turned the key and the engine grated as he started down the road towards Cherry Hill. It would be the first time he would step foot into Cherry Hill.

After a short ride, the car pulled up to the gate. A single guard stood watch and waved the vehicle through upon seeing Scarlet. She managed to compose herself as they passed.

"Don't worry Jerad we'll park in the back. It's the closest door to my office anyways," Scarlet said, leaning over Bergden and smirking eagerly at the guard.

A steady rain moved in as the pair raced to the door with Scarlett hanging off his arm. Bergden wasn't sure why she had brought him here, but he doubted he'd find a better way to locate Ridgway than in the heart of the prison. Getting away from a drunken, horny woman might be the biggest problem he faced. After a few attempts at flipping the switch, Scarlet composed herself just long enough to turn on the hallway lights. Each light slowly flickered to life as Bergden followed Scarlet down the hall. She careened from wall to wall as Bergden was led by the hand towards Scarlet's office.

Inside, Scarlet's office was not so different from his own at Pemply Station. Mounds of unfilled papers scattered across the desk, a half-eaten salad and empty mug were all the friends she needed as a Regime desk jockey. A row of filing cabinets was staged behind her with a listing of the prisoners at Cherry Hill. Bergden needed to somehow get access to those cabinets.

Scarlet sat on the corner of the desk waving her finger in a come-hither motion. A halfcocked smiled burgeoned as she motioned for Bergden to sit beside her.

"I've always wanted to make love on my desk at work," she

cooed.

She began to writhe along the top of the desk knocking over piles of papers. She crawled towards Bergden unbuttoning her blouse. Bergden began to sweat as he gazed at this beautiful woman, who was not his wife, lust after him. He took a step back and looked to the door. If he needed to escape would he be able to? The guard at the gate would be suspicious. He sighed and as he walked towards her, he asked for forgiveness under his breath. He outstretched his arms then heard a peculiar sound. He picked Scarlet's head up and realized that she had passed out. A gentle snore was all that came from her sending a wave of relief though his veins.

He searched frantically through the cabinets in the prison directory until he came across a single manila folder with the abbreviations AR on the tab. Opening it up, he saw the dossier for Andrew Ridgeway

Subject: Andrew Ridgeway

Date: Unknown

Cell: 369 (Moved Per Request)

Subject is in stable condition after being absconded by the Dealers. He has not responded well to stand interrogation techniques. Most of the guards reporting he doesn't speak, nor does he eat and if we do not find a way to get him to cooperate, he will likely perish from malnutrition. I have stated in the past that Andrew Ridgeway would require advanced medical evaluation and I appear to have been right. Even after a few days of persistent interrogation he still remains quiet. I believe a visit with Dr. Vossen should soundly cure whatever ails him. Despite his attempts to thwart my interrogation, I must admit I admire his persistence to the cause.

Cmd. Liam Grimm.

He must be in Singer Psychiatric Ward, Bergden cursed to himself. Carl had mentioned there were two targets to check. Ridgeway had been in Cherry Hill, but not for long and now resided in a place far more sinister than any prison.

He looked over at the passed-out woman and for a moment felt a pang of sorrow. He had done worse things in the name of the Regime and he was prepared now to do anything for his family.

CHAPTER TEN

Alyssa slumped down, sinking slowly into the worn, leather chair, exhausted from her day. She had been teaching at Blackwell Academy for nearly six months already, but the days felt longer. Each morning, students came eager to do their best to undermine her. She bemoaned being an instructor for the first time as her lessons felt frivolous and hollow no matter how she tried. The students continued to ignore her instruction and mocked her in bated breaths, aware that she was not part of the Regime's elite. She imagined the stories their dutiful parents told them about her wasteful life, how she was more a detriment than a boon to the Regime and that someone born outside the walls of Blackwell should nary spend time educating their children. The sounds of their back-alley scolding as her teaching prowess was constantly on trial. Finding refuge in the teacher's lounge was but a brief respite from the realities of her situation.

"Looks like schoolmistress Crane has had a wallop of a day?" a woman's voice said jokingly.

Alyssa craned her eyes upward from the couch and saw her friend Cara hovering nearby pouring her and Alyssa a cup of coffee.

"It's probably a bit stale, but you need it," Cara said, passing the saucer to Alyssa. The bitter, almost chalk-like taste of the lounge coffee swirled down her throat and into her belly immediately prompting an angry growl from her stomach. She placed the cup on the nearby table and closed her eyes hoping to put the events of the day behind her as she let the warm liquid permeated through her body resting gently on the bottoms of her feet.

"Cara, why do the students not like me?" Alyssa lamented. "I try and try to make them understand that I want only for them to learn and be productive members of society. Yet, I am treated worse than the rats that run the sewers!" Alyssa fought back tears knowing better than to let anyone in the Regime's elite schooling academy see her cry. Crying remained a sign of weakness and to be weak was tossed aside, a forgotten soul in a bitter hell.

"I just don't know what I should be doing differently." She wiped away her tears, trying to hide her face in shame.

Cara sat down next to Alyssa, pulled her head to her chest, and gently stroked her auburn curls and rubbed her back. "They just don't see you as their superior. No doubt their parents have influenced their malleable, little minds. I've seen their parents on many occasions at gatherings. Terrible folks. The whole lot of them," she said, hoping to pry Alyssa away from her foul mood.

Alyssa knew Cara could say whatever she wanted. Cara was the daughter of a Regime general and a well-known woman of promiscuity among the Regime's higher profile leaders. If anyone gave her grief, she could cause more than her share of problems for the antagonist. She received lavish gifts from her forbidden lovers and for her, working as a school mistress merely passed the time. Although they were worlds apart, Alyssa still managed to embrace her offer of friendship. Cara would offer existential advice on how to thrive in the Regime often far beyond the typical, more pedestrian insights provided by the other faculty members. Most were so entrenched in the ideology of the Regime to offer any tangible or prudent guidance that required Alyssa to raise her standing. Yet, Cara stood by her and for that Alyssa was grateful as she had little in the world to be thankful for.

"Are you going to get to see your son today?" Cara asked, with an overtly fake sense of optimism that today would be the day James would be reunited with Alyssa.

Alyssa shook her head and cupped her hands over her face hiding the fact that it had grieved her so.

"I don't know, but it has been weeks since I've seen him. The commander keeps assuring me that I'll get to be with him permanently, but I don't know. The commander and his wife are so cold and calculated with each step they take and rarely do I ever see any emotion from either of them. It is truly a challenge to determine what is fact and what is the falsehood that spills from their lips."

Cara grimaced as she learned the foulness of the lounge coffee swallowing hard before dumping the rest of the mug's contents out the window and into the courtyard. A chorus of curses and openly wished maladies rang up from the unfortunate people below. The complete disregard for their position made Alyssa laugh a little.

"Can't say I've met the good commander's wife. What is she like?" Cara asked as she leaned out the window and mocked the pedestrians below with a gentle wave.

Alyssa scoffed.

"Can I say frigid bitch without making it sound like an

understatement? When we first met, she was kind and understanding, but as time progressed, she's treated me with a less than ideal temperament. She is constantly looking me over. I feel as though I'm judged on everything that I do. She's not as bad as Dr. Vossen, but I'm not sure that's a compliment."

Cara pressed her fingers to her chin in deep thought before coyly smiling at Alyssa. "Does she think you're sleeping with the commander?" she questioned, inviting gossip from her friend.

The thought that Jocelyn saw her as a possible home wrecking adulteress certainly crossed her mind on more than one occasion, but that assumption was poorly drawn for a litany of reasons. Not the least of which was that she had rarely seen the commander since being plucked from Singer. Each day was the same as the last. Hari would pick her up from the academy, a meal would be prepared for her and she would go to her accommodations without so much as uttering a single word to the mister or misses. On occasion she'd get to see James, but mostly she just stayed to herself.

"I think she fears that I am, but I can safely say that I have not. In fact, he hasn't even suggested such a thing for which I am quite grateful." A heavy sigh escaped her. "I miss Bergden and James more and more each day Cara. What can I do to ease my fears? Perhaps if I knew that Bergden still took a breath, then perhaps I could breathe a little easier each night knowing that we would one day be reunited."

Suddenly, Cara lit up and bounded over to Alyssa.

"Come with me to the Chancellor's Victory Gala on Friday night! I think it will cheer you up. Plus, you'll get some exposure to the Regime's elite. Daddy says that even the chancellor might come and grace us with his presence."

Alyssa's face turned scornful as uneasy hate brewed within her. She had yet to personally meet the man that ruined her life, but she despised him with every breath he took.

"Meeting the chancellor is the least of my desires. He's the reason I'm in the mess as it is!" Alyssa snapped before quickly repenting. "I'm sorry, Cara. I know I should not speak ill of him. I put myself at risk each time that I do."

Cara rolled her eyes.

"Honey, do you really think Chancellor Kroft had any personal knowledge about your family's arrest? He's so far away from the reality that is Blackwell that I dare say he is scarcely in charge anymore," she scoffed. "Commander Grimm probably runs the show at this point."

Alyssa's anger became redirected towards Cara.

"Yes! That bastard runs the whole show, does he not? He has the last call and the service my husband put forth for the Regime was brushed aside without a second thought! Bergden fought for the right for the Regime to exist and was cast down as a villain."

Cara motioned for Alyssa to lower her breath pressing her finger to her rose-colored lips.

"You haven't met Kroft, have you?" Cara asked, shocked that the commander hadn't introduced the two.

Alyssa, still bitter, shook her head no vehemently.

Cara continued. "Let's just say the chancellor is not exactly at the peak of his physicality. He has Dr. Vossen working day and night trying to find mystery cures for his ailments."

Alyssa could still picture the types of "cures" she had been working on and shuddered in fear.

Cara continued "He's a shell of his former self and those mandatory radio broadcasts you hear? I've been told that he no longer really cares about them and delegated it to someone who sounds like him. He's too busy living the high life than leading."

Cara continued to amaze Alyssa with the secretive connections she seemed to maintain with the Regime's higher society. If the average person knew the dirt that she did, they would quickly find themselves in a shallow grave or on a cell floor in Cherry Hill but being the attractive daughter of a Regime general had its perks.

"The idea of a Regime gala does little to quell the pain inside, Cara. Besides, I'm not one for overly done dresses and cavorting with high society. Pretending that I give extra concern to the elite's petty bourgeois struggles and their maddened feelings towards the rest of society. I doubt more than one of them has experienced the pain that I have at any significant level."

Cara rolled her eyes.

"It couldn't have been *that* bad Alyssa. The past is called the past for a reason. You can learn from it, but don't dwell on it and you can't go back to it. If Bergden were still here he'd probably tell you the same."

A slow boil of ire rose within Alyssa. She wanted to lash out at Cara for her ignorance but realized that she would have no knowledge of the hardship being in the position that she was. Lamenting her ignorance wouldn't bring Bergden back to her or her old life. She had to play within the boundaries set and if she were to win the game she'd have to play along.

"Do not take this as condescending as I know you can't possibly fathom what I'm about to tell you and, but I feel this conversation is long overdue. You are my friend after all, and you deserve insight into who I am and why I feel the way I do towards our dear old chancellor."

Cara gently gnawed at her lower lip in anticipation of Alyssa's confessions.

"Each night and many times throughout the day, I flash back to when I was on that cold, wet floor of my cell. I can picture the fanatical intensity in the eyes of my oppressor as I lay naked and vulnerable. Enduring strike after strike and a bevy of verbal abuse each waking moment. It haunts me whether in the darkness of night or the brightest of days. But despite all of the anguish in my heart, I persevere for the love of my husband and son. That is why each waking moment, I agonize over the thought of Bergden's death or the fear of never seeing James again. It is also why I hate the Regime so."

The revelation struck Cara hard forcing her to a chair across from Alyssa gripping the arms tight in exasperation. The news that someone close to her ever found themselves in such a damnable position alarmed her to the core. Growing up surrounded by those who found themselves only seeking the benefits of the Regime's tyrannical rule numbed her or rather shielded her from the firsthand knowledge of individuals who ultimately suffered more than anyone could possibly surmise. She'd be taught her whole life that only real enemies of the state spent time in a place like Cherry Hill and being isolated in the Regime's most revered strongholds made that knowledge a nonnegotiable fact.

Cara stammered for a moment seeking a response. Her lips remained pursed until suddenly her eyes lit up once more.

"Okay, hear me out Alyssa. As I said, there are going to be some high-level people in attendance at the gala tomorrow evening. If anyone would know where your husband is, it would surely be someone there, and I can help you get your foot in the door!"

The commander and his wife showed no interest in assisting her and were recently downright hostile to her overtures to putting the pieces of her family back together.

Commander Grimm was about as elite as one could get without being the chancellor, but perhaps there would be someone there who could assist. The hard part would be convincing Commander Grimm that her being at the gala was a good idea. It was almost not worth the effort.

But she'd feel awful for not trying.

"I will go to the gala with you," Alyssa said, exhaling a breath she didn't even notice was being held. "The commander will get the ultimate say in the matter though. I just hope he's as understanding as you are Cara. He strikes me as a man with little patience for such things."

Cara yipped in glee and hugged Alyssa.

Alyssa just prayed that the commander was as forthright about her aspirations as Cara was. As Alyssa held Cara in her arms she looked up at the clock.

Five o'clock. Alyssa thought.

"I've got to go! I'm going to be late and then I'll never get to go to the gala" Alyssa said as she picked up her handbag and raced from the room and out of the building to an awaiting cruiser.

Alyssa arrived at the commander's estate a little past seven in the evening which meant she was nearly an hour later than usual. She stared at the enormous abode as the car wound down the lengthy driveway until turning sharply in the governor's turnaround. She thanked the driver and made her way up the stairs only to be greeted by a grim-faced Hari.

"Mrs. Crane, the mister and misses are anxiously awaiting your arrival. They almost certainly did not anticipate tardiness. I just wanted to be the first to warn you that they may be in a sourer mood than normal," Hari said, quickly ushering Alyssa up the stairs and into the house.

She barely had a moment to take in the situation as Hari thrust her towards the dinner table. The commander and his wife sat in silence at each end of the long wooden table. Small intricate runes were carved into the wood and a thin sheet of glasses placed on top. It was a different table than the one she had become familiar with.

"I suppose it is too obvious to say you are long past when you are supposed to be home," Jocelyn chided as soon as Alyssa's backside touched the chair. "You are to alert us when you are going to be late. If I hadn't made it clear before then it is to be crystal clear now. Understood?"

Alyssa nodded in silence as Hari served her the first course. It was a simple salad and a bowl of clam chowder. She was starving but resisted the urge to dive in until the commander and his wife began to eat.

"Now my dear," Commander Grimm said to Jocelyn, bringing his wine glass to his lips. "She was unaware as I do not recall making such demands in the past. Going forward though, I'm sure she'll be extra cognizant of the time."

Jocelyn shot him a piercing glance. She clearly was not a woman who appreciated being undermined, but she managed to shrug away any stress before returning her focus to Alyssa who had caved and began to eat her salad.

"Dare I ask why you were later than usual?" Jocelyn questioned in a snarky tone.

Alyssa looked over to the commander and back to Jocelyn a mouth full of lettuce spilling out from between her lips as she couldn't resist digging in any longer.

"I was at the school speaking with Cara about the students," she answered, trying her best to work up towards asking the couple for permission to attend the gala.

"The students?" Jocelyn questioned, sharing a passing glance with the commander affirming her suspicions before returning her gaze back to Alyssa who by now had taken another rather substantial bite from her salad. Her mouth once more overflowing with food.

Alyssa used the food as a distraction while she formulated a proper way to address the matter of the gala with the commander and his wife. The pair likely knew what she did, but as long as she shoveled food away, she bought time to build her courage, but suddenly something unexpected occurred. Something she could not have anticipated.

"Alyssa, while you are eating, Jocelyn and I wanted to ask you something," the commander murmured, trying to hide his disgust for Alyssa's onset of less than tasteful table manners.

"Yes, Alyssa. Liam and I are cordially inviting you to the Regime's annual victory gala tomorrow night. It is an event of extravagance and indulgence, but more so a way for you to meet those who run the government and get face time with them," Jocelyn said with a strange sense of excitement.

"Are you serious?" Alyssa said, her eyebrows raised in astonishment. Never for a second did she think that getting to the gala would've been possible.

Commander Grimm rose from his chair and took a position next to Alyssa at the foot of the table placing a hand on hers as an added measure of comfort as she processed the information.

"We believe it is the best way for you to become familiar with those who are running things in the Regime and to become better acquainted with the chancellor and those whom he chooses to surround himself with," he added.

Alyssa smiled agreeably and began to think of reuniting with her family before Jocelyn brought her back to reality.

"Alyssa? Are you still with us?" Jocelyn looked over at the commander and smirked. "Is the gala the dreams of a forgotten little girl Alyssa? I feel as though I could bet with measured confidence that there were no such balls in Oyster Bay. This gala is more important than perhaps you realize."

Oyster Bay had not been the pinnacle of culture as Jocelyn had insinuated, however, the elite was no less self-consumed. The gala was essential and probably quite the contrary to Jocelyn's opinion of Alyssa's knowledge on the matter. If at the gala Alyssa were to find someone who could help her get back to her family, she would do so without consulting the commander and no matter the cost. She had tired of his prodding around when it came to her affairs. Soon would be the time to end it.

"Oyster Bay had its fair share of inwardly focused elites that I can assure you, but no I have never made a personal appearance at a gala before. As you can imagine, I'm overtaken with joy knowing that I can finally take part in the festivities for once," Alyssa said as she began to rise from her seat, excusing herself from the rest of the conversation.

Commander Grimm tilted his head and appeared to study Alyssa as she smiled. He could tell the smile wasn't just due to the invitation, but Alyssa dare not invite suspicion into her ulterior motives behind her excitement.

He was too shrewd of a man not to notice.

"Care to tell us how you already knew about the gala before our invitation was presented?" Commander Grimm asked, not taking his eyes off of his chowder.

The idea that she would have to confess the circumstances around her friendship with Cara and the reasoning for her excitement sat poorly with her. The commander likely knew of Cara and the type of *lady* she presented to the public. He was after a well-connected individual and as Cara noted in their earlier exchange, she was indeed intimately familiar with the Regime's most powerful men. Alyssa became apprehensive about sharing any sort of information with him as she trusted him less and less each day. Until she received affirmation that her son's prohibition from contact ended, she'd preserve her cautious slant towards her hosts lest she give up any of her true motivations.

Alyssa sat quietly thinking of a proper way to address the commander's question. "Tell me how you know Cara Rutari?" Commander Grimm had preempted her excuse with an exact strike on his line of questioning.

Alyssa felt her throat fall into her stomach. "She's a fellow school mistress at the academy. She teaches a class in arithmetic to the same age group and we share coffee between lessons. Nothing else," Alyssa answered flatly, hoping her version of the truth would end the line of questioning.

Commander Grimm rubbed his eyes and shared a moment of eye contact with Jocelyn who by this point was just finishing off her last glass of wine. In their mutual silence the two seemed to agree that the conversation was to continue without Jocelyn in attendance.

Alyssa sat frozen with fear until a panicked knock rapped on the door outside of the dining hall. Hari burst into the dining hall and fell to the floor gasping for breath. Commander Grimm raced over to help the old servant to his feet.

Hari struggled to get up from the floor trying desperately to regain his composure. "I'm sorry to interrupt your dinner, but I have urgent news concerning our household," Hari strained as Commander Grimm helped him to one of the dining chairs.

Jocelyn gave Hari a glass of water and knelt down next to him. "What is it Hari? What is so urgent?" she asked.

Hari downed the glass of water and took a deep breath, finally regaining his wits. "Chancellor Kroft is on his way here at this precise moment!" Hari cried out. "The checkpoint down the backroads reported his personal escort only a few minutes away!"

Commander Grimm glanced over at Jocelyn and then over at Alyssa, who remained at the table trying to her best to keep calm. Jocelyn leaned in and whispered something in Commander Grimm's ear before returning her gaze to Alyssa. Alyssa sat confused at what the chancellor's arrival meant for her, but clearly, she was either not wanted or was to be the guest of the world's most powerful man.

"I can go to my quarters if you'd like. I will remain out of the way and not utter a single word. I promise. I doubt very much he'd want to see me anyways," Alyssa offered to Grimm.

Much to her surprise, Grimm refused.

"That won't be necessary Mrs. Crane. You'll join Jocelyn and me with the chancellor and his entourage. He'd likely get suspicious if word of your presence reached the table considering the continued efforts to locate your husband." Grimm rubbed his chin intently. "The only thing that I ask is you remain quiet and if the chancellor addresses you keep your answers short and vague. Understood?"

Alyssa nodded her agreement. She had heard Bergden speak of the chancellor dozens of times. Bergden's respect for the chancellor died off shortly after the end of the war when he abandoned those who fought and died for him. He'd often speak of the tremendous economic revival that was promised and how the people came to follow him blindly even though the signs of tyranny were there right from the get-go. The gradual surrendering of personal liberties, the appointment of suspect government officials and the embargo of goods from countries that were supposedly defeated. Alyssa herself never saw it coming and had been worse off because of it save for the fact she found Bergden.

After a few moments Jocelyn and the commander took their leave and exited the room to greet the chancellor. She sat in silence as the time passed until Alyssa overheard the sounds of the chancellor and his entourage entering the mansion. The chancellor's voice bellowed from the atrium as Alyssa sat nervously waiting to meet him.

"Hari, has the chancellor visited us before? He has not been present for the entirety of my incarceration here. Why visit at such an hour?" Alyssa asked the old man as he rushed to clear the table to get drinks prepared.

"He comes at all hours because he can. He has intruded even as you've slept safely in your bed. He's a cunning man that likes to check up on his trusted advisors. Even one as important as Liam. After all this mansion used to be his hunting house before he gave it to the commander as a prize for his efforts during the war. He knows it quite well I'm afraid."

Alyssa was shocked to hear that the chancellor had visited right under her nose. "And the nature of such a visit when he calls upon the commander?"

Hari finished pouring the wine and leaned in close taking Alyssa's ear. "Acquiescence of those whose power stretches beyond his own."

The cryptic meaning behind his words puzzled Alyssa, but before she could continue the door into the dining hall flung open and in walked the chancellor flanked by Grimm and Jocelyn. His entourage trailed close behind taking measures to secure the room.

The chancellor wore a simple uniform, much different from the portraits that were scattered around the Regime, consisting of a woolen, hunter green petticoat and gray trousers with a single medal pinned across his heart. His hair was a wintry mix of whites and grays completely slicked back. He sported a well-trimmed mustache that extended out past the corners of his lips with a slight curl. Alyssa startled as his guards began to search her person.

"Who is this lovely young lady, Liam?" The chancellor greedily eyed Alyssa, causing her to shift uncomfortably in her chair.

Alyssa and Grimm locked eyes for a moment before turning to the chancellor.

"This is Alyssa Crane. She'll be joining us for evening drinks and conversation. We've been hosting her for a few days before she returns to Blackwell."

The chancellor smiled before taking a seat across from Alyssa, and without waiting another moment, he took the chalice to his lips, the wine disappearing with each swill until only the empty glass showed.

"Delightful year I'm sure!" he cooed, waving Hari over to refill his glass. A deep red almost violet liquid collided with the glass as Hari poured from the bottle.

"It's prewar, sir," Grimm answered. "I keep a stash in the cellar for special occasions. Tough to find grapes that give such a pleasant aroma when swished about the crystal. The vineyards were destroyed during the fire bombings, of course."

The chancellor drank again this time leaving wine in the glass. The red liquid swirled about his glass like a whirlpool of blood as he set the glass down hard on the table. It was at this moment, this precise moment, that Alyssa realized that the chancellor had arrived suffering from a fairly severe case of consumption.

"I see you've come to us in a manner of great cheer, dear chancellor," Jocelyn mocked, but the chancellor took no notice of her tone and continued to smile as he took another drink from his glass.

Kroft gave a crooked, drunken grin before beginning his dive into the happenings around the Regime. Alyssa noticed that the chancellor finishes each glass of wine with great haste and faster than the galls before, and she was not the only one to notice, but Grimm and Jocelyn let their guest continue on without interruption. Kroft told them of the laws he was planning to enact. Increasing his powers, eliminated the already useless parliament, but most alarming was the expansion of the military. Since the end of the war, Kroft had decreased the strength of his military in favor of increasing the enforcement officers and inquisitor ranks.

"Well chancellor, I must say you've come to us in quite a good humor," Jocelyn said with a sigh, finally able to speak after Kroft droned on for what felt like forever.

"Considering the news, I've received today I should say it is a cause for celebration!" he responded, a resplendent grin mocking Jocelyn.

Jocelyn looked over at Grimm who stared back at her emotionless clearly unaware of what news the chancellor spoke of.

"What is the great news Albrecht? My agents haven't told me

of anything out of the ordinary occurring." He sipped from his glass and without looking up expressed his displeasure without being included. "As your top military commander any gap in intelligence could be fatal."

The chancellor leaned in on the table as if to whisper to the group spilling a portion of his wine in the process.

"We've located the headquarters of the terrorist organization known as the Remnants. Everyone last one of them!" He leaned back and smiled, cocking his eyebrows in a show of bravado. His smug expression appeared to set a fire in Grimm.

"A washed-out factory town called Harvick just a few hours from here. Our agents have informed me it is quite the little rat's nest, and now I intend on playing the role of the exterminator," Grimm gushed. "A plague of rats is best removed by fire; don't you agree Alyssa?"

Alyssa became startled as Grimm's knee jostled the table. The room was silent, but she could see the news alarmed both Grimm and Jocelyn and in spite of their efforts to hide their emotions, both grimaced and swallowed hard doing little to hide their reactions from the drunken Kroft.

Something about the news troubled them, but Alyssa knew not why. All she could do was sit and wait.

"How did you come upon that knowledge?" Grimm questioned. Kroft shrugged his shoulders and frowned.

"Dr. Vossen was able to extract the information from a few invalids at Singer Psychiatric Ward and our intelligence agents confirmed their statements. That woman is quite the wonder of interrogation. A master of the medical profession."

It was at this point that something changed within Jocelyn. Alyssa could sense it. The chancellor had struck a nerve with the commander's wife and now was the time that those innermost desires, the emotions tucked away for a moment such as this would emerge.

Jocelyn pursed her lips and slid the glass away from her chair. Alyssa's eyes darted between Grimm and Jocelyn. The tension thinning to the point of breaking.

"Dr. Vossen? A medical professional? Surely you jest. She's hardly one I would link to the medical profession. It's an insult to the good doctors we do have. Although I dare say those are few and far between now," Jocelyn snapped as she rose from her chair.

Kroft furrowed his brow then suddenly smiled as if pushing away his anger.

"Of course, a medical doctor! Those men, those terrorists, clearly suffered from a level of delusion making them unfit for the society I created. What healthy person could do the things they've done? Deranged and dangerous they could not stay in the great society we've built."

Not satisfied, Jocelyn pressed the chancellor.

"Because they chose a different path, they are suffering from a malady of the mind?"

The chancellor shook his head and looked to Grimm for supporting words.

"My dear, maybe another topic is in order? Chancellor Kroft is our guest after all," Grimm said, trying to intervene.

She held out her hand silencing him and continued to berate the chancellor.

"Tell me, what treatment did these sick men receive?" She glanced over to Alyssa fully aware that she experienced Dr. Vossen's sadistic version of medical science. "Forced hypothermia? Starvation? I imagine those patients fared quite well under her "

Kroft slammed his fist down on the table, spilling the wine from their glasses.

"How dare you question Dr. Vossen's work? Those anarchists were just a few of the dangerous individuals that are intent on collapsing my utopia. I don't question the methods that Dr. Vossen uses to cure her patients. I've given her unlimited authority to try any and all medical treatments to solve the terrorist crisis. It will only be a matter of time until our people are rid of this disease and we can live in peace."

The chancellor rose from his chair and straightened his jacket.

"I must admit I'm a bit alarmed regarding your concern for Dr. Vossen. She provides substantial greater value to the Regime than you ever have Jocelyn. Commander Grimm, I assume you only keep her around for her satisfactory wifely duties?"

Commander Grimm shot up from his seat, finally showing any emotion. "Chancellor Kroft you go too far. I think you've had too much wine and I must insist you take your leave. You are of course welcome to use our guest room. I can have Mrs. Crane moved."

Alyssa could not believe the disregard Grimm had for his own wife. If ever a man should speak to her like that in front of Bergden, they would surely be regretting those words many times over. Grimm could only insist Kroft take his leave and offered her room. She glanced to Jocelyn. An intense anger burned from her eyes as she stared daggers at the drunken chancellor who had clearly worn out his welcome a long time ago.

"Perhaps you are right Liam, but I will not do so in this household. I could not possibly deprive Mrs. Crane of her quarters and to remain her might prove dangerous to my personal well-being," Kroft said as he lifted his nose at Jocelyn.

Suddenly, Kroft walked towards Alyssa taking hold of her hand. She found herself blushing of embarrassment as the chancellor brought her hand to his lips. As he placed a gentle kiss upon her hand, Alyssa looked past him at the astonished Grimm and Jocelyn.

"I do want to apologize to you my dear. It is a matter of circumstance that you've seen this side of me, but I hope we can meet again. Perhaps next time I can see if your voice matches your beauty."

Without uttering a single word Alyssa nodded and watched as the chancellor departed with acknowledging Grimm or Jocelyn and when the doors were shut, and with the cruiser lights gone only the three remained.

"That man infuriates me, Liam, and tonight was the worst it's been. His mental health is in decline and he's an alcoholic. I can't wait—" Jocelyn realized that Alyssa still stood in the doorway. "At least he's taken a liking to you, Alyssa. You must be very proud. You don't have to say a word and the most powerful man in the world is kissing your hand," Jocelyn said, scoffing.

Jocelyn bid Liam and Alyssa good night, leaving Alyssa with Grimm.

"I hope I didn't offend her in some way," Alyssa said.

Liam placed his hands on her shoulders in a gesture of comfort. "She'll be alright. There is far more to her than you know and her reasons for disliking the chancellor are her own."

Alyssa turned to head towards her quarters.

"Alyssa," Grimm continued, "soon you'll understand why Jocelyn does the things she does and says the things she says. I wish I could discuss it more, but there is much to be done. For now, try and get some sleep."

Alyssa walked into her quarters, closed the door and let her mind race.

CHAPTER ELEVEN

Bergden leaned on the balcony railing, most of the balusters were either broken or missing from neglect. He kicked a piece of broken concrete and watched it fall to the courtyard. He took a moment and listened to the sounds rising from the street below. The rush of a trolley and the clang of its metal wheels as they clung precariously, yet without fail, to the track. The hustle and bustle of people heading to work trying desperately to ensure they were not late. For the first time in a while he felt a moment of peace, of moment solidarity within himself. He knew that eventually he would have to resume his pursuit to mend his broken life, but at this moment the universe slowed, and he basked in the glow of the morning sun.

As the sounds of the morning rush died down, Bergden returned to the kitchen and poured himself another cup of coffee and awaited the arrival of Carl who by now was headed towards Bergden's apartment to debrief him on the next steps of the operation.

Bergden stood awaiting orders from a man he thought he had known. The discovery that Carl wasn't who he claimed to be was surprising. Bergden had been so immersed in the comings and goings of his own life that he never took notice. For him, the purpose of joining the cause was ultimately self-serving in nature. He hadn't a need to know the true Carl Sonderberg. All that concerned Bergden was that his family was somewhere in the city of Blackwell waiting for him. Alyssa and James were too strong to not find a way to survive. He just needed to do his part and the Cranes could return to a healthy life.

If the Remnants would let him have a normal life after this was over.

Suddenly, he heard a knock on the door. The morning calm and relaxation were ripped away and quickly replaced with overwhelming, unnerving anxiety.

What if it wasn't Carl? He asked himself as he pulled out his pistol.

What if Draven found out he returned to Blackwell and with the enemy no less?

Bergden wasn't ready to take that chance. He cocked the hammer back and crept closer to the door. Step by agonizing step, foot over foot he approached doing his best to remain silent.

Breathing deep, doing everything he could to stay calm. If it was Carl, he'd want to make sure he didn't accidentally blow his head off.

He leaned against the door ever so gently and pressed his ear against the wood to listen.

For a brief moment he heard nothing aside from the hushed shuffle of boots. He thought it might be just another tenant and debated about returning the balcony, but a muffled voice called out from the other side.

"Bergden?" He heard Carl's voice from beyond the oak door. "Mind answering the door. This place is under constant surveillance. I would rather like to avoid drawing any additional attention to myself by being seen outside your door."

Bergden edged open the door and the waiting Carl rushed past him and into the apartment shutting the door hastily behind him. "Your old neighborhood isn't what it used to be, Bergden. The Regime turned this place upside down after you escaped looking for any sign of you or your family. Leadership kept a close eye on the place for weeks until you were pronounced dead."

He had to admit the thought of his own death had crept into his mind from time to time.

Not for lack of wanting to live. Life had thrown him his fair share of challenges, not including his current predicament, and he had managed to get through each for better or for worse; the 'worse' of course never completely ruining his existence, which, all things considered, he now stood toe to toe with.

In spite of the unavoidable contemplations of his death, Bergden was happy to be home even for just a few hours.

Carl checked the back rooms, shuttered the windows and flicked on the kitchen light the faint amber light casting a glow. Pulling up a chair, Carl lit a cigarette and lipped a long, exasperated drag. Bergden couldn't recall Carl being a smoker, then again, he found out he barely knew him. The man whom he used to know was a strait-laced moral center in a world without one. When society crumbled, he would show Bergden that not all the people the Regime saw as enemies were truly bad. It was that mentality that guided Bergden down a different path.

"Getting into Singer is going to take some finessing. You won't be able to just get the mark drunk and waltz in. Singer is a fortress.

The Regime puts its most hardened criminals and mental patients behind those concrete walls. Takes a reason to get into the prison."

"And how do I escape?"

Carl rubbed his cigarette into an ashtray and went to pull another from the pack disappointed when he came up empty. "Getting into Singer is hard, getting out might be impossible."

"Impossible? Why the hell would you send me in there knowing I won't come back from?"

"Impossible isn't the right word. A better way to put it might be, a monumental task the likes of which you've never faced."

"You'll forgive me if that does little to assuage my fears," Bergden retorted.

"Duly noted. Now, let's get down to business. "Carl urged.

He laid out a picture of a man with a scarred, worn complexion. Bergden didn't recognize him but noticed the two deep scars. Each a reminder of a man who fought in the war. One above his left eye and the other running the length of his chin. He was a middle-aged man probably only a few years older than Bergden, but significantly greater in stature. Faint blond hair, a boxed chin and a nose that looks as though it suffered its fair share of breaks. It was a mug that only a mother could love.

"That's one ugly son of a bitch Carl. Looks like he's been through the ringer a time or two," Bergden said.

Carl laughed and picked up the picture tucking it away.

"Ivan Komarov is the plant. Part of the forced immigration after the war ended in the east, he joined an early version of the black jacks before being unceremoniously discharged after assaulting an inquisitor. He made a habit of punching out Regime underlings when he got a chance. You can see why he's on our side."

"So, can I ask how he fits into the plan? I don't imagine he's going to help us just stroll right into Singer," Bergden remarked.

"In a manner of speaking? Yes. He will be able to help you go right through the front door. After discharge he escaped and met up with some resistance Singers eventually falling onto my lap. We were able to change his dossier and get him a position as a guard at a psychiatric institute. Since Cherry Hill came up empty, our last, best hope is that Andrew Ridgeway is alive somewhere in that hellhole."

Bergden heard little about the maximum-security mental hospital. A term he used loosely. Patients, another term used loosely, were housed by the nature of their illness. The worst housed in the basement under the bedside care of Dr. Ana Vossen. Cherry Hill often served its purpose to house hardy Regime enemies, but to make someone disappear, that's what Singer was designed to do. Make a person nonexistent.

"Ivan is eager to play a role in the coming revolution Bergden. He's been hidden under the Regime's noses for years operating in plain sight," Carl said, grinning.

Revolution? Bergden thought to himself. The Regime's stranglehold on society needed more than an ideological tour de force from a handful of saboteurs to knock off the long gathering rust of revolution. The average man, woman and child needed to feel the flame inside and push aside their fears. A revolution required the people to storm out into the streets and use the power of overwhelming numbers. Bloody days would follow, but a price must be paid for freedom. That fire did not burn in the streets, it did not burn in the hearts and minds. It did not burn at all that he could see. The flame of freedom snuffed out by Chancellor Kroft himself.

"Revolution is a strong term Carl. I too want to do what I can, but you can't possibly believe this will spark a total uprising? We both walked those streets. We've seen the complacency of the people. We helped drive them to it. I'm not proud to admit that, but I can recognize that it's a serious obstacle to full political upheaval!"

Carl rubbed his chin frustrated by Bergden's words.

"Bergden, releasing Ridgeway will trigger events beyond your understanding.

We've been planning huge changes for the people in Blackwell. You are a major catalyst to those changes, but not the only one. We need all gears turning at once if we hope to succeed. I need to know you're all in with us Bergden."

Bergden remained silent.

"I know it isn't easy to accept, but let me remind you that this is the only way you'll get to see your family again. You can't do it alone and I can't help you if you don't help me.

Understood?"

The tone hinted at a threatening proposition should Bergden refuse, but for him it meant a chance to be reunited with his family and if that came at the expense of a tyrannical dictatorship well that was just a bonus if they succeeded. If the coup failed, but he still saved his wife and son, then it didn't matter. His family was his world.

"Don't worry Carl I'm your guy, but I just want some sort of reassurance that Alyssa and James are still alive and well. Can you give me that? I need to know that what I'm fighting for is still worth fighting for. "

Carl took a moment nodding his head.

"They are alive and quite well. Alyssa is in the care of a high-level member of a Regime double agent and James should be in his custody soon. I trust that is enough?"

Bergden grimaced. "For now. What's the plan?"

Carl pulled a manila envelope from his rucksack. Taking a knife, he unsealed the envelope and scanned the document before taking the half-lit cigarette and burning the small piece of paper and any evidence that the Remnants were operating in the area.

"Ivan is going to meet you near the corner of Grant and

Pederick at 8pm. Don't worry, it's far enough outside of Pemply Station's jurisdiction you won't be recognized. Ivan will place you under arrest so you can pass unscathed into Singer Prison. From there, it'll be up to Ivan to get you to the deepest levels of the prison and hopefully to Ridgeway."

Bergden sat dumbfounded, less than impressed Carl's plan.

"You're telling me the plan is to place me in cuffs, march me inside and just see how it goes? That's crazy. Singer isn't a place to just wing it, Carl."

Carl winked. "Crazy enough to work?"

Bergden vehemently shook his head to the negative.

"No, not crazy enough to work. Just plain crazy." He sighed. "But I'm crazy enough that if it gets me back to my wife and son then so be it. I hope you have a backup plan to get my ass out of there should it go south. Another thing, why can't Ivan just bust out Ridgeway himself?"

Carl sat silent for a moment rolling his neck in exasperation resulting in an audible crack.

"Let's just say Ivan is at the hospital for an alternative purpose for the resistance.

He can get you to the inmate look up and you'll have to take it from there. I'm sorry Bergden, but that's all I'm at liberty to discuss for now. Here are your new background documents."

Bergden studied them closely. A new name, another back story and a set of medical records that could lock him away forever.

"These will get you into the hospital no problem. You'll be a perfect candidate for Dr. Vossen."

Bergden scanned the rap sheet.

"A serial rapist as a result of a mental disorder? You have me being convicted of raping a female inquisitor. Not everyone with mental health issues does such things," he complained.

Carl shook his head.

"Kroft believes that anyone who would do what you did to an inquisitor would have to be mentally ill."

Bergden let out a frustrated sigh. "Eight o'clock."

The evening came faster than Bergden had hoped. Leaving his home for what he feared would be the last time, he pulled his brim low and walked out into the familiar thoroughfare. The sun was down and the streetlights on. People were still coming and going as usual, but a bitter, unseasonably cold autumn chilled the air. Bergden walked at a good pace trying not to grab the attention of the passing black jacks. He took a final look at his complex. A gut-wrenching sorrowful reminder of his life coursed through his veins.

For the first time in years, he cried.

Walking inconspicuously became nerve-wracking by the time Bergden reached the corner of Grant and Pederick. A single, softly illuminated streetlamp was all that let Bergden know that he had arrived. A nearby pub had just let out the afternoon work crowd and began preparations for the evening shift. He thought of the picture Carl had showed him and scanned the faces as they exited onto the sidewalk.

Where is that son of a bitch? Bergden asked himself, peering down the darkened streets.

Suddenly, a towering imposing figure, the last patron of the group, emerged from the closing pub. It was Ivan, he couldn't forget a face like that.

"Ivan?" Bergden asked, trying to keep his own face hidden.

The big man only nodded silent and gestured towards the alley behind the pub, which by now was devoid of any light whatsoever.

"You'll get in the cruiser and do as I say, Mr. Crane. Do not say a word. Is that understood? He said in a heavy eastern accent. "At any point we might be followed or watched. We abort."

Abort? Bergden thought about the word. Carl hadn't mentioned anything about the what ifs of such a plan, only the outcome. Bergden kicked himself for not pressing for more details. If forced to abort, they were likely already dead.

Bergden kept his focus on Ivan as he held out his wrists and watched as the cuffs were placed around them. The sound of the lock turning into place on the cuffs meant he was fully committed. A nervous tingle raced down his spine culminating at the tips of his toes before getting into the back of the cruiser.

He had never felt more fearful of a failed mission than he did now. What if the Regime ambushed their cruiser? Ivan had the only key to the cuffs. It would be like serving up lambs to the slaughter.

The cruiser started towards Singer and all was quiet until suddenly Bergden saw a series of lights flashing down the main avenue towards what appeared to be a checkpoint. His heart skipped a beat as the car approached the gate. Bergden swallowed hard expecting the worst, but without warning Ivan tossed a black bag over his head.

His vision now gone; he was completely reliant on the enigmatic Ivan. "Remember, do not say a word. We're approaching a checkpoint. I'll do the talking; you just sit there and be quiet," Ivan commanded.

Bergden listened as the window wound down. The flashing lights were the only things he could see through the darkened sack. His heart raced and his pulse inevitably jumped. He muttered silent prayers to himself.

"Where are you taking this man?" the officer asked. Bergden thought he recognized the voice. Bergden could hear Ivan turn in his seat, likely giving a passing glance to his "prisoner."

"Singer. Mentally ill rapist and general no good son of a bitch. I can show you his papers, officer...?" His voice trailed off as he waited for the black jack's response.

"Lieutenant Draven, and no. Just make sure he gets his in

Singer. Find the biggest, thickest baton and make it hurt. Dr. Vossen likes her patients *tenderized.*"

Bergden heard Lt. Draven tap on the glass.

"You'll be all better soon, you crazy asshole," he laughed.

Bergden contained his fury the best he could. Mere feet away from the man who ruined his life. His blood boiled hearing they promoted Draven to his former position. Here he was outside of Pemply Station jurisdiction, probably plotting his next hostile takeover and Bergden had to refrain from stomping his face into his boot heel. His wrists pressing against the cuffs, Bergden did everything in his power to keep composed.

"Don't worry lieutenant. I'll make sure he gets what's coming to him."

The big man turned and jabbed Bergden in the gut. Bergden winced under the bag and gritted his teeth. Ivan played his part perfectly.

"Move along," Bergden heard Draven order.

The cruiser started back up and as it headed down the avenue, Ivan removed the bag briefly to check on Bergden before slipping it back over his eyes.

"Sorry, but just a precaution. Never know who you'll run into at those things. One of those bastards could've recognized you. Saw a few Pemply Station badges there. Black jacks are stretching their jurisdiction further and further past their home stations without check.

Kroft uses them more than the military these days. "Bergden stayed silent festering internally about how close he came to Draven. He would get his revenge, but for now he needed to stay focused. Revenge would be a moot point if it came at the cost of never seeing Alyssa and James again. Staying alive and getting through Carl's mission remained a top priority. Even if it was only a means to an end.

Thankfully, the rest of the ride went uninterrupted and the cruiser came to a stop outside of the outer gate. Ivan turned and removed the bag from Bergden's head.

Bergden blinked his eyes as he adjusted to the spotlights beaming down from the towering palisades of Singer Hospital, the medical institution looking more like a castle than a hospital.

"We're here now, friend. I'll have to turn in your papers and no bag, but we can use the late-night entrance. Less security."

Ivan wore a big smile on his face as he helped Bergden from the back of the cruiser. It was a moment he had been waiting for, and to help kick start the revolution must have brought him great pride. Bergden often forgot how bad the people in the east had it during the wartime years; and the post war was arguably worse. Forced immigration followed by debilitating labor to build Kroft's cities. Back breaking was a mild way to put it so to see Ivan finding joy in the mission was surprisingly warming.

"New patient? What is here for?" the guard at the back gate asked without even looking, instead, focusing on the daily newspaper. The headline read: *Kroft Named Person of the Year.*

Ivan shrugged his shoulders at Bergden, the lax security apparently a surprise to the big easterner.

"Last name Jarek. Mental illness leading to sedition and crimes of assault and rape. I guess he cornered and raped a female inquisitor. He's been identified as a perfect candidate for Dr. Vossen. According to the admission documents, he's to be housed on level seven. He'll never see the sunlight again in his miserable life."

The guard looked up at Bergden and sneered.

"Get that piece of human garbage down to the lower levels and lose the key. I doubt anyone will care if we forgot he existed. I'm sure the good doctor will have a devil of a time breaking this one. Find that cure," the guard said, laughing.

Ivan nodded, and as the door switch buzzed, he pushed Bergden through. On the other side, Bergden got his first glimpse of the inner workings of Singer Psychiatric Hospital and he had underestimated how depressing a hospital in the Regime could genuinely be. Chain gangs were forced to march in a circle in the waning hours of the day for no purpose other than to facilitate exhaustion and study the effects. Men and women were hanging upside down on the walls, most clearly succumbing to the rushing blood to the brain. There was a glass encased cell that appeared to be intentionally overcrowded. Men and women with clipboards noting the patient's reaction while ignoring their pleas for help.

My God I had no idea the extent of the atrocities, Bergden thought as he was rushed along by Ivan. He couldn't recall if any of the people he captured were sent here. He had always tried to be lenient with those he felt were truly innocent. The thought of someone like that ending up here gave him goosebumps.

"We'll take the elevator down to the seventh floor. I'll give you more instruction when we get closer to the bottom."

The elevator arrived painfully slow. The sounds of agony filled his mind as his imagination began to run wild. The bottom floor housed the absolute worst the Regime had to offer. He could only imagine the physical and psychological horrors that awaited him.

The descent maddened Bergden more than the waiting, and a fear of failure crept towards his psyche. Mission failure meant he would never escape. Branding as a rapist of Regime personnel likely reinforced, he would die down here without seeing the light again. He refocused on the task at hand and held his breath as the lift chains churned and wound their way up as the elevator car worked its way towards the lower levels.

"Just about there," Ivan muttered. "Typically, only one guard manages the floor at a time. I just pray the doctor isn't in. Rumor is that she only takes orders from the highest authorities in the

Regime. Anyone else though and it's a waste of resources when the only way out is this elevator."

Bergden glared daggers at Ivan. "Only way out? How the hell am I supposed to escape with Ridgeway?"

Ivan let out a laugh and clapped Bergden's back with a massive hand. "The only way out that they know of. There is an old drainage tube that I uncovered in the back of a rarely used storage room down here. On my lunches I'd sneak down there and see where it went. Comes out right onto the riverbank. Hope you can swim."

He laughed again and clapped Bergden's back causing him to shudder. "I kid. There will be a boat there. Take that and head towards Harvick. I'll make sure Carl knows you've made it out. I'll instruct him to wait for you and Mr. Ridgeway down the river a way. It is supposed to storm tonight so that'll help cover your tracks. Now give me your wrists."

The cuffs fell to the elevator floor with a bang that permeated through the silence. Bergden rubbed his wrists relieved to finally have the metal away from his skin.

"Good luck!" Ivan cheerfully said as he shoved Bergden into the hallway, waving as the elevator doors closed and the car began to ascend.

He was alone once again and Bergden felt a sense of dread in his bones. The hallway lights flickered on and off. Shadowy figures danced in the darkness. Somewhere a pipe leaked. The constant drip of water echoed as it struck the pavement. Perhaps the most haunting part was the silence from the cells. He'd be in enough jails and prisons to know that prisoners rarely kept quiet even during lights out. These so-called patients made no sounds.

The walk through the seventh floor became maddening. The cacophony of sounds followed each footstep and as he approached the first cell, he took another breath before beginning his search. He pulled the crumpled picture of Ridgeway from his back pocket. He'd forgotten he had it and thankfully he wasn't searched upon entry. Carrying a picture of the most prominent member of the Remnants probably wouldn't go over well.

Dodged a bullet there. Bergden realized putting the picture back in his pocket.

Suddenly, from down the hall, he heard a door open and observed a bright light illuminate the poorly lit corridor. Bergden hastily searched for a place to hide as a figure emerged, but his feet felt like cement. He stood frozen in his tracks. The feminine figure turned and walked away from his position, and as it did, he grasped the fact that he froze rather than react. He got lucky again.

He passed by each cell, staring into the darkness looking for Ridgeway. None of the patients responded to his presence. Most content to lie on the cold damp floor not acknowledging him in any way. The sign of the patients in many of the cells was the putrid stench of human waste that hung heavy in the air. It was hard to discern if the scent of death had been mixed in.

The search for Ridgeway continued as he crept further down the hall until suddenly a hand materialized from a darkened cell. Bergden bent down and looked in trying to see who had grabbed him. Finally, a man pulled himself closer to the cell door.

"You must leave! If the mistress comes back here, she will surely break you!" His wretched hands gripped Bergden's shirt tight pulling him closer to the bars. "She does not like unwelcome visitors. She is extra hard on them! You must go!"

Pulling himself away, Bergden took a closer look at the man. It appeared that he'd likely outdone his years on earth. Long, ragged brown hair with a matching beard hid his face. Yellowed teeth and cracked lips curled into a smile as Bergden looked at the face of a man suffering from madness.

A few cells down another voice called out to Bergden. This one was much more coherent.

"You're here for me, aren't you?" His voice cracked and he yanked on Bergden's shirt. "Please God tell me you are here for me. Another moment in this vile place and I'll crack like the rest of them."

Holding up the photograph the features were unmistakable even if they were buried beneath a host of ratty hair. He had found Andrew Ridgeway the last surviving general of the Coalition.

"General we need to get you out of here. Are you able to stand?" The man pushed himself up to his feet and fell into the iron door before steading his gait. "She's got the only keys to the individual cells. If you challenge her, you must not yield. She's the devil's mistress if you ask me. You'll need to kill her and get the keys."

Bergden gave a silent nod and headed to the office. As he passed further into the prison, he realized that the cells were only the beginning. Large, brightly lit rooms lined the opposite wall, an observation window carved neatly into each. Approaching one of the windows, he watched as the woman he saw earlier whipped a bound man on the floor, blood rushing towards the center drain. The walls were soundproof, and he found himself staring as the woman berated him before appearing to question her prisoner. He was witnessing a brutal interrogation, not a medical procedure.

"God damn," Bergden whispered, but as he did, the woman reacted. He looked at his hands and panicked. His left wrist had been pressing an intercom button when he had leaned against the wall. He watched as she tried to make out who was on the other side of the observation window. He ducked down and crawled towards her office in an effort to cut her off if she decided to sound the alarm. He crept in and locked the door behind him.

"Does Dr. Vossen have a guest in the midst? Surely you know visiting hours are long past!" she said as her heels hit the pavement, a sharp point at the end of each. "I must admit hide and seek is not my favorite game. Why don't you come out and see if we can examine you for signs of malady?"

Bergden didn't move, instead keeping his head low and below the glass. The clank of each heel as it hit the walkway was getting closer and closer. He knew he was going to have to act fast. The office was devoid of anything remotely resembling a weapon. He grabbed a letter opener and waited to ambush her.

The sounds of her footsteps stopped. The only sound he heard was that of his own breath. Then suddenly, the window smashed behind him sending Bergden scrambling to the other side of the office. He turned to meet his attacker. She grinned wildly as she reached down to unlock the door. He hurled the letter opener, striking her hand and pinning it against the wall, but she didn't cry out in pain. Instead she pulled the blade from her hand and tossed it. She crashed through the door and tackled Bergden.

"Now that's a game I like to play!" she cooed as she jammed her blade-tipped heels his thighs. Bergden cried out in agony as he pushed her off and limped to the door, trying to regain his composure. She gave chase and kicked him in the back, the blade sinking into the flesh. He fell into the wall and turned to face his attacker. She wore a maniacal grin as she rose up to strike him again, but this time he dodged and struck her side. She doubled over in pain but continued her pursuit.

"I love this. Now, this is an innovative treatment!" She raced over trying to outmaneuver him, but again he dodged and struck her sides. The skills he learned in the Regime military were coming back to him and it couldn't have been soon enough.

She kept coming at him, blades flying. He dodged and ducked as much as he could, but the longer this continued the more time he wasted getting Ridgeway out of the Singer Prison and greater the risk of her sounding the alarm.

He decided to try a different tactic.

A more direct approach, he thought as he dodged another blow before rushing her, tackling her to the floor with a thud.

"That's more like it," Ana proclaimed as she dug her heels in tight, but as she did, he took a grip on her throat. He felt the blades inching further into his sides, but he refused to loosen his grip as his warm blood poured down his sides. He stared down at her, her eyes widening, but so was the smile. It was like she enjoyed her fate, but after a few moments the smile faded as the realization of her own demise settled in.

She removed the blades from his side and struggled against his weight. He pushed through the pain and felt her windpipe crush beneath his grip. She began to frantically kick and thrash about, but it was too late. Bergden tumbled off of her as her final breaths escaped. He had bled out from the wounds. He gathered his waning strength and he crawled back to the office to get the keys. They were hung neatly above the former mistress's desk lamp. He forced himself to his feet and wrestled for the keys. He stumbled back out into the hallway and dragged his weakening body to Ridgeway's cell.

"Got the keys," Bergden said as he fumbled with the lock, his vision fading from the blood loss.

He opened the door and Ridgeway rushed out to hug him. He stepped back; his hands covered in blood. "We need to get you out of here," Ridgeway said as he started to help Bergden to the elevator. Bergden pushed himself away pointing to the other end of the hall.

"Down there. Closet. Ivan said the closet," Bergden said, nearly collapsing.

Ridgeway picked up Bergden and the two men trudged towards the opposite end of the hall. The other prisoners soon realized what had happened and pleaded for respite. Bergden could hardly respond and watched as Ridgeway gave another prisoner the key.

"Wait till we're out then open the doors. Then strike like the four horsemen. Make them pay for their crimes," he commanded.

The man nodded and gave a chest to head salute. "Yes, general. Coalition now! Coalition forever!"

"They'll provide a distraction while we escape. Hopefully, they can take a few of the bastards out in the process.

Bergden mumbled a reply as he continued to lose his strength until they got to the end of the hall. A nondescript closet greeted them.

"Here?" Ridgeway asked, trying to hold up the struggling Bergden. Bergden could only nod his affirmation and fell to his knees.

"Come on mate, we've only got a little further. Is this where we're going?"

Bergden pointed to the open tube at the back of the room. By now Bergden wasn't even sure if he was nodding or just going into shock. He tried to help himself as Ridgeway pushed him into the tube and followed quickly behind, the sounds of the cells opening the background with the whoops of the escaping prisoners.

Bergden crashed down to the rain-soaked ground and saw the boat that Ivan had mentioned.

"I guess this is our ride out of here. I'll help you but try to stay with me. Things are going to get a bit bumpy," Ridgeway said.

But it was too late and as he was lifted into the boat, the night sky went completely black.

A few hours later Bergden awoke in the back of a car. He tried to lift himself to check his surroundings, but his arms felt like rubber.

"Good to see you awake," a voice exclaimed. "Thought we'd lost you back there."

Bergden shielded his eyes from the morning sun. He looked up and saw Ridgeway hovering over him, bandage in hand. Ridgeway continued, "Carl managed to stop the bleeding thank goodness, but you'll be weak for a while." Ridgeway held out his hand. "I wanted to thank you for rescuing me."

Bergden pushed himself up and gripped Ridgeway's hand weakly and turned to see Carl driving the car. A pang of nausea forced him to lay back down.

"You guys shook the bees' nest with that stunt you pulled," Carl bellowed.

Bergden pulled himself to a sitting position. "What happened?"

Without a single word, Carl threw a newspaper into the back seat.

Bergden picked up the paper and read the headline, *Hospital Riot an Inside Job?*

"Riot? Did someone see us escape?"

Ridgeway laughed. "No, mate. I let the animals out of their cages. Led to a riot. I'm hoping they find their way to Harvick. I wanted to get my people out before Carl's contact does his job. You gave me the window by killing that bitch, Ana. Witch damn near had me broken, but seeing you overcome her snapped me back to reality. Lots of broken souls in that prison."

Bergden nodded, still weak from the blood loss. He struggled to speak. "Where are we headed?"

Carl turned around and smiled. "Back to Harvick. There's work to be done."

CHAPTER TWELVE

The clouds came and went without purpose, without reason. They took no particular path as each passed in front of Alyssa's window. She had become accustomed to trying to see the world through them. She imagined the skyscrapers of Blackwell, the gentle rolling hills of her parent's farm and even the figurines James kept on his shelf with each cloud that silently crept past. She'd become bored with her life at the commander's mansion and the constant back and forth with Jocelyn was a tedious exercise in power control. Alyssa had gotten more adept at combating Jocelyn's often condescending approach with her personal resolve. It had become all about perception. Her time with Dr. Vossen was a topic of dinner conversation with the chancellor, but for her it had fortified her personal strength. She had resigned herself to doing the worst in order to achieve the best outcome. For Alyssa, that outcome was the reunification of her family. Not just James, not just Bergden, but all of them together living in peace.

I would do anything. She thought about what those words meant as another cluster of clouds rolled past. In her life she had accepted a level of risk that allowed her to be steady, to be happy, enough. When she chanced upon the ad for a roommate when she came to Blackwell, she was delighted. When she first fell in love with Bergden, she was happy.

When James came screaming into the world, she was happy. Years had passed and she was happy, but the moment the world came crashing down she did not act. She ran and accepted help from all others and she was not happy. She had been content to live the past year of her life in a bedroom with only intermittent visits with James, her son living in fear that he'd never get to see his parents again.

For this she could not stand, and she decided to act.

Taking a final look at the clouds, she turned and crept into the hallway. Commander Grimm was to be away giving a sermon on the merits of Regime reeducation, but Alyssa had not heard from Jocelyn since the day before yesterday. She was strangely aloof from her husband, and for a moment this angered Alyssa. Alyssa had resigned herself to doing anything to get her family back and Jocelyn could care less about hers. Even if the commander was a stoic and cold man, he was still the man she chose to marry.

Alyssa only made it to the staircase before she heard a voice. "Mrs. Crane?"

It was Hari. She had totally forgotten about Hari. The thought of running came to her mind before realizing that even if she could outrun the older Hari, he'd be obligated to report her to Grimm.

"Oh. Hari. I'm sorry I just wanted to go and get something from the kitchen. I have a terrible thirst," Alyssa lied.

Hari saw right through it. "You've been here a year and today is the day you've decided to service yourself? All you have to do is ring the bell. You know that." He narrowed his gaze. "What is it you are truly doing, Mrs. Crane? None of the masters are in the house."

Alyssa looked at Hari and quickly grasped the situation. Hari had dropped the subtlest of hints.

Or so she hoped.

"Fine, I'll be honest with you, Hari, since you've been nothing but good to me." She sighed. "I'm going to go get James. I'm going to flee to the countryside. I'm going to find Bergden and we are going to take back our lives. We'll live in the Coalition. I don't care if they are destitute from the war. It beats living under the heel of everyone who does not but seeks control."

Hari looked around trying to see if any of the other servants were watching or nearby before returning his attention back to Alyssa.

"The keys to the black cruiser are under the driver's mat. It's the car Liam keeps ready in case he needs to take off in a hurry."

Alyssa leapt over and hugged Hari catching him by surprise. "You have no idea what this means to me!"

Hari gestured for Alyssa to calm down.

"The main road to Blackwell will take you through a checkpoint, but Liam follows a back road through the reserve and enters near the Skids. It's dangerous there, but you'll avoid detection. Can't say whether or not those black jacks would recognize you. I can't very well say its worth, but you'd better get going."

Alyssa smiled and pecked Hari's check with a gentle kiss.

"I don't know when the masters will be back, but I don't suspect until nightfall. Be mindful of that," Hari warned, but Alyssa was already on her way to the garage.

The garage held ten cars. Most appeared as though they'd never even seen a road.

Only one car faced a door, a black Regime cruiser.

Great, she thought, but it was her only option as the keys to the rest were nowhere to be found. She used a pulley to lift the garage door and took a seat in the cruiser. It was like nothing else she'd ever been in. Soft, black leather bucket seats, darkened windows and even a handheld radio. She'd driven before, but never a car this nice. She just hoped to keep in one piece as she sped from the garage.

Taking Hari's advice, she took the back way into the city without event. Arriving in the Skids in the middle of the day. Thankfully, the streets weren't too busy, but that didn't keep her from running a few stop signs until she came out onto the city's main thoroughfare, Victory Boulevard. The road would take her the whole way to Regime Headquarters.

She took the first left out of the Skids and realized that she was close to Cara's apartment. She decided to pay her only friend a visit.

Alyssa pounded on the door and after a few moments she could hear Cara scramble to the door cracking it open a hair.

"Alyssa? What the hell are you doing here?" Cara asked.

"I was in the neighborhood and I figured I'd stop in on our off day. If there is such a thing in the Regime," Alyssa said.

Alyssa tried to get a peek at what was past Cara and saw movement. "Are you not alone? I thought you lived alone?" Alyssa asked.

Cara looked back and pushed out into the hallway wearing only a towel.

"I have a friend over. He's not staying I promise. I wouldn't break the Regime rules like that. Lord knows what that would do for me," Cara said with a wink.

Alyssa thought of Marcus and Sia. She remembered what they endured to live the way they did and ultimately what happened to her once dear friends.

"Just be careful Cara," Alyssa warned. Although she barely had room to judge. She was after all using a stolen car to blindly look for her son.

"He's a black jack lieutenant. He's not going to say anything," Cara said with a devious grin. "Besides, he tells me that he's due for a promotion to station chief any day now. I've been with higher ranking men, but let's just say he plays the game much better." Alyssa rolled her eyes.

"What's this lieutenant's name?"

Cara played coy then caved. "Rocco. He's stationed over in Pemply. He comes to Craven once and awhile and looks me up. I'm sure he's just using me to get my contacts, but I promise he works for it," Cara said, winking.

The name was familiar to Alyssa, but she couldn't place her finger on it. He was a black jack with Bergden for sure, but still how he fit into the situation was misplaced.

Suddenly she remembered.

"I've got to go, Cara. I'm sorry to bother you. Just pretend I wasn't here okay. I'll see you at the academy."

Without another word, Alyssa turned and ran for the stairwell forgoing the elevator. If Rocco saw her and recognized her then not even Grimm would be able to save her. She'd spend her days in Singer and face Dr. Vossen once again. This time though she wasn't sure if she'd see the light of day or even live through the night. Worst of all she'd never get to see James or Bergden again.

She rushed out into the street and saw an inquisitor loitering near the cruiser. The female inquisitor taking down the plate numbers before trying to peer through the darkened windows. Alyssa looked up and took careful note of the streets at the intersection.

Victory Boulevard and Minske Avenue, she thought. *Easy enough.*

Taking in her surroundings, she noticed a statue of Kroft holding a book. There many statues of the chancellor dotted throughout Blackwell, but rarely did he have a book. That would be her landmark if she got lost. She decided to sneak away from the scene and return for the car later. The academy would only be a few blocks away, and if James was anywhere, it would be there.

The streets began to buzz with the after-work crowd. The first shift of workers pouring into the streets. She praised her luck as she soon realized that the academy should be empty save for the reeducation wing. If the kids were kept there, then she'd be able to waltz right in and use her credentials to save James then she could start anew.

She kept her brown low and her eyes on a constant shift looking for any signs of trouble. Heightened to the sensitivity of her situation, she needed to keep a low profile at least until she arrived at the academy. From there she would just have to approach the facility confidently. As if she belonged. It was rare to have a schoolmistress working after hours, but she doubted the Regime would punish anyone for working longer hours and for free.

"Doesn't look like anyone is home," Alyssa said to herself as she approached the outer gate. The academy's security was nominal. The building itself was four stories, her classroom was on the third floor and the reeducation barracks on the fourth. The Regime cared little for children outside of their place as future supporters, citizens, and soldiers. Terror attacks on schools were unheard of probably due to the negative publicity that would follow. She knew little of their cause outside of what Bergden had told her. The reality was that the schoolchildren were in more danger from the Regime than any resistance attack.

A single, unarmed guard stood at the gate. She recognized him as one of the regulars that rotated throughout the academy.

"Schoolmistress Crane. What can I help you with this fine day?

I think you of all people would know that classes are out for the weekend. You shouldn't take for granted the few moments of leisure afforded to us," the guard said. He was a younger man, almost too young to carry the gun at his hip, but Alyssa decided that her feminine charms might come in handy.

She gave a flirtatious smile and placed her hand softly on his shoulder.

"I left a few things at my desk that I need for the remainder of the weekend. It'll only be a few moments," she said, smiling again.

The guard shrugged his shoulders. "I suppose there isn't a reason you can't. Just try not to take too long. If the Headmistress would stop by, we'd both be in deep trouble."

Alyssa hadn't thought about Headmistress Longmire and the possibility of her presence at the academy. *Surely, even a woman as frigid as Gretchen Longmire had better things to do?* she thought to herself as she thanked the guard and proceeded into the school.

The halls were empty save for the occasional maintenance worker, and for that she was thankful. She hadn't been to the reeducation children's barracks, but she knew the way.

When she wasn't behind the desk or writing on the chalkboard, she was contemplating how to get James out of there. It dominated her thoughts, her daydreams and with each waking moment James spent in the Regime's custody, the greater the chances he would forget who he was and what he could be.

As she approached the glass door that led to the barracks, she froze. She thought of what she had done to get to this point. Things she wouldn't typically have done, she did and without a second guess. She was proud of herself.

She couldn't wait to tell Bergden of her newfound freedom. She checked the handle and swore under her breath as it wouldn't move. She pressed her hands against the glass to fight the glare and saw two children race past the door, then another group of children followed by another three. Then she saw James race past. Instinctively she called to him and pounded on the glass. James and another boy had stopped in the hallway.

"Mrs. Crane?" a familiar voice said behind her. The icy trill of the woman's tone sent a shiver down her spine. "Mrs. Crane, I can't believe my eyes. What exactly are you doing here?"

Alyssa turned to face Headmistress Longmire.

Turns out, she doesn't have anything better to do. Alyssa thought as she put on her best smile.

"Headmistress. Yes, I was picking up some items from my desk. Nothing more." Longmire grinned the widest grin Alyssa had ever seen. Alyssa instinctively took a step back from Longmire subconsciously distancing from her steely visage.

"Strange that you should find yourself near the children's barracks. The very same barracks that house your son whom you complain has been away from you for too long." She steadied her gaze and stepped closer to Alyssa. "I know you speak with Cara about your personal trifles. You cannot deny that. Do you know what I think?"

Alyssa instinctively bowed her head in submission, but she felt different. The normal submissive Alyssa could not take hold for that's not how she truly felt. Shaking off her impotence, she regained her composure and fought off what usually was second nature to yield to her societal superiors.

Her perception of her own reality had changed. That perception changed the moment she left the mansion. She was grasping on to the shreds of what remained of her independence clawing it back from the edge of oblivion. An independence she never knew she lost.

Longmire's voice jarred her from her private revelations.

"Mrs. Crane I am speaking to you and if you know what's good for you, you'll answer me!"

Alyssa stood in silence then darted her eyes back up to meet the gaze of the now angry Longmire. "No Gretchen, but please do indulge me. I'm always interested to hear your thoughts on matters that do not necessarily concern you. I've taken a great deal of pride in my ability to zone in and out of our conversations, taking care to rejoin it when it most conveniences you. "

Her tone caught Longmire utterly off guard, leaving the headmistress in a daze. It was one of those rare moments that a person who is used to abusing their power, was left speechless. Alyssa watched as Longmire swallowed hard and braced for the inevitable dressing down.

"I will not stand for this insubordination! You do not get to speak to me that way, ever!"

Alyssa rolled her eyes forcing a gasp from Longmire.

"Go do whatever it is you need to do." Alyssa pushed past the Headmistress and back to the barracks door. "I'm getting my son out of this hellhole and there is nothing you can do to stop me."

Longmire stormed away without uttering another threat leaving Alyssa alone. Alyssa tried the door again and swore under her breath as it refused to budge, but her mood lightened as James raced around the corner, turned and smiled.

"James!" Alyssa cried out in glee as James sped to the door.

"Mom! What are you doing here? Never mind, it doesn't matter. We were given the evening to have fun. It's like something we never get to do and we—"

Alyssa cut him off.

"James, listen to me. Does the door open from your end? Give a pull and see if it moves."

James nodded emphatically before trying to pull the door from the inside. He grimaced and sank to the floor as the door still would not move. Not a single inch. "I can't open it, Mom. What should I do?" James asked.

Alyssa studied the room behind James and noticed a small alcove with a few sets of keys hanging a series of small hooks. "Grab those keys and try them in the lock. You have to hurray James, mommy doesn't have much time." Alyssa looked over her shoulder. The faint sounds of footsteps echoed from the hall. Longmire's for sure, but as she listened harder, there were several others with her.

James frantically tried each key into the keyhole and turned. Alyssa could feel the pressure of Longmire approaching, and she urged James to try key after key until finally she heard a click.

"Got it!" James called out. "What do you want me to do?"

Alyssa turned and saw Longmire, flanked by a squad of black jacks rushing down the hallway towards her and James. James stood impatiently, shaking his hands waiting for his mom to tell him what to do.

Alyssa sighed. She couldn't risk James because of her newfound bravado. She would have to wait...for now. "Run back and play James. Mommy will see you in class on Monday, okay?"

James looked past his mother and saw the group of people running down the hall. "Are you in trouble?" James asked.

Alyssa saw Longmire's reflection in the glass. Her time had at last run out. "No. Mommy will be just fine," Alyssa said, not knowing if she was lying or simply hoping that she wasn't.

James frowned and turned away. She wanted to smash through the glass, wrap him up and never let go, but Longmire's commands forced her to change her plan.

"Mrs. Crane stay right where you are! You are under arrest," Longmire ordered.

Alyssa smiled one more time at James who had returned to playing with his friends. Now she had to focus on getting herself out of a predicament.

Longmire and the black jacks were nearly on her when she

turned.

And ran.

She sprinted for the stairwell and burst through the door. Foot over foot she hurried down the steps making gains on the now pursuing black jacks. She could hear the four men bark out orders. As their boots pounded the pavement she started to hurdle over the railing before pushing through a door and onto the second floor. The hallway was clear to the other end. She would use the far end stairwell and get down to the street.

That was of course until more black jacks showed up. "Mrs. Crane. You are only punishing yourself by running," Longmire chided.

She turned into a vacant classroom and looked out a window and down at the playground. She stepped out of the window and took a deep breath.

"Wait!" Longmire yelled as she stormed into the room, reaching in vain at Alyssa as she fell to the ground below.

Alyssa hit the ground and a sharp pain shot up her leg. She winced as she pushed herself to her feet and turned back to the school. Longmire was hanging halfway out the window cursing Alyssa.

"There will be no Commander Grimm to save you this time," Longmire barked.

Alyssa gestured an insult to Longmire before limping off into the streets. Knowing that the black jacks would be close behind she needed to get back to the car and back to the mansion. Rounding the corner the sounds of sirens filled the air. Word had gotten out. She was a fugitive.

She followed the path she took to the academy and kept a step ahead of the sirens. Pushing through the pain, she didn't bother to try and blend in as she entered the crowded streets. She needed to get to the cruiser, but the next shift of workers left out, filling the sidewalks. She pushed her way through the crowds dodging inquisitors who no doubt took suspicion to her haste.

"You there, stop!" a woman's voice called out. Alyssa paid no heed and pushed into a grocer and rushed through the isles to the back of the building. Ignoring the grievances from the store owner, she plowed through the back door and into the alley. She could see the cruiser only a block away. She parked and the inquisitor from earlier was nowhere in sight.

"Get back here, Crane!" Longmire's voice boomed as a cruiser whizzed down the alley.

All this because I wanted to see my son? Alyssa thought to herself as she made the final sprint to the black cruiser.

Her hands shook violently as she thumbed for the key. The sirens were getting closer.

She began to sweat until finally the door opened and she threw herself into the driver's seat. Pushing the pedal to the floor, the cruiser sped off, tearing down the street and towards the way she had arrived. Looking into the rearview mirror she saw as two black jack cruisers were in hot pursuit. The roads wound through the woods as she raced towards the mansion. The black jack cruisers coming alongside her ramming the sides of her vehicle. She struggled to maintain her steering until the sounds of gunfire rang in her ears.

Were they shooting at me? Alyssa thought to herself. She had never been shot at in her entire life. Bergden had told stories about the feeling of the wind of a bullet that just missed.

As another round smashed through the back window, she suddenly knew what he meant. There was a moment of terror as she believed all who had never been shot out felt, but much to her surprise, that quickly subsided, replaced with an almost faint rush of adrenaline. Another bang, and another until the car veered wildly to her left. She fought against the cruiser until the vehicle ran into the hillside stopping her in her tracks. The black jack cruisers took up a perimeter around her now disabled vehicle.

"Enough! Get out of the damn car and put your hands above your head!" one of the black jacks ordered. Alyssa looked out at the guns trained on her, then reached into the glove compartment. Without taking her eyes off the black jacks, she felt around the compartment.

Her hands came to rest on the cold steel barrel of a pistol. Slowly, she eased the gun out and rested it on her lap. She closed her eyes trying to weigh her options before realizing that what she contemplated was nothing short of suicide.

Taking a deep breath, she shoved the gun back into the car and stepped out of the cruiser her hands held high.

"Turn and place your hands behind your back. No sudden movements, or we will fire," the officer said.

Alyssa put her hands behind her back and fell to her knees. She wanted to cry, and she wanted to wail in agony, but she couldn't. There were no tears. There were no cries of anguish. She kneeled stoically waiting to be cuffed.

Alyssa watched as another car emerged from around the bend partially hidden by a cluster of pines. Both she and the black jacks turned their attention to the new car coming, but as it came to a stop, Alyssa knew precisely who had arrived.

She grimaced at the sight of Commander Grimm's cruiser.

Hari hurried out from the driver's side and jogged around the trunk of the vehicle to the rear passenger door. Opening the door, Hari took a step back allowing the commander and his wife to exit the car.

"That's enough," Grimm said as he motioned for the black jacks to lower their weapons.

Yet, each maintained their persistent aim on Alyssa angering Grimm.

"You heard what your commander said! Lower the damn guns or there will be hell to pay. Do it!" Jocelyn barked. She took an aggressive step towards the black jack nearest to her and grabbed him by his coat. "Are you deaf?"

Suddenly there was a stare down between the black jack and Jocelyn. A silent struggle of egos and the unspoken acknowledgement of duty. The black jack was chasing down a perpetrator and to Grimm, despite his authority over him, he was impeding an arrest.

"What is the meaning of this?" Greta Longmire said as she exited the back of the black jack cruiser. "Liam, this woman is under arrest, and you are obstructing Regime affairs!"

Liam pushed aside and strode confidently to the Headmistress, who was only now realizing the tone she had used with the commander of the Regime Enforcement Officers in front of the entirety of the Regime. Before she could beg forgiveness, he was towering over her.

"I am Regime affairs, Greta. You are in charge of a school and the education of the people of the Regime. I am in charge of their safety. I am in charge of whom they arrest, and I make the ultimate decisions when it comes to how they conduct themselves." Grimm ceased and walked up to each black jack staring briefly into their eyes. Alyssa could see the fear in their eyes as they realized their mistake.

"Each and every one of you people down your weapons, get in your vehicles and go back to your stations. Turn in your badges. You are now on unpaid leave as of this moment. Is that clear?"

There was no hesitation this time as the collective sounds of guns hitting the pavement filled the awkward stillness that hung in the air.

"Greta, you will stay with me for the moment. The rest of you get out of my sight!" Grimm commanded.

The black jacks packed their cruisers and sped off in the direction of Blackwell. "Can I ask what this young lady did to warrant a high-speed chase through a population center, causing one of my personal vehicles to be utterly destroyed and a small platoon's worth of guns to be drawn?"

Greta looked over at Alyssa, who stood motionless still holding the commander's pistol.

"She had a gun. You can see right now; she had a gun!" Greta said, panicking.

Liam turned and looked at the gun in Alyssa's hand. He nodded, and Alyssa dropped it to the pavement.

"So that's how this got started? Forgive me, but I find that her possessing that firearm is only a result of the initial cause of these events. Now, I'll ask one more time Greta, and you'll do well to be honest with me. What happened to cause all this?"

Greta stammered before taking a deep breath to regain her composure. Alyssa deviously smiled at the Headmistress. She knew that no matter what was said, Alyssa would no longer be at the academy, so why not revel in watching Greta Longmire twist in the wind.

"Insubordination. She was attempting to free her son from the academy's reeducation barracks. When prompted for an explanation, she told me that it was none of my business, and she proceeded to speak ill towards me. Certainly, that is grounds for arrest and prosecution."

Liam Grimm stood motionless for a moment before turning to Alyssa who stood bloodied and battered from the accident.

"Get in the cruiser with Hari and Jocelyn. We will speak about this later. As for you, Greta, if I ever catch wind that you are using black jacks as your personal gestapo again, I will make sure you are relieved of your post one way or another, clear?"

Greta shot a challenging smirk.

"You don't have the authority to remove me from my post." Grimm leaned in to whisper in the Headmistresses' ear. "One way or another."

Longmire could only nod in agreement as she turned to get into a cruiser only to realize they had all departed.

"How am I supposed to get home?" Longmire asked the commander.

"You can walk, can't you?" Grimm replied without turning back.

Alyssa watched the entire scene unfold from the back of the cruiser's window before snapping back to the front as Grimm approached the opposing passenger door.

"Take us home, Hari, and put up the privacy window," Grimm ordered.

A small, tinted window crept up from the headrest, separating Grimm and Alyssa from the rest of the cabin.

"I suppose you are going to kick me out of your home, make me quit at the academy, or put me back in Singer," Alyssa asked, her voice sounding defiant. "None of these things will come to pass. You will, of course, have to deal with Greta Longmire on your own at the academy, but I do not believe she will be much of a problem going forward," Grimm reassured her.

Alyssa sat confused. She had broken every rule he had put into place when he first rescued her from Singer and Dr. Vossen. She had spent almost a year of her life bemoaning the fact that she could not see her son or know the whereabouts of her husband for fear she'd be kicked to the curb only to find out that once she mustered the courage to go out on her own that there would be no consequence? Something wasn't adding up.

"I violated your trust and broke your boundaries. Yet, I will not face retribution?" Alyssa croaked.

"When you first arrived at my home, I told you that you were not a prisoner," Grimm reminded her. "That you could come and go as you pleased, but only asked that you stay confined to particular areas of the manor when on the property."

Alyssa scoffed.

"I was resigned to the first floor for nearly three months. The doors were locked.

How is that not a prisoner?" she bellowed.

Liam Grimm shook his head.

"The only thing you were a prisoner to was your mental astuteness of the situation you found yourself in. You listened and obeyed because that is who you were when you arrived," Grimm reasoned. "The thought of my authority within the Regime frightened you and drove that mentality. But as I said you could've come and gone, but you never figured out how. You never thought to put your preconceived notions behind you and do what it is you thought was best for you."

Alyssa thought about her first days at the manor. Not once had she even considered simply asking to go.

"Why keep James from me?" she questioned. "If I was so free, why could I not just simply be reunited with my son and husband?"

"James was taken to a reeducation center, and that is not within my power to abscond him from that facility," Grimm admitted. "I command the black jacks. Authority over the academies belongs to the woman you chose to anger. James will be fine but seeing him will be that much harder."

Alyssa became angry with herself, but as with before, it subsided. She had done what she wanted to do once and could do it again.

"Why be deceitful? Why not tell me I could do as I wished and when I wished it?" she asked. "You told me when dinner was, you told me to dress in fancy clothes, and you gave me specific instructions every step of the way. Why lie?"

Grimm grinned.

"Choosing to listen to my direction was a matter of your own doing, nothing more. You could've ignored me or wore rags, but you listened to me out of fear. Whose fault is that? You are what, twenty-eight, twenty-nine, thirty?"

"Thirty," Alyssa answered bluntly.

"An adult both legally and naturally. Truth be told, I would've thought it would've taken you another year to do what you did today," Grimm conceded.

"You were expecting this?" Alyssa demanded. "Why do this to me? Why...why...?" Alyssa nearly broke down, but her strength pushed her tears away.

"I knew at some point that your desire to see your family whole again would prevail over your submissive instincts and mold you into a healthier, more mentally fit individual. I saw it as you writhed around on the floor in Singer drowning out the humiliations bestowed upon you by Dr. Vossen. The potential to be superior and more resilient than you ever were."

The privacy glass suddenly began to descend, and Jocelyn's face appeared. "We are almost to the manor, Liam."

Alyssa sat shocked by the sudden revelation that the past year of her life had been somehow at the behest of Grimm and that some ulterior purpose lay in the shadows. She had more questions than answers now, and the world seemed a much darker place. Her suffering, her agony of her lost family part of a greater whole that she has yet and may not, to understand.

CHAPTER THIRTEEN

The sun warmed Bergden's face. The blue sky and snow-white clouds hung softly above, embracing the ebb and flow of the summer breeze. The grass waved, allowing him to drift further and further into tranquility. The day became night and the stars glowed brightly, illuminating the landscape around him. In the background, he could hear the voices of James and Alyssa becoming louder and more joyful. He sat up from his grassy knoll and looked around trying to locate them. His eyes darting through the lush landscape.

"I'm here Alyssa! I'm here James!" he cried out into the night, frantically searching for his loved ones.

The stars darkened and the sky blackened. As he ran through the grass, it quickly died around him. His dream had become a nightmare. Trees fell barren, and dark creatures flung themselves from the shadows at Bergden as he ran. He did not know where he was running, but there he saw them.

Alyssa and James standing beneath Kroft who had taken form as a titan.

His family called out to him, "He'll crush us!"

"No!" Bergden screamed as he leapt across the world with hand outstretched. He was nearly there until...

"Bergden? Wake up man. I know you're still recovering, but we've got to meet up at the tavern."

Andre stirred him from his nightmare. He grinned ear to ear as he helped Bergden to his feet. The bleeding had long stopped, but the wounds from Singer Hospital ached at every step. He realized he was back in the dingy apartment in Harvick. The salmon-pink curtains, that even he knew were out of style, had gone missing from his last stay. The old fridge finally gave out and smoked. Despite the deplorable state of his apartment, it was better than being in a cell. Of course, just as he settled back in to rest, the Remnants called upon him once more.

"Coffee?" Bergden asked, wincing and forced himself up from the cot and walked towards the bathroom which now was missing a door.

Andre walked over to the kitchen counter, the wood worn from years of neglect and started to brew a pot. A surprisingly familiar and pleasant waft of fresh coffee grounds filled his senses as he brushed his teeth. He filled his lungs with the aroma and smiled softly. It was a moment of normalcy, he wanted more of those, but with his family at his side.

Walking out into the living room he saw Andre topping off a small, porcelain mug. "Can I ask what happened to my apartment? Go away a few days and look at it now. Who steals curtains?" Bergden asked, gesturing to the windows.

Andre laughed.

"It isn't exactly your apartment so when you're not here, pretty much any old person can waltz in here and use the place. Probably a couple of junkies hawked whatever they could. Those people get pretty jacked up. The drugs out here aren't watered down like they are in the cities. I guess you might say they have the good stuff."

Bergden shook his head then shrugged his shoulders. He had no personal belongings to his name and kept any money on his person at all times. If a couple of low-level crooks made off with cheesecloth curtains, why should he care?

He grabbed his leg as a shock of pain raced to his knees. He slunk down onto the stool. Still shaking from the pain, he brought the hot cup to his lips and sipped for a long time. The warm, nutty flavor of the coffee helped him to forget the agonizing pain he was in.

"Crazy dream you woke me from Andre. I'm glad you intervened though. It was getting ugly. When a dream turns into a nightmare, that's the worst if you ask me. That simple transition can ruin the whole damn day," Bergden said, holding his mug out for another pour.

Andre poured more coffee into Bergden's mug. "What was it about?" Andre asked.

Bergden smirked as he brought the mug of coffee eagerly to his lips. "No idea. Just that my family was in it, and a giant Kroft. I'm sure that it means something, but I've never been much for spiritual revelations from a subconscious state. I'll chalk it up to blood loss and fatigue."

"My grandma used to say that dreams were the pathways we were meant to walk and that our earthly forms kept us grounded," Andre offered.

Bergden thought for a moment about his dream and shuddered. If that was his path, then he did nothing right in his past. He knew that his misgivings, a polite way to put it, would haunt him for the rest of his days, but he hoped to make up for it every chance he got.

Andre helped Bergden get dressed and head to the tavern. It

was an overcast day that seemed to threaten rain every waking minute which remained par for the course for the town of Harvick. A proverbial black cloud followed its denizens as they spent their entire lives trying to subsist and avoid the Regime's attention. But today appeared different. The streets were empty, and the food carts tucked away from sight. Even the beer vendor took the day off. "The town is more deserted than usual today. What gives?" Bergden asked Andre.

Andre stopped and pulled Bergden closer to the wall.

"Rumor is that the Regime caught wind of our operations here after the riot at Singer," Andre whispered. "It's got the people here spooked. With everyone on edge most feel it is safer to hide. If the Regime finds us here, there won't be any hiding from them."

The apocalyptic scene was easy to imagine for Bergden. The tanks rolling in and unleashing their payload. The people dragged from their homes unceremoniously executed and their belongings pillaged. The Regime won't round up resistance found outside of the city. Too much work needed to get them all back. Instead, the women would be ravaged, the men killed and the children...well...the children sent to be reworked or is it more commonly known, brainwashed. No graves would be dug, and the town burnt to the ground to be forgotten, a distant memory. The papers the next day would praise the brave men and women of the Regime for taking on and crushing a terrorist stronghold. The people in Blackwell would simply shrug their shoulders and their lives would move on.

The tavern differed from the rest of the town. The entire resistance movement jammed into a single building. Ridgeway stood at the back of the bar talking to Carl, a grim look on their faces. Roderick was serving a smorgasbord of bacon and potato cakes.

Ridgeway pushed through the crowd and took his place on the

old stage in the corner gesturing for everyone's attention.

"Alright people listen up. We've got a lot of work ahead of us and not a lot of time," Ridgeway announced. "Carl, would you please brief the group."

Carl came to the stage his expression somber.

"First and foremost, I want to thank Bergden Crane for giving us this opportunity by rescuing the general. His bravery will not be soon forgotten. Second, we've lost contact with Ivan at Singer Hospital after the riots," Carl said, looking at the faces in the room. "As a result, the plan is going to be delayed. As soon as we hear from our contact in the ministry--"

Roderick slammed down the plates sending bacon falling to the tavern floor.

"What do you mean we've lost contact with Ivan?" Roderick demanded. "You don't think that blowing up that fucking hellhole is important? Ridgeway led as many of those miserable bastards out as he could. Can't waste an effort like that. That's twice now it's been delayed. We might not get another chance. "

The fact that the hospital was a target for explosives surprised Bergden, but to hear it was postponed piqued his curiosity and amid the arguing, he raised his question. "What happened the first time?" he pondered.

Carl looked over at Ridgeway then at Andre who gave a slight nod. "Think by now he deserves to know," Andre said before pursing his lips.

Carl paced for a moment. "Your wife is what happened, Bergden," Carl confessed.

Bergden pushed through the crowd to Carl.

"What do you mean Alyssa is what happened?" Bergden demanded. "Why does she have anything to do with this?"

"The cause is why Bergden," Carl retorted, "You are an asset. Most importantly, I know you want the same things we do. Over the years, I saw it. I saw a man that sought freedom and peace for everybody. I couldn't just let Draven take you, but when he took Alyssa, I feared you wouldn't help us. I—We needed you."

Bergden shook his head again punching his fist into his palm. "Where's my wife Carl? Where's James?"

Andre stepped in. "They are safe, both of them. That much we can say. We can't reveal their location because it would compromise our Regime contact. But I assure you she and James are in good hands."

Could he really trust any of these people? Bergden thought. He barely knew anyone and apparently that included Carl. His imagination raced as he wondered if he had staged the evidence that led to the arrests of Sia and Mark. Did Carl use the black market as a trap for Alyssa? All she ever did was buy things the Regime hardly took notice to with all the other problems in Blackwell. He raided hundreds of homes and barely bothered with alcohol.

"What happened to her in that prison? Tell me the truth Andre," Bergden asked, waving away Carl.

Andre swallowed hard and gestured for Bergden to follow. Andre took Bergden back behind the and away from the rest of the group.

"She was beaten, nearly broken on the seventh floor," Andre stammered. "Dr. Vossen handled the interrogation."

Bergden's heart sunk. He saw the evil Dr. Vossen propagated in Singer Hospital and the anguish on the faces of the people there. Knowing that somehow Alyssa escaped was the only thing keeping him from a total and utter meltdown.

Carl appeared in the doorway.

"We didn't know where she was, but our agent Ivan recognized her. He was able to secure her release through one of our turncoats," Carl said.

"Turncoat?" Bergden questioned.

"Our Regime insider. He promised to keep her safe and assist us in going forward with the plan to take down the Regime once and for all. You have my word that she will be safe. In fact, she's probably in the safest place a person could find themselves when shit goes down," Carl reassured.

Whether it was exhaustion or the unwillingness to continue to press for information, Bergden conceded and the group went back to the waiting resistance fighters.

"I just want to be reunited with my family Carl. That's it. Just tell me the plan," Bergden said, defeated.

Carl nodded approvingly and helped Bergden back to his feet. The pair walked over and pulled down a ragged document from an old, tin can. It was a faded blueprint of the Regime headquarters, probably an outdated blueprint, but still functional. The basic tenets of the structure were there including all areas supporting the structure. The architecture behind the famed Regime headquarters was quite unique. During the construction, a river was diverted to create the canal that ran from the city limits to the base of the building. The water is used as a backup power supply and fills the numerous fountains nearby.

Bergden remembered his first time gazing upon the fabled fountains of the Regime. The image of watering spewing from Kroft's mouth brought about a rare smile.

"The plan is to eliminate the Regime headquarters," Carl started, "Destroy what is left of the government and implant Ridgeway as the new chancellor. Our agents tell us that the city is ripe for revolution. We just need the catalyst."

Bergden laughed out loud at the absurdity of the suggestion.

"That's your plan?" he mocked. "A coup that begins with the destruction of a building that was built to withstand a hundred thousand bombs, install Ridgeway, a guy that likely has been forgotten by the people in Blackwell and hope they rally behind him completely after obliterating their lives? I've seen the inner workings of the Regime, I've been the wolf, and I can tell you that it will not roll over and die. Too many people in the right positions have it too good with the Regime in power to let it slip away without a fight."

The room was silent, but Bergden could sense the determination and mounting resentment against him.

Roderick stood up. "Like you? You were a black jack lieutenant, and yet you were stabbed in the back. You should be dead, not standing here before us! "Bergden stood his ground.

"I want what you want. I want justice, freedom and peace, but the Regime is going to need a swifter kick in the ass than what you've proposed. The roots of evil run deep in Blackwell. A tree cannot be destroyed without tearing up the roots," he urged.

Ridgeway gestured for the room to remain calm.

"The plan is to attack the Regime headquarters on the day of the Anniversary of the Victory Parade. The tenth anniversary of the Regime's victory seems like a fitting day to open their eyes," Ridgeway said and pointed to the map. "As you know there's a waterway that runs under the building that is unsecured. This might be our only chance, Bergden."

Unconvinced Bergden rubbed his head and remained silent.

"I saw your wife at Singer Hospital, Bergden. I saw the torment in her eyes, the things they did to her. She was violated, mutilated, but she was strong. I saw hope and compassion in a world where both are in short supply. She persevered against all the odds," Ridgeway insisted. "I don't think I need to tell you that she's special, Bergden. She's stronger than she realizes, and people have a positive attraction to her. That's what we saw in her and that's what you see in her too. The only way you'll ever be able to live without worry is if we can accomplish the impossible. But we cannot do this and expect to succeed without you. We need to know, are you with us?"

Bergden thought for a moment. The impossibility of the situation overwhelmed his sense of logic, but Ridgeway had a point. He was still an outlaw, still sought after by the Regime, and the only sensible way to be able to live in peace with his family was to destroy the very monsters that created him.

"It's a long shot, but I'm willing to take it," he conceded. "Just tell me what I need to do."   Before they could respond, the door shot open. A young woman, her mood frantic and her eyes wild rushed to Andre. "The Regime is coming. It's a hit squad. Less than a mile out!"

Andre shot glances around the room before racing out into the street.

"Saddle up. Take positions on both sides of the street. We're going to have to pin them down," Carl ordered.

Roderick pulled a submachine gun from behind the bar and handed it to Bergden, gesturing for him to follow.

"We're going to take a spot on the rooftop above the tavern," Roderick said, pointing to the adjacent roof. "We'll carve up those bastards before they know what hit them."

No stranger to the nature of war, Bergden still felt uneasy about the rooftop. The walls were short and the path off was singular. He stared off into the distance trying to make out what the Regime was bringing to the party. Roderick handed him a set of binoculars.

"Half-track with a platoon of regulars," Bergden said.

Roderick craned his head trying to get a good look at the oncoming Regime fighters. "How can you tell? I can barely make out what I'm seeing."

Bergden pointed to the dust clouds.

"There's a pattern in the clouds for each type of vehicle. The half-track is slow, but not as weighty as a tank. There will be a .50 caliber on the roof of the truck cab. Anyone a decent shot here?"

Bergden yelled down to the street.

Across the way, a woman called over with a scoped rifle in hand.

"Natalia is probably the best shot," Roderick offered. "Her dad was a sniper in the Coalition. Wounded during battle, he settled in Harvick dedicating his life to getting back at the Regime." Roderick lowered his head. "He died about a year ago, from too many tumors but taught her everything he knows. She's always out in the fields taking target practice."

Bergden waved his arms to get her attention. He signaled to check how many Regime soldiers were with the half-track. After a moment of peering through the scope, she pulled back and hesitated before turning towards him.

She mouthed. "Fifty"

Almost twice as many fighters as the Remnants and heavier weapons to boot. He studied the surroundings. Most of Carl's fighters had taken positions on higher ground, which was good, but others hid by concrete walls that were crumbling to begin with. A .50 caliber round would eat right through it and deliver a fatal shot to anyone on the other side.

"Signal to Carl to have those fighters move into the alley. Those walls aren't going to stop the rounds the Regime is packing."

Roderick glanced over the edge and nodded in agreement. He whistled for Carl, and within a few moments the fighters scrambled for better cover, guns leveled at the street ahead. Now all that was left was the agonizing wait for the Regime's men to arrive.

"Wait until the half-track is underneath us before engaging from the roof. There's no top-down armor on those things. If we don't wait, our rounds will plink right off and do nothing but attract their attention, got it?"

Roderick cocked his weapon giving it a final once over. "Got it," he said.

A few minutes later the Regime hit squad arrived and en masse. Bergden kept his head low as the half-track entered the town. He painstakingly raised his head just enough to glance down at the oncoming group. A group of soldiers led the way for the half-track, its gun manned by a single gunner. He looked over at Roderick. He was gripping his gun close to his chest and muttering a prayer before looking over at Bergden. This was about as close to a battle that Bergden wanted to be since the war. He just hoped to come out alive. "Open up!" a voice cried out from below, and the sounds of machine guns cracked.

Bergden flipped over and saw the half-track working its way down the street. The rest of the Regime's men went scrambling for cover. The sounds of rounds striking the thick metal plates of the half-track were not welcomed.

"Wait for the half-track to get into position!" Bergden countered, but it was too late. He crawled over to Roderick's position keeping his head low as small arms rounds. He looked over at the sniper Natalia as she began to pick off Regime soldiers one by one. Bergden hoped she could keep from being compromised. The roof's cover was limited to a three-foot concrete wall. The .50 rounds would make quick work of the cheap masonry.

Bergden crawled to the back of the roof and scanned the alley below. There was a back street that ran along the rear of the main avenue before turning back out into a residential area. Glancing back, he saw Roderick taking aim at the Regime soldiers below. Roderick nodded to Bergden as Bergden began to climb down the fire escape to the street below taking care not to attract the attention of the Regime soldiers. He could hear the clack, clack, clack of the .50 caliber gun as it opened fire. The gun let loose a barrage of lead at the rooftops sending chunks of brick and mortar flying into the air. He just hoped that Roderick and Natalia found cover in time.

Ducking behind a dumpster, Bergden studied the Regime's

positions. Most were up in front of the half-track taking shots at the Remnant fighters in the main street. The .50 caliber gun continued to spew rounds at an alarming rate. He needed to flank that gun and fast if the rest of his comrades had any hope of survival.

He kept low as he reached the corner of the block. He poked his head around and saw that the path to the back of the half-track was wide open. The entire platoon had pushed forward to take ground, leaving the flank exposed. During the War, the Regime rarely made such a blunder, but for Bergden their lack of foresight gave him the window of opportunity he needed. He checked his gun, sprang up and dashed for the back of the vehicle. Under cover of the booming .50 caliber gun, he made it without drawing any attention.

Climb up, take out the loader, then the gunner. Bergden thought as he planned the maneuver. One slip up and he'd likely be dead, and the resistance members would soon follow him to their graves. He crept up the back of the half-track while the gunners focused on the task at hand. He approached slowly. Inch by inch he crawled toward the unsuspecting men until he could see the men's mouths moving.

"What the hell?" Bergden could see one of the gunner's mouths before he reached up, and with a swift turn of the neck, he sent the soldier limp to the deck of the half-track. Despite the attack, the main gunner still pressed on, unaware that anything had happened until the last of the ammunition ran out. He turned to chew out the loader, but to his surprise Bergden landed a right cross sending him reeling. Before he could recover, Bergden was back on top of him pulling his goggles down from his eyes, disorienting the soldier. As he recovered, Bergden landed another punch, this time connecting to the chin and knocking him unconscious. Instinctively, he reached down to end the man's life.

His memories of the war hurtled into his mind. The men and women he killed, the destruction he wrought. It was too much to bear. Bergden fell to his knees right on the deck.

Pull yourself together! He pushed himself as he pounded the sides of his head. The nightmarish remembrance of those who were felled by his hand crippled him. Rocking back and forth, he struggled against his own mind to regain composure until suddenly the sounds of mortar rounds brought him back to reality.

He stood up and watched in horror as a mortar round struck Roderick's position, then another near Natalia. He rushed to reload the .50 caliber gun to turn the tables on the unsuspecting Regime fighters.

He brought the gun's power to bear. With devastating effect, each round crashed through flesh and bone, tearing away what numerical superiority the Regime had at the onset. Bergden held down the trigger, the iron barrel glowing like the coals of a fire and nearly melting away from the intense heat. When the final round escaped none were left standing.

"God damn Bergden!" Andre whooped. "I thought we were going to be overrun!"

The rest of the resistance fighters emerged from hiding. A noticeable decrease in their ranks became apparent.

"Check for survivors and tend to the wounded," ordered Ridgeway as he pulled away rubble to check the pulse of a downed comrade.

Bergden regained his senses and walked towards the building where Roderick had been positioned, his ears still vibrating from the vicious boom of the .50 caliber.

"Roderick?" he called up to the rooftop. "Roderick, you up there?"

No response.

He climbed the fire escape which had avoided the brunt of the blast until he reached what used to be the rooftop. In the corner lay Roderick slumped over his rifle blood pooling beneath him.

Bergden rushed over to check his pulse, but not even a faint heartbeat remained. He sat down next to the lifeless resistance fighter. The details of Roderick's life eluded Bergden since his arrival in Harvick. Yet it no less pained him to see his body lay dead. He went to painstaking lengths to keep Bergden safe and for that he was eternally grateful.

The opposing rooftop fared little better, but the mortar round missed its mark by just a few meters allowing the elusive Natalia to come away unharmed. Her sniper rifle on the other hand was not as fortunate.

"Not sure where I'm going to drum up another one of these!" Natalia yelled across the rooftop as she held up the mangled rifle. "Everything alright over there? Roderick you okay?"

Bergden shook his head as he looked back at Roderick's body and sighed. Natalia knew the worst had come to pass for Roderick.

Hours after the attack, the bodies finally were buried, the debris removed from the street and the remaining resistance fighters huddled once more in the tavern. It went without saying, but the somberness of the crowd deflated any excitement over the upcoming mission. As Natalia passed around shots of whiskey in the memory of the dead, Carl stood once more in front of the careworn group.

"Thirteen. That's how many were killed out there today. Thirteen. I didn't think I have to say it, but we need to make sure they did not die in vain. We lost some good folks out there today, but we bested the Regime, and while that won't bring back the lost, it must count for something."

A grim reality set in for Bergden. The Regime had been stirred, and the defeat of its own would not go unpunished. As he sipped on his whiskey, he pondered the possibility of the Regime sending a follow up force or would they just bomb the town into oblivion?

Harvick provided little to Blackwell and harbored known

members of the Remnants. It only made sense for the Regime to wipe the pathetic shanty town from the face of the earth.

Carl continued his diatribe against the Regime and ranted about how the Coalition's rise would be swift and exacting. Justice served to the Regime's party members wouldn't be justice, but retribution for the perceived atrocities of a single entity. Bergden caught himself smiling at the absurdity of it all. Everyone likes an underdog and wants them to win, but when it doesn't happen it's expected. When an underdog wins it's a miracle.

We're going to need a miracle, he thought.

"When do we strike at the headquarters?" Natalia demanded.

The rest of the room erupted again. Emotions taking control of a process that required strategic insight and a high degree of focus.

Carl tried to calm the crowd.

"We will get our revenge brothers and sisters, but we must exercise patience," Carl urged. "Our contact stated that we cannot move until they believe we have the greatest chance to succeed. I know what happened today weighs upon our souls, but restraint is needed!"

The crowd continued to argue for another hour until the sun began to set. The day's events were trying, but Bergden could hardly unnerve himself to move. He felt as though the deaths of everyone in that street, Regime or resistance, was blood upon his hands.

"You really shouldn't blame yourself," a soft voice called from over his shoulder. It was Natalia. She stood over him with a glass of whiskey.

"Care if I sit?" she asked, gesturing to the seat across from Bergden.

Bergden nodded choosing to sip on his glass without uttering a response.

"I know what it means to kill another person Bergden. I did my fair share of horrible things during the war. My father taught me how to shoot at a young age. I'd shoot small game. You   know, squirrels, birds or whatever, but I remember the first time I trained my scope on another human. The image of him in my cross hairs sent a chill up my spine."

"Pulled the trigger?" he asked grimly.

She shook her head.

"No, it was the neighbor boy, but it was then I knew I could do it if I had to." A heavy sighed left her chest. "When the Regime came to my village, the Coalition had long abandoned its efforts there. People were taking sides. Naturally, violence broke out."

"I'm assuming you took part?" Bergden asked.

She smirked, insulted by the tone.

"Who wouldn't? I fought for our freedom just like they fought for their lives," she reasoned. "It was a personal priority. It was the first time I took a life and I have no regrets."

Bergden laughed and threw back the rest of the whiskey.

"I have taken life away from hundreds of people and regret every single one. Not a day goes by that I don't let it burn at my soul," Bergden admitted. "In fact, it was one of the last conversations I had with my wife before our lives were turned upside down. Never let death become your norm. It is what makes us human. It is what stokes our desires to be alive. I just hope God can see it to forgive me."

Natalia threw back her whiskey and nodded in agreement.

"What you did today though saved a whole town. Don't forget that," she noted.

Natalia left and again Bergden was alone at the table until Carl and Ridgeway joined him. Carl poured the three men another round.

"Thank you Bergden. You may have just saved the Remnants with that act of heroism. Listen, I know you have particular qualms about War, but the price of those Regime soldier's lives could lead to our salvation and the freedom for millions of people," Carl said.

Bergden remained silent, choosing his whiskey over conversation. Ridgeway pulled his chair closer to Bergden.

"I need to know you're on our side, Bergden," Ridgeway insisted. "The gravity of what we are about to undertake cannot leave room for doubt or else we're all dead."

Again, no word was spoken. Causing Ridgeway to look to Carl and gesturing for help.

"I worked with you for how long Bergden? Six, seven years?" Carl maintained. "I know what happened today weighs heavily on your shoulders, as it should, but you must recollect your thoughts. Think of Alyssa. Think of James."

The mention of his family stirred Bergden.

"What about my family Carl? When are you planning on letting me see them again?" Bergden questioned. "Or are they dead, and when we're done, you'll toss me aside? Which is it Carl? If we are as close as you think you'll tell me straight away when I get to wrap my arms around them!"

Carl and Ridgeway sat still, trading glances as Bergden wept over his glass of whiskey. "Bergden, I promise they are alive, and when the mission is completed, we have a cottage set up for your family on the outskirts of Harvick. There you can live in peace."

Bergden grimaced. "The two of you just don't get it, do you? If any part of this plan fails, Harvick and probably the Remnant movement, is doomed. In fact, I'd wager the Regime is sending over a squadron of bombers at this very moment to wipe us from existence."

"What do you mean?" Carl asked, surprised.

Bergden couldn't believe what he was hearing. Did Carl honestly believe that there would be no repercussions to today's events?"

"Once Kroft gets word of the hit squad's defeat, he'll burn down Harvick and slaughter everyone just so the news doesn't get out." Bergden sighed. "Look, whatever plan up your leaves you might want to move forward, or else we're all going to die horrible deaths."

"Fine. You are going to lead a strike team into Blackwell, Bergden. Is that what you wanted to hear?" Ridgeway bellowed. "Your attack is coinciding with the festivities at the same time as another phase of the plan is commencing."

"Ivan's destruction of the prison?" Bergden questioned.

Ridgeway shook his head.

"We've been unable to get in contact with Ivan. He's presumed dead," Ridgeway admitted. The prison isn't the primary target."

"So, what is it? Another bombing?" Bergden probed.

Ridgeway walked over and pulled the map down from the wall. "The parade route begins in the western districts near Pemply Station. You are the most familiar with it, and that is where we begin, but it is also the most critical stage of the attack."

Bergden studied the map carefully. He saw his old apartment building, the café where Alyssa got her morning coffee, James's old school, and of course Pemply black jack headquarters. The building itself ran alongside Victory Boulevard straight to the headquarters several blocks away. The parade would wind through the streets with various stopping points, but it all began at his old workplace.

"They'll recognize me there. I know it has been a while, but I doubt the whole station just forgot a lieutenant. Besides, any access I had has been revoked I'm sure. My ID, my keys, none of it could possibly pass muster anymore."

Ridgeway pulled a small satchel from his jacket and tossed it to Bergden. "Your keys are in here. Obviously, the ID wouldn't work, but there is good news. Since the parade starts at Pemply, the station will likely be largely empty."

Holding the keys strangely felt familiar to Bergden, as if he was about to return to his former life.

"What's my goal once I'm inside?" Bergden questioned.

"Arms and explosives," Ridgeway exclaimed. "You will lead a squad of four, including myself, into the Regime Headquarters. Plant explosives in the canal support, then blow the fucker. That's the plan. Simple as that."

The plan was simple when spoken, but the execution was another matter based entirely on circumstance. For Bergden, if he was spotted in Pemply Station, then the entire operation would fail and end with his death. If by chance he made it out of Pemply Station with the squad, they'd likely run into security at the headquarters, which if not quelled quickly, would lead to an unwinnable battle.

None of this seemed plausible to Bergden and the fact that there was yet another phase to be completed worried him. That phase was entirely out of his hands and the only thing he knew was that it involved some Regime benefactor. For Bergden, it was a wait and see approach. He just hoped that wherever Alyssa and James were, they were safe.

CHAPTER FOURTEEN

"Tell me again why we aren't able to just bring weapons and explosives with us?" Natalia asked from the back seat of the unmarked Regime cruiser. The resistance members in Harvick had been saving the Regime cruiser for a special trip to Blackwell.

Today was a banner day.

Bergden sat in the passenger seat watching as the world raced by on the way to Blackwell. The countryside was in stark contrast to the dismal, broken streets of Harvick. The death and destruction left in the wake of the Regime's raid ushered in a moment of quiet solidarity for a resistance movement he had long sympathized with, but rarely took seriously. The end game remained the same for Bergden despite taking it upon himself to fight on behalf of the Coalition.

Find Alyssa and James. Bergden reminded himself.

Carl sat in the driver's seat focusing on the empty highway. Most of the Regime's supporters in the rural areas had long made their way to Blackwell to witness the Victory Parade. For years, Bergden donned his uniform, put on the cap, and carried his rifle down the streets of Blackwell, high-stepping his way to the chancellor's mansion. During his early days in the Regime, he took great pride in the uniform and what he represented, but as more atrocities were revealed he took a different path. A walk back to his apartment in shame to look at his beautiful wife and young son in the eye and say what he did was for them. When he became a black jack he didn't have to march, but that disappointment persisted. He hoped that whatever the outcome of this mission, it put an end to that feeling.

"There is a single checkpoint into Blackwell from this direction. Considering what happened the other day, they'll be looking extra hard at incoming vehicles," said Andrew Ridgeway. "If they opened the trunk and saw a cache of weapons, they'd execute us on the spot."

Satisfied, Natalia sat back in the seat checking her watch. The car had left Harvick two hours earlier with the intent of reaching Blackwell at the beginning of the festivities. The checkpoint would be undergoing a staff rotation. If they timed it right, it would be at the end of the shift for the group pushing the car right through and to the station.

Bergden knew the drill. The more robust checkpoints would do an entire search of the car on any given day, but on the day of the Victory Parade, the goal was to get hammered. Every man and woman who wore the uniform propositioned themselves to getting sloppy drunk after the parade left their sector. Pemply Station turned into a seedy nightclub after the last boot fell. Debauchery ruled into the night and when the morning light arrived it was business as usual, with a ridiculous hangover and a boat load of bad decisions tagging along.

"We're about ten miles out from the city limits. Just to be clear. The plan is to escort Bergden into Pemply Station, wait for him to get the weapons and explosives stashed in my locker, then meet him in the alley. The car will then take us to Regime Headquarters where the fun will begin. Understood?" Carl asked, his eyes still focused on the road.

The plan seemed simple enough, but the Regime made it a habit to remove simplicity from the equation. Waltzing into Pemply Station usually was reserved for those who were under arrest or those who made the arrest. Station Chief Patton made it clear that civilians took a risk coming through the double doors. He once watched a guy who just wanted out of the rain get his teeth knocked out by a baton before getting rushed out. Protecting and serving the public was a myth for black jacks. For Bergden it meant pretending to be arrested while Carl escorted him inside. Carl donned his black jack uniform. The black and blue jacket, the rider's pants, boots and even the high-crested cap. The whole nine yards. Bergden even noticed Carl had been promoted since Bergden was forced out, a few more bars along the breast showing as much. Lord knows what he had to do for those few pieces of tin.

"What's the plan once we arrive at Regime headquarters?" Bergden asked, concerned about the loose nature of the plan. He hadn't been filled in on the rest of the plan and judging by the mixed reactions, it was by design. Carl and Ridgeway mulled over letting him in on the details.

"Alright, the plan is to have you, Natalia and Andre plant the explosives at the base of the headquarters," Carl ordered. "While that is happening, Ridgeway and I are going to head to the Regime broadcasting station and announce to the world the death of Kroft and the fall of the Regime."

The shock of the simplicity of the plan overwhelmed Bergden.

"Removing Kroft and destroying the headquarters won't be enough. The Regime plunged its claws deep within the people of Blackwell for too long," Bergden countered.

"These are the options the resistance was given. A choice must—rather *has*—been made, Bergden, with or without your participation. Removing Kroft is just the beginning. The people will join us, and the Coalition will emerge from the Regime's shadow. That I can promise. Its retribution will be swift, and justice wrought," Ridgeway exclaimed.

Bergden sat in silence, wondering if Carl truly embraced the understanding of the dangers associated with replacing one totalitarian government with another. A different name served only to mask the inherent similarities of a government swept into power through massive upheaval. Suddenly, the sound of low flying planes drowned out the radio broadcast. Carl pulled the car over and the squad stepped out to watch as a squadron of heavy bombers soared overhead.

"Where do you think they're going?" asked Andre, holding his hand up over his brow to get a better view.

Bergden watched as the bomber squadron soared past. "Harvick," he said without emotion. The defeat of the Regime at Harvick beckoned retaliation.

Ridgeway and Carl looked at each other before racing to the car to grab the radio, desperately trying to get the signal to work.

"Whoa, whoa you can't use the radio," said Natalia, cutting the two men off from trying the radio any further. "If you call using the radio it'll compromise our position. The Regime has eyes and ears everywhere. Have we forgotten that?"

Carl placed the radio back on the receiver and watched as the bombers flew out of view.

"You can't just let them die," Andre insisted "Get on that radio and warn them."

Neither Carl nor Ridgeway made a move for the radio.

"The blood of the people of Harvick will be on your hands," Andre warned.

Bergden walked back to the car. He knew that even if they could warn the people of Harvick, most wouldn't escape.

"For the cause, Carl? Worth a whole town getting wiped off the earth for the cause. Men, women, and children dead or buried alive in the rubble? That's what the worth of your cause?" Bergden questioned.

Bergden knew the answer. Yes, the deaths of innocents paled in comparison to autonomy and freedom from the Regime. No one in the squad had much to lose. Carl had no family, Andre and Natalia lost their families and Ridgeway, well, he seemed okay with losing everything for a shot at power.

Bergden just shook his head at the silence, and the car again went on its way. He just prayed that a warning made its way to Harvick that it was about to rain fire.

The remainder of the trip no one said a word, but as the cruiser approached the checkpoint the mood changed. Bergden could feel the change in attitude in each person. The somberness of watching bombers heading off to destroy your home was displaced with the resolve of revolution. The checkpoint marked the first of several significant hurdles to the ultimate goal.

Carl brought the car to a stop at the checkpoint. Luckily, soldiers manned the checkpoints.

Not a Pemply black jack in sight. Judging by the soldiers' body language, their tired sluggish movements were signs of a long day's work, the shift nearing an end.

"Papers please. I'm assuming your heading in for the parade?" the soldier asked, scanning the cruiser's passengers. Bags hung low under his eyes. The private clearly exhausted from manning the checkpoint for hours on end.

Carl handed over the paperwork. Taking the paperwork, the private walked over to his commanding officer. After a few tense moments and suspicious glances, the private returned and passed the paperwork back to Carl.

"You're good to go. Just avoid Victory Avenue, but you know the drill, lieutenant. There are inquisitors on staff today, so make sure your guests follow their instructions, and there won't be a problem. Have a good day."

He stepped back, saluted, and waved the cruiser through the gate. A collective exhalation of relief rushed out from the group. The first major hurdle conquered, and the cruiser continued into the city. Bergden wondered if it was a matter of luck or good timing that propelled them through the checkpoint without incident and onto the next challenge, Pemply Station.

The city was a flurry of activity. Vendors lining the causeways selling pro-Regime propaganda, food and portraits of Kroft. Banners fluttered in the gentle breeze whispering through the city streets carrying with it the glory and might of the Regime. The cruiser wound its way through the congested streets until opening up near Pemply Station. The parade patrons cleared a wide path for the black jacks as they strolled the streets. Bergden watched as an Inquisitor stopped a couple at a food truck to question them about the day. The blazing red uniforms doing little to hide them in a crowd.

"The entrance is up ahead. Bergden here are your new papers and identity. It'll work to get you through should Carl be stopped and questioned," Ridgeway said, passing Bergden the dossier.

Bergden scanned through the papers. He was to be a fishmonger from the nearby lake town of Meca. His temporary name, Jason Darby. Booked by Carl for alleged ties to the resistance through "non-material" evidence. Typical non-justifiable cause used by black jacks across the Regime.

Pemply Station appeared empty as the cruiser arrived, the majority of black jacks were out on patrol or providing extra security for the parade. Black jacks got paid overtime to play security guards for a few hours.

Easy money, easy job. Bergden remembered the eight-hour day of blending among the citizens of Blackwell, reveling in the tremendous public awe often induced from the persistent stream of the Regime's war machine. Bergden once marched in step with the others and secretly a part of him wished he still did. He'd live a life of guilt to see his wife and son safe once again. But, passing thoughts were that, passing. "Keep your head low Bergden. I'll check us in and let you into the staff areas," Carl said, leaning in close to disguise his motivations to anyone who might be listening.

Carl escorted Bergden into the station. Bergden noticed that the place hardly changed in the two years since his disappearance. The same obnoxiously large portrait of Chancellor Kroft greeted visitors. The gentle hymn of the Regime anthem subtly reverberating in the background over the loudspeakers. Propaganda driven reminders tacked to the walls leading back to the employee only areas a constant reminder of who you work for, who you lived for.

At the receptionist's desk Carl showed his badge and with a nod from the secretary whisked Bergden past the offices and to the back of the hall. There was one thing that Bergden noticed had changed.

Lt. Rocco Draven.

The name on the door made his blood boil and for a second, he thought about lunging in before Carl pulled him aside into his office.

"The weapons storage is locked, and the only key is now kept with Station Chief Aberdeen," Carl said, peering out into the hallway making sure they were in fact, alone. "You're going to have to go into the locker room and grab it. He keeps the only spare in locker number *69* right next to the showers."

Bergden nodded. "And if there is someone in the showers?"

Carl swallowed hard and took a deep breath. "Do what you need to do to get that key."

Bergden crept back into the hallway, looking from his right to left. The ordinarily busy station remained a ghost town due to the parade. The walk back to the locker area eerily felt too easy for him, but as he entered, that feeling soon disappeared. The showers were on and a thick layer of steam clouded the room. Bergden proceeded into the muggy showers with caution.

Bergden froze when a figure emerged.

"Sorry, I like good steam after days like today, but you know all about that, don't you, Bergden?" an all too familiar voice called out from within the shroud.

Bergden tried to see where the voice had emerged, but his field of vision was too dense.

"I gotta say," the voice continued, "I'm surprised you came back. After we couldn't find your body, we left you for dead," the man sneered. "Your wife and son weren't as fortunate. Son should be a full-fledged, walking, talking Regime neophyte by now and the misses? Well, most don't leave Cherry Hill. Unless of course it is in a body bag."

Finally, it dawned on Bergden, who was speaking to him from within the locker room. The man that single handedly ruined his life and began a steady downward spiral into a personal hell that would culminate in the destruction of everything he once held true.

Draven. Bergden cursed.

"Why don't you show yourself and be a man for once?" Bergden grunted. "The things you did to me, to my family and to the countless other innocents. You need to stand for what you've done. Come out and let me have my vengeance."

He scanned the clouded room and caught sight of a figure

moving among the lockers. Bergden raced blindly to the spot and stopped. The locker stalls were empty.

"I know this might irk you, but I don't know what the hell you're talking about. If anyone's done anything to your family it was you, not I. From my recollection it was you that betrayed the Regime. It was in all the papers," Draven chided.

"You framed my wife and sent our lives into a spiral Draven," Bergden snarled. "Why? I know we had our differences, but why drag my wife into this? My son?"

Again, Draven darted through the steam cloud. Bergden tried again to get a bead on Draven's position.

"Perhaps you should ask someone who knows. The article said you were a collaborator for the Remnants. I thought you would bleed yourself dry for the Regime. I had doubted the veracity of the story until this moment," Draven offered.

Bergden managed to eye Draven as he stooped down behind a row of lockers.

Gotcha you son of a bitch. Bergden thought as he lunged towards Draven.

Racing through the steam cloud he nearly reached him until the silhouette of a pistol appeared.

"Take it easy, Bergden. I know we're in the showers, but you don't have to make a move on me. I'm not into that sort of thing," Draven quipped, jabbing the pistol into Bergden's gut.

Draven's face passed through the cloud, a snarky grin greeting Bergden. The same familiar face. The slightly crooked nose from when he fought another black jack in training, the stubbly goatee and the high and tight. Bergden wanted to sock him right in the mouth.

"I'll be honest, Bergden, I really don't know why you're here, but you won't be leaving. Not alive anyways. I must admit I've been dying to do this," Draven declared, cocking the hammer back on his sidearm.

Backed into a corner, Bergden felt desperate, but instead of trying to flee, he did the last thing Draven expected. He attacked.

Grabbing the barrel of the pistol, Bergden yanked it from Draven's grip sending it skidding across the steam-soaked tile. The two men grappled, wrestling for position and slamming to the hard floor. Bergden struck Draven across the jaw. The impact of the blow sending shock waves of adrenaline-fueled ecstasy through his veins.

The showers running, Bergden threw Draven into a set of lockers, sending them sprawling to the floor with a metallic bang. Draven straddled Bergden, pummeling him with blow after blow. Bergden managed to free his arms, blocking another strike and landing a right across, staggering Draven. Bergden, slow to get up, forced himself to his knees the taste of blood resting on his tongue.

He watched as Draven winced, blood pooling at his feet, his jaw broken from the blow.

"You have no idea how much my family has suffered from what you've done, Draven. I've been separated from my wife and James for nearly two years. You wanted to know what I'm doing here? I'm here to find my family and regain what's left of my life. The life you stole from me."

Draven smiled through blood-soaked teeth.

"Maybe you are crazy after all, Bergden. You get your revenge, leave me bloodied, then escape?" He laughed, choking on blood. "You're going to be disappointed."

Bergden frowned. "That's not good enough, I'm afraid."

Bergden leapt atop the wounded Draven and proceeded to pound the battered black jack onto the tile floor, each strike cracking the tile. One blow after another, Bergden let loose his rage until he pulled away from the motionless body of Draven, the fatally wounded man's blood circling a nearby drain.

The sound of the water being turned off immediately redirected Bergden's attention towards the showers.

"Lieutenant Crane. I must say I'm amazed to see you here," the man's voice called out from among the steam.

As the cloud began to dissipate, Station Chief Aberdeen emerged, holding a key.

"Chief. I suggest you turn and leave. I don't know what your part was in all of this, but I swear you'll be next," Bergden warned. He rose to his feet, his mouth bloodied from the fight with Draven.

Aberdeen walked up and much to Bergden's surprise, embraced him.

"I'm sorry about what happened to you, Bergden. I didn't believe the accusations, but you have to understand there was nothing I could do," Aberdeen lamented. "I have my own family to feed and people to protect. I'm just sorry it came at the cost of yours."

"There wasn't another way," Bergden said, gesturing to the lifeless Draven.

"I know, Bergden. I will have to deal with that, but for now, I presume you are looking for the weapon's storage key." He held up the key and placed it in Bergden's hand.

"How did you know?" Bergden asked.

Aberdeen shrugged. "A reckoning comes with little warning sometimes, Bergden, and I do not want to be on the wrong side of history."

Bergden took the key and looked to Aberdeen but could not speak.

"I've let Carl know, and now you must go. The rest of the station will be back soon, and I can stall them, but not for long. Get what you need and go," Aberdeen suggested.

Bergden looked down at the lifeless former black jack.

"Why are you helping me? Why risk everything?" he asked,

looking up at Aberdeen.

The Station Chief took a deep breath.

"I'm not proud of it and I hope my inaction is rewarded, but I suspected all along that Draven was setting you up. He had the backing of my superiors including Commander Grimm. I know you and your family are innocent. Should men like Draven come to power, it will mean the end of men like you and me," Aberdeen said, pointing to himself. "I tried to do right by the world where I could."

The locker room door swung open and Carl rushed in, trying to catch his breath. "We've got to get moving, Bergden. The radio says there are a few units on the way. Parade traffic will slow them down, but not for long."

Bergden looked at Aberdeen and nodded before running to the door. The Station Chief had always entrusted him with making the right decisions. Now more than ever Bergden believed that the right choice was finding his family and putting a nail into the coffin of the Regime.

Carl and Bergden grabbed a few machine pistols from the weapons storage and went through a back exit into the alley. The car sat running while Carl and Bergden passed out guns and ammunition. The shrieking sounds of sirens echoing down the street.

"That's our cue. Let's go!" Andre shouted, slamming his palms on the hood and gestured to the door.

The cruiser sped off towards the Regime headquarters five blocks away. The canal entrance sat beneath the bridge leading up to the building itself. Wrought iron streetlamps symmetrically lined the roadway leading to the heavily fortified guard house a few hundred yards away from the main gate. Barricade after barricade lined the bridge leading up to the grand doors that marked the entrance. Dozens of Regime soldiers loitered about paying little interest to the group's car as it approached. The car came to a stop a block away just as the parade turned down the main boulevard on the final stretch to the chancellor's mansion.

As the team piled out of the car, Regime headquarters stood before them. The chancellor commissioned its creation during his third year in office, the stone imported from conquered lands as a testament to the Regime's fortitude. At each corner rose a palisade topped with the crescent of the wolf. In the center, a towering bronze statue of Kroft atop a dire wolf stood ominously above the city of Blackwell. The tip of Kroft's cap was the tallest man-made point in the entire Regime.

Bergden set foot in the headquarters only once before in his young life. Years ago, he received the promotion from brown cap to wolf guardian, and to this day it's the only time he's ever met Kroft. Not that he thought of the man. Even at his height of loyalty, Bergden saw Kroft as the beginning of a new world for the people. Rising to prominence on campaign promises of higher wages, greater freedoms and opportunity, those proclamations couldn't be further from reality. Instead of opening the world to the people, Kroft slammed the door shut. Cutting off all manner of culture or diversity in favor of a more silver-tongued approach to nationalistic superiority pushing the population away from globalization and into the arms of totalitarianism wearing the guise of a prosperous yet internalized democracy.

It has to come down, Bergden thought, craning his eyes skyward.

"Bergden, Natalia, and Andre wade through the canal until you reach the gates. That's the entrance point," Ridgeway directed, pointing to the base of the building where the canal disappeared.

"How are we supposed to get in? We don't have any cutting equipment," Natalia noted.

Carl smirked. "Ivan. He's working on the tunnel entrance as we speak. General Ridgeway and I are going to stack out the radio station until we see the fireworks. Good luck."

Bergden climbed down over the embankment and watched as the cruiser sped away, leaving the trio to their own devices. Andre took point and Natalia took up the rear. Over the past few weeks Bergden's combat instincts crept back into his mindset. The canal left them over exposed, but not knowing another path, he pushed on in silence.

The water was cold and the current swift. Bergden felt the rush of the water press firmly against his knees as he pushed through the strength of the current. His step was a challenge and every inch laborious. If the Regime soldiers up on the bridge took notice, they'd be dead in a matter of seconds and the mission a failure. The canal afforded little in the way of cover and the depth of the water would slow any attempt to run.

"Keep your steps short and your head low," Bergden suggested checking to make sure his machine pistol stayed above the rushing water.

Natalia and Andre kept low as they passed beneath the bridge while it rose above them. The myriad of cross beams and support structures shielded them from view as the car approached the canal tunnels entrance. The canal itself served as a cost-effective means to power the building. A small, yet powerful hydroelectric infrastructure sat nestled in the basement. Bergden expected the structure to have at least some Regime presence.

Kroft couldn't be that arrogant, he speculated.

Outside, the group was able to gain ground until they saw Ivan cutting away at the bars of the gate.

"Bergden, it's good to see you again!" Ivan exclaimed. "These bars are a bastard but I'm almost through with the torch."

Natalia stepped up and peered into the tunnel. "Any resistance up ahead?" she probed, trying to get a clearer view of the building. The sounds of rushing water masking any chance of hearing the drop of booted feet.

Ivan shrugged his shoulders.

"I can't be sure. I'm not familiar with the headquarters guard schedules. Probably no more than any other part of the building," Ivan suggested.

"We'll find out once we get through, won't we?" Andre said, pointing to the last few remaining bars.

Ivan laughed and pressed his hacksaw to the iron. "I suppose we will."

After a few minutes, the final bar was cut sending up a splash of water as it fell into the rushing canal. The squad moved into the tunnels a faint glow hung in the distance.

"I'll go up ahead and see what we're dealing with," Andre said, pushing ahead of the group.

Bergden, Natalia and Ivan waited patiently as Andre's figure faded into the dark tunnel. After a few tense moments, Andre returned.

"The area is clear. I think the water is masking our entry so be prepared once we get inside," Andre said.

As they entered the chamber, Bergden saw little evidence of Regime patrol. No footsteps, no spotlights, no nothing. Just the hum of the generator, the rush of water and the subdued glow of a few utility lights.

It was the perfect entry point.

"Alright, Carl said to place an explosive on the generator," Ivan said, rushing over to the generator. He unpacked his bag and placed two small devices on the generator. "These explosives are designed to explode with a low frequency radio receiver. Carl had this switch created." Ivan held up a small remote-like device. "Once we get out of range all we need to do is click and thirty seconds later…boom."

As Ivan finished connecting the ignition charges, double doors at the top of the stairs that lead down to the water swung open. Two guards emerged, surprised by the intruders. "Who the hell are you? You can't be in here. This area is restricted," the guard threatened, lowering his pistol taking aim at Bergden. Before the other guard could draw his sidearm Andre ducked behind a wall and aimed his machine pistol at the first guard.

"Drop the gun," Andre ordered.

Ignoring him, the guard pulled the hammer back on the pistol. Bergden felt the muzzle staring down at him and as he looked around for anything that might help his current predicament, he realized Natalia had disappeared from sight.

"Drop the gun or your friend here is going to die. Is that understood?" the guard retorted, not once taking his eyes from Bergden's position.

Bergden watched as Natalia dropped down behind the guards from the catwalk. She threw the butt of the gun into the armed guard's jaw, sending teeth and him to the floor. The other guard dodged her attack and raced to the door. Natalia gave chase. Ivan went back to arming the explosives at the support structures, and Andre emerged, guns drawn.

Bergden sighed in relief as Natalia caught up with the guard before he could set the alarm sending him sprawling to the cement with a thud. The group hadn't been exposed and the pace that Ivan worked sped up. Andre, Bergden and Natalia watched as Ivan worked his magic to set the explosives until suddenly the alarms blared. The guard, whom they had all thought was knocked unconscious, crawled and struck the alarm that hung by the twin doors.

"We're about to get company!" Bergden yelled. "Take positions and keep Ivan safe at all costs."

In moments, more Regime guards charged in and opened fire at the scrambling resistance fighters. Bergden leaned out and returned fire missing the mark before ducking back behind cover.

At least a dozen guards took position above them and a steady stream of gunfire rained down on their position.

"There's too many of them!" Natalia cried out, trying to return fire.

Bergden knew they couldn't hold out for long as the Regime soldiers laid down heavy covering fire, moving closer and closer with each passing second. Soon they would be able to flank the fighters. A primary tactic, but effective against small arms fire.

Bergden watched as Ivan dodged fire jumping from beam to beam placing the remaining explosives.

"Natalia is down. She's down!" Andre wailed and as he sprinted to her side, he too was struck. Andre tumbled in a heap grabbing now motionless.

"Are they moving Bergden?" Ivan called out, setting the last explosive. "Can you see their position?"

He shook his head. "We're on our own Ivan. We need to move," Bergden ordered.

You're with your family now Andre. You with yours Natalia, Bergden thought as he made his way to the tunnel entrance.

"Ivan, we're running out of time!" Bergden cried out as he fired towards the advancing guards.

Ivan rose from the final explosive charge and nodded grimly. Looking back at Natalia and Andre one more time before taking cover, Ivan signaled Bergden to follow him back through the tunnel. Under the cover of fire, the pair climbed into the narrow passage, fighting the current, trying desperately to get enough distance to set off the explosives.

As they pushed through the current, the sounds of gunfire echoed down the canal.

"You're going to have to set it off Ivan. They're gaining too fast. We're sitting ducks out here!" Bergden shouted above the sounds of rushing water, forcing his way through the current.

Ivan looked back and grinned at the Regime soldiers in pursuit.

"I don't know the effects of the explosion on this tunnel Bergden. Could be crushed, or we could drown!" Ivan cautioned as he held up the remote.

Bergden glanced back and saw the Regime troops entering the tunnel. At this point even if they managed to get out of the tunnel, they wouldn't make it far before the entire city was on top of them. Blowing the joint was the last, fateful option.

"Do it!" Bergden roared.

Ivan flipped the switch, his eyes wild.

"We've got thirty seconds until it blows. We won't get out of the tunnel in time—" Ivan's words were cut off with a flash. A roaring ball of fire hurdled down the tunnel sending Bergden and Ivan face first into the canal waters. Under the water, Bergden saw the bright, fiery glare of the flames above. In a moment, they retreated, replaced with the rumble of the collapsing building.

Bergden rushed to his feet.

"The end of the tunnel is up a head," Bergden cried out before a rush of water raced behind them from the second shockwave picking the two men up and launching them through the tunnel through the breached gate and out into the canal. Bergden turned, taking a breath and watched as the building continued its collapse. The sides immediately came down, the gothic styles disappeared beneath a wall of dust and those trapped inside buried in the rubble. The dust reaching out into the canal and over the two men.

Bergden tried to regain his breath, and as he did someone grabbed his shoulders and dragged him to the shoreline.

"Get in the car!" a woman's voice called out from the car. "Ivan, get in the front. Let's go," she persisted.

Bergden tried to wipe the soot and dust from his eyes to get a better look at the woman as he blindly hurried up the embankment and into the back of a waiting cruiser.

"Who are you?" Bergden asked, still disoriented from the blast.

The cruiser began to move.

"My name is Jocelyn, and if we don't get the hell out of here, we'll all be thrown in Cherry Hill. Now hold on, we're not done yet. We've got another passenger."

Bergden's vision was finally clearing. "Where's Carl? Ridgeway?" he asked.

He could make out the look of desperation in her eyes. "Waiting on your wife and son Mr. Crane," Jocelyn said. "Waiting on your family."

CHAPTER FIFTEEN

The night air felt good. The gentle breeze brought with it an eager chill, but for Alyssa it was the first night in many months that she could enjoy the balcony and stare up at the illustrious celestial beings. What made the night truly special was not the sense of harmony she felt with her place on the earth, but the fact that James sat next to her. That's what made the night a night like no other she'd experienced in a long, long time.

"What are those three stars, mom?" James asked, pointing to three brightly shining stars neatly tucked in a row.

Alyssa turned her gaze to the stars and smiled.

"During the winter those stars are even brighter than now. One of my favorite things to do as a kid, even now I suppose, is to watch the sky at night."

James turned and looked adoringly at his mother.

"What do you think about when you see the stars mom? I like to think there is a whole world up there looking back at us! I just hope they know that we're good people too!"

She laughed and gently whisked the hair away from his eyes as he tried to get comfortable, settling in for the night next to his mother. The site of his innocence warmed her heart. Only a few days earlier she questioned if the commander would allow her to see him again, but he kept his word. The commander's controlling nature eminently irritated her, yet despite his apparent contempt of her situation, he always honored his word.

As James slept Alyssa thought about Bergden and where he might be or if he was still alive. The commander mentioned in passing that Bergden's whereabouts were unconfirmed, but she struggled to overcome the difficulty of believing such a thing. The wife of a black jack, she knew that the Regime kept tabs on its own and Bergden was no exception. A year's passing did little to ease her weary mind about her beloved husband and the thought the Regime covered up his death or locked up without a key brought her to tears. For the sake of James, she kept her tears at bay. The boy needed strength and she was stronger than ever.

Suddenly, the door on the neighboring balcony swung open. The commander and Jocelyn emerged in a fit of anger. James woke up and Alyssa ushered him into the room closing the door behind her. She ducked her head and leaned against the balcony wall trying to listen in to the couple's conversation.

"Those bastards in Harvick are one step too far into the plan, Jocelyn. I told Carl that when he found out the location of Andrew to let me know and I'd take care of it. Instead, he busts him out himself, sending the prison into a riot and almost compromising the entire operation."

Alyssa tried to comprehend what she was hearing. Was the commander more than he seemed? And who was Andrew? Where was the town of Harvick? She had too many questions to not listen in.

"I know Liam, but you have to understand that the resistance operates when it is most opportune. The mole we planted at Cherry Hill Prison is dead as a result, but the plan moved forward, nonetheless. There is only one more stage of the plan that needs completing. Then you can go and do whatever the hell you'd like."

Jocelyn talked to the commander not as a spouse, but as an unwilling business partner. Alyssa always did question the nature of their relationship. True, it was common for spouses to grow distant over time, but the love that sprang to life in a younger age rarely dissipated without cause. A years' time did little to squash her hopes for reunification with Bergden.

The thought of his embrace sparked harmonious swells of adoration in her heart. She prayed that day would arrive soon.

"Jocelyn, I think we should just tell her what needs done. She's strong enough, and when she is thrust into situations that are uncomfortable and push her limits, she will know how to react. I've seen it in her eyes," Liam insisted.

Jocelyn immediately interjected. "Her endurance is not in doubt. I've seen what I need to see, and I know that despite her gentle exterior, there is a ruthless avenger desperate to rise out from the ashes," Jocelyn declared. "She's been pushed hard and for too long. I worry she could crumble under the pressure of what she is about to do."

The commander shook his head, grabbing Jocelyn on the shoulders.

"We don't have a choice now. With the group moving out of Harvick, everything has already been put into motion. At the gala, when the time comes, I can remove Kroft's guards, and she will do the rest."

Jocelyn pushed away from the commander.

"I just hope you're right, because if only one part of the plan comes to fruition the whole thing will collapse. No one will be spared. None of them and especially not us. You're putting your faith in the hands of a woman that you barely now. Hoping, praying that she'll react the way we need her to."

The commander walked over the balcony door.

"I know this may be difficult to believe, but I know her better than you think. She will perform the task; you just need to be there for the pickup. Understood?"

Alyssa peeked out over the wall. She could see the commander shaking his head and rubbing his chin in frustration. Clearly, the two saw two different sides to the issue and Alyssa was dying to find out what precisely that issue was, but neither continued to speak. Jocelyn marched past the commander and slammed the door behind her. The commander walked to the edge of the balcony and lit a cigarette. One, long drag later he flicked it over the balcony and went back inside. Whatever the commander and Jocelyn were up to, she'd have to figure that out later.

The day of the Victory Gala arrived before Alyssa knew it. She had been looking forward to spending time away from the commander and Jocelyn. She regretted having to leave James with Hari, but the old man took a shining to her son and treated him as his own. Cara told her during the week that the gala was the party to be at if she wanted to ever get ahead in the Regime. Alyssa hardly cared for politics and just saw it as an opportunity to learn more about Bergden. The commander assured her that among the Regime's elite, someone must have some information.

After last night however, she wasn't so sure.

James sat on the edge of the bed reading one of his textbooks as she picked out a dress.

Earlier in the week Jocelyn helped her pick out a blue dress, but the night before soured Alyssa on the idea and instead she went for a ruby dress. It hung from the shoulders and flowed gracefully down her sides. A pair of elbow length black, velour gloves accented it well with a black onyx necklace she found in the dresser drawers.

"Close your eyes James, mommy is going to try on a dress and when I tell you to open them, I want you to say the first thing that comes to mind, okay?" she said, giving him a kiss on the forehead. James rubbed it away like most small boys did and held his hands over his eyes.

A few minutes later, Alyssa emerged and gave a polite curtsy before twirling the dress left to right.

"Can I open my eyes yet?" James asked, hands still pressed firmly to his face, his childlike grin pushing through outstretched fingers.

"Now!" Alyssa playfully commanded. Again, she swung the dress to and fro. James squealed with excitement at the dress.

"Beautiful!" James proclaimed, jumping from the bed to embrace his mother. She knelt down and held him close, kissing him again.

"Your mom is going to a ball tonight, James. Do you think this dress will be okay?" Alyssa playfully asked, already knowing the answer.

James emphatically shook his head yes.

Alyssa smiled approvingly before hearing a knock on the door. Her smile faded as she went to answer, praying that the commander and Jocelyn weren't on the other side. Instead stood the withered face of Hari. He grinned at the sight of her dress.

"Looking ravishing Mrs. Crane. I'm here to take James to the library for studies while you're at the gala. Is that okay?"

James reluctantly agreed and dragged his feet as he walked to the door. "Love you, James," Alyssa said as he walked away.

Within moments of turning back into the room Alyssa heard a

familiar voice.

"I see you went with the red dress. Jocelyn said you'd pick the blue, but red is the preferred color of the Regime elites."

It was the commander.

"I rather enjoy the gloves too. I'm not a fashion connoisseur mind you, but I've seen Jocelyn wear similar attire to these things. I on the other hand am relegated to my wartime garments for the chancellor's regale. Amazed they fit after these past ten years."

Alyssa stood in silence almost regretting her choice of dress, the conversation from the balcony still fresh in her mind. The commander looked as he always did, like a man with power. His Regime uniform was freshly pressed with his medals adorning the left breast.

Thin blue lines faintly outlined the otherwise predominantly gray woolen material of the officer's uniform. The sign of the wolf embroidered onto the opposing shoulder.

"Are you ready to head to the victory gala?" the commander asked, holding out his gloved hand.

Alyssa looked around for Jocelyn. "Where's Jocelyn?" The commander smiled grimly.

"She's feeling under the weather tonight. You're to be my date for the Victory Gala. I certainly hope that is agreeable to you. I know there are many Regime leaders there that would take pleasure in meeting you."

She nearly balked at going with the commander but remembering why she planned on attending in the first place. Upon her recollection she instinctively took the commander's hand—and his offer.

The ride to the chancellor's mansion, where the gala was to be held, felt longer than usual. The commander barely uttered a word instead of choosing to focus on the road as the sun set on the horizon. The menagerie of deep reds, blood orange, and violets harkened to a fairer time for Alyssa. Colors that only nature could produce. Her dreams could not hope to match the palate of Mother Nature's artistry.

For the next fifteen minutes, she felt at peace once again as the car cruised across the paved roads into Blackwell, passing through a military checkpoint without cause for concern. Her harmony lasted until she saw the outskirts of the chancellor's estate. An immense plantation plopped into the midst of a bustling city. Rows of soldiers lined the driveway as it led to a governor's driveway in front of the home. A two-story fountain made in the image of the chancellor himself flowed. The up lighting illuminating the otherwise dark stoned face of Kroft.

"This is where the parade ends Alyssa and the chancellor will give his broadcasted speech. You'll have front row seats, I'm sure," the commander said as the car came to a stop outside the front door. A soldier offered to valet the car.

"There's so many people here," Alyssa whispered, astonished by the significant number of patrons that seemed to buzz in from all directions. "I'll be lucky to get a drink I'm sure."

The commander leaned in and whispered. "I promise you'll see who you need to see. You have a purpose here, my dear. I will make sure you realize that purpose."

Again, the conversation from the balcony came to mind. Were they referring to her when they spoke of "her?" How could they not be? Coupled with the fact that Jocelyn conveniently missed the Regime's largest party of the year, something was afoot, and while she did not know what, Alyssa felt confident that it would come to pass tonight.

The commander led Alyssa into the main foyer of the home. A crystal chandelier hung high above the guests as they entered, the walls decorated with pieces of art from all over the world. Most would be considered illegal but in the home of the chancellor exceptions were made, and despite his typically bombastic approach to self-adoration, not a single portrait had been raised.

Each guest was given a glass of champagne as they were greeted by the servants and a small plate of hors d'oeuvres. The hall, packed with flowers from all areas of the globe, guided guests towards the main ballroom. A floral cornucopia of scents rushed through her nostrils, immersing her in a state of euphoria. Flowers were rare in the city of Blackwell and the smells harkened her back to her youth in Oyster Bay. She hoped to take James to what remained of her childhood after they found his father.

"Alyssa!" an excited voice called from across the room. It was Cara dragging her date over to see her friend. The poor man looked beaten as the eager Cara pushed him towards the commander and Alyssa.

"I love your dress!" Cara proclaimed. "This is my date. Colonel Wells of the fifth...fifth. What was the name of your group?"

The man frowned.

"Fifth Armored Battalion and Cara you need to stop announcing me as a colonel. My father is the colonel. You're going to get me arrested for impersonating a higher rank."

The commander smiled at Cara.

"Cara, you'll do well to keep watch over Alyssa, won't you? Jocelyn couldn't make it tonight and she's new to the gala scene."

The commander began to stroll away from the two women. Alyssa ran over and grabbed him on the shoulder.

"Where are you going? You can't just leave me here. I don't know any of these people."

Grimm snickered. "I'll keep an eye on you," Grimm assured Alyssa. "Cara has a way with the Regime elites. If you want more information about Bergden you'll stick close to her. Just be mindful of who you speak with. Naturally, not everyone here is who they claim to be."

The response was cryptic enough to send a shudder down her spine. Who could she trust, if anyone in this crowd? Commander Grimm warned her about Cara and yet he let her go.

Cara led Alyssa through the crowd introducing her to the debutants of Regime high society. Most of whom she had been intimate with at one point or another. Her knowledge of the Regime impressed Alyssa. If knowledge was indeed power, then Cara wore the crown and wore it well.

"The chancellor should be coming down here in a few minutes, Alyssa. That's the one person I've yet to introduce myself to," Cara gushed. "How do I look? Think he'll notice me in the crowd?"

The dress Cara wore would catch anyone's attention. Low cut in the back, her slender frame barely masked by the yellow, lace fabric that made up the bulk of the dress. The dress cascading down the front, barely covering her breasts. The dress attracted attention, good and bad, from anyone who gazed upon it. Whether that attention was what Cara sought was a different matter.

Through the crowd appeared Headmistress Longmire, and without fail, her gaze caught Alyssa and Cara. The contemptuous Longmire pushed past other Regime party members to confront the two schoolteachers.

"I'm surprised to see the two of you here," Helga said, staring disdainfully at Alyssa before turning her attention to Cara. "The Regime's parties are usually reserved for those of us with class.

Cara rolled her eyes and Longmire took notice. "Did you fuck your way to the party, Cara? Judging by your dress I'll assume you did." She looked back at Alyssa wearing that same look of disgust. "And who dragged you from the gutter? I figured you'd be half across the continent—"

Helga stopped mid-sentence as the commander put his hand on Alyssa's waistline. "Headmistress, I see you've met my date for tonight," Grimm said, eyeing Longmire.

Longmire put a hand to her chest in surprise.

"Commander Grimm, I was unaware that you knew our dear Alyssa," she snorted, adjusting her pillbox cap. "She's a fine school mistress. I assure you she receives only the highest marks as an educator."

The commander grimaced and held up his hands putting the brakes on the conversation.

"Please enough with the patronizing language Longmire. I doubt it is much of a secret that you hate younger, prettier women that are a threat to your ego. Just do us a favor and stand somewhere else. The chancellor is about to make his entrance. I'd prefer not to be seen with the lower echelon of the Regime if it's just the same."

Dejected, Longmire stormed away from the trio.

Cara wrapped her arms around the commander. "Thank you, commander. The headmistress can be such a vile woman."

He gently removed Cara's arms from around his shoulders.

"I have no doubts that you used your body to gain leverage in the Regime, Cara. The headmistress can be gruff, but make no mistake, she is well respected in the Regime for her intelligence and astute insight. Granted, pointing out that you use your body for gain hardly is astute."

Cara crossed her arms and shot the commander a snide glance.

Alyssa knew Cara had a way with men, though that allowed her to push the boundaries. Alyssa saw that even the commander, who had the authority to make Cara's life miserable, took a light approach to her crass behavior.

The crowd gathered at the bottom of a grand staircase. The bannisters and railings were solid marble topped with ornate ivory bulbs. Two great spotlights crossed beams at the top of the steps, and as each member of the chancellor's inner circle descended, lights followed each step until each reached the crowd below.

"Quite a sight, isn't it, Alyssa?" Cara whispered. "Such debonair people. Even with the brutalities of the Regime, they exhibit a sense of regal self-indulgence that puts them above the rest of the world. The brightest of their days are our darkest. Remember that Alyssa and you'll go wherever you want to go in the chancellor's world."

The words stunned Alyssa. Cara hardly seemed the type to be a Regime diehard, but her eyes glazed over with the thought of seeing the chancellor. His charisma was an opiate for the people. As he approached the crowd, roaring applause erupted. She found herself clapping despite her anger towards the man that facilitated her husband's disappearance. She watched as the chancellor began his descent down the staircase. Clad in white, the chancellor wore no medals, no markings of the wolf, nothing except a white suit. His hair greyed, and eyes were a piercing blue. It was the first time Alyssa had ever truly laid eyes upon him in his public glory.

"Ladies and gentlemen, thank you for attending the tenth annual Victory Gala!" he announced, much to the delight of his guests. "I've been told the parade is under way and that in just a few hours will make its way right to our doorstep. Isn't that a delight?"

The crowd around Alyssa beamed with excitement, but she felt nothing. She felt no inclination to smile or applaud. The memory of Bergden came to the forefront, and for but a fleeting moment in time she pushed forward, intent on confronting the chancellor.

"That's not very wise," the commander said as he pulled her back to reality. "You'll have your chance to speak with him I'm sure. Be patient and you will be rewarded. Trust me."

Alyssa slinked back away from the staircase and to the bar. As the chancellor spoke, she gathered her thoughts. The commander seemed sure that her time would come when she would find out the truth about Bergden, but whose side was he on? She watched as the commander mingled with other Regime leaders. He maintained the same stoic face throughout each conversation, as if to hide a truer nature. A man with his power wielded influence and yet he walked about as if he were bored or in a strange way, contrite to be in his position.

"Your friend is a real piece of work," Cara said, throwing back a martini and signaling for the bartender to make another. "He's a powerful man though, Alyssa. You'd do well to stick close to him. I've got my eyes on a greater prize."

Cara gestured to the chancellor who by this time began to cavort with the guests. A drink in hand, he made pleasantries with everyone. He particularly liked to address women, young women placing his hands on their waists and speaking softly to each. Alyssa held back her gag reflex as she watched these poor women unwittingly swoon to a grotesque, monster because of his power.

"You really want to sleep with the chancellor? What good could come of that?" Alyssa questioned.

"What good could come of it?" Cara responded. "He's the most powerful man on earth. If I can get him to spill secrets, then I'm made."

It was delusional thinking like that. Alyssa worried the Regime would have Cara killed or tossed into Cherry Hill Prison. Cara may have her proclivities, but she was the only friend Alyssa had. Watching her go headlong into such a poor decision pained Alyssa. She had to put a stop to it.

"Cara, if things don't go as planned, they could kill you," Alyssa whispered. "You don't think you'd be the first to sleep with him thinking you'd get leverage, do you?"

Cara thought for a moment and shook her head. "It's a risk I'll take Alyssa. I have no desire to stay a school mistress the rest of my life, and fineries such as my dress do not come on such a salary."

Alyssa shook her head.

"You can't possibly think that's a good idea," Alyssa scolded. "Everyone in Blackwell has to work Cara, it's the law. "

Cara scoffed.

"You don't believe that do you? I suppose you wouldn't know what it was like to meet the Regime high society. Those are laws for lower class ruffians like you, not me. I thought you were my friend Alyssa. You're a smart girl, look around you and tell me that everyone works."

With that Cara rushed off towards the chancellor leaving Alyssa alone once again until Helga reappeared at her side, drink in hand.

"Alyssa, she'll get what's coming to her if she stays on her path. That I can promise you," Longmire snickered.

Alyssa sighed. "I'm sorry about what the commander said earlier. He didn't speak for me." Helga frowned.

"I've known Liam for years," Longmire said, studying her champagne glass. "He does that for those he cares about and I respect that. You should be grateful to have a man of his position supporting you. I know when to leave well enough alone. Cara on the other hand does not curry favor within the Regime as much as she thinks. She believes that sleeping her way to the top is how you get ahead in this world, but that couldn't be further from the truth."

Alyssa gestured to Chancellor Kroft as he mingled through the crowd stopping to kiss the hand of each beautiful woman he encountered. "But the chancellor looks like he's searching for a woman over there."

Helga shook her head.

"He's the chancellor. Nothing more than abuse of power," Longmire chided. "I'll let you in on a little secret Alyssa. His health is failing. A mixture of constant paranoia, indulgences, and a steady stream of venereal diseases will bring all but the strongest man to his knees. If it weren't for the doctors, I'd swear he'd be dead already," she chortled before sipping her champagne. "God, if he went, I don't know what would happen. I believe our dear friend Commander Grimm is next in line to lead the Regime."

For Alyssa, the activity in the room came to a screeching halt. The sounds of laughter and merriment fell away as Alyssa looked over at Commander Grimm. His stoic form stood listening to the chancellor. About what, she could only guess, but she could see through the stone like expression. The anger his eyes betraying him as he listened to the chancellor. She had seen that look in a man's eyes before. Bergden sat many mornings at breakfast quietly wrestling with his real perceptions of the world.

No more would she sit and watch the world tear Blackwell's men from the inside out. She decided to act on her intuition.

"Excuse me head mistress. I must attend to something," Alyssa said, leaving the bar and making her way towards the commander.

"Commander, aren't you going to introduce me to the chancellor?" she asked, squeezing his forearm voraciously causing the commander to wince.

Commander Grimm turned, shocked by her presence. "Mrs. Crane, what a surprise," Grimm said, forcing a smile "I had thought you had taken your leave to the bar for a drink." Alyssa grinned, maintaining eye contact with the chancellor. "Of course, Chancellor Kroft. This is my date for the evening, Alyssa Crane," the commander said, clearly perturbed by the interruption.

The chancellor sauntered forward pushing aside his two bodyguards to get a better look at Alyssa. Alyssa, for the first time, had a close-up of the man himself. His eyes were a pale gray, crow's feet masked the monstrous man with the guise of wisdom. His smile was a reminder of how insidious a human could be doing little to hide the look of lust that he greeted her with.

"What a precious individual, Commander. Jocelyn finally had enough of your insufferable approach to life's delights?" Kroft jested to Grimm before turning his attention to Alyssa. "You know my dear, the commander leads a boring life, choosing to rest his laurels in politics rather than the earthly pleasures that you have no doubt partaken in."

Alyssa feigned embarrassment. "There are many earthly goods I have not had the pleasure of tasting."

"Let me be the bounty to fulfill those dreams," he boasted.

She nearly threw up in her mouth.

Commander Grimm put a hand on the chancellor's shoulder.

"I think you give me too much credit, chancellor," the commander joked. "I live a much more loathsome existence than you could possibly imagine. Politics notwithstanding."

The chancellor laughed then placed his hand on Alyssa's casting aside Grimm's hand. "My dear, won't you join me for a drink in my private booth?" Kroft asked, his voice darkening.

He did little to mask the fact it wasn't an offer, but rather a command. Alyssa followed the chancellor to a private booth where another woman was waiting.

Cara. Alyssa released as she entered the booth.

"Alyssa, I'm so glad the chancellor found you!" Cara exclaimed with glee. "I told you he wanted to meet us."

The chancellor grinned and rubbed Cara's lower back.

"So, you know each other? Wonderful," he said.

Wonderful, Alyssa lamented as she took her seat, a server quickly providing another glass.

"I'm so glad you could join us Alyssa. The chancellor was just telling me that his troops located a pocket of resistance members in a nearby town—what was it called?" Cara asked the chancellor.

"Harvick," he confirmed.

"That's right, Harvick. Anyways, the chancellor said we would soon be rid of them, isn't that right?" Cara asked, rubbing the chancellor's forearm.

"Well, my dear, when I find embers, I stomp it out. We cannot allow a fire to go unchecked and as we speak there are planes on their way to destroy the town. It'll show the rest of those defiant bastards that I'm not playing anymore of their partisan games," Kroft growled.

The town of Harvick sounded familiar to Alyssa. She knew she'd heard the name in the past but couldn't quite put her finger on it.

Cara giggled before raising a glass gesturing towards the chancellor. "To the final elimination of the resistance in Harvick!"

Alyssa half-heartedly raised her glass before throwing its contents back. Suddenly she remembered where she heard the name before.

Harvick, she thought.

"Excuse me, chancellor, I must use the washroom. I will return soon. I do very much enjoy your company," she lied.

"Please do, I wouldn't want to go looking for you," he warned.

Alyssa got up causally and tried to walk with haste towards the washroom, all the while scanning the room for the commander. He found Commander Grimm near the men's room.

"Commander," she said, exasperated.

"Had enough of the chancellor, have you? That was over faster than I expected," he admitted.

"Har—Harvick," she managed to blurt out.

Grimm took her by the elbow and walked her away from the crowd. "What do you know about Harvick?" he demanded.

"I heard you on the balcony last night," she confessed. "Only parts of what you talked about, but I can remember Harvick, and there is something you should know."

The commander's pleasant demeanor melted away as he gripped her arm tight.

"You eavesdropped on my conversation with Jocelyn? Tell me,

what did you hear? Tell me now!" he demanded.

Alyssa tried to pull herself away but Grimm resisted, bringing her even closer.

"Please," Alyssa pleaded. "I don't know what is going on here, but the Regime is going to bomb Harvick."

The commander's face softened as he looked at Alyssa then his attention shifted to something behind her.

He pulled her close and whispered. "The chancellor's guard is going to take you to him. Do not succumb. You are strong and that is why you were picked. Be strong. I wish I had more time to explain but follow your instincts. Whatever they tell you, you must do."

The guard tapped on her shoulder, but Alyssa still struggled to figure out what the commander's words meant. What did he mean she had been picked?

"Please follow me Miss Crane," he ordered, grabbing Alyssa by the wrist.

She resisted for a moment looking back at the commander, who could only nod before disappearing into the crowd.

The guard took her, not back to the table with Cara, but past the dining section and up the grand staircase. She could feel the eyes of the rest of the party following her as she was dragged away from the ballroom. The music faded the background as the guard stopped outside a set of large, wooden, double doors.

"The chancellor is waiting for you inside. My advice? Do what he says and don't try anything stupid. From what I hear he doesn't last long these days. There are towels near the wet bar to clean up with," the guard mumbled before pushing her through the doors.

The room was beyond lavish. Large red curtains were drawn closed blocking the outside light of a two-story window. An immense mahogany bed adored with extravagant, ornate designs clearly reflecting old world stylings. A separate bar area and a roaring fireplace completed the spectacular suite.

"I hope you like it Mrs. Crane," the chancellor's voice called from the other side of a large wingback chair. "Please come join us."

Alyssa hesitated as she approached the chair. A long dress lay nonchalantly on the floor that she recognized to be Cara's yellow gown. The chancellor sat, his shirt undone, relaxed in the large, leather wingback chair with his legs crossed. Cara lay across from him on a velvety chaise lounge. She had stripped down to her garter, her breasts free from her corset.

At the sight of her topless friend, Alyssa turned towards the door.

"Where are you going?" The chancellor gestured to the king-sized bed. "I insist you join us."

The words from the guard echoed in her mind as she slinked back toward the lounge area. He had probably seen the scene play out dozens of times and the ones who resisted likely faced a terrible fate. The chancellor wielded his power on a whim, and she dared not challenge him. James still needed her.

"Of course, Chancellor Kroft," she said, taking a seat next to Cara. Cara smiled seductively at Alyssa trying to get her attention, her eyes signaling for Alyssa to take off her evening gown. Alyssa turned her attention to the chancellor who sat waiting patiently for Alyssa's response. Despite her misgivings, Alyssa decided to play along, at least for a while.

She undressed, careful not to reveal her naked form to the chancellor, but as she continued to shed her clothing, he came over and placed his hands on her hips. His cold flesh caressing her hips to her lower back sent chills of horror up her spine. "Cara, why don't you come kiss Alyssa's neck?" he insisted, taking a step back and pulling Alyssa's hair to the side exposing her supple nape.

Alyssa closed her eyes as Cara approached, trying to drown out her imagination of the things to come. Hoping to distract herself from the situation, she pictured James and Bergden playing in the apartment. She focused on the memories of her life that kept her going all this time. Then she remembered the words of the commander.

"Do not succumb. You are strong," he had said, "That is why you were picked for this task. Be the strong woman we know you to be."

She stepped away to the surprise of Cara and the chancellor

"Why don't you two get the fun going? I have a surprise I think you'll both like."

By this time the chancellor had his pants around his ankles, and as he stepped out from the pair of slacks, Cara smiled at Alyssa and turned, exposing herself to him. Alyssa faked a smile and stepped away towards the chancellor's wardrobe.

"Don't take too long Mrs. Crane," the chancellor purred. "I wouldn't want you to miss out on the fun."

She gagged again as she searched his wardrobe for the perfect item, a black leather belt. Emerging from the wardrobe she saw the chancellor taking Cara from behind. His pale, naked form moving back and forth in vigorous motion. Her taught, perky form contrasting with the disgusting body of the chancellor. Alyssa took a deep breath and pressed forward towards the pair who by now were lost in one another, Cara truly embracing the chancellor.

"Close your eyes, Chancellor," Alyssa whispered in her most seductive voice. She ran her hands down her chest, the cold leather of the belt running along his shoulders and up to his neck. Then, she pulled tight. The belt digging into the astonished chancellor's throat. Cara fell from his embrace and stood in horror as Alyssa pulled the belt tighter and tighter.

The belt pulled tight; Alyssa dragged the chancellor from the lounge. He swung wildly about trying to get a hold of the belt or Alyssa. The pair fell backwards over the high wingback chair sending it crashing to the floor, the chancellor trying in desperation to call out. The struggle continued for a few moments until the chancellor lay motionless, a stifled gurgle the only thing to escape his throat.

"Alyssa! What did you just do?" Cara cried out as she came to the chancellor's side. "He's—he's dead! You fucking killed him!" Cara went running for the door, but Alyssa cut her off, standing between her and escape.

"This was meant to happen Cara. The past year of my life led me to this moment and there is nothing that can be done. I suggest you back away from the body. I promise I will take all the blame," Alyssa said with a cold, blank stare at Cara.

"You killed him! You killed him!" Cara cried as she pushed past Alyssa, finally reaching the door. But instead of the guard, there stood Commander Grimm, his gun pointed with a silencer attached.

Alyssa stepped back, her hands in the air. Cara continued to cry and shout about the chancellor's demise.

"Hurry up and put your clothes on." He gestured towards Alyssa. "Cara you too!" But Cara ignored his commands.

"Cara, you have to put your clothes on do you understand?" he demanded, this time pulling the hammer back on the pistol.

She continued her hysterical crying over the chancellor's body and damned Alyssa for her atrocious act until the sound of a muffled bang left the commander's gun. Cara slumped to the floor next to the lifeless body of the chancellor, blood pouring from a coin-sized wound in her head.

"Liam, you didn't have to shoot her," Alyssa snapped as she continued to put on her clothes.

Ignoring Alyssa, Commander Grimm went to the bar pulling down on an unlabeled bottle. Revealing a hidden door beside the wardrobe that swung open.

"Go! Follow the passage to the alley below and there will be a car waiting for you." A pounding came on the chancellor's door.

"Open up! By order of the chancellor's guard. Open up this goddamn door!"

Alyssa turned and ran down the staircase not looking back even for a moment. The dimly lit, stone steps causing her to stumble in her high heeled shoes, but she pressed on until arriving at a door at the bottom. A door that would not budge.

"For God's sake please open!" she begged, pounding on the unsympathetic stone. The realization that she had just taken a life setting in. She continued to strike the stone door until it opened sending her careening to the darkened street.

"You'll be alright. Get in, we have to hurry!" a strange voice said from the shadows.

Fighting through the agony, Alyssa thrust herself onto the back seat trying to regain her composure. Wiping away her tears she realized who her savior had been.

Jocelyn sat in the car waving her in. A man sat in the front seat she did not recognize and as she entered, she looked in the rear cab.

There sat Bergden. He was covered in soot and dust, but she knew her husband when she saw him. He smiled and leaned over. The two embraced, tears rolling down their faces. Alyssa pulled away to get a better look, but she could not, he would not let her go.

"Carl and Ridgeway are making the announcement from a secret location. Once the word gets out, the Coalition will launch its attack. You have no idea the favor you just did the world Mrs. Crane," Jocelyn said, eyes glued to the road.

She could care less about the world. She just wanted to be with her family and nothing more.

CHAPTER SIXTEEN

Bergden found Commander Grimm at his desk on the second floor of the mansion. The office overlooked the very meadow Bergden had watched James play. He wondered how many times Grimm did the same. Despite the relative safety of the countryside estate, Bergden burned inside knowing that Grimm had watched James grow while he was in a hovel a hundred miles away in Harvick. The only comfort he could glean from the situation was the knowledge that Alyssa was with James and safe.

"I see you found my personal study Mr. Crane. I would invite you in, but I see you've already taken the liberty," Grimm mocked.

Bergden took a seat and thumbed through a few papers left on the side table. Most were stories or poems that appeared to be composed by the commander himself.

"Had you closed the door I would've knocked. Besides, I

believe I'm owed a moment of your time after what you've put me through. The things you made me do and the pain Alyssa experienced," Bergden replied.

The great chair slowly turned away from the window. Grimm wore a sardonic grin as he leaned over to snatch his works away from Bergden. "I'd appreciate it if you would not go through my personal work," he said, shuffling the papers into a locked drawer. "Helps me pass the time."

Grimm got up from the leather desk chair and circled the large desk over to a map of the world that predated the War. The Regime was nothing more than a blip on the map at this point. Bergden was still a citizen of the old nation. In fact, judging by the surrounding countries, he hadn't even been born.

"I meant what I said, Liam. I am owed a discussion with you. One way or another you're going to give it to me" Bergden pressed as he rose from his seat to approach the commander. "Why? Why was I chosen out of the millions to do your dirty work?"

The commander smirked.

"What's so funny?" Bergden demanded. "I find nothing funny about this. Not in the least. My life is in ruins."

"The fact that you truly believe that all of this was done because of you. That everything the Remnants worked for was facilitated through you. That's what's funny."

Bergden stood confused but continued to probe for answers.

"I was framed, taken to a resistance stronghold, then did the hard labor to free Ridgeway. None of this was possible without me. That's why I stand here a chaotic and increasingly angry man."

Liam Grimm smiled and leaned in to whisper into Bergden's ear. "I'm going to let you in on a little secret Mr. Crane. A secret that I'm sure Mr. Sonderberg would be more than furious for my sharing. Do I make myself clear?"

Bergden nodded in agreement. He was ready to agree to any

terms to understand why the past year and a half of his life had to be the way that it was.

"You were not the primary target Mr. Crane. It was merely incidental that your report reached my desk. After the late Mr. Kroft gave his proclamation regarding the use of internal investigations, it was in short order that I received a report about a lieutenant in Pemply Station that was undermining the Regime as was his family."

Bergden shuffled his feet dispersing his anger. "That wasn't true though. I would do no such thing."

Again, Grimm produced a devious grin. "Forgive me when I say that how was I supposed to know? You were nobody to me and when a person of your rank is alleged to have done something horrible against the Regime, it would only behoove me to investigate."

"And what did your investigations yield?" Bergden asked impatiently.

"That a private, who held a personal vendetta against the lieutenant, provided a report with falsified evidence that alleged that very same lieutenant was working with resistance saboteurs to collapse the Regime. It is only ironic that eventually that statement would be true, but at the time we knew it to be false."

"Again, how does this come back to me if your investigations showed Rocco Draven was a liar?"

Grimm shook his head. "It didn't come back to you, but during the investigations I was already knee deep in Remnant activity. I had chosen a new path and the success of the revolution required a coordinated approach to toppling the Regime. You are right Mr. Crane, you were not trying to undermine the Regime in any significant manner, but there was a member of your family that I felt we could use."

Alyssa. Bergden realized.

"Your wife proved to be the perfect candidate. Behind your back she was soliciting material goods from our people. She wouldn't stray too far into the revolutionary cause. Not without prompting of course. But she proved to be a malleable individual probably a result of her natural intuition for submission. We needed an asset we could control."

"Humans naturally estimate what they can control including you, Liam," Bergden snapped. "No matter what you did, no matter how you influenced her, Alyssa is the only person who can control her inner self."

"Perhaps your beloved was a hot-bloodied rebel right under your nose," Grimm countered.

Anger boiled inside Bergden.

"You had her tortured by Dr. Vossen as a result?" Bergden bellowed. "You're sick and maniacal. I should kill you where you stand."

Grimm held up his hand to calm down the now furious Bergden. "The warrant for your arrest was not on my order and the string of events that led us to this very spot began before I realized it. Carl rescued you, and my men thankfully absconded with your son and wife. Alyssa was taken to Singer and James to the academy barracks. Rest assured; your wife was in no serious danger with Dr. Vossen. I had the situation completely under my control."

Without warning, Bergden backhanded Grimm, sending the commander tumbling into the map.

"I suppose I deserve that, but Alyssa showed me that she was quietly resilient and, when pressed, could overcome any situation. It would take time, but I was going to build her into the perfect sleeper agent. It wasn't until a few days ago that the fruits of my labor manifested in her bold attempt to liberate your son."

Bergden stood slack jawed. He began to realize that Grimm had pinpointed Alyssa to be the catalyst for the revolution.

"How did you know she'd kill Kroft? What made you think she had a killer instinct hidden away?" Bergden questioned. "She'd never shown it before in all the years we were married. Why now?"

"She never had to show it. You were there, weren't you?" Grimm reasoned. "It wasn't until the prospect settled in that you were not going to be there that she took it upon herself to take action. Quite a remarkable change really, and she'll be better off for it. As far as Kroft was considered, it was a gamble, but I knew the odds were in my favor."

"How so?" Bergden asked.

"A beautiful young woman that old pervert couldn't resist would put the now hardened Alyssa into a situation she would not want to be in. We just needed to groom her and put her into a position to succeed," Grimm admitted. "The hope being she'd take the appropriate action, which thankfully she did."

Grimm walked back to his desk and poured two spots of brandy. One for Bergden and one for himself, which he threw back in earnest.

"She is the most important person in the history of Blackwell right now. She killed a man that shackled humanity for a decade under a yoke of false impressions, paranoia and terror. You should really be proud," Grimm gushed.

Bergden took the brandy and stared down into the glass swirling the amber liquid and watching its clash against the sides like ocean waves upon a rocky shore. The gravity of the commander's words took him from reality for just a brief moment, but it felt like an eternity. His wife had been manipulated into becoming a person she was never supposed to be, or was this the person she truly was? Had she somehow been saddled with the belief that a conciliatory approach to life was her way of survival and not happiness? He wanted to run to her and embrace her, but there was still one more question to find answers to.

"What was my part in all of this? Where did I come in?" Bergden asked before lifting the glass and engorging himself on the entire pour.

Grimm gestured for the two men to sit back down. Grimm's brow furrowed. "As I said earlier, this is funny because of how you feel you fit into the equation. You were useful, there is no denying that, but you were not essential to the cause. Actually, I doubted you'd survive the initial arrest and when Carl suggested you break into Cherry Hill and then Singer, I laughed. I had doubted your ability to withstand both missions and I would've bet good money on you being arrested before even getting inside. You defied the odds, but rest assured it isn't as though we didn't have a plethora of agents who couldn't have done the same."

Grimm sipped on his brandy as Bergden tried to swallow what he had just heard.

"I was expendable? What about rescuing Ridgeway, killing Dr. Vossen or defending Harvick?" Bergden demanded.

"Killing Dr. Vossen I suppose was a bonus, but she wouldn't have lasted long anyway once we liberated Singer. I must admit, helping the Remnants push back the Regime at Harvick was a great benefit to the cause, although the chancellor would later have troops come back and obliterate the town."

Bergden couldn't believe what he was hearing. He didn't want to consider it. Had he spent the past year and a half of his life working for the Remnants because he was manipulated into doing so? No, he wouldn't believe it.

"Surely emancipating General Ridgeway was—" Bergden began to ask before Grimm interrupted.

"Please Mr. Crane. I said you were useful, but none of those things were critical to the success of creating a revolutionary catalyst. Ridgeway's only job was to get on the radio and tell the good people of Blackwell, the heart of the Regime, that their leader had fallen, and that the Coalition was coming. The good general will be useful in the transition, but after the government has been reformed, he will no longer be required."

Suddenly it dawned on Bergden. All this time he believed that the Remnants and the Coalition forces that remained would swoop in and bring a civil war to the Regime, but that wasn't it. That wasn't it at all.

"You. It was you. You are going to supplant yourself as the new chancellor in the Regime, aren't you?"

Grimm nodded, agreeing with Bergden's revelation.

"Once the infighting settles down, I will emerge from the ashes and rebuild the Regime. Of course, the Remnants will protest my new role, but once they see the power I will wield I am sure they'll be more than willing to work with the new government. I will ensure they have prominent spots in the government and work to create a new, better tomorrow," Grimm said.

"Does Carl know about this?" Bergden asked.

Grimm grinned ear to ear, and that was all Bergden needed to see. The Remnants had been played for fools just as he and Alyssa had been. Liam Grimm, a man who he feared, used his power and influence to justify his role in the revolution and the Remnants bought it.

Bergden turned to leave in silence, never to return to the lands of the Regime ever again.

"Before you go Mr. Crane, I have a gift for you. In case you were curious about Mr. Sonderberg's part in sparking the revolution," Grimm said, grinning as he held out an off-white envelope. "Read it once you are on the road. Get a hundred miles out. You'll thank me for waiting. "

Bergden took the envelope and walked out the door, never to return.

*　　*　　*

Alyssa watched James play in the meadows in the mansion courtyard. The blades of grass danced in the wind as the sounds of his laughter rose above the springtime breeze. She smiled as James rolled around and tossed loose stones over the hillside squealing in delight as each crashed into the creek below. Moments like these were precious to her now. The image of her young boy playing in the sun etched into her memory as life seemed to be returning to normal.

But for her, there would be no return to the past.

She had killed a man and started a revolution. She had changed, and she fought with whether or not those changes were for the better. She felt colder, more calculated than she had ever felt before. Buying alcohol from smugglers felt like a trip to the market compared to the things she'd been through. The scars from Dr. Vossen and the manipulation at every turn had changed her forever. Bergden hadn't had time to see those changes, but she wondered how he'd see her. If he would still love her as he had always loved her. He had been through the War. He had seen atrocity and lived through it, yet those things haunted him. Would the things she'd seen haunt her too?

"James, make sure you don't stray too far," Alyssa cautioned as the young boy disappeared over the hillside.

"He'll be alright," called a familiar voice over her shoulder. "Nothing down there but a shallow brook and a few frogs."

It was Hari.

"Before you speak, Mrs. Crane, I want to apologize to you. I want to say I'm sorry for the hell Mr. Grimm put you through. Wasn't right of me not to speak up," he lamented, struggling against his own sorrow.

Alyssa craned her neck to try and get a better view of James before turning her attention to Hari. The older man had been crying. His eyes red and watery, and the cuff of his shirt soaked from wiping away his tears.

"You don't need to be sorry, Hari. I doubt I would've made it without you," Alyssa comforted. "You helped me through these dark days."

Hari smiled and sighed with a gentle grin. "If I had known the extent of what his plans were, I would've intervened. You're too sweet a soul to have been put through that."

Alyssa knew she should be mad at anyone who had been involved in her forced mental reformation, but could she really be that angry? She was after all a stronger person than she had ever known. She tried to reason with herself that despite the events of the past year, she would be better off for it and if that meant the people of the Regime were too, then her sacrifice, even if it was involuntary, would be worth it.

"Don't worry, Hari, I'll be okay, but have you seen Bergden? I'd like to get the hell out of this place and on with our lives. No offense."

Hari laughed and embraced Alyssa.

"I can't blame you Mrs. Crane," Hari conceded. "As for Mr. Crane he was speaking with Mr. Grimm and should be around shortly."

From around the corner of the chateau, Bergden appeared.

"Speak of the devil. The Cranes are always in the right place at the right time," Hari joked. "I'll let you go. Don't be afraid of calling Mrs. Crane. You are always welcome in my company." Hari again embraced Alyssa before departing, stopping briefly to tip his cap to Bergden as he approached Alyssa.

"Bergden!" another voice called out from the front door. It was Carl and General Ridgeway. Both men were in Coalition uniforms and appeared as though they had gotten a proper shower and shave for the first time in months-something Bergden planned to do as soon as they got to wherever it was they chose to go.

"Carl," Bergden responded bluntly before turning back to the cruiser. He called for James, who came rushing up the hill to greet his parents before he was ushered into the back seat of the waiting cruiser.

Alyssa watched as Carl took Bergden by the shoulder and turned him to speak. "Bergden. You and your family are welcome to stay. In fact, we could really use you and Alyssa to help us rebuild and regain the trust of the people. Two former, loyal Regime citizens turned revolutionaries paints quite the damning picture of Chancellor Kroft and his cronies, don't you think?" Carl offered.

Alyssa was handed a folder from Bergden, who ignored Carl's offer and proceeded to begin packing what few possessions they had left into the car before finally acknowledging Carl and his proposition.

"I think you know damn well why I am not staying here Carl. Why Alyssa, James and I are going to go as far away as possible from you and the rest of the Remnants," Bergden bellowed. "Good day and good luck with your bloody revolution."

"Bergden. Please just listen to me," Carl pleaded, grabbing his former partner by the elbow. "There is a place for you in the new government, the new order of things. We need men of your caliber to restore order and put down what remains of the Regime."

"Never could I put my family through more suffering, and with the city turned into a war zone I want to get them as far away as possible," Bergden boomed.

Alyssa could see her husband was angry. Not just with the Regime, but with Carl, with the commander and with himself. She felt the sorrow in his voice, and she knew that Bergden blamed himself for what had happened to their family, but she knew the truth. She knew that they had been caught up in something much bigger than themselves and there was no avoiding it aside from death. She realized that the moment she met the chancellor and understood that they were either going to be part of the future or waste away.

She didn't realize the impact the Cranes would have on the fate of Blackwell.

Carl continued to try and convince Bergden of the merits of staying. "The city will soon be under our control, Bergden, life can return to normal, and because of your service to the Remnants, you'll be pardoned for your actions during the War."

Alyssa could see the fire in Bergden's eyes. He had always been particularly sensitive and aloof to his role in the War, but never had he been challenged on it in such a way.

"Pardoned for my actions during the War?" Bergden barked. "I fought for what I thought was my country. I fought to protect those I loved. Never had I thought the Regime would change the way it did. I did not fight to kill. I fought for what I thought was going to be a new and better world. For equal rights among my fellow man. A fair wage to live on, but most importantly, I fought for my future family."

Carl shook his head.

"I'm your friend Bergden, you don't need to lie to me," Carl scolded. "We all fought and killed. That is the nature of war. You were excited by the prospect of war when it started. So was I. I think it was that bond that made us such close friends."

"You're not my friend Carl. Not anymore. To be honest, I'm not even sure you were ever a friend. Somewhere along the line you saw me, and you saw Alyssa and made your move. I want to tell you that you disgust me. I want to tell you that I hope the worst only comes for you, but lucky for you, I've seen enough bloodshed and sorrow for a million lifetimes," Bergden lectured. "I never want to see your face again."

Ignoring Bergden Carl continued. "I've known you for years, Bergden. Of course, you are my friend and we need you now more than ever. A friend would stay and help us. A friend would look past what needed to be done.

Bergden said, holding up a manila envelope, shaking it at Carl. "A friend would never put his friend through the hell that you did."

And with that Bergden took his position in the driver's seat. Leaving Carl to shake his head and retreat into the mansion.

Alyssa breathed in the spring air as she stood outside of the mansion gazing up at its immense gothic façade one last time. The estate had been both a prison and a home, but more importantly a center of personal awakening. That wasn't to say she'd miss her life here, but she would walk away with a new appreciation for who she was and her inner feminine strength. It was a unique gift. A gift that she could use to solidify the bonds with Bergden and James. A gift that she decided then and now to use to better the people she met along the way.

"So where are we off to?" Alyssa asked as she pulled the passenger door side closed. She saw the envelope in her husband's grip. "What's in the envelope, Bergden?"

"I think it's best if we pack up the cruiser and head down the road. Then we can talk about it," Bergden said, turning the ignition. Alyssa nodded and watched as the mansion began to disappear in the distance. As she watched in the rearview mirror, she felt tired. Everything that had happened over the past day finally caught up to her and within moments she was fast asleep.

She had dreamt of her youth in Oyster Bay. She remembered wanting to be an artist, wanting to create and share her creations with the world around her. Then she recalled the destruction wrought by the weapons of war before suddenly waking to watch the sun begin its long descent over the horizon.

"How long was I asleep?" Alyssa asked. She glanced back and saw that James, too had fallen into slumber.

"A few hours. I imagine you needed the rest, all things considered. Lord knows I need to catch a few hours too."

Alyssa rubbed her eyes, wiping away the haze of sleep.

"I can take the wheel if you want. That way you can get some sleep too," she offered.

Bergden shook his head.

"It is okay. I can manage a little while longer," he replied.

The two sat in silence as the cruiser wound through a valley, over a bridge and into a thicket of forest. It was a beautiful sight. Alyssa had never seen such serenity in all her days and hoped that wherever Bergden planned to go. It would be just like this.

"I hate to ruin the moment Bergden. The world is showing us such beauty now, but I must ask. What was in that envelope?" Alyssa asked, suddenly remembering what had spurred Bergden to move with such haste.

He sighed. She saw the struggle he fought to try and gain the emotional fortitude to speak.

"It was Carl," Bergden sighed.

"Excuse me? What did Carl do?" Alyssa asked.

"He was the one who sent in a report to internal investigations and reported me dead to the Station Chief. Not Draven. Carl started all of this and worked with Grimm. We—I mean, you were the reason he submitted false allegations against me," Bergden lamented.

Alyssa was taken aback.

"Me? What do you mean me?" she retorted.

"Grimm used you to remove Chancellor Kroft and to elevate himself into chancellor. But none of this could have happened unless Carl filed that report. Alyssa, I killed an innocent man because of Carl's lies. Rocco Draven was scum and detestable, but he didn't need to die. I saw the fear of death in his eyes as I took his last breath from him."

Alyssa sat in silence, unable to find the words to appropriately respond to what she had just heard. So she did the only thing she could do in such moments.

"So, where are we going?" she asked.

Bergden smiled.

"I figure a stop in Oyster Bay will be the start. Then we can go anywhere we want. As long as we are together, that's all that matters."

Alyssa peered out as the sun made its final goodbyes behind the mountains. "That's all that matters."

Thank you for spending time with The Cranes of Blackwell. I hope you enjoyed reading it as much as I did writing it.

For more of my stories, go to jdkellner.com.

— *J.D. Kellner*

ABOUT THE AUTHOR

J.D. Kellner's affinity for science fiction and fantasy attracted him to the writing world. When not working on his next novel, J.D. writes musings and short stories for his website, jdkellner.com. Outside of the literary world, J.D. spends his free time with his family and friends enjoying life to the fullest. J.D. Kellner lives with his family in Pittsburgh, Pennsylvania.

Astrid was brought back to restore balance in the city. Cursed with a past she can barely remember, she fills her role as an assassin with ease. Astrid realizes she knows dangerously little about the place she lives and the people she kills for. As her trigger finger begins to fail her, she fears she might be labeled as Unworthy next. When an enigmatic doctor draws her into a rebellion, she won't just have to save the city—she will also have to decide what it truly means to be human.

Summer Wilkins, the official spokesperson for the Reformed United States, is still grieving the loss of her son when a shocking murder rocks the city. After her husband is implicated, she's drawn into a rebellion that's ready to do anything to find out the truth behind the new Inevix patches being distributed to the public. Murder, mystery, and politics abound as Summer finds out that the biggest secrets are being hidden in her own family.

CPSIA information can be obtained
at www.ICGtesting.com
Printed in the USA
LVHW020827141120
671493LV00004B/67